WHAT'S LEFT
BEHIND

AANIYA PATEL

Library of Congress Control Number: 2024912956

ISBN: 979-8-218-46162-1

This book has entirely fictional characters and a storyline made from the author's imagination. Certain locations are mentioned, but any similarities in characters or plots to the real world are coincidental.

First printing, 2024.

Printed in the United States of America

To my 6th-grade self,

who started this story and wanted to see it till the end,

and to every child with a dream

ONE

THE FACTORY

WHEN THE APOCALYPSE started, I thought it was just a dream. I was at school when the news broke out. Chaos filled the halls. People cried in agony as their limbs were torn apart. Nobody knew what to do. It felt like a nightmare, and it still does.

I'm sitting on a bus with both my friends and strangers. We all have a common goal—find a home. It seems easy, but it hasn't been. Each place has a group that they want to protect, and we never fit in. I'll have hope for something better, but it always disappoints.

The bus rears to the side of the road. Their heads turn in unison to our bright yellow vehicle. It's been one year since the apocalypse started—one year of gains and losses.

A broken-down factory rests in the snow that's built up a few inches. Pine trees surround the metallic building whose big rusty windows at the top and bottom expose the insides. For the most part, it looks abandoned. It's one of the only buildings for miles. All the others are crumbled, destroyed, or looted.

I stand up to face the people. "We all know what to do. The sun is setting soon, so we'll stay here for the night. Keep your weapons drawn and stay alert."

Emily Rivers opens the bus doors. The dead begin their way towards us. I'm the first one out. Dylan Sanchez follows closely behind, and Angel Stone is next, hopping off the stairs. There's hope in my heart for something here. We're running out of food and water. This factory is something we need desperately.

I lay my footprints onto the untouched snow. Any sign of someone coming here *today* is impossible. The snow sparkles, and I almost feel bad for ruining the clean surface. One of the creatures draws towards me. With my knife, I stab into the side of her skull. Her gray eyes stare off as the knife comes out, and she meets the ground.

Dylan and Angel kill the other ones in seconds.

"That's strange," I say as white fog puffs out of my mouth.

Zombies rattle the fence that ties their arms away. Their skin is ragged and falling off. The dirt and blood on them stain the snow.

Dylan steps closer to the fence. "Yeah, that is strange."

"It's a waste of time, says Angel. She wields her blade and slices one on the far right. "I can't believe people would—"

Her path stops as an arrow nearly pierces her head. Now she's silent with a terrified look. There's no movement in any of us. Another arrow flies behind her and falls into the snow. I turn around to see the culprit.

"How about we don't kill the scarecrows," a girl says, appearing from behind the bus.

She wears a black jacket with mud stains. A bow clutched in one hand, the other ready to pull out a knife. A quill sits on her back stocked with arrows.

"We don't want any trouble," I say with my hands up.

She looks at my belt, almost barren if not for the knife and revolver.

"We just need some food and water."

She doesn't feel threatened by us—unless in her silence she's plotting our deaths.

Another person comes out from behind the bus. This guy has the confidence of a mouse. He holds a gun with plenty of ammo strapped around his chest. His cargo pants have a knife peeking through one of the pockets. Following him is a girl with a gray linen shirt. Her black hair is in a high ponytail, and the snow's light makes the tips look brown.

"Who are they?" the second girl whispers.

The first one turns her head, but her eyes never leave us. They never leave me.

"I don't know."

I must make a good impression. They have us in a tricky spot. One false move could be our last.

"Who are—"

"I'm Hailee," I interrupt Angel before she blabbers something bad. "That's Dylan and Angel."

Dylan gives a small wave and Angel looks at me, annoyed.

"Todd?" a familiar voice says from near the bus.

I look back and see Jason Reyes wide-eyed as he steps onto the snow.

"I knew I recognized that face of yours," he says, grinning.

Todd looks surprised as he walks past me and up to Jason. They share a side hug.

"You know this guy?" asks Dylan. His eyes look at me, but I can only offer the same confusion.

Angel walks towards them, surprise on her face. "No way!"

"We went to preschool together." Jason's eyes are lit up.

3

I hold in my laugh.

"Todd Ellis. I'd never imagine you making it this far," says Angel as she shares a hug with him.

"Honestly," he begins, his voice raspy like a young teenage boy, "neither did I."

"So, how did you?" Jason questions.

Nobody else says anything. The two girls are silent as are the people on the bus. I wouldn't hurt our chances of finding help by questioning them anyway.

"Well, we were in Lincoln when the outbreak started. I was attending my sister's engineering match," Todd begins. "Avery was on the team."

Avery, the second girl, smiles just barely.

"We hadn't gotten through the first round when a ragged-looking human came barging through the doors."

"One of the dead isn't hard to take," Ava Monroe chimes as she walks towards Dylan and me. She looks at the girls, and they look back at her, neither person showing a smile.

"See, we thought it was just some cosplayer tricking us. My dad was telling him to knock it off, and—" Todd pauses. We already know what's next. The calls of the wind are interrupted as Todd takes a deep breath and continues.

"You can guess what happened next," his voice thickens. "Everybody went into full panic. A couple more of those things stumbled in, and then things got crazy, fast." Every few seconds he glances around, analyzing our faces.

"Before I could think, I was running out the back door with Avery and a few others. I didn't know where my sister was or anyone. I just had who I was with. Joseline was going on a run when she saw us in panic."

I look at the first girl who seems to live up to the introduction. Joseline. Her hand hasn't moved from the bow.

"And I guess that's how we became a group," he finishes with a half-smile and a dorky expression.

Everyone just stares at each other. Todd looks down at the snow, kicking it around. "I'm sorry, I made everything sad," he says, breaking the silence once again.

"No, it's okay," I mumble. "We've all lost people we love. It's just how the world is now."

His expression doesn't lighten up, but he looks at me and nods his head. The slightest nod that I wouldn't have noticed if I wasn't really looking.

"You guys said you needed food and water? Well, we don't have much to give," Joseline says, bringing up a new topic. "We went to find a bunker just a mile down that was said to have supplies in it."

"I'm guessing you didn't find it," Ava implies.

"Actually, we found it. It's just—it requires more than what we have."

"We can help." Dylan turns to the girls, stepping closer to them. "As long as you share it with us."

They exchange looks, wary ones.

"The bunker could have a lot of food, plus we could really use the help," Avery whispers into the ear of the girl. She takes a deep breath in, concentrating on how to reply to our aid.

"Fine," she mutters.

My stomach churns at the thought of food in the bunker. The cold and empty road has made it hard for us to find anything. We've been living off of snacks like raisins and canned fruit.

"Thank you," I say, unable to contain the smile on my face.

"Let's go inside, people are waiting for us." Joseline heads off towards the factory. There are more people?

We follow behind her and enter the building. Odd shades

of rust form on the walls and windows. As everyone spreads out, I see a few tables with ammo and weapons lying across. Other tables have random items like balls, coloring utensils, and woodworking tools. Tall lockers stand empty in the right corner, rustic wood covers the floor, and an odd scent of blood and iron fills the area.

"This is pleasing," Angel says as she looks around.

The girl doesn't take the comment to heart and says, "It's the best we have for now."

Avery blows a whistle with her fingers. People flood from the left and right of the factory. They must have been hiding near the doors of the small additions. Those additions could be holding their food and supplies—the stuff we need.

There's a metal staircase at the back of the building. The sun shines a mosaic of white light onto the steps. The stairs lead up to a small room, and another door is below.

There's an old man and two young kids on the right. I check twice to confirm the view. The kids, who are identical, have brown hair and sharp green eyes. They stand on either side of the man who seems to be in his late sixties. He has light brown trousers and a brown sweater on. His skin is wrinkled, whether that's from his age or the apocalypse. The formation of a white beard stands out against his tan face.

He smiles at us. He smiles at strangers. Everyone else in the room has given us looks as if we're bandits, but him. He approaches us with the twins by his side.

"We've needed new company, Joseline. I'm glad you are bringing them in," he says.

"They're not staying. They're going to help us open the bunker, and then they'll be gone," she replies.

I've grown comfortable with those words. Everyone on the road tells us the same. We're all so desperate for anything, but I can tell this factory doesn't have much anyway.

"I'm Anthony. It's nice to meet you."

"At least *you're* welcoming," Angel says.

Anthony lets out a chuckle and then introduces the twins. "This is William and Charlie."

"It's CJ," one kid mumbles and looks at Anthony with a funky look.

"Yeah, and I'm Will," the other says, staring at us.

Besides the twins and Anthony, I notice a few other people. Their ages are much closer to mine. It's hard to believe that I'm seventeen already. I can still remember the volleyball matches, late-night sleepovers with the team, and even the Air Force Base where we found Dylan and the others. And yet, one year is still not enough to find a place to call home.

On the left, there are three people—two men and a girl about the age of Emily. One man has a pale face and shiny black hair with eyes that match, and the other has a rough golden beard.

"Sarah, do you mind showing these people around?" Joseline insists to Sarah, the girl on the left.

She has light blonde hair that's tied into two loose braids. Behind her lenses are bright blue eyes. She wears a gray shirt and a belt holding a knife.

Her eyes plead with Joseline, but she doesn't budge.

"Yeah, okay. Follow me," Sarah says, defeated. Her hand signals us to follow.

We pass the tables piled with junk and walk into the dimly lit segment where she waits. There are just two doors, one leading outside and the other soon to be found.

"So, this door leads outside, and this one," Sarah says like a kid who is forced to present in class, "leads to our tech room." The doors are pushed open, and she enters the room filled with computers and boxes with wires.

"Woah," Jason gasps as he walks into the room. A grin appears on his face as he heads to the computers. Three black screens reflect the scars and bruises on my face. Jason searches around, looking for more excitement.

"Nothing turns on though. We never had time to set it up," Sarah says. Her mouth lingers open like she wants to say more.

Jason's smile doesn't fade until Ashton Evans decides to speak.

"Quit dorking about the computers, nerd."

I look back at him. He's tall enough that I can see his face clearly amongst the crowd. "You're begging to be left for zombies, Ashton."

He scoffs with a smile and then looks away.

"So far, we haven't seen any eaters around in bulk. We think they're clumping up—we just don't know where," Sarah says as she looks out the window.

"Eaters?" mocks Angel. "What are *Eaters?*"

"The…monsters out there? The ones who eat…people?" Sarah stumbles over her words.

When we met Nathan and Kira, Angel did the same thing. She questioned every inch of their time. How they killed the dead, found food, how they survived.

"You mean the dead?"

"Eaters, the dead, whatever. Let's continue the tour," I say, cutting off the tension.

"Right, yeah." Sarah rushes out the door. "On to the next area."

Jason takes one last look at the computers, at something that could've been.

The door slams behind us. The people who were staring at us then now stand at different tables working on something or talking amongst themselves. Different items are spread across each table. How did they possibly manage to live in this run-down factory for almost a year?

"Now, I know there's not a lot of rooms in the factory, but it's home. We manage to survive and that's what matters." Sarah leads us to the room on the other side. "I mean, we've been here since almost the beginning."

The beginning.

We were living in the school for the first month. My parents were still alive, we had adults protecting us, and life wasn't as bad.

"So, how'd you get all your supplies?" Noah Dias, one of the other members from the Air Force Base, asks from the back. He and Ava were with Dylan at the start. "We were on the road for weeks. The only buildings we did see were wiped clean."

"Unless they're the ones who took out those buildings," Madeline Francis says. She was one of the best receivers on our volleyball team.

"Oh yeah," the girl says, "that was us."

Her voice dampens. "If you guys need anything, or if you want to talk to Joseline or whatever, we can totally help you." The girl proceeds to ramble about her group in a bashful tone.

"You can calm down, Sarah. We're not here to hurt you," Dylan chimes.

She laughs nervously but doesn't say anything. At this point, we arrive at the right section that's identical to the left. Two doors on the walls.

"Let me guess, one leads outside?" Angel asks.

"Yeah," the girl replies. "The other leads to our storage. That's where we keep our food, weapons, etcetera."

Leading us inside, we see racks almost full of weapons and

meds.

"As you can tell, we're running out of food," she says with a sigh and leads us out quickly.

"Now we have two rooms left and that will conclude our small tour." She smiles to help fix the uneasiness around us.

The staircase from a closer view looks ready to break at any second. A small office is at the end.

"This is where Joseline stays. She's the one who managed to keep us alive over the year."

We file into the cramped room. Angel and Noah on my left and right. A black and white picture of a man, who looks like Joseline, hangs on the dark gray wall. A desk with a non-operating computer sits on the right, and old papers are in front of us. Along with those is a wide piece of paper with sketches of the building in pencil. Arrows point in different directions and words scramble across.

"Let's get out quick. She doesn't like anyone here," says Sarah as she starts guiding us out. "The last room, if you guys guessed, is where we all sleep."

"Finally," Angel mutters.

Elbowing her in the side, I whisper, "Quit it."

She glares at me, and I flash a smile, then my eyes focus back on Sarah. She walks down the steps carefully. Her dark boots are silent on them. The eyes of the other people make saying anything feel like a crime.

"I probably shouldn't show you where we sleep 'cause you won't be staying here," Sarah says.

Her words strike me. I don't know why I assumed otherwise. We're just getting some food and leaving. I try to keep my face the same, not letting a sign of shock appear on it.

"Oh, come on! We're helping you with that bunker. The least you can do is let us sleep here for *one* night," Angel exaggerates.

"Sorry." She shrugs. "Josie's rules, not mine."

Frustrated emotions fill our circle. Whispers of the group sound behind me.

"What seems to be the problem?" Joseline asks, nearing our group.

Angel steps closer to the girl. "You want to know what the problem is?"

I stop her before she takes a step. "Look, we haven't had a decent place to stay in forever." The right words must be said so that things don't get worse. "We just thought we would be sleeping here since you know—we're helping you?"

"Yeah, I see," Joseline responds. "Well, we don't have many open beds left. I'd like to keep the space open in case of an emergency."

"You can't take any of us?" I ask.

"Yeah, we can. It's up to you who you want to stay, I'll allow four of you."

Only four of us. Four of us can have a decent sleep, while the rest sleep on the bus, just like yesterday, and the day before.

"Pathetic," mumbles Angel. Others whisper to each other.

My mind doesn't falter. After all, we came here for food and nothing else. "Let's figure this out then."

Joseline and Sarah are already leaving, and a few from the group have sat down on the eerie steps.

TWO
THE FIRST PIECE

ASHTON AND MARLON were the first to ask, but their tone made it seem like they *deserved* it. Nathan and Kira didn't bother asking. We've only known them for a few months, so maybe they didn't want to start anything.

The lack of food must be dragging us all down. Nobody tries to fight for a bed. Most of us don't mind sleeping on the bus, but the problem is the food.

Dylan glances at the others. His head held high. "Since we're helping Joseline open that bunker, it's best if those helping are the ones who stay in the rooms."

"And remember," I begin, "we're just her guests. Our goal is to open that bunker, and then we're leaving."

For an odd reason, I can feel the factory people eyeing us. Like they know our fate and are just waiting to see if we can conclude it ourselves.

"I wish we didn't have to move. We've been moving so much—" begins Angel.

"I promise you. We'll find a home." I may have said I promise, but I don't know if it can be kept. The others heard me say it too, so the pressure is on me now. "So then, who's going to help Joseline tomorrow?"

Angel and Ava offer themselves up first, and I accept. I'm surprised Ashton hasn't said anything, though it's probably because he doesn't trust their group yet. Madeline also asked to go. She said she can help if someone gets hurt.

"I'm going to go talk with that Joseline girl. I'll be back soon," says Dylan. He doesn't wait for a response and heads off.

"In the meantime, does anyone have an idea as to how we're opening that bunker?" I say, picturing some sort of iron wall in my head.

"Back at the camp," Noah starts, "before everything went to hell, my dad was one of the engineers. He taught me how to open the bunkers near the camp. They could be similar to the one we're dealing with now."

The Air Force base. My memories of it are clear. The blood bags and feeding the zombies with our dead friends. The houses and buildings with people who promised they'd be nice to us, only to learn that none of them wanted us there, especially after what happened.

"Go ahead then, tell us how to open it," Angel pipes. A cheesy smile appears on her face. She must be the most excited out of us all. Whenever we had matches, she was the one to bring all the food.

"Okay, so there were three number codes around the camp, buried underground. Each had a set of numbers, and on the bunker, there were three pin pads," Noah explains. "The codes were on a map. Only close members of the group were able to access it. If this bunker is anything like the one over there, I'd say we should be looking for those codes and some kind of map."

Noah's mouth curls as he locks eyes with Angel. "What're you staring at?" he asks, playing dumb.

She turns away, a flustered look on her face. "Not at you, Noah."

Her cheeks are red, and she's fixing her sitting position. Some of the others giggle to themselves. Luckily for the two, Dylan's already walking back to us with information.

"What's so funny?" he asks.

"Nothing," Angel replies. "Noah's just telling us how to get into the bunker."

Dylan sits down next to me, and I ask, "Did Joseline tell you anything?"

"Well, long story short, this place was a factory where men worked in the 1850s. They built an underground bunker for bombings and attacks, but also to help runaway slaves. After the war, they used it as a tornado shelter—or a shelter for other natural disasters. It's loaded with food, water, and other supplies, or it should be. Joseline said there were three keypads on top of the bunker, but she doesn't know what the codes are or where they are."

My head twists to see Noah accomplished with himself. He pushes back his almost black-colored hair and tries not to look too cocky.

"I'm guessing you know where it is?" I question.

"Yeah, I do," he replies.

I hold my breath, trying to contain my happiness. "Then that settles it. Angel, Ava, Noah, and Madeline will get the room tonight so that they can go to the bunker with Joseline and the others tomorrow. The rest of us will sleep on the bus and stay here."

Dylan will probably go with them, but I know he'd rather sleep on the bus.

"I won't promise that others won't be going to. If we need to find those three codes, it could require a lot of us to help."

Most of the others don't seem fazed. They're not happy or sad, just there. Some are relieved to have a decent stay, while others look like they want to sleep for a week. I can't say anything to help them, I just hope that things will get better.

I was up longer than I should've been. I was starving and cold. Joseline gave us more food for the night, but it wasn't enough to fuel us. The snow was tumbling around, filling the night with the sounds of ghosts. The only thought that came to mind was about the bunker filled with food and supplies galore.

After many miles, we finally find a stop, but something feels unsteady. There isn't enough room for us here anyway, and Joseline's group has themselves figured out.

Goosebumps rise on my arms and legs. Besides food, I need a blanket. A big warm blanket. Sitting across from me is Emily. Before the apocalypse, we used to share the same bed. It was comforting to be beside my sister.

She lay peacefully on the bus seat, her busted purple winter coat spread on top of her. Funny how we all own things that originally weren't ours. Her coat was found in a mall some weeks after what happened at the Air Force Base.

When one of the zombies ripped my sleeve off, I abandoned my denim hoodie. I found a black jacket at one of the shops we looted in the same mall. I'd always wanted one of those, and it would've sat there anyway, waiting for someone else to pick it up.

Sitting up from my attempt at sleeping, I undo my ponytail. Everyone says that humans evolved from apes and fish. I wonder if we'll evolve too. I know we have adapted before, but is my body really going to change? My hair is still greasy, my body hasn't handled the cold yet, and a cure for these zombies is still to be found. Maybe it's just my ignorance thinking.

Emily and I sleep on the second set of seats. In case of emergencies, Emily can drive us away, and I can deal with the harm. There's a seat in front of me. It protects me from the cold wind seeping through the cracks of the door, but the window still breaks the warmth. For Emily, it's the driver's seat that encloses her.

The freezing window blows its frigid air against my head.

"Not much of a cushion," I think to myself.

My mind continues to wander afar. How long would it take for us to open the bunker? Are we leaving anytime soon? Can I trust Joseline and her group? I don't want to stress, but stress wants me. I feel like I can't conquer it. Even at night, it keeps me up.

Stress was kinder that night. I must've fallen asleep in my thoughts. The fiery sun glows on my face. It forces me up. My hair feels slightly messy and my neck hurts from the bad posture, but that's normal for us. I wonder how the others slept in the room.

I stand up and adjust my belt. My revolver must've fallen out of it and onto the floor during the night. I slowly pick it up, still tired like every day, but I remind myself why I'm here. For the bunker. The bunker will bring us food and warmth.

My arms stretch to the sides. A thick burn clogs my throat. In the corner of my seat is my almost finished water. Chugging it down, my body yearns for more, but the bottle is empty in seconds. Not much help there.

Feeling a bit better, I turn around to see if anyone else has woken up. Jason catches my eye. He sits alone, three rows back, and looks out the window, gazing off to who knows where. My eyes dart to the right, and I see Dylan putting his sniper on the top compartment. He then ruffles his hair and glances my way.

"Morning," he whispers.

The sun must've woken us all up. His green eyes sparkle against the yellow light.

"Good morning," I reply with a weak smile. My eyes shift away as Emily rises.

"Morning guys." There's a hint of annoyance in her voice, but that's typical for her; she hates waking up.

My legs bend as I catch the seat. "Let's head inside after everyone is up."

Dylan nods and falls back into his.

The sun beats down on the bus forcing others to wake up. The group is small, much smaller than last year, but it's not because they died. Many left to find their families and pursue their own ways of surviving the apocalypse.

Nobody minds because it feels safer to have fewer people anyway. Kira and Nathan are the only ones who we've added.

We wake up the rest of the sleepers. They're all annoyed, but I would be too. Our dreams are the only place we can escape this reality. Nobody wants to leave them.

My body still feels asleep in a way. I need an adrenaline rush to boost me. Or just some caffeine, but in the apocalypse, I'm even lucky to find a can of food.

I try to ignore my old life. If I think too much about it, I'll keep seeing it. Images of coffee now appear in my head. Hot coffee, warm sweaters on, and sitting by the fireplace.

Oh, how I miss my old life. All I had to worry about was what I was going to wear to school to show the other girls that I had style. Still, they never really saw anyone except themselves.

I do a quick head count. Nine are on the bus and four are in the factory. Emily slips into the bus seat and opens the door. Cool air spirals in sending chills down my back.

"I can't wait for spring," I groan to my sister who smirks.

Dylan and Jason follow behind as I step down. The snow still holds our footprints from yesterday, but it's all squishy and wet. It lies there, being a nuisance to everyone. I tramp through it and find myself in the factory.

"Good afternoon," one twin cheers. The other one sighs and corrects the first one.

"It's morning, idiot."

They whisper to each other with laughter and annoyance.

"Good morning you two," I reply.

Their mirroring image makes telling them apart difficult. I don't bother trying to find out. They walk away as Anthony approaches.

"Sleep well?" he asks us. "You all must be hungry—I wish I could help."

"Don't worry about it. We'll find something soon," I reply.

One of the twins starts calling for him, and the old man leaves, but he gives us a warm smile before turning away.

"Let's go find Joseline," says Dylan as he looks around.

Jason is already wandering off. It doesn't take long to find her as she and Noah are right beside us. They stare at a big plaster on the wall. I noticed it before but never had the chance to look at it.

"Oh, Hailee. How was your night?" she asks.

"You know—same old," I reply.

She looks at me funny and laughs a little. "Our groups are still wary of each other, you know. It's only a matter of time before something breaks out."

I'm taken aback. "Are you trying to say something?"

"No, I'm just warning you. I want us to work together."

Her tone makes me question this whole thing. I guess I should talk to some of the group. Not all of them are on board with this. I see Ashton and Marlon laughing away in a corner.

"Yeah, I'll talk to them," I say with reluctance.

Dylan looks at me, and his face mirrors what I'm feeling. Even Noah has a confused look.

Turning back to Joseline, Dylan says, "So, we're looking for a map. Where do you think it'll be?"

"I say that it's in one of the floor tiles," Noah says. His foot rubs over part of the flooring.

A smirk crawls on my face. "Yeah, that's definitely a place."

Joseline gazes at her office. "After all this time being here, we haven't noticed anything abnormal about the factory. If there really is a map here, they hid it pretty dang well."

She must know about something; I'll just have to pry to find out.

"So, Joseline, when did you all *actually* get to the factory?" I ask. Maybe if someone had been here before, they could've stolen the map.

She thinks for a second. "About a month from the start of this whole mess."

Enough time for someone to sneak in, but how would they know of the map so fast?

"...And when you got here, did you see or find anything strange?"

She looks away, her eyes remembering something. I stare at her waiting for a clue.

"A few days after we started living here, I went up into the office to see what was there," she begins. "I saw this metal box. I tried cracking it open, but it wouldn't budge. There was a keyhole on the top. But I stored it away—there were other things to deal with, and I can't remember where I left it."

"In the floor tiles," says Noah, laughing at himself.

Now my smirk is an embarrassed grin. "What's up with you and floor tiles?"

"They're just convenient places to hide stuff." He shrugs, facing the floor.

"I figured it out. Thanks, Noah." Joseline bolts to the tech room.

We follow her, barely keeping up like little chickens following their mother. Noah has the same sly smile he had when he was talking about the bunker.

When we open the tech door, Jason and Todd stand messing with some wires and parts of the computer. They're startled as Joseline speeds to the computer on the left.

"What are you looking for?" Todd asks, looking at his precious items being rummaged through.

"I stored this metal box somewhere"—her fingers trace over different parts of the setup—"here, in this thing."

A big box is next to the monitor, and she places it on the floor.

On its side, Joseline pulls off the top and reveals what's inside. The motherboard, power cables, and everything else fit together perfectly. A small space is left open. It's just the right size to fit a box, and as predicted, the metal box is there, dirty and muddy, but okay. The first piece to our puzzle.

My heart skips a beat, but I don't let myself get too happy. With excitement comes failure. The key is still to be found, and then we'll have to search for the codes. It'll be a while until we get the food.

THREE
SEALED TIGHT

JOSELINE AND I bring our groups together near the staircase just like yesterday.

"I need you all to look for a key," I begin. "Our hope is that it'll open this box."

Joseline displays the metal to everyone. "We need to get this bunker open quickly. This winter was terrible, and it took a lot out of us. The stuff in there can help us build back up."

She looks at me and then my group who occupy the right side. "Some of you have brought concerns to me about Hailee's group. They'll only be staying here until we get the bunker open. Then we'll be back to normal. For now, you all need to keep your eyes open. The sooner we find the key, the sooner we have food."

The crowd whispers amongst themselves. Others nod their heads, and soon the group is scattered. A single thought keeps swimming in my head. What if the bunker doesn't have anything? I'd be putting these people through a lot just for nothing.

Without any food, my mind feels like it can only think negatively.

"Hey, Sarah!" I yell to the blonde girl sitting next to the storage room. "You think we could eat something? None of us have had food in a while."

I notice her glance at Joseline and look back just as fast.

She hesitates to speak, her eyes darting across the floor. "Yeah, I think we have something."

"All right, you're not getting in trouble for this, right?"

"No—no, it's fine. Come with me."

She leads me into the storage room. It's barely visible with only a light coming from the sealed window. It's like the one at the base. A medium-sized box sits alone in the corner.

"Thirteen of you?" she asks, approaching the box.

"Yeah, thirteen," I reply.

Already, she knows how many of us there are. I can't tell if it's because of trust or worry. She hands me the exact number of bars on a small tray.

"You can just give the tray to Anthony when you're done using it," she says and leads me out to the main room.

I go around to everyone and hand out the bars. First, Angel and Madeline. They were talking with Kate Davis, another girl on the volleyball team.

Ashton and Marlon were next, then Todd and Jason. Todd understood when I didn't give him one of the bars.

"I've had plenty already," he said.

Dylan stands by the window with Ava and Noah.

As I approach, my arms stretch out, offering the few bars left. "Hey, Sarah gave me these for us to eat."

"Finally," Ava says, grabbing one. "I was wondering when they were going to give us food."

I smile and turn the tray to Noah and Dylan.

They both grab one and in sync say, "Thank you," which is then followed by small chuckles.

I don't waste time trying to talk to them. I'm hungry too. As I head off, I hear Ava behind me.

"Hailee," she whispers and takes a step closer.

My body turns reluctantly. "Yeah?"

"Let's get out of this place soon."

Her face shows a disguised fear. These two groups haven't become close. I don't know if they ever will, but I know I'll look after my own.

"Don't worry."

The mood seems to have lightened a little after the meal. Even I feel better despite the bar being cold and hard. Like Sarah said, I give the tray to Anthony, and he puts it away. Now the wrapper lay in my hands.

I look around for a trash can. It may be the apocalypse, but I still have decency. I see a big green garbage bin through one of the factory windows. A thin layer of snow on top.

"There," I think to myself.

This can be an excuse to check out the outside. I haven't done much of that yet. After a final look around, I head towards the doors.

"Hey, Hailee," Kate calls from behind me.

I turn around and see her cheerful smile. Her height always catches me off guard. "Where ya going?"

"I thought I'd throw this in the trash can and look around a little outside, you want to come?" I suggest. It'll be nice to have some company, especially if any of the dead are lurking.

"Hell yeah. My mom would be proud of us."

Kate's mom was an environmental scientist. She left for a trip over the weekend when the apocalypse started, and Kate never saw her since. The same story goes for a lot of us here, and for others like me, our parents died in a bus crash at the start.

I've gotten over it now, though it didn't seem possible back then. There were still others who cared for us, living people who protected us. The adults are gone now, but they would want us to keep fighting.

We arrive at the dumpster and throw out the trash. From the outside, the people in the factory are hard to see. The windows are tinted, so you can't make out anything.

"Where should we go?" Kate asks, shifting her weight to look around the trees. She approaches some of them with light steps.

"Not sure," I reply and follow her lead. "I just hope—"

The sound of crying cuts me off. I look at Kate who seems like she heard it too.

Her body stops moving. "You hear that, right?"

I stay silent to hear the sound better. A whimper, a small girl's whimper echoes in the woods.

"Yeah."

"We *have* to check it out," pleads Kate.

With the key on my mind, I keep thinking that this person will have it.

"Let's do it," I reply and head towards the trees.

The cries get louder as the empty forest carries her call.

"Help me. Please," the girl sobs. "Please! Help me!"

We share a look of agreement. This girl needs our help, so we might as well. The snow holds our steps as we trot down the slope. Anyone can follow them and find us.

By this point, the girl must be right around the tree. She's been crying all this time, but now she's stopped.

I gesture to Kate to go left, and I go right. She nods and

sneaks to the side.

Our eyes find each other, but no girl is around.

"Where did she go?" I whisper and look around at the repeating scenery. Everything looks the same, and there's no girl anywhere. The cries start up again, and we look down to see a cassette tape.

Before either of us say anything, a sharp kick flings Kate, and then me, forward and hurdling downhill as snow clumps onto us.

In seconds, I fly down the slope. The ice freezes the bare parts of my body. The hill feels miles long. I can't help but regret everything now. What have we gotten ourselves into?

Trees sprawl across the pathway. I hear Kate whimper in pain as she hits something big. I don't want to look.

A thick tree stands in my way. Frozen in fear, a sharp pain blasts through my hip. I steady my vision to find something, anything to hold onto. With no mercy, I continue to be dragged down. The view of the snow blackens.

We make it to a stop—meaning I have no idea where we are. A rocky, dirt-filled cave entraps us. Snow covers Kate's hair and clothes. I can only assume it's the same for me.

"Oh god," she says, winded. "That girl is dead once we get out of this hole."

I'm guessing Kate's rage was too loud as a pack of zombies appears from a slit in the cave.

She mumbles something but I don't bother asking. I reach to find my knife. The typical feeling of the blade is nowhere. Not in my pant pocket, my gun belt, or my jacket. It's nowhere.

"Please tell me you have your knife?" I ask her as the dead get closer.

She pats herself down, and I already know her answer by

the anger in her sigh. "It's gone."

There's no room in my head to be frustrated. We both start scanning through the items on the floor for a possible weapon. A stick behind me seems fit for a knife.

In enough time, I flick back around to see one of the dead inches away. Swiping his foot, he falls to one knee. He isn't as tough when he can't walk. I poke the stick through his skull.

My mind flusters as I struggle to pull it out. While twisting it around, a picture of a landscape on his shirt catches my eye. There's a large mountain with tiny people trying to push it. The mountain faces the sun while the people stand in the rain. It's happy and enjoying the sun's warm rays as the people try to move it helplessly.

The stick slides out, and the picture vanishes from my view.

Kate has found a small boulder, and she now uses it to smash a zombie's head against the wall. His brains stick and then skid down like mashed potatoes. I see another one coming my way. I fix the weapon in my hand and stab the woman right below the chin. The end of the stick pokes out the back of her head.

Another zombie peeks out from the side. I pull out the stick and jab the end through the zombie's skull. Most of them are down now. I see Kate swipe the leg of one of the dead in front of her. The same technique as me. Kira taught us it. She picked it up at a training session with Nathan for the army.

The rest of the dead split evenly between Kate and me. I walk over to the first, an old man, and stab him. Pulling the stick out, the end injects into the other one, a middle-aged woman. With a sigh of relief, I glance at Kate. She's focused on one of them. Another one comes from the same direction with teeth prowled open.

"Watch out," I yell drawing his attention. When he looks

at me, the stick crashes into his head.

Finishing off, Kate smashes the boulder into the last one, and the growling silences. At first, it wasn't loud, but now the beating of my heart is all that's heard.

I catch the wall behind me and let myself drop to the floor, my lungs out of air and blood splattered across my clothes.

"Just for some trash," Kate sighs and leans against the wall. I look up at her and begin laughing.

"Hey? is that the—"

"Holy shit," I interrupt. "That's it."

Kate's already looking down at the zombie, and I'm right behind. His neck holds a chain with a silver key.

My arm reaches out and yanks the key off of his neck. "It was down here all along."

"We've got luck on our side," she says and follows with a fist bump.

We climbed our way out of the cave. It was more than difficult as the opening was at the top. My hands felt numb, and my body ached. I didn't think about the crying girl—or whoever had kicked us down the hole. Amid all the chaos, our attacker wasn't on my mind, but now she's all I can think about. She could be lurking anywhere. Ready to send us to another infested cave of the dead.

We step through the front doors. Snow and mud cling to Kate's thin green winter jacket. Everyone's heads turn towards us as we walk into the factory. I smile weakly while Kate lets out a sigh of relief.

Most of them continue back to what they were doing, but Joseline and a few others walk up to us.

"We have a present for you," says Kate as she looks at me. "You got the key, right?"

I nod my head. "Of course." My hand, red from the grip, opens to show Joseline the token of victory.

"Where were you guys?" she asks with a hint of worry. Her brown eyes are entranced by the key.

"Let's just say it wasn't fun. Someone is lurking around here in case you didn't know," Kate replies.

Todd raises his hand for a high five. "Nice one guys!"

"Thanks," I say through a smile and slap his hand. Kate stares at him for a second, debating if she should. Todd's smile wins, and she slaps his hand.

"I guess now we open that box," Joseline says.

Todd follows behind her and says, "Yeah let's do it."

They lead the way over to the staircase while Kate trails away. She said she would wait with the others.

Joseline's door key flips around in her hand, and when we arrive at the door, she doesn't wait to put it in. The dirty metal box is sitting on the desk, waiting to be opened.

It feels as though a boulder has been lifted off me. We'll finally get the map and open the bunker.

Joseline picks up the box, her finger tracing over the key-hole. "Let's hope this works."

She inserts the silver key into the slot, and the top clicks, then the small door opens. We all look up at each other and smile.

"Well, open the map up!" Todd spits out.

"I will—calm down."

There is hardly a smirk on her face as she pulls out a paper. The map is folded up, the edges are cracked, and the color looks ancient. Carefully, she reveals it. The backside faces Todd and me.

"Let us see," he says, trying to peek over.

"Okay, okay." She puts the map down flat. "I think we

found where our bunker codes are." Her mouth finally cracks a smile.

There are three shapes placed a few inches away from a small building, which must be the factory. A map key is in the corner along with a compass. The front doors, or what I think are the front doors, are facing south. My suspicion is confirmed in the key. The building on the map symbolizes the factory.

There are different land symbols, and the three shapes that symbolize Code 1, Code 2, and Code 3 are written. The last thing I see is a map scale showing one mile as an inch. Before I can measure the distance between them, Todd's stomach grumbles.

"You hungry?" Joseline asks him.

"Uh—of course, I am."

We laugh, and Joseline folds the map up. "We can study this later, right now we should let Hailee rest," she says.

I know resting is a better choice, but the eagerness inside of me doesn't want to wait.

"Yeah, okay."

The two of them hurry down the stairs and find a seat. Before I follow, my eyes draw to the people below. Angel sees me and rushes over.

"Where were you," she shouts.

"I'll tell you some other time."

Her body leans against the railing at the bottom. I hear her scoff, but she doesn't leave.

"Well, are we still going to the bunker?"

My eyes fix on her leather jacket, a thin black shirt is hidden under. It never crossed my mind that we planned to go today.

"We need to round up everyone—we won't be able to go today," I say.

Her eyes contort into confusion. "Why not?"

"Well, that box with the map, it's open now."

"So?"

"On the map, the codes are miles away."

Even I wanted to go today, but by the time we make it back, it would be night, and with whoever kicked us down the hole, I don't want to cause any harm.

"So, how are we going to find them then?"

I smile to hide my head turning its gears. I wish all the answers would come to me like they do for Jason, but I don't think they ever will.

"I don't know."

Angel and I round up our group and some of the others.

"We won't be making it to the bunker today," I begin, staring at their faces. "When we got the map out, it revealed the codes."

"So, they just slept in this place for nothing?" asks Ashton, a harsh anger in his voice.

Despite his aggression, I know he's right, and it makes this all worse.

"Yeah, we can switch out the people, but we'll end up being here for longer than we thought."

I don't want to stay here, and they don't either, but from the aching muscles to the wimp legs, I know that we're all exhausted. Getting some rest is the best thing to do right now and finding the bunker is something for tomorrow.

"I promise we will get the food and be able to eat," I say, knowing they're all annoyed at me now. "I need three different groups. This way, we can all go to the codes at the same time and be able to get to the bunker sooner."

"Whatever. Let's get these groups assigned then," the same voice groans.

Ashton glares at us through the crowd, but I try to ignore him.

Joseline brings the box in front of everyone and opens the door. "All right everyone, eyes on this," she says, unraveling the map and placing it in the middle.

Everyone sits down in a circle, and she begins piecing it out. "There's three shapes. The triangle, circle, and square." She points to each shape as she speaks. "They're the codes for the bunker. So, let's assemble those groups."

I point to one of the shapes. "It looks like the triangle is the furthest one. Madeline, Noah, Angel, and Ava can go for that one since they slept here and have the most energy."

They each nod their heads, and I write their names on the map.

"Todd and I can go to the triangle as well since we know the area the best," says Joseline.

My fingers move quickly to keep up with them. "Okay. The square is the second furthest, who wants to go for that one?"

Nobody answers, so I scribble my name. "Okay, I'll go."

Dylan volunteers after, a stern but hopeful expression on his face.

"We'll go," Kira says for both her and Nathan. Nathan looks at her irritated, and she smirks.

"Okay us four will go to the square."

Joseline eyes me. I can tell she doesn't trust four people from my group to find the square.

"You can trust us, Joseline."

She nods, but her eyes still search for something. Giving up, she looks back to the map. The room gets silent. Her group doesn't trust us, and mine doesn't trust hers either.

Breaking the tension, I ask, "And who wants to go the circle?"

31

Avery offers herself first with Sarah next.

"Okay anyone else?"

"I'll come with," says Emily.

Jason watches my pencil and waits for me to finish writing before saying, "Yeah, I'll go as well."

Ashton smirks from the back and says, "I'll go too. You guys will need me."

"Then that settles it. We all know where to go, right?" I ask them, finishing off Ashton's name, and they all nod.

Glancing at Kate, her mouth lingers open like she wants to say something.

"What about the rest of us?" she spits out.

I didn't realize that neither Joseline nor I would be present to keep people in check.

"My people are well-behaved, as long as yours are too, it won't be a problem," Joseline says before me.

Kate doesn't look away from me.

"You won't have to worry, I trust them."

FOUR

SEPARATE WAYS

I PUSH MY HANDS into my jacket pockets. My body still hurts from the tumble down the slope, but I'd rather think about other things. The cold winds fling my ponytail to the left. The short strands in front of my face go wild in the air.

The square code is a couple of miles out, but if we follow the plan, we can be back once night hits. My cheeks feel numb and cold as we trench through the snow. Any light is shaded by the gray clouds.

My knife was by a couple of trees, and when we found it, I tucked it away hoping it wouldn't get lost again.

"Just two miles—can't be that hard," says Nathan behind Dylan and me.

Kira scoffs. "I doubt that." The paper is yanked out of Nathan's hands and into hers. It's a hand-drawn map of the original which is with Joseline.

A part of me wishes we'd taken the bus, but there's no road out here to drive on anyway. Joseline and the others have that as well. I've given a lot of trust to them, and they've done the same for us. I'm starting to think we have a chance of staying with them, and even if we don't, we'll still have food and water.

"I told you," Nathan says.

He zips up his black jacket halfway, then proceeds to wipe the fog appearing on his glasses. "I'm not that dumb."

I look at Dylan who is smirking by himself. I can't help but smile too.

"If we go fast enough, we could make it in 40 minutes," I say.

"40 minutes?" Nathan complains. "I ran a mile in eight minutes. If you mul—"

"We're not running out here," says Kira.

"But we could."

Running may sound great, but when the dead arrive, we would be too tired to continue. "You're just going to waste your energy."

"Oh c'mon, Hailee," protests Nathan. "We could beat all the other groups."

"It's not a race." Kira stares in disbelief as Nathan pushes past Dylan and me.

He taps Dylan on the shoulder, who then looks at me like he's waiting for approval.

I shrug my shoulders. Nathan and Dylan are strong, they'll figure it out. "Don't get lost, I guess."

* * *

"How much longer?" Angel stares out the window and into the gray sky.

"A few more miles on the bus, and then we'll walk for a mile after," Joseline answers. The bumps of the road shake her voice as she speaks.

Angel lets out a huff and crosses her arms.

"Just think about the food," Noah says, fixing his eyes onto her. "Or you can come sit by me. I'll keep you company." His smirk is almost creepy, and Angel can't help but feel awkward.

"That was cringe, dude," says Madeline from the driver's seat.

Noah looks down at his hands and shakes his head.

"Way to go, Noah," Ava says elbowing him in the arm. "You lost the girl."

"She'll like me eventually," he retorts.

They both sit on the seat across from Angel. Nobody sits in the back, and Madeline drives the bus. Joseline and Todd sit at the front.

"Keep dreaming."

Angel is quick to move up towards the front. Getting to know the others will be less awkward than this.

It doesn't feel like they're making any distance with only snow and gray skies for a view. After what feels like an hour, trees start showing up and all the driving becomes worth it.

Madeline parks the bus on the side of the road. Hills surround the right side and stretch out further down.

Joseline steps down with the others behind her. "Now we just walk a mile out and we'll find the code."

Madeline takes the keys and follows the procedure to close the door. Pull the emergency latch, close the doors, and then lock it. Everything that Emily taught her.

Joseline leads the group, Todd by her side, and they head up the hill. It's steep, all of the hills are.

"You hear that?" asks Todd, pausing in his tracks.

Joseline makes it to the top and sees the zombies on the other side. Their growls seem even louder in the pit of the hills.

She strings up her bow and says, "This'll be easy."

* * *

"There's about two and a fourth of a mile left," says Jason, clutching the drawn map tightly. "We can reach it in about 50 minutes if we're fast."

"This fucking wind is getting on my nerves," Ashton mutters. "Can't we find a resting place?"

"You volunteered to go," says Jason. Despite the breeze, his eyes are wide and alert.

"Yeah, 'cause I'm hungry, and you guys need me."

Nobody replies. They're either too cold or plain annoyed. The wind is picking up its pace, blowing directly in front of the group. Jason and Sarah have pink faces.

"We're all hungry," Avery mumbles. Ashton scoffs and walks ahead of the group.

"What do you think's going to be in the bunker?" whispers Sarah to the girls.

Avery replies, "Probably some cans and expired food." Her eyes never meet Sarah's.

Emily shoves her hands into her pockets. "Let's hope it's not expired."

Avery stares down at the repetitive snow. "Yeah, we can hope."

"I think we should hope that we don't get sick from this wind. I can't imagine what the other groups are going through as well," says Sarah as she too turns to the floor.

"Well, technically, we have the most walking distance, so we probably have it the hardest," Jason adds.

"I thought we were supposed to be walking not talking," Ashton shouts. He mutters something after, but nobody listens.

Jason scoffs, and Avery rolls her eyes, but they all stop talking. They may not agree with Ashton, but they know the silence can help them move faster. The wind, as if it were playing with them, slows down too.

* * *

"Wow! You guys made it so far," Kira says to the two who sit on a rock.

Nathan gasps for air. "We would've made it further if it weren't for this wind."

"He's right," Dylan says, out of breath.

"Let's keep going," I say, holding my hand out to Dylan.

He grabs it and picks himself up. Nathan uses Kira's hand to do the same.

"We can rest in a few."

"All right, let's go," Nathan commands, taking the lead.

They weren't joking about the wind. It's hard to move at all, and at this pace, we'll be late. I'm sure the others are facing this too.

"The bus would've been nice," Nathan mumbles.

I glance at him, but the gusts of wind force me to look back down. "Joseline's group needed it more."

"Plus, there's no place for the bus to travel on," says Dylan.

"Still would've been nice."

I cross my arms and tuck my hands into my armpits hoping it minimizes the frostbite. I remind myself once more of why I'm doing this.

* * *

"Stay together. There are not a lot of them right now, but

there'll be more," Joseline says with the bow pointed at the small crowd.

Together, they walk down the hill and into the divot with the zombies. They kill those ones with ease, but now they stand in the middle with trees all around.

One creature emerges from the left. All the hair on his head is stripped away, his skin is nearly fleeing from his face, and his eyes can penetrate a soul with one look. He's terrifying.

An arrow plunges into his skull, and his body stops in its tracks. He falls to the floor, his eyes wide open. Joseline walks over to the zombie and yanks the arrow out of him. The blood is thick and mixed with parts of his fat. She wipes the liquid onto his torn beige shirt.

"There'll be more."

Everyone is on high alert. Each of them analyzes a portion of the woods. Their backs together.

Angel wipes her hand onto her shirt. She always had a problem with sweat even in the cold.

Another zombie peers out from the right. Todd brings up his gun, aiming for the zombie, but is pushed away by Joseline.

"No noise," she whispers to him, wide-eyed.

He nods his head and lowers his gun. Angel steps between the two and up to the zombie. With a grunt, she severs the top of his head. Her sword cuts through like cake, and the man falls.

More zombies flutter in like bugs crawling for food. Their teeth are ready to gnaw into their next meal. Ava takes her knife out, gutting the zombie in front of her. Its insides spew out from the sides like water from a faucet. Then with one knife in the zombie's abdomen, she takes out another knife from her jean pocket and sticks it into his head. The zombie freezes. She pulls both knives out in a clean motion. White smoke drifts out of her mouth as she exhales with relief.

Another zombie limps over to Noah who's already aiming at him with his gun. He pulls the trigger of the silent weapon, striking the zombie in the forehead. Its eyes stare blankly at him, and then it falls. The snow stains a dark rosewood color. A smell reeks from the surface of the zombies.

Another comes from the shadows of the trees near Todd. He stares at the thing, scared like a boy who just saw a clown. The zombie approaches him in the blink of an eye, and he trembles with fear as he pushes its shoulders. He trips while trying to grip his gun strapped around his back.

Fumbling around, he finally gets the gun around and finds a grip on the trigger, but recalling what Joseline said, he instead bashes the end into the zombie's head. He lets out a sigh and wipes his forehead that's developed a scary amount of sweat.

Madeline stares at the mess with a worried look. He laughs off the nervous pit in his throat. Turning back around, she sees a zombie headed for her.

"Eat this you cockroach," she shouts and shoves the man to the ground. Kneeling next to him, she stabs her pocketknife directly through his dry, yellow eye. She snorts. "I got him right in the eye."

In the middle of a battle, they can't help but laugh. More growls are heard, and Joseline turns around to see the creature headed for her. Using the arrow she pulled from the first zombie, she injects it into the bottom of his chin, piercing through his grim head and out the other end. When the zombie goes limp, she yanks the arrow out and shakes the brains off.

* * *

"We're almost there. It's like a half of a mile left now," says Jason, taking a glance at the map and then putting it away. By now, all their faces have gone numb.

"We get it," Ashton complains. "You don't need to remind us every second."

The cold makes the trip almost unbearable, but they know they need to do this for the bunker. A few more minutes and they will make it.

"Of course we get the windiest route," continues Ashton.

Emily looks at him, tired of his denying, pessimistic self. "They're probably facing the same weather as us."

He scoffs. "Your sister is ridiculous for making us go right now."

"Hailee just wants to find food for us all. You said it yourself, you're hungry, and you volunteered," Jason says. "Maybe if you stopped complaining, we could get there faster."

Ashton stops walking and looks down, his eyebrows furrowed. They all watch, exhausted from his hatred and denial. He turns back to them.

"I get it, you all are tired of me."

Jason doesn't hold back. "Well, obviously when you act like a bitch."

There's an eerie smile on Ashton now. He glances down at his sneakers and then at Jason.

"Maybe you'll listen to me now."

In a few steps, he's in front of Jason with his eyes staring him down. If not brown, they could be the color of the devil. Perhaps the devil himself has possessed Ashton's body now.

Nobody expects his hand to curl into a fist and dig into the kid in front of him. Jason is knocked down, and his cheek flushes with color.

The blow puts a ringing in his ear, and he looks around, dazed.

The three girls watch in horror with shouts trying to stop

the beast. Ashton mounts on top of Jason, keeping him down and landing more punches. He mutters stuff to himself as he throws each fist. All the anger he's built up is being sent towards Jason.

The kid sticks to the ground, trying to find a way to stop Ashton. His knife and gun are compressed beneath his body. His mind, which he used to call smart, tries shifting its gears, but nothing is coming up. One thing he does know is that his body will start putting up defenses soon.

He gives up searching, and the pain starts to go away. The idea that he deserves this now plays in his head. He thought he was just helping the group, but to Ashton, he was being a dick.

Nobody says anything. Ashton realizes what he's done, but it doesn't make him feel guilty, it makes him feel powerful. He wipes the snow off his coiled hair and sniffles.

"You wanna follow me now?"

Jason doesn't move. His eyes stay shut, and the snow seeps through his jacket.

"Ashton—what the hell did you do?" Emily cries as she steps closer to the two.

The other two girls are quiet. After all, they don't know Jason, but they do know something. It's in the distance, nearing them. It's someone.

Someone who walked all the way over to them—through the long snowed prairie with trees scattered about. Someone with a gun pointed at Ashton.

Someone who says, "Get off."

FIVE
SYMPATHY

KATE CROUCHES TO level with the twins who stare eagerly at her. "How about you two go hide," she says, noticing their hyper bodies, "and I'll come look for you?"

They glance at each other and run opposite ways. She doesn't bother closing her eyes because they won't care.

At night, the other day, some of the factory people introduced themselves. Kate tries to recall the names. Was it Tyler and David? Tim and Damien?

Tyler and Damien.

She remembers the way they introduced themselves too. One was optimistic while the other skeptical, but despite their personality differences, it seemed like they had an unbreakable connection. Kate wishes she had something like that.

"I don't know how I feel about this bunker thing," Tyler says, pursing his lips, "and that group is big. They could easily ambush us—or even kill us."

Damien laughs. "I think they're fine."

He brings his hand to Tyler's pale cheek.

"You gotta stop worrying. Joseline trusted us, and she trusts them too."

Damien's rough chestnut-colored hair stands upright. He takes his hand back and crosses his arms.

Tyler stares at the window. There's a layer of condensation that blurs the outside. "Worrying is all I can do. I wish I had those meds now."

"It seems like you're more worried about those guys than the literal apocalypse."

"I'm worried about that too," he says, looking back at Damien and smiling. "You remember how my dad had the Chinese barber shop?" He picks at the back of his head where his black hair has grown to be shaggy.

"Is it the one by Savannah—with the boring decorations?"

Tyler scoffs. "They're not boring."

"Yeah, but your dad could've at least used some color."

Tyler's smile fades.

"I didn't mean it like that."

"No, it's fine," says Tyler, his voice low. "I always told him that too. But what I was going to say was my dad taught me how to cut hair, and I think it's time your beard goes. Then I can cut my hair too."

A frown crawls onto Damien's face. "This is my baby. I can't let it go."

"Change is good for us all, Damien. I don't want to let go of this pre-mullet either."

He looks at Tyler's hair and then feels his own beard. "That mullet is pretty nasty, isn't it? Maybe you're right."

Kate begins her seeking for the twins. There aren't many

places to hide in the factory, so it won't be hard. She heads to the tech room first. Even if her eyes were closed, she still heard the door closing to her left, so it is only proper to check there first.

"It looks empty," she thinks, her eyes scanning around. It almost seems like neither one is there until she hears a small giggle.

"Where are you, bud?"

She peeks behind the desks and boxes and then sees that the room isn't quite a square. There's a little divot in the right corner. Approaching the area, her thoughts are confirmed. She sees the brunette kid crouching on the ground. He laughs some more and then runs out the door.

She finds the other one hiding in one of the lockers to the right. She can't take all the credit though. The twin she found before helped her. They both giggle, almost the same. Kate can't tell them apart, but they don't have to know that.

One of them glances at the door to the storage. The look is enough to tell Kate that he's hungry.

With the two behind her, she leads them to the door. "You guys want a snack?"

"Sarah said there isn't enough food for us to steal," one of them says bashfully.

Kate recognizes the small freckle above his lip, the one that Will doesn't have. That's how she'll tell them apart.

"Relax, we can share something small. Plus, it's not stealing because we're a group, right, CJ?" she replies, heading inside.

The sun peeks through the small windows, but barely any light comes through. The wind has died out, or perhaps it's waiting to strike.

"What do you feel like eating?" she asks CJ who's looking around with worry.

"The dark scares me..."

She barely snickers to herself, but there's no response from her. CJ doesn't dare a word either.

Kate peeks into the boxes. There are candles, bricks, old car parts, and more junk. The other twin stands outside, telling himself that he is the guard in case anyone comes.

Her hands cling to the racks as she searches. That's when an odd patch of the wall catches her eye. It's behind some of the racks on the right. The wall is dark gray and smooth, but the spot seems different. Kate's curiosity takes her over. She walks to the corner and sets aside the racks. The patch is clear now. A lighter gray with a grainy surface. Her fingers slide around the textures, looking for another clue. An indent in the patch rubs under her hand, and she pulls it.

It's a zombie, a kid zombie with bones seeping through his grim skin. He looks up at her, and she stumbles back. CJ, still unaware, looks for any sort of food in his interest. When the child catches his eye, he goes silent.

A shriek fills the room, and CJ's face flashes with fear. As the zombie starts crawling over to Kate, she shoves her boot into his face, breaking a small part of her heart as she does.

The kid reminds her of her younger sister. The one she hasn't seen since the day before the apocalypse. She knows she must kill this zombie even if it's harmless. It couldn't do damage to her, but even the beautiful ocean carries deadly things, and the harmless zombie could lead to more.

Still on her bottom, she looks around for something to kill the little guy with, but he has no strength. No muscle to help himself up. He's weak and starving. Poor kid.

Poor *kid*.

After rummaging her hands across the floor, she finally finds an old pole to her left, the size of a katana, and picks it up.

Now, she'll have to shut her heart off and tell herself that if she lets him live, she's just trapping the real kid within him.

With one strike, the kid is already on the floor and limp. His soul is finally free. CJ looks at Kate, scared and confused. She killed the monster, but it doesn't feel that way.

Tyler and Damien rush in first, Will shortly behind them. They all surround Kate as she remains in her sprawl.

"Cyrus," says Damien, his voice breaking.

He rushes over to the child and pulls him into his arms.

"Cyrus," he whimpers again. His eyes, which match the child's, blink the tears away. His face is identical too.

A pit develops in Kate's throat. "I'm sorry, he was—he was one of the dead when I found him."

Damien contemplates staying silent. "It's—it's not your fault."

And with that, Kate still feels weighed down, like there was something she could've done.

"I don't know what I was thinking," Damien says under his breath with tears filling his eyes. He sets the child down. "Could you just bury him?"

He doesn't wait for an answer and rushes out of the room with Tyler behind him. Only he knows what truly happened to Cyrus. They pass by Anthony and Marlon who hurry into the scene. Their eyes are on Tyler for answers, but he sweeps past them.

"What's happening in here?" calls Marlon as he walks by the racks and finds CJ standing next to Kate. She still sits on the ground and stares at the dead child. Damien's wish plays in her head.

CJ turns to Marlon who looks down at Kate. Before he can say something, he sees the body of the starved child lying right outside the compartment.

There's a pain in his chest. Before, he and Ashton were the kids who picked on others. Before, they were predators and kids like Cyrus were prey. And now, they are all prey. They're prey to the zombies and the inescapable virus they carry. Ashton may put on a show, but even he knows that he is just another fish in the sea.

Marlon holds his hand out for Kate, like a signal to put herself together. They're a group after all. She looks up at him and thinks about it.

"We need you, Kate. Get yourself together," says Marlon, his eyes never shifting away.

Their hands meet, and Kate lifts herself up. "Thanks." Her voice is quiet, frail. "We should—bury him."

Anthony looks around and finds tools on the right. "There are shovels over here."

He picks up the rusty shovels covered in dirt and brings them to the two. Marlon takes both in one hand.

"Be safe out there," Anthony whispers before holding CJ's hand and leaving.

Marlon picks up the dead kid in his other arm, and when Kate doesn't follow him, he calls, "You coming?"

She inches towards him, looking back at the tunnel. They walk out of the doors on the sides, and the cool air seeps into the factory.

There are dozens of thoughts in Kate's mind, most of them questions. Her mom always said that every question has some sort of answer, we just need to find it, but she can't find an answer for these ones. Marlon wouldn't know and Damien won't want to tell.

The only question she *can* ask is, "Where should we bury him?"

His heart breaks apart when he notices the tears in her eyes.

"Over here," he says, walking up to the trees on the left. They form a sort of U-shape, perfect for a burial ground. "The grave will face the sun when it sets," he says.

It's not because Cyrus was a child, but because Kate cares. White smoke puffs out of their mouths, vanishing into the air. He gently sets down the kid and drops one of the shovels.

He doesn't understand why Kate cares so much about a random kid, but there's a feeling inside of him that he can't name.

When Kate doesn't try to help, Marlon knows he has to say something. "Kate, he's in a better place. You didn't kill Cyrus, you killed one of the dead. And to me, that's just saving the world."

Their eyes are locked onto each other. She doesn't want to accept the truth. She wants to blame herself, and it's not because of Cyrus, but her sister. Maybe she's hiding in a spot like Cyrus, just waiting for someone to set her soul free.

"Yeah right," she says because the only way she can help herself is by being sarcastic.

Marlon stays persistent. "How could anyone have known that he would be in there?" He shovels hard into the ground, pulling out a big pile of dirt with snow on top. "There was nothing we could do to save him. God knows how long he was in there."

"It's not about Cyrus," she whispers, "it's about—"

"Your sister. I just know someone has found her. Your sister is young, but she's smart, and she would've saved herself. I should know, one day she outsmarted me when we played chess."

Her face shifts to the side, letting the cool air calm her down. She wants to say something back because the usual Kate would never let an argument go until she won. But now? She wasn't just Kate Davis, the artsy, talented girl. She was Kate Davis, the girl who held a heavy heart for people she didn't know.

She digs the dirt in big piles, trying to drive the memories of her sister away. They both shovel fast with Cyrus lying next to them. The handles for the shovels are cold but it doesn't stop them. The hole reaches almost two feet deep. Their arms are sore, but they continue. They both have their reasons. Neither says a word. They don't need to.

The hole has become big enough to hold a kid. Marlon picks Cyrus up in his arms. His eyes are closed but Kate still remembers his stare. She imagines his eyes as he rests in the hole, the snow already covering him up.

"Rest in paradise little man," Marlon mumbles and picks his shovel back up. The dirt hits his legs first, then his abdomen, and then his chest. His head is last, and eventually, the spot is filled back up.

They pat down the area with their shovels, making an even grave.

Kate doesn't look any better, and Marlon can tell. He wants to say something to her, but no words come out.

As she looks at the grave he walks up to her, and for once he feels sympathy. He wraps his arms around her hoping a hug will cure it all. She stands there, confused, but allows it. Her arms tighten around him, and they stand there with the snow sprinkling around.

Realizing where she's at, her arms drop, and she wipes away her tears. Marlon feels almost accomplished as he watches Kate go back inside.

SIX

THE SAVIOR

THE PISTOL MAKES no noise, but it's there and pointed at Ashton. The man's footsteps are almost silent as he approaches the others. Ashton looks at the person and contemplates his choice.

He has a green beanie on, and his skin is pale like the snow. One of his eyes matches the sky while the other matches the ground. Freckles spot around his face, but they're hard to see.

With a sigh, he repeats, "I said, get off."

Ashton looks back down at Jason. His plan to be in charge failed. Life is more valuable than being on top, but he still plans to have both. Obeying, Ashton gets up and glares at the body below him. White snow has begun covering them all.

A large slit is open and bleeding on Jason's face. His nose is dripping too, and his right eye has a purple tint around it. Ashton seems to be calm now.

Jason's hands froze pink from clenching the snow. He thought this was the end, this would be his death. His eyes shift to the man that helped him.

His age seems close to Kira's and Nathan's. As the beanie comes off, his red hair is exposed. The color is like Madeline's, and it curls at the front. His lips are a deep red.

Something catches Jason's eye. Some sort of sound player is hooked onto the belt of the man. When he sees Jason looking at it, he hides the player behind his brown jacket. His sweater and pants are both dark gray.

Ashton backs up slowly, and he does something he thought he'd never do. He puts his hands up. A fiery rage builds up in his mind. He despises the idea of this newcomer. Just another block in the way of his power. He focuses on the pistol—he knows he won't die, but the thought of the trigger being pulled makes him behave.

"You can put the gun down, I ain't doing nothing," Ashton says.

The man glares at him for a few seconds. He shows no mercy and points the gun further up, now at Ashton's head.

"Don't try me, kid," he replies.

The gun flicks to the left, like a signal to the three girls on the right to help Jason up. They follow with no noise, and Jason stands with an arm over Emily.

Perhaps the silence grows on him because he puts down the gun. Ashton lets out a sigh of relief and brings down his hands. He rubs the blood on his knuckles away, both his and Jason's.

The man stands tall, not letting Ashton's gaze affect him. "What's up with the fighting?"

"It's not your business," snaps Ashton.

The man scoffs but doesn't reply. He knows what Ashton did. He was watching most of it. Jason stays silent, still trying to understand the last few minutes.

"I'm Elliot," the man says, looking at the girls. "Elliot Francis for those who want the full name."

Nobody dares a smile, but they still introduce themselves.

As his eyes go down the line, Jason mumbles his name with a hint of blood in his mouth. Then Elliot looks at Ashton who glares back.

"I'm out of here," he says and trots away.

"What a piece of shit," Elliot whispers. His eyes flick back to the girls.

When no one speaks, Emily fills the void. "You could say that again."

He chuckles, exposing his pure white teeth. "So, what are a group of teens doing out here in this weather?"

They contemplate telling him. In the end, people who save you could just be doing it for praise. They end up hoping for something after.

"It's this code for our group," Sarah blurts.

"A code for—" Avery begins, looking around until she gets an idea, "for this pharmacy."

Elliot's eyes don't leave Sarah, and his voice hardens. "All right."

The four look at each other in relief. Jason stops leaning on Emily, trying to tell himself that he's okay. At the time, his adrenaline blocked the pain, but now he can feel every bit seep into his body.

"So, you're going to continue to find this code?"

The group looks at each other. Can they trust this new guy? Should they just abandon him after he saved Jason? None of them say anything. Their eyes look everywhere but at him.

Elliot smiles at the ground. "It's okay I won't come along. I have a group of my own that's probably worried about me."

When none of them respond, he takes the hint and says,

"Okay then."

His eyes glance towards Jason before taking a step. "Don't let another kid beat you up again, all right?"

Then the man walks off, back the way he came. They wait for him to be far into the prairie before turning away.

Avery is the first to speak. "I don't trust him."

They walk once more, and this time following Ashton's steps. Emily grabs the map that fell on the floor and wipes the snow from the back. They wasted too much time because of the beat-up. They could've already been heading back, but now, another mile remains. Jason keeps his hands in his pockets, shutting out the world around him. His wounds have stopped bleeding, but the grime from before still surrounds his face.

Fifteen minutes pass by, and they arrive at the code—or what's supposed to be it. A crumbled building surrounded by trees is in front of them. Rubble lies everywhere and only a few parts of the building remain. The place is a disaster, but it makes sense. The code won't be easy to find here.

"This'll be fun," Avery says, stepping forward to take a better look. "How the hell will we find the code here."

Sarah groans and heads for the building. "Might as well start looking now."

"Sarah, be careful," Emily calls out, almost taking a step.

Before Sarah can register her words, a creature stumbles through the broken door. He lurches for Sarah who kicks him to the ground. Then she searches for a weapon.

A piece of rubble, the size of a soccer ball, sits by her feet. She grabs the boulder and smashes it into the zombie's head. The creature tumbles to the ground, his skull bleeding at the top.

Sarah's breath is heavy and quick. As she turns around, she

lets out a weak grin. The girls smile with her and follow her motion to come.

The snow is untouched, meaning Ashton hasn't arrived yet, nor has Elliot.

There are two parts to the building. One looks much more intact than the first. They step through the doorway and onto the wood floor. All the roof is gone except for parts in the corner, the windows are shattered, and the walls are almost gone too.

"We should split up. The code is probably under some of these rocks," says Avery, walking over to a mountain of rubble. Her hands stain from the dirt and dust as she picks apart the pile. They watch her try to put a dent into the large mountain.

"Maybe we *should* work together," says Emily, walking over to her and pulling a rock.

Another rock is taken out by Sarah. "This is going to take forever."

Jason takes his jacket off, walks over to Emily, and reaches for a boulder. With the four of them, they manage to shorten the mountain in a few minutes. Now, the rubble they pulled is spread out on the floor.

Sarah goes in to pull another rock, and as it leaves the pile, the rest of the stack collapses. Dust flies around, and Jason coughs as his lungs breathe it in.

Emily steps carefully through the flattened pile and digs in the middle to find a code, but there's nothing there besides the floor.

She shakes her head in defeat and heads over to another pile much smaller than the previous one. The boulder pile sits next to one of the walls of what seemed like a factory. She quickly digs through and scraps her hands in the process.

They all sift through the piles, working together, but they

come out empty-handed.

Jason walks to the closed door on the other side of the building. "Let's check over here."

When he steps inside, he sees the faded checkerboard floor and a pile of metal sheets in the corner. Heading further in, Avery and Sarah follow behind.

They spread out and look in every corner. The walls of this section are still together, there are more clumps in the ceiling, and parts of furniture are scattered on the floor. The building is barely smaller than the other.

Emily walks in last and heads over to one of the metal plates that's alone. It leans against the wall. She pushes the sheet aside, revealing a small handlebar.

"I think I found it," she shouts with a rush of elation.

The others come to her, and she pulls the handle. A patch of the tile connected to hinges lifts from the ground.

Dark stone shaped in the form of a circle and a thick rim sits in the perfectly dug tunnel. Engraved in the middle is the code.

"4, 5, 7, 8," Jason reads aloud. "We should write it down."

His eyes scan the area and see a pen sitting by the floor of a window. The thought of a trap flashes in his mind, but that happens often. He's always worrying about something.

As he squats to grab the pen, he catches a glimpse of a black object through the window. It's like the gun that Elliot pointed at Ashton. Elliot steps into the frame, and a shock runs down Jason's spine. He wonders if he should even look up. It could be the weapon that ends his life.

There's nothing around him to help, and even if he were to find something, it would be no use. A bullet would meet him instantly. Jason raises his hands, just like Ashton, and stands up slowly. There's Elliot in the same position that he was in, but

Jason stands at the end of the gun instead of Ashton.

"Look, Elliot, we just need this code. We'll be gone and away from you in no time." He fights to not let Elliot, nor anyone, hear how scared he is. "Just let us go."

Elliot chuckles, "And why would I do that?"

Emily, Sarah, and Avery look cautiously at Jason. They don't interfere because they know it won't help.

"You want something, I get it. Just tell us what and we'll hand it over," pleads Jason, staring Elliot in the eye.

The hole of the gun is traumatizing. Jason can imagine the bullet flying out in a second. Then he'd see black, his thoughts would disappear, and he'd forget all that's happened.

"I don't want something. I want someone, and I want four of them."

Four people. That's what *they* are. But why does he want them? Is it for an army—lab testing?

"Why?" Jason asks, his voice loud and steady.

He hopes his courage will free them because inside he is trembling. His wounds sting from the piercing wind. His mouth still has a dash of blood, and his face feels swollen and broken.

"Let's just say they have a task to fulfill."

The tension throbs against them. They want to help each other escape this mess, but how can they? Avery sees a long and skinny piece of scrap metal just a foot away, but if she even moves a bit, Jason could be dead.

Her fist opens. The skinny fingers with long nails are ready to pounce.

Elliot glares at her, and she doesn't realize it. Her face is fixed on the metal piece.

His mouth curls at the end, and he pulls out another gun. This one aimed right at Avery.

"Don't try it." His eyes, if they weren't evil already, flash with something terrifying. "Now, drop your weapons."

Emily looks at Avery and Sarah. She doesn't intend on dying today.

"We'll get out of this," she whispers, dropping her knife. The hidden one in her boot will be of use now.

Jason hears the knife thud on the floor, and he shakes his head in defeat. His gun is all that's visible, and all that he drops.

Avery throws her combat knife to the ground. The built-in taser breaks apart. One of her prized builds.

Sarah pulls out her dagger. Now none of them have weapons, or that's what Elliot is supposed to think.

"The other ones too. I won't hesitate to shoot you all."

Jason whispers to himself and then chucks his knife. Emily pulls out the weapon from her boot.

"Perfect. We may leave now."

SEVEN

THE FROZEN RIVER

AS THE WIND grows stronger, it picks up the snow with it. The sun sits just over the mountainous lands, ready to sink through the horizon and allow the moon to replace it. The winter times are the worst. Less day and more night so the dead can attack us easily.

"We have to get home before it's too dark," I say, clutching the map closely.

Trees and stones glisten against the golden light. The cold pierces my skin. Every so often, my eyes dart around, hoping to see the code. Four numbers plastered onto something.

"We'll make it," assures Dylan.

I look down at the map. It feels like we've been out here for hours. The sun is testing us, but I'll do anything for that food.

"I hope so."

The square lies above a river, but with this cold, it must be frozen. The flowing water will be gone. We won't know if we're close until we see it.

With a final look at the map, I roll it back up but keep it in my hands. My drawstring isn't here to hold it. "We're not too far."

I hear a growl, and soon enough, a creature steps out from behind a tree. It's a woman with a large sweater and jeans that are ripped all over. Her hair is dark brown and wet. Her hair is wet! Her clothes too.

My mouth curls into a smile. "She must've come from the river. That means it's close by."

My nose isn't pierced as I approach the zombie. Her scent is weak. The knife stabs right above her ear, and her bobbling head stops. I yank the blade out and don't bother closing her green eyes. My legs have already started a jog, and when I call out to the others, we begin running through the trees.

Everyone beams with joy as we pass by pine trees of all sizes. The needles sprinkle white flakes onto our heads.

The floor squishes and squirms under our feet. The icy water left over from the snow seeps into my boots, but I don't mind it. The code is in our reach.

I arrive first at a large river. There's ice all over with snow on top. The only way to the other side is by crossing it.

"I'm glad we're here. My feet aren't going to hold for long," says Kira, out of breath.

"God, you're weak," Nathan remarks. He chuckles as Kira glares at him. "Anyway, how are we going to find this thing?"

Besides the cold river, there are only trees and a mountain. The code could be up there. A few open areas, free of ice, are still on the river. The water projects a deep blue aura around the snow. It's almost as if the Aurora Borealis found its way here.

I snicker to myself, grasping the beauty of it. "Well, let's cross this first. The code can't be far from here."

The patches of water grow as they scale down the river, and at the end, the ice is barely there.

"It won't hold for long. Let's be careful."

I lift my leg and hover it over the ice. Erasing my thoughts, my foot finds a spot, but my weight is still on the other foot.

As the fear of slipping towers upon me, I take the step with hesitation. My body balances on the ice.

I twist my head to look at the others. Dylan gives me a confident smile and Nathan stares plainly. My legs move as my mind draws blank, every step increasing my panic.

Now I stand alone in the middle of the frozen river, a tension suffocating me. Luckily, it's not much longer of a walk. I'm carried across the river by my legs. My hands are bright red and numb, my hair flows with the wind, and my heartbeat accelerates.

A few more steps, three, two, one. I feel like jumping right off the ice and onto land, but I contain my excitement and step off with caution.

Dylan follows the same route that I took with just as much patience and steadiness.

He leaps a foot or two and makes it onto the land, sighing with relief. We look at each other, glad the other one made it. I only met Dylan last year. I've only known him from the apocalypse, yet I feel like I've known him for my whole life.

It's a cliché thing to say, but it's true. Somehow, we just connected in a way that I haven't with others.

I break the gaze and look at Kira.

"All right," her voice quakes, "I'm—I'm coming over."

She stares at the ice for a moment and wipes her hands on her jeans.

She hasn't gone yet; every time she tries, her head shakes and she takes a step back.

When she sees us watching her debate with her thoughts, she says, "Sorry, it's just—drowning is my biggest fear."

"Just go already," says Nathan. His eyes avert to us, and he mouths the word, "Chicken."

She looks back at him and hisses, "I'm not."

With another long breath followed by an exhale, she leaves her footprints in the snow and draws closer to the ice.

"Okay, I'm going. I'm going right now. I just—no, I am going to walk onto that ice and—"

"We don't have time for this," Nathan mumbles and pulls her onto the ice. It holds them both well until a small crack appears.

The tiny fracture will grow big in seconds.

Muttering something under his breath, Nathan runs with Kira still in his hand.

As they reach the land, their hands separate, and they turn around to the river. The ice splits in half, a rippling sound carries through. The water flourishes between the rift.

"Way to go," says Kira, not bothering to look at him. He chuckles and starts walking into the forest.

"We'll figure out a way over," I whisper to her. "Let's focus on this code."

"Yeah, okay," she says and follows Nathan's track. When she disappears into the woods, I turn back to Dylan.

"Hopefully we're all alive after this."

He grins and heads towards the path. "We have you. I'm not worried."

The trees lead up to the mountain. If the code is up there, someone might not make it. I ignore the aching pain in my feet and continue to stomp through the thick sludge.

My knuckles are bright pink, and my ears feel burning cold. We get past the first couple of layers of trees, and the dirt rises rapidly.

"Hurry up," Nathan calls to us.

"We're trying," I say while trying to pull myself up.

"Here, I'll boost you," Dylan offers. I know I can do it by myself, but I can't turn down his offer.

"Okay, thanks." I throw the items in my hands onto the ledge.

He locks his fingers and hangs them below his waist. I put my muddy shoes onto his hands, feeling bad about getting them messy. The dirt crumbles as I find a grip and pull myself up. Nathan and Kira stand on a flat terrain, a path shaped within.

Once I'm up, I turn around to help Dylan. He wipes his hand against his cargo pants and grabs mine. His body flies up with ease.

"Let's see the map, Hailee," says Kira.

I pick my things up and open the map. No landmarks, signs, or anything to tell where the code is. There's only the square a few inches away from the factory and the river right below.

Kira glances to the side. "It has to be around this mountain. Let's split into two."

She looks at Nathan who stands a few feet to the right of her, and then back at me with pleading eyes.

"I'll go with Kira. We'll head west, you guys head east. If we don't find anything we'll come back—"

My eyes search around for a landmark. A distinct stick near Dylan catches my eye. I reach over and grab it.

"—here."

It pierces into the ground and sticks upright.

"If one of us does find the code, we'll head the way of the others and find them," Dylan adds.

"You guys keep the map, you'll need it more," says Nathan

as he leads Dylan on their path.

Kira scoffs, giving Nathan a final look. "Let's go."

We turn around, and I smile at the chemistry between the two.

They act like my parents. My mom was the head of the household. She worked for hours supporting us. My dad, even though acting tough, knew it was true. God, I haven't seen them in a while. I had found them at the start of all this. A lot of us did.

They made a foolish decision to go to the city because we needed more supplies. None of us "kids" could say otherwise. Ms. Mack was one of the only adults who stayed back. They died on that bus after an attack. My parents weren't there when we found the vehicle. The others saw their parents dead. It was one of the worst days for us all.

Emily occasionally mentioned their existence. "There's a chance they're out there," she would say, but we both had a clear idea of what happened. We just never let it affect us.

"You okay, Hailee?" Kira asks.

Her pale blue eyes stare keenly at me. I look up at her, wanting to say what, but I just shake my head.

"Oh, it's nothing. This code—it's gotta be around here."

She sees through me. Her stares continue for what feels like minutes. The pressure falls off me when she sighs and looks away.

Mud, dirt, and brown snow collect on my winter boots. My left hand still clutches the map, and my back feels stiff. When we get the chance, we need to move to warmer land.

"This snow is killing me," Kira says. "I could use a hot bath right now."

"Me too."

We continue walking, or at least I do as Kira stands behind

me. I turn back to her.

She wants to say something, she just doesn't know how to word it. Her head drops to the floor as she puts her sentence together.

"Hailee, you know the factory can't hold us all. We're going to have to leave soon. Somewhere warm so we don't get sick."

I nod my head. Why does everyone keep repeating this? It's obvious we're not staying with these guys, but it'll be like this until we get the bunker open.

It feels like I'm always waiting for something. Something I can't get, and when I finally do, a new problem arises. Everyone must be getting irritated. I am too.

"Maybe the South," she says under her breath. I look at her. "It's warmer down there, maybe—maybe there's something or someone."

"Yeah, the South sounds nice."

Hope for somewhere safe. Somewhere with walls, houses, food, and water has been all I think about for the past months. Maybe that's what keeps me going. The hope for a better life.

My thoughts vanish at the sound of a zombie.

A woman growls as she limps over to us. Her eyes are a diluted gray, and sections of her hair are stained dark brown. Her mouth flails open, ready to dig into my body. I look to Kira, letting her take part in some action.

Before, areas used to be filled with zombies, and now? Just stragglers. Except in the cave. The dead ones in there had to be planted. Something's off about the woods behind the factory.

Kira moves forward, holding her pistol in her right hand. Her arm stretches out, and the point of the gun aims at the woman. With a slight pull of her finger, she sends the bullet into her head.

The zombie falls, and her eyes stare up at the crossing sky. I step around the creature and continue forward, staying cautious for more.

The sun still sits inches above the land. We could have been heading back by now, but this scavenger hunt is taking up our time. Luckily, we're following a trail. Perhaps we'll find the code here.

How is Angel's group or Emily's going to survive through the night? I must not worry. They're all smart. They know what to do when things get rough.

"What do you think of Joseline—Todd, and the others?" I ask.

Kira's dirty blonde hair rustles against her jacket as she looks at me.

"I think—" she pauses, her eyes fleeing to the floor, "I think they want to help us because it'll help them. I wouldn't put our full trust into those guys."

Her words remind me of just yesterday when we met the factory group. Joseline only agreed to help us because we could help her.

"Yeah, I don't plan on it."

It falls silent again until a tree rustles nearby. Neither of us is near any leaves. There's no growling or a zombie in sight. I can't help but think about the tape recorder and the guy who pushed us. Maybe we aren't the only ones on the mountain.

"You heard that right?" asks Kira, looking around.

The silence surrounds us. I don't risk making a noise, and instead nod my head, looking down at the slope. Almost like a hallucination, I hear our names being yelled by Dylan. Then the branches of the trees rustle and commotion echoes through the woods.

"Nathan," Kira chokes.

My feet drag on the ground while my mind races. This must be a prank. Kira's steps are light behind me. As we inch towards the commotion, everything begins feeling like a dream.

In seconds, we're running back through the path, hoping that the worst has not come.

EIGHT

THE LOG CABIN

JOSELINE TOWERS OVER the dead zombie with the bow clutched loosely between her fingers.

"Let's keep going."

She lets the arrow slide back into the quiver and straps her bow back. The map is back in her hands. "Dammit, which way was it?"

She mumbles something else as she looks around.

"Okay, let's not lose hope," Todd says. He walks up to Joseline and looks at the map. "We have to head west."

His head glides up. "The sun sets west, and with an account of our location, we'll have to head this way."

He marches just right of the sun that sits above the trees. After a few steps, he turns around. "Y'all coming?"

The others hold in their laughs and follow the confident man. The woods absorb them in seconds and leave darkness throughout.

"I hope we find the code soon," Angel says. "Getting lost

in the woods would be a nightmare."

"Don't worry. I'll be here to save you," Noah replies, drawing closer to Angel.

She gives him an unsure look.

"Yeah, sure." Instead of moving away this time, she stays. "This bunker better be worth it."

"It will," Joseline responds from further up. "Have a little faith."

"I remember when my brother and I used to go camping in woods like these," says Madeline, easing the tension. "It's crazy how we had *lives* before this. We went to school and played volleyball. I could walk outside and not fear getting eaten by my used-to-be friend."

"Your point?" mutters Angel.

"My point is that we shouldn't live in total fear. Just because some dead people have taken over the world doesn't mean we can't live. If we allow them to control our lives, then what's the point of living? We should have fun, especially you, Joseline."

Joseline scoffs. Her eyes are locked on what's ahead. "Fun killed people I loved."

"Look, I don't have my family either. I've lost everything, but that's not stopping me from having a life, from having a soul. I don't want to be just some survivor; I want to be alive! Let's do something." She thinks for a moment. "We could blast some music and have a dance party, or we could play truth or dare. Maybe we could find some alcohol and get drunk."

"That sounds epic," Todd chimes. Madeline shoots him a dirty look, but she softens up after thinking about his words.

"Yeah, it does."

"How much longer?" Ava asks from the back.

Joseline looks at the map. "About fifteen minutes."

"Let's play twenty questions. I'll go first," says Madeline, looking up for a moment. "All right, I have something."

She waits for them to ask but it falls silent. "C'mon, ask a question."

She turns around to look at them. Her eyes file through each person hoping one will speak.

"Is it alive?" asks Noah.

"Nope."

"Can you wear it?" Ava throws out.

"Yeah, I guess so."

Todd's eyes glint despite the gray sky. "Do you have it on you?"

"Yep."

"Can it hurt people?" Noah questions.

Madeline knows they are getting close. A wide grin floods her face. "Yes, it can."

"It's your knife, isn't it?" asks Angel.

"Ding, ding, ding!"

They laugh, some to make Madeline happy and others with true intent. The wind has begun to settle down as if the group having fun makes it happy.

The conversation dies, and Madeline says in failure, "Okay, I guess that was boring."

The sun beams a couple of inches above the horizon. The clouds grow foggy, and the bitter cold has softened.

A zombie growls from the left. Everyone looks towards the sound.

"I got it," Madeline says. Her hands grab the knife tucked behind her shirt. Then she processes how she wants to kill the zombie. Through the neck or the temple?

The temple it is.

She pushes the blade into the zombie, its eyes locked onto

hers. Then, as the knife comes out, blood oozes down its head. The body falls to the floor. Madeline combs her red hair back and sighs.

This is going to be a long walk.

"We're getting close," Joseline says, taking a glance at the map in her hands. Her hair holds small flakes of snow illuminating her eyes and rosy cheeks. The end of the pine forest is nearing. Soon, it will be flat land again, and soon, they will be at their destination.

"This is exhausting," Angel complains. She looks around, eager to find where the triangle code could be.

"You could say that again," says Ava, "and we still have to walk back."

Joseline views the trees and dull sky. "Okay, quit whining. Think about the food in the bunker. Think about what this is all for."

Angel steps past Todd. "I think the woods are clearing up."

The rest of the group slows down behind her while she continues.

"Angel, wait up," Noah calls from behind.

"Come on! I think I see it!"

They start to run as the trees disappear. The wind blows in her face and carries her blonde hair. They shout to her, but the joy in her mind drowns it out. She runs to the end of the forest, her shoes covered in snow and mud.

Once she passes these trees, her code will be right there. Her running slows down as she fixes her knife position.

"Wait, Angel," Noah calls again. A small plate is placed in front of her. She doesn't notice with her excitement bubbling inside.

"Wait!" he shouts. She takes one more step and then looks

back.

God, I just want to see the—

Her mind goes blank as she hears the click of the plate. The difference in the ground makes it clear what's below her. As she glances at Noah, her face is filled with worry. The others make it to her, realizing what's happened.

"Don't move." Noah's palms are out, hoping his steadiness will calm her.

He looks around for something that would distribute the same weight. Twigs and branches are all that's in sight.

Todd notices the large log on the left with spikes all around. It hides beneath the trees. He doesn't open his mouth, not because he doesn't want to alarm them, but because he is too scared to.

Ava looks to her right and sees a large boulder embedded in the dirt. She sprints to the rock and falls to her knees. Her fingers peel at the dirt, but it's no use. Instead, her knife lodges into the sides, and the boulder moves around.

"Here," she says and hands it to Noah.

He heads back to the plate. "I'll place this down, and you'll need to walk off as it drops, okay?"

Angel nods her head. Her body doesn't want to move. Any step taken could be her last. Noah places the boulder down to Angel's feet, and then he scoots it closer to the plate. Luckily for Angel, she didn't have both feet on. Noah slides the boulder on while Angel reluctantly steps off. She looks around waiting to see something come for her, or maybe an explosion.

Waiting for the trap too, Noah keeps his hands on the rock. His eyes look up at Angel who towers over him. As he inhales, he lets go of the rock and steps away.

Once nothing happens, Angel lets out a sigh of relief and says, "That could've ended badly."

"Yeah, if it weren't for Noah and Ava. Where's the appreciation?" asks Madeline.

"Yeah, whatever," Angel remarks. As the thought of his kindness plays in her mind, she decides to give him a special gift.

Noah can barely hold his smile as Angel pecks him on the cheek.

Some of the others whisper as Angel walks away.

Noah grins and turns back to follow Angel.

"Let's be careful, there's likely more," Joseline says and walks with Noah.

The rest of them follow, carrying their aching feet, bruised shoulders, and tired bodies to survive. Angel arrives at the last few trees with Noah and Joseline right behind.

A log cabin sits in the middle of a plain field. Snow lays on the dark pine roof that matches the small windows. The wind howls and kicks the snow in the air. A shadow swipes through the tint of the window on the right.

Angel sees the figure, a girl. "Did you see that?"

"No, what happened?" Noah peers at the house.

"There's someone in there." Her eyes never leave the sight.

"Nothing Ms. Stone can't handle."

She appreciates his compliments, but it frustrates her that he rarely gets the seriousness of a situation. "Right."

Her mind runs in circles. "Do I steal from her—or should I try to negotiate with her? Ugh, stealing would be so much more fun, but Hailee would be pissed."

The rest of the group catches up to the three of them.

"You said someone is in there?" Joseline asks, looking sternly at the cabin.

"Yeah, I saw her face," Angel replies, turning to Joseline. "And if we have to fight, I have no exceptions."

"That shouldn't be necessary."

"Well, let's go," says Madeline, walking to the path that leads to the cabin. The pebbles crunch under the snow, and the trees whistle about as if they're warning her. She looks around for traps, but nothing is obvious.

"Trap free. Well, so far," she shouts.

They catch up. All of them gleam with hope for the code and the possibility of food and water. As they approach the cabin, Joseline is the first to make a move. She takes a step onto the wooden stairs and examines the door. Planks are boarded up, preventing anyone from going in or out.

Joseline glances at Angel and says, "Must be the person you saw who did this."

Angel steps past them and says, "Here." She wields her blade at the wood. "You might want to move."

Joseline steps down, and the others move back. With all her strength, she pulls the machete down and crams it into the wood. Only a tiny crack.

"Dammit, I'm not risking this," she says, pulling her knife out and dusting the wood particles off.

"Yeah, you're right. We need an axe. Or a screwdriver to get the bolts out," Todd says, eyeing the planks. "Maybe there's something in the back."

"Let's hurry. I'm getting hungry," says Madeline. She looks to either side of the log cabin. "I'll go with Josie and Todd—it's cool if I call you that, right?"

Joseline shrugs but stays silent.

"Okay, so us three will go left and you three can go right. We'll meet up in the back."

Everyone agrees, and they part ways. Angel, Noah, and Ava are on the right side.

"So, you guys have been cramped up in that factory this

whole time?" Madeline asks as they begin their way. She seizes this moment to get intel.

"It hasn't been that bad. We have each other, so it's bearable," Todd begins. "What about you all? Where have you guys been?"

"Well, we've been all around Nebraska, but we started in Cheyenne," she replies.

"You're from Wyoming?" Joseline asks.

"Yeah, a shit state home to some shit people." They laugh as Madeline notices something on the left. "Is that an axe?"

"Seems so." Joseline eyes the object. The axe sits in plain snow with no footprints. Was it left the night before?

Joseline and Todd follow Madeline who eagerly steps towards the tool. As she reaches the axe, she feels the snow below her crumble.

The shock hits her before she can say anything. Her eyes have already closed, but she can feel her body slipping down.

Joseline runs to the girl in seconds, and her hand catches Madeline's.

The snow falls, revealing the net it was sitting on and a pit full of spikes. Todd comes shortly after, and he grabs Madeline's other hand. They pull her up as the snow clings to her dark denim jeans and beige long-sleeved shirt.

She gets a grip on the ground and turns around to see what could've ended her life.

"Someone is really out to kill us," she says, out of breath.

"Yeah, that means no more wandering off," Joseline insists. She glances at the axe sitting on the other side of the trap. "Stay here, I'll go get it."

Her feet press down on the snow before making each step. Each one could be a bomb waiting to be ticked off.

"Got it," says Joseline as she grabs the axe. "Let's hope this works."

"What happened?" Ava asks the group when they meet in the back.

"It was another trap. If Angel is right and there is someone here, we might end up fighting them," Joseline says, holding the axe in her hand. Only a plain wall and a small rustic window at the top are on this side of the cabin.

"Seems to be nothing over here, let's circle back."

When they reach the front, Joseline hands the axe to Madeline. She raises the weapon over her shoulder and walks to the boarded door. Without a second thought, the axe flies through the boards. The first few are cracked, and she loads the weapon up again.

One board breaks and hangs by the screws still in the door, then another, another, and the last. The door stands bare now with the broken planks dangling on the side.

"Be careful, she could be anywhere," Angel whispers to Madeline.

She looks the door up and down. Her hand falls onto the doorknob, but there's a moment of hesitation.

"Guys, I think we found our code."

Her feet step back, revealing the door to the group. A small triangle has been carved into the center. The numbers 9, 3, 4, and 6 scraped within.

"9, 3, 4, 6," Ava repeats. "That's definitely it."

Todd pulls out a pen from under his shirt. He jots the numbers onto his arm.

"Smart," applauds Joseline as she pats him on the back. "We can leave now."

"But what if it isn't the code?" asks Angel. "We still have time—we could look around for more food."

Nobody protests. Madeline takes it as her queue and puts her hand back on the knob. The door creaks open, and dust fills the entryway. A dark and empty inside awaits them.

"I don't trust this place," she says before entering.

Her eyes scan the room while Joseline inches behind her. The cabin reeks of blood and iron.

"Anyone have a flashlight?" Madeline calls.

Ava reaches into her small backpack and pulls out a circular object. "It might be dead," she says while handing the light to Madeline.

She powers it on. It flickers a few times, and then the light is gone. Madeline scoffs and slams the flashlight on her palm.

"It's fine, I guess," she says nervously and hands it back. "The dark doesn't scare me."

The others crowd around the door. A candle lay on the side table. She picks up the matchsticks and shakes them. The clacking sound of sticks brings light to her eyes.

With one strike, the flame is lit. The golden light is waved around. The fire spreads down slowly, and when it reaches midpoint, Madeline brings it to the candle. The wick ignites, and she blows out the match.

"Can I help you?" an older man queries from near the staircase. He shines his flashlight on them and holds a gun with his empty hand.

Joseline steps to the front and holds the map behind her back. She hesitates to speak.

"We have plenty of food and water if you guys were just stopping by," he says, his southern accent cutting through, "and there's no need for that."

Madeline looks up at him, his height startling. "Then why is it here?"

"Emergencies. Come, I'm sure Zara won't mind company."

"Wait," Angel shouts from the back. She pushes through the others. "Why was the door boarded up if you guys are in here?"

He looks at the door. "So that people think there's nobody here. Seems like y'all weren't fooled."

"I saw your friend pass by the window. Also, what's up with that trap in the woods? You nearly killed me."

"Angel." Joseline eyes her.

"What? This guy gives me the creeps," she mumbles.

Turning back to the man, Joseline says, "We'd appreciate anything."

They follow him up the stairs by the back wall. The cabin is small, and the walls are covered in dirt, or what looks like dirt. The smell of blood is piercing as they walk further into the house. It's not like the blood of the dead—it's fresh blood, almost like human blood.

NINE

IN THE WOODS

THE THREE GIRLS stare at each other, none of them making a move.

"And what if we don't?" Avery finally spits out.

Elliot smirks and perks his gun up a bit higher. "Don't play dumb. Line up, and let's go."

He waves one gun to the side, and their hearts fill with distress. Avery looks at Sarah, and they mumble something to each other.

"C'mon, it's going to be night soon."

He hops through the window with his guns still raised. Jason backs up but never takes his eyes off the weapons.

The girls reluctantly walk to Elliot. Jason looks at them, then at the perpetrator. If he follows him, who knows what will happen, and what would the others think? The gun is tempting to grab.

When Ashton beat him up, it almost felt nice. Like a snap into the reality of the world. He decides to grab it, but before he can, Elliot fires his gun. He misses.

"Don't test me, kid," he says.

Jason scoffs, his face darkening. Images of what could've been fly through his mind.

"Hurry up, I don't want it to get dark."

Elliot pulls out a long chain with handcuffs attached from a hidden bag under his coat. He clicks the cuffs on to each person. Emily, Sarah, Jason, and Avery.

There are two extra cuffs attached to the chain, both closed. Elliot had thought out his scheme before coming. As he clicks the handcuffs onto Avery's hand, she spits on his face.

He remains still and wipes the insult away with his sleeve. His lips twist into a smile as he tugs on the chain. Something digs into each of their wrists. It's hard to notice them, but each of the cuffs has spikes on the bottom.

"You guys don't listen, do you? You'll want to be careful with these. One rough tug and it'll pierce you." He rounds up the weapons into the corner and says, "You won't be needing these."

None of them respond. There's only one person out there who could save them, but he must be long gone. Elliot starts leading them into the forest.

"It's a long walk so don't drag behind."

Jason's head flicks in every direction, searching for an exit, a way to get out of their doom. There are only trees and snow around.

"Where are you taking us?" asks Sarah as the wind whistles.

"Away."

She persists, "We have a group to go to."

"So do I." He's quick to respond. There's no use. Nothing can save them.

Jason's cuts sting more every second. A brutal drum is

bouncing in his head. Their heads hang low as the silence falls upon them.

The woods aren't terrible with the sun shining down. Though, the pines make it hard to even see the sunlight. A growl from the dead disturbs the quiet.

"Stay here," Elliot says as he hauls his gun. He searches the woods for a trace of the sound.

Just another idiot.

The snarls get louder as the zombie approaches.

In the corner of his eye, he catches the arms of the creature and shoots. The bullet pierces the zombie's forehead. He chuckles and goes back to find the four.

The winds cause his skin to dry and his eyes to water, but beneath the sound of it is only silence. He puts his gun back in his jeans as he walks.

"It's too quiet," he tells himself but continues walking back anyway.

Footsteps pound against the snow. There's no time for him to listen as a body tackles him to the ground, launching his gun at a nearby tree. A teenage voice groans as they try to leap for the gun. Elliot grabs their foot and drags them through the dirt.

Ashton Douglas.

He kicks Ashton to another tree and heads for the gun. His hands are numb against the cold while his heart accelerates.

Ashton's head bleeds, but it doesn't bother him as he jumps for Elliot. He falls to the ground and drops the gun once more. Ashton yanks out his knife and misses the cut as Elliot rolls to the side. He pulls himself up and stumbles to one of the trees, looking around for an opportunity to strike.

Ashton tries again to slice at Elliot, but the man ducks and knocks him to the ground, and the keys fall out of his pocket.

Ashton turns to the side and stabs the knife into Elliot's thigh.

Elliot cusses out and sends a knee to Ashton's nose. He flies back and loses his knife. Bright blood drips down his face as he searches for his weapon. It's cut short as a boot crushes against his hand.

"Not so tough now, huh?" Elliot speaks through spit.

Ashton watches as the man glares down at him, the knife only a few centimeters away from his hand. A wicked grin is plastered on Elliot.

"This isn't the end," Ashton thinks.

He remembers what Marlon taught him during practice and uses his free hand to pull Elliot's leg.

The man crashes flat onto the dirt, and a sharp ring blasts through his ear. Ashton finds the knife and crawls on top of Elliot.

His blue and brown eyes stare at the pointy blade. A distraction to take out his weapon. He draws out the gun and fires two shots. One misses, but the other plunges into Ashton's shoulder.

Ashton falls back, clenching the wound. His head is pounding, and his arm tingles, yet the pain doesn't come. His body gives him another chance.

Elliot aims the gun at Ashton as he walks to him. With no other choice, Ashton launches the knife like a football into his shoulder. The pain in Elliot's arm paralyzes his muscles, and he drops the gun.

It'll only make him weaker if he listens to the pain. Elliot pulls the knife out. There isn't time to regret his choice, he has another weapon now.

Left helpless, Ashton runs into the woods.

"What a coward," Elliot thinks.

He looks up to the sky, catching his breath, but Ashton will be back.

As expected, feet shuffle behind him, and Ashton holds up a branch to his neck.

"Drop your shit," commands Ashton. His body may hurt, but he needs to take this guy down.

Elliot sighs and looks down at his fisted hands. The knife is still in one, with his own blood on it.

"I can't do that," he says and yanks Ashton over his shoulder. Instead of trying to go for the heart or brain, he stabs into Ashton's arm. Blood rushes through the cut as Elliot attempts to saw through the flesh.

Ashton screams in agony. He loses the feeling in his fingers first, and then his forearm, his elbow, and soon all of it is gone. The arm is still attached, but his nerves are shattered. If Elliot doesn't kill him, blood loss will. This is his end, but he won't let it go to waste. He shivers the pain away and picks up the gun next to him, still on the ground. He shoots. He shoots again, again, again. There's nothing.

Empty.

Startled, Ashton kicks Elliot aside and barely picks himself up, Elliot laughs maliciously as he walks towards the beaten kid whose breath is barely there. Emptiness fills the spot of his hand. All he feels is the weight of the dull limb. He couldn't help the others, and now he's going to die. He shakes his head and runs towards Elliot, chucking him to the floor.

Ashton's reminded of one of his last matches. He broke his arm then when the opposite team played dirty. But that didn't stop him, he beat the kid up.

The knife falls to the ground while Elliot fires a bullet. As they fall to the floor, Ashton's body shakes. The fever is spreading throughout him. He can't win this time like he did on the field. He's dying, and he knows he won't make it.

His body barely moves. It tries to get on top of Elliot, but nothing budges. He tries to punch, but it comes out as a weak throw of his arm. Ashton falls over next to Elliot. The blood of his weak arm spills. It leaks onto the cold ground and allows for every part of his body to try and save him.

The blood on Elliot's face has started to dry, and he stands up with unstable legs. He grabs his gun but leaves the empty one and Ashton's knife. Something is whistled under his breath, and then he glances at Ashton who holds onto his arm. With what energy he has, he tries to stop the bleeding.

"This could have gone better for you," says Elliot as he runs away, leaving Ashton alone and helpless.

The cold evening settles into his skin and all the pain his body ignored then now comes haunting back. His breathing slows down while his mouth clogs up with blood.

He imagines himself on the field again. Marlon would throw the ball to him. The cheerleaders and students would be shouting as he scored. They'd win the game because of him.

* * *

A zombie growls in the distance.

Elliot says, "Stay here," and begins walking into the woods. They wait patiently for him to leave, knowing now is their time to run.

As he disappears into the woods, Jason turns his head and says, "We need to leave now. Elliot will be back."

The rest agree and look at the path they traveled along.

Avery views the spikes just below her wrist. "These chains aren't coming off. Running is our only option—at least until we get to our weapons."

"All right let's get on with it."

Jason forgets about the pain. His mind has been playing through hundreds of scenarios for escaping. His freckles are covered by crusted blood and purple spots.

Examining his surroundings, he makes sure that this is the right thing to do. With the spikes on their handcuffs, it'll be hard to run—and worse to escape Elliot.

The sound of a gunshot booms through the woods.

"Quick!" Jason shouts.

He doesn't know what Elliot will do if he finds them escaping, but while he's distracted, this is their chance. They all pick up their feet and head back the way they *think* they came. Keeping in sync raises a problem. If one of them goes too fast then the others will trip. Too slow, and the rest get yanked back.

The sun has set into the trees leaving a deep yellow tint over the air. With it, there's a new silence after the gunshot, an eerie silence. A quiet that means something is about to occur.

They don't know if the direction is right, but what they do know is that they need to get far away from Elliot. Who knows where they would be if the zombie hadn't come?

They run fast with their hands in front of them. Heavy, the chain weighs down their arms. They pull through the pain knowing they must survive. Pain is temporary, but dying is permanent. Death is like a contract you can never get out of. No matter how hard you try, you're stuck in an endless loop.

Now there are sounds of commotion and more gunshots. Elliot's voice is noticeable, meanwhile the other sounds familiar.

"You guys heard that right?" Sarah comments, timidly. The others nod.

"It's just Elliot fighting the dead. C'mon, we have to go," Jason urges. The chain tugs as he tries to run. "What? Don't tell me you want to help him."

"No, it's not that," says Sarah.

Emily and Avery stare at her, while Jason scoffs and waits.

"Just hold on for a second."

She zones out, looking at the floor. Her ears ready to catch another sound. There—two gunshots. A familiar voice shouts in pain.

Her eyes scan the trees. "That voice isn't Elliot's."

"You're right," Emily chokes out. Her ear faces the commotion. "That sounds like Ashton."

Jason shakes his head. Hearing his name, he recalls what had happened just a moment ago. Even then, that's not all that Ashton has done to him.

"So what? He deserves what he gets."

"No, we have to go back and help him," Sarah replies. She and Emily try walking.

Avery doesn't budge. "I'm with Jason on this. He's a dick. We shouldn't waste our time on some dude who doesn't give a crap about us."

The girls turn back.

"Look, he may suck," begins Emily, "but he's been with us since the beginning. He's a human, a survivor. And lately, we've been needing more manpower." She focuses on Jason.

He lets out an angry sigh. "Fine. But if something happens, I'm booking."

Avery shakes her head and mumbles, "Whatever."

They start to run back, but no sound calls out. No trace of Elliot or Ashton. Only trees bristled with snow and a sky covered in gray and yellow. Their footprints distort their old ones as they tramp through. They make it back to where Elliot left.

"All right let's find him and go," says Avery.

The branches rustle, and the snow sprinkles down like sugar. They walk in the direction of Elliot's disappearance, hoping to see Ashton just around the corner. Blood drops have stained the snow near one of the trees.

A louder scream wails out, a terrifying scream like a man being lit to flames. Now, even Jason has started feeling wary, but he won't show the others that.

"This isn't good. Ashton doesn't sound well," Sarah's voice trembles. "We have to find him."

"All right!" Jason groans. "Let's go then." He walks up to the tree with blood, dragging the others along.

"They've got to be close," Emily says, looking down at the blood. "It's fresh."

The woods stall them by sending out a zombie.

"Shit," says Jason at the sound of the creature.

They turn around. Each time they do, they have to spin in a circle. Any other way and they'll end up in trouble.

"Okay, I have an idea. Avery and Emily cross from the back of it," he begins. They question his plan. "C'mon. We can use the chain to slice its head off," he shouts as the man limps to them.

"This better work," Avery whispers.

Still confused, the others go along with the plan. Emily and Sarah take the right while Avery and Jason take the left. They work quickly, bringing the chain against the zombie's neck and swapping spots in the back, creating a loop around the zombie. Now that the chain between Jason and Sarah is tied around the neck, the zombie can only look around helplessly.

"Pull!" Jason shouts. They pull on their handcuffs, and the spikes dig into their wrists. The chain wraps tighter around the neck. They pull harder, gritting through the pain. Release.

The head of the zombie twists. The skin is ripped and blood spills out. The head hangs on, barely attached to the neck, but the creature still falls. They sigh in relief and bask in the success of teamwork as another one approaches.

"Round two," Avery says, ready to take the zombie. Just as she's about to move, Jason stops her.

"Wait," he says. His ears drown out the wind to listen to the growls of the woods. "There's too many. We can't fight them all. We could bleed out."

"He's right. We should look around for a weapon instead," Sarah says, her eyes searching the floor. They start to check their surroundings as the creature gets closer, bringing its friends too.

The snow glares back at them. Why would it be hiding a weapon?

"Guys," Jason says as the zombie raises his ragged hands for him. He inches backward.

Avery turns to the monster and kicks his leg. The zombie falls to his knees and looks at her, ready for a new snack.

Sarah pushes his chest, and he falls back from the blow. Emily stomps on his head, but it lifts again. She pounces with a grunt.

His skull forms a crack, but his eyes stay open. She pushes for one last time. The man stops moving, and his head has caved in. Before they can relax, another one prowls out from the left.

The trees shake as the sound of shuffling carries through the leaves. They all look at each other.

"Let's just leave the zombies, we gotta save Ashton," Emily says. She jogs into the woods, and the others follow with no choice.

The blood on the ground leads them to more trees. While following it, Emily looks up and sees the zombie Elliot killed and the tape recorder. She doesn't bother grabbing it, Ashton is still out there.

There's a soft whimper behind one of the trees. They walk in a line, looking everywhere to find the kid. Emily spots him in a small clearing with one hand over his arm. He tries to speak, but his blood strangles him.

"Oh my god," Emily cries out.

Sarah sees him as well and leads the other two towards the scene.

Jason kneels next to Ashton and says, "Holy shit."

Thoughts race in his mind. Memories of all the times that Ashton bullied him. He shakes his head in disbelief.

Ashton looks at them with his brown eyes, though the color has lost its richness. His skin has paled while his body has given up. He notices their chains and cuffs. He wants to say something, but he knows it will waste the only few breaths he has left.

Jason swallows the heavy pit developing in his throat. It's sickening to look at Ashton. The almost severed arm, the bullet in his shoulder, the cut that stretches from his ear to cheek.

He gently pushes Ashton to the side, allowing him to disperse the blood inside his mouth. A small key lay under him, and Jason picks it up.

"Ashton…" says Emily as she sits on her knees.

He spits out the blood he can, but it still clogs deep in his throat. "You—have to go," he chokes out as he settles back down. "Don't let me become one of those."

His voice is desperate. The confidence and strength are all gone, and the malice behind every word has changed to regret.

Jason's eyes turn foggy red. He pushes his emotions down. Yes, he wanted Ashton gone, just not like this. Not by sacrificing himself. Ashton's supposed to be the bad guy. He's supposed to be hated by everyone, yet Jason's overwhelmed with emotion.

Ashton looks at the gun. "No am—mo."

Jason nods his head and reaches into his shoe. He pulls out a bullet that Elliot never found and looks at the weapon. After a blink, there's a tear falling down his face. Then he pulls himself together and grabs the gun.

The wind dances around, knowing that now is not the time. Jason takes one feeble breath in. Emily, Sarah, and Avery watch, shifting around to make it easier for him. They know Jason has to be the one to do this.

He holds the gun up, his finger barely away from the trigger. Ashton looks at the weapon. His body feels cold and empty. The disease inside is trying to break out, trying to take over. He may not look like it, but he's fighting another battle, a battle against himself.

Jason's hands shake as he aims the gun at the body. The spike digs into his new punctures, but misery is all he can feel. Ashton closes his eyes.

Both want to say more but are clouded with feelings and pain.

Jason pulls the trigger. The bullet launches into Ashton's skull. His eyes were being taken by the virus, but at least now, they died with some amount of human left, unlike the unfortunate ones out there. Jason doesn't say anything. He had so many words to say to Ashton, yet he said nothing.

"We have to leave," he croaks out and tucks the gun into his shirt. His face is almost unsteady trying to hold back the emotions, the hurt he is feeling. Without a sound, Jason hands the small key to Emily.

She nods her head and turns to Sarah. With the key gripped awkwardly in her hand, she unlocks Sarah's cuffs. Sarah takes the key and unlocks the others.

"He's gone. Just like that," she quivers and then throws the key to the ground.

They can't help but stare at the dirt. It's the only place they can find comfort. Jason wipes his hands against his face and lets out a heavy sigh. The zombies from before emerge out of the trees.

He looks towards them and knows he has to run. Not just because of the zombies, but because of the feelings inside.

Emily notices him already going and quietly says, "But what about Ashton?"

"We have to leave him," replies Jason, and he darts into the woods.

Avery shakes her head and starts running.

The other two take a final look at the boy. His eyes are shut, but his face is still alive. The zombies have already caught up. They can't bring him. They can only run, and so they do.

TEN

DOWN THE STREAM

AS WE RUN, we pass by a large square stone. The numbers 3, 7, 2, and 4 are printed on it.

"Is this—?" Kira pauses, examining the stone built into the mountain. Dirt covers the edges, and a dark moss grows near the two and four.

"The code? It seems like it," I begin. Right now, Dylan and Nathan are more important. "Just try to memorize the numbers, we have to get to the guys."

Kira nods her head and reads over the numbers. I repeat three, seven, two, four in my head a few times hoping it'll stick with me.

"Okay, let's hurry," she says looking at the path. The trees cover any sight of the river below, but the sound of crashing water is there.

"Hailee!" A muffled voice shouts. The trees clamor, and the voice never speaks again.

We look at each other and head downhill. The mud is slick

and sticks to our feet with every step. One quick move and it could send us tumbling down. My hands cling to the trees as we trot, trying to secure a grip when I can.

Kira has started speeding down. It feels like I'm walking in water. With Kira going this fast, she could fall at any moment.

"Kira, wait!" I shout. She tries to stop herself but loses her footing. The brown mush catches her feet, and she rolls down the mountain.

"Kira!" A dryness suffocates my throat.

I'm mindlessly jogging down. The trees stand as my good friend. I pass by dozens of them. Most are pine and spruce. They rustle again, and then there's silence. Kira must've fallen all the way, but she couldn't be dead. It's too short of a fall, right?

The ground thickens under my feet. "I'm reaching the bottom," I think.

Kira calls out to Nathan.

I look around the green leaves hoping to see his dirty blonde hair. "Nathan!"

All I can hear is the river again. We're all separated. We're all alone in a place we don't know. Sticks crunch behind me, and my body flings to the noise.

I see the grueling creature in the shadows of the woods. It was a mistake trying to take out my knife. A rock peeking out of the ground sends me tumbling.

My head leads me down the hill until I start rolling. I can feel pebbles of rocks hitting my face and tree branches scratching and clawing at my hands. Luckily, the rest of the mountain is a short and flat distance. The moment lasts seconds, and I reach an end on my side.

I pick myself up and look around for the group. If I shout, zombies will come. It's not worth the risk. My knife fell out of my hand. I feel a warm sting on my forehead, but it's just a scratch. I rub my hands on my jeans to get rid of what I can. Everything hurts. There must be bunches of dirt all over me.

I feel so dirty.

The rush of the river clears my thoughts. I have to find the others and be cautious. The trees shuffle around as a large body falls through. I turn to the noise and back away. The body can be anything. Anything except the others.

The zombie from before reaches the bottom. He lays on the floor, stomach down, and glares up at me with wretched teeth ready to sink into my jacket. Realizing my only weapon is a revolver, I head down the river in hopes of finding something else. Maybe Dylan or one of the others is nearby. The zombie gets up sluggishly.

There's a sharp log to my right. I glance back to see the position of the creature. He's walking now, making slow distance. His legs are bent at odd angles, and his body slouches to the right. The stick is hefty, but it'll be an advantage against him. He steps closer, unaware of his fate. The log smacks into his skull. Black blood oozes from the wound. One blow is all it took as the dead one falls.

"Get off me kid!" a man shouts. The sound is almost quiet from the flow of the stream.

"Nathan," I call back.

Now's the time to use my gun, but I'll keep the stick with me too. If worse comes to worst, this is my best shot. I sprint down the river. There's a small boat house. Snow covers the wooden roof. I see Kira as I pass by the shack.

"Kira," I say with relief.

She looks back at me, her sunken eyes full of fear. Dylan steps out from behind her. Thank goodness they're safe.

"Where's Nathan?" I ask them, expecting to see Nathan

come in from the woods.

Kira pulls out Nathan's black-rimmed glasses. "I—I don't know. His glasses."

"It's okay, Kira. He's not gone. Nathan's a fighter," I reply.

But the truth is, the people harassing us are more cunning than they seem. This isn't going to be an easy group to deal with, especially with us running out of supplies.

Water crashes around within the stream. We look towards the sound. It must be Nathan. The ground below us turns to slush as we pass over.

"Nathan!" Kira shouts, her voice breaking down.

"Nathan, where are you," adds Dylan.

Further down the stream, a shadow dances in the water.

Running to the commotion, I call back to the two, "He's under the ice."

Nathan and another figure are struggling below. Cold air roams above the platform. I drop my revolver on the ground and use the stick to pry open the ice. Who knows where this river goes, and who this person is.

The ice lets out a splintering sound. Cracks form around the hole I make, but Nathan has already moved further down the stream.

"Meet him at the end," I shout and get up, fatigued.

Locating the edge of the ice, I squat over and shove the stick under. Maybe if Nathan can get a hold, he can pull himself up. A body hits the stick, but I can't make out who. They kick the stick out of my hand, and I watch as it sinks to the bottom.

Now what?

Nathan pops up from the water. His blonde hair is soaked, and his scarred hand holds onto some rocks below. I push my hand out. He barely grabs it and tries to pull himself out. His head is just an inch above water.

The figure emerges too. It's a girl around our age. Her hand is holding a knife. I look towards the symbol located near the blade. It's not the Air Force Base symbol, but a snake with yellow eyes instead. She slices at the side of my wrist, and blood drips into the river. My hand weakens. I can't hold on for long. I bring my other hand out, and Nathan grabs it.

His dark blue eyes stare at the girl who goes back into the water. He kicks at her, and she clings on tighter. The water seeps between our hands, and my grip loosens. Dylan and Kira stand behind me.

"Nathan!" Kira cries.

Nathan smiles at her. The worry is still in his eyes. "I missed you too. Now help me."

I try to hold onto his hands, but I'm losing him. The girl rises from the water again. She sucks in all the air she can hold. Her green eyes seem to glow as water drips from her long eyelashes. With the knife in her hand, she tries to slash my arm again, but I let go of one hand to dodge the attack.

Dylan falls to my left and holds onto Nathan's arm. The currents splash against the girl, and she sinks into the water, holding onto Nathan's waist.

There are sounds of zombies behind Kira. Her body flicks to the noise with her gun pulled out. My head barely turns to see her. She aims at a young woman and pulls the trigger.

Looking at the gun, Kira heads towards the edge of the river. She points the weapon at the dark shadow of the girl. The water ripples her figure, washing around Nathan. She fires and misses as the girl squirms around.

She fires another—if she continues, she'll waste our bullets.

"There's no use. Just try to pull me up," Nathan shouts as another wave crashes against him.

Dylan and I nod and use all the strength we have. After

going days with barely any food, my energy is weak. Luckily, Nathan has moved a few inches above the water. Even if our strength is little, we're getting him up, and that's what matters.

As the water splashes against us, I feel our hold weakening again. If I lose my grip on Nathan, he could get carried further down the stream. Another wave of water hits our hands, and Nathan starts sinking.

I try to find a better position, but with every move, the water is ready to break us apart. More zombies tumble down from the mountain, all of them covered in dirt.

"Don't let go, I got these guys," Kira says.

I can sense the fear rising inside her. On the outside, she might put on a secure picture, but within, she's scared she'll lose the only person she has.

She raises her gun and shoots one of the zombies. I focus on Nathan. No matter what, I can't let go of him.

The girl below must've found something to latch onto because Nathan is sinking rapidly now. Her hands find Nathan's shoulders, and she pulls with a powerful force. My body feels numb, and my fingers are just pieces of junk now. Arms sore, hands tired, fingers slipping.

Dylan is holding onto one of his arms, and I'm barely holding onto his fingers.

Kira's gun shoots nothing, and I hear her say something beneath her breath.

"I left my gun over there. It has some ammo left in it," I shout.

Leaving the zombies, she bolts for the gun. They turn in her direction, but when they see us, they continue their path. Kira comes back, shooting the zombies as she moves. After a few bullets, the gun is empty again. More creatures come from the woods. Nathan notices them and a look of disappointment spreads across his face. His eyes trace to each of us and then to the water.

"It's pointless. You guys just have to let me go," Nathan chokes.

The words strike me hard. Someone who was always irresponsible and headstrong giving themselves up.

I shake my head in disbelief. "No, we aren't going to leave you."

"Hailee, you have no other option," he replies. His hands have become limp. He moves around still trying to fight the girl below.

Dylan tries to grab his arm. "Nathan, c'mon don't give up."

"Just leave me. I'll find you guys. I promise." His neck sinks into the water.

Kira draws towards us. "Nathan? What are you doing?"

"Kira, I have to do this." He looks at the zombies inching closer. "You guys have to run! I'll find you!"

Then with a hopeful smile, he pries free from our grip and sinks into the river. His and the girl's dark shadows scurry along the stream.

"No," Kira cries out. Tears flood her cheeks. She drops the gun and tries to run to him. "Nathan!"

I grab her hand before she can get far. My legs tremble as I stand up, swallowing the pity in my throat. Dylan pulls out his knife.

"We have to go," he says while killing the zombie close to him.

I try to force Kira to run, but she refuses. The one person she loved the most was snatched out of her hands, and she couldn't do anything about it.

"If you stay here, you'll die. Nathan wouldn't want that."

Her eyes glare at me. "Like you know *anything* about him."

She breaks her arm away from mine and walks up the stream. Her hands wipe tears off her face.

Dylan kills another zombie, but they outnumber us. He retreats and catches up to us. We run fast, and the zombies drag behind.

Our legs race until we find thicker ice on the river. Getting back on the right path will take some time, but it's safer. The zombies are slow in the cold. Some have lost interest and others just can't keep up. Nathan pulled Kira over the ice, now who will help her?

I can imagine how she feels. After losing my parents and Ms. Mack, I realized that not everyone will stay alive, not everyone is going to live. But this time, it was my fault. I sent us out here knowing someone was in the woods.

"We'll find him," I say. My hand rubs her shoulder, and she doesn't take it off this time.

She wipes away her tears and stares at the river.

Dylan steps up first. He takes a short breath in, looking at the sky. The sun is dipping into the horizon, and the night will greet us soon. We should've gone earlier. I thought I'd let the group get closer to Joseline's, but it was a mistake. This was all a mistake.

Dylan presses his foot down on the ice, testing its strength. "We should hurry."

There are no water patches on this ice. Maybe this time it won't crack. Maybe it'll show some mercy. I nod my head and follow behind him.

He makes it across, and I signal Kira to go.

There is no caution in her steps, no reluctance, and soon it becomes my turn. It's just like last time—a few steps and you're over. Don't think Hailee, just go. It's less scary this time around.

"3, 7, 2, 4," Dylan says as I step off the ice.

Recalling the stone, I repeat the numbers back.

His nose is pink, and his chestnut hair holds small sprinkles of snow. He stares at the trees while I look at the snow. Once we find our old footprints, we can trace them back. Most of us, at least.

ELEVEN

MISSING

THE OLDER MAN brings them upstairs. They follow, holding onto their weapons with high alert. As they venture up, they all notice the blood. The railing leads up on the left side, a few poles missing. The cabin is old and disturbing, but it's safer than outside.

"Zara!" he calls out.

Once up the steps, there is a long hallway with a boarded-up window at the end. There are only a few doors, and the one at the end seems the most eerie.

Behind the closest door on the right is a person shuffling around. The knob turns, and a young female steps out.

She wears a black leather jacket, and the top half of her hair is tied into braids leading back. There is a small cut on her nose with dry blood.

"Newcomers?" she says, peering out the doorway. With a foot out, she examines them carefully. "You guys just needin' some food and water?" Her accent is light and almost forced.

"Yeah, if you have any to offer," replies Joseline.

The rest of the group waits beside her. It's better to stay silent and observe, even if the encounter feels off.

"We sure do. Come on, let's get you guys something to eat, and then we'll pack you up some more," the man says. He ushers them down while the woman goes back to hiding.

"We didn't get your name," says Joseline, following quickly after the man. Though she sounds nice, she doesn't trust them. After all, they're lending food for nothing. That's hard to find in the apocalypse.

"You can call me Thomas."

"Thank you, Thomas," she says as Thomas starts walking to the kitchen.

The sharp smell of blood comes piercing back. The man can smell it too.

"Monster must've wandered in," he says, scratching his mustache. "That smell ain't nice."

While chuckling, he points them to the wooden table and chairs. "Y'all can take a seat right here. I'll come prepare you guys somethin' while Zara packs up some more food."

Thomas hurries to another room and brings two more chairs. For being much older, he still has his muscles. His cowboy boots clank against the dusty floor as he walks. Once he leaves the kitchen, the group huddles closer.

"This place is great," Todd says with a grin. "I can't wait to eat something!"

"Yeah, well don't get your hopes up. Something isn't right here," Ava remarks.

"We should just take our food and leave." Noah covers his nose with his hand. "And that smell, that's not of the dead. The dead don't smell like fresh blood."

Ava nods, glancing at the stairs. "Noah's right. That smell

is almost like *human* blood."

"Well, I'm starving. I'd eat anything," says Angel.

It's hard to think about the bad when there's no food to fuel your mind. None of them want to be desperate, but some are willing to accept it and others aren't.

"Let's see what they offer," begins Joseline. "We need this food, so just be alert. Fighting might be our next option."

Thomas returns with six small trays of what looks like bacon. However, the strips are thicker and have a vibrant shade of red. The smell is worse now.

"Hope you don't mind the scent. Our seasoning is getting old. Not to mention our meat supply is damn low. We might just have to go vegetarian." His accent strengthens when he laughs. What's left of his hair is blonde with gray hairs peeking through.

The others laugh too, but not for the same reason.

The meat lays on the dirty plate, waiting to be eaten. Todd picks up his fork and uses more strength than normal to cut a slice.

"So, where's the meat from?" Joseline asks. If before she wasn't suspicious, she is now. "I mean, did you guys have a cow or something?"

She stares blankly at her plate. Something tells her not to eat it. Todd lifts his piece. As he brings it to his mouth, his nose burns from the putrid odor.

Thomas looks around and says, "There are packs of rabbit meat by Omaha. Zara and I looted what we could find. Gotta survive somehow."

"Omaha, huh? That's a few miles away, right?" continues Joseline. Her eyes catch Todd's, and he stares at the meat. She tries to shake her head, but it's no use.

Thomas laughs, this time louder. "Don't worry about the

meat, kids. It's safe to eat, we've been eating it for the past few months, and look at us. Perfectly fine."

His reassurance warns Joseline more. It's true—his skin looks healthy, his hair is clean, and it's almost like the apocalypse never hit him. She looks back at Thomas and sees a large knife covered in red behind him.

They remind her of someone from before. A group they had run into, but those guys should be long gone.

Looking back at Todd, her concerned eyes don't stop him. He places the meat in his mouth. Then there's chewing. They all watch his face, waiting for a reaction. His face scrunches like a prune, and then it rests. The chunk is gone, and his mouth is stained red.

"So?" Madeline asks.

Before he can express himself, a cry comes from the room under the stairs. Small thuds rustle the cabin. Thomas' face grows cold and almost angry.

"Must be another one of those monsters. Let me go take care of that," he mutters.

Instead of going from the front, he heads into the room. The cries are thunderous, but they're not of a zombie's growl. They all know it's the cry of a human.

"You guys hear that," Ava asks the others. She places her hand over her knife, ready to strike.

"Yeah, that's a human," replies Angel. She pulls out her blade, holding it below the table.

Todd takes another look at his meat. "Crap, that's not rabbit meat, is it?" he questions through a gag. His eyes flick to Joseline, and they both know what has happened.

"Let's leave," says Noah, pulling out his pistol and looking around.

Madeline stands up, holding in her disgust. "Yeah, and I

vote now."

She heads for the front door. Her footsteps skid across the wood. Thomas is talking in the other room, and his boots shuffle around. Shouting booms through the cabin.

As the others stand up, Zara's footsteps are heard coming down the stairs. Madeline reaches for the doorknob, and the others stand behind her in a low stance.

They may not know who these people are or what they do, but they know they need to leave. Escape this place that could end their fate.

As the knob is turned, a bomb rolls into their vicinity.

Red gas hisses out of the inside. Coughing and low mumbles fill the room. They try to search for a way out, but the gas blinds them. Madeline feels a sharp sting in her arm and warm blood flowing out. She lets go of the knob and clutches her bleeding hand. Her sight of the door is lost as the bomb blurs her vision. The drowsiness is overwhelming. Their legs tremble, and they meet the floor. All of them are helpless.

Within the red air, Joseline sees somebody being dragged away. She's far too tired to get up. Her body feels paralyzed. Everything in her tells her to stay awake—to get up and fight, but she can't. One by one, they are absorbed by the dangerous sleep. Their eyelids are held down by weights, and their mind is blanketed by darkness.

Whatever happens is not in their hands anymore. All they can do is hope for something or someone to save them.

Hours later they wake up. A debilitating headache in each of them. Ava is the first to get up. She glances at the back window, and the sky has set to black.

"Guys?"

She shakes Noah who lay asleep next to her.

Angel rubs her eyes, trying to make sense of what has just happened. "Oh God, they took Todd," she says as she picks herself up.

Hearing his name, Joseline bolts up. Her hand stops short of the door when she feels an emptiness on her back. One peek at the others and she knows what has happened.

"They took our weapons." With aching legs, she rises from the floor. "We need to get out and find Todd."

Her eyes dart around for some kind of protection. In the small kitchen, she begins rummaging through the cabinets. Only half-empty cans and boxes. Something shimmers in the corner by the fridge. One of Ava's knives.

"At least it's something. C'mon, we have to go now," she says, approaching Noah.

He rises, a bewildered look painted on his face. On his feet, he looks around the cabin and asks, "What happened?"

Madeline scavenges through the living room. Decorations clatter together, pillows fall to the ground, and chairs are pushed astray.

Joseline reaches for the door covered in blood.

"It's boarded up," Madeline says, looking at her hand. "All of the exits are."

The same noise from before pounds against the back door. They all look towards the sound. Angel heads to the noise, but Joseline stops her.

"It's not safe."

The banging grows as if whatever is in there has multiplied. It's hard to ignore the door as the shaking intensifies. The rusty screws won't hold the pressure. Cracks spread across the door until it splits in half.

Five zombies splatter across the floor. Most of them have a limb or two cut off, and the rest are in chains. Inside the room are tools of all sorts—saws, knives, hammers. Each covered in fresh blood.

"What the hell," says Madeline.

She and Angel stumble backward, barely missing the claws of the dead.

The zombies stare with hunger at them. Their faces still look like humans—they must have died recently.

Joseline steps up and stabs into the first man. As he tumbles down, she crouches and pushes the knife into the top of his skull.

The other zombies flare their teeth, trying to grab her. She backs up. There are too many for her to take on at once.

Madeline finds a vase on the floor and picks it up as one of them draws near her. The vase is sent flying at the creature. It shatters, sending the zombie to the floor. The pain doesn't affect him as he rises back up, one arm gone. She flees into the living room, hoping for a way to save herself.

Joseline follows and pierces the knife into the zombie. It falls to the ground as a legless one crawls towards her.

His long, outstretched arms grab her leg, and she falls to the floor. The knife slips out of her hands too. There may be no weapon with her, but her legs are still intact. With a kick, the zombie gets a taste of boot. His head bobbles back and tries to bite into her again. Madeline finds the knife and sinks the blade through his skull.

One of the zombies with no arms stumbles to Ava. Easily, she trips the zombie, and he meets the ground.

"Over here!" Noah calls out to Madeline. She throws the knife to him, and he jams it into the creature.

Another one creeps over to Angel. The bottom half of his leg is gone, and he uses one knee and a hand to move. She slams it to the ground, allowing Noah to kill it.

The last zombie leaves a trail of blood as he walks. His thighs are nubs, and he has a bite mark on his abdomen.

As they all look at the helpless man, they can't help but feel pity. His body stumbles around, and his face still has its brown color. If it weren't for the walking and lost limbs, he'd still look like a human.

Ava shakes her head in disbelief. "Must've been the last to turn. Poor guy."

"These people aren't sane," says Noah, approaching the man. The body stops as the knife is pushed into his head.

They stare at the mess below, and Noah hands Ava her knife back.

Joseline walks further down the living room. The only way out is the front door. All the windows are boarded up, and now the front door has been shut off too.

By the kitchen, snow has found its way inside. There's a small hole. Something they hadn't noticed when they checked the back of the cabin.

"Look, there's an opening," Angel says. The others find her staring at the wall.

"Will we all fit?" asks Noah.

Out of all of them, his masculine body makes him the biggest.

Ava approaches the opening. "Even if we can't, the wall is probably weak."

"You're right," says Joseline, squatting down to the hole.

There's only snow out there, and a fresh layer of it too.

"Nothing's outside. Let's get this done quickly."

She looks at the group, examining each to see who is best to go first. "Ava, you're the smallest. You should go."

Ava complies and lies down. She swats the snow away and crawls through. White powder fixes itself onto her shirt, but she still slides through with ease.

"Okay, now can you break the wall from the outside?" asks Madeline, her voice muffled through the wall.

"I can try."

Ava steps back and kicks into the wall. Dust sheds down, and the wall cracks. Her leg aches, but she pushes through.

A section of the wall crumbles away, and now the hole is big enough for them all.

The rest of them make it through safely.

Joseline is eager to go. "Let's go find Todd now," she says, looking for footprints.

"Josie," Madeline says. Her eyes wait for Joseline to stop moving, but she doesn't. "Josie!"

Joseline glares at her. Her nose is bright red, and her hope is slowly crashing.

"Look above—you know we can't go out there and expect to find him. Not like this."

Joseline shakes her head. They know Madeline's right. The sun is already gone, and the night has arrived. In the night, the zombies come out. Joseline knows that best.

"No. I can't just leave him, not with those guys," she says through a depleted voice.

"We can find him, just not right now. We need to get back alive," Ava adds.

"I get it, you guys have only been with my group for a few days, but Todd is my friend. I don't care if you think it's better to leave him. He's been with me since the beginning of this, and I wouldn't forgive myself if I left him all alone."

"Look, Joseline, I've known Todd since I was four years old. If it were any other situation, I would say we should find him, but look around. It's night, and we barely know where we are," Angel says and rubs her shoulder.

Joseline swats her hand away. "I can't leave him."

"Where would you even look for him?" asks Madeline. "They'll just take you too, and who knows what they'll do. We can't afford to lose more people."

Joseline feels her heart breaking. A part of her knows that they are all right. The memories of Todd flash through her head. The way he smiles at anything, his positivity, and his words, including what he would say right now.

"Just go, Josie. You can't die too."

And she does. With hesitation, she heads down the path to the parked bus. The others follow behind her, leaving a gap between them.

She knows she'll never see Todd if she leaves this place, but she also knows that going after him could risk her life. It has always been about being strong and making the right choice, yet all she wants is to see her best friend's face again.

Noah glances back at the cabin, looking at the numbers. Without Todd, they will have to memorize them.

"9, 6, 4, 3," he repeats, viewing the numbers in his head.

Madeline tries to walk closer to Joseline, but Ava holds her back. There's no use comforting her.

The wind howls through the silence. It's almost like the cries of the man in the room, perhaps like the cries of Todd too.

TWELVE
TOGETHER AGAIN

DAMIEN DECIDED TO tell Marlon and Kate about Cyrus. They would be left with questions, and he didn't want to harm their chances of being a group.

His brother was bit a few months into the apocalypse. It was one of the first deaths of someone he loved, and Damien couldn't handle the pain. He told the others that he buried him, but in truth, he hid Cyrus in the compartment. Nobody would hear or see him, so it didn't matter.

Kate was stunned, not just by his story, but by his honesty. "When we love someone, we do things we know are not sane. We are driven by love, and we can't stop that," she said to him. He appreciated her sympathy and went off on his way.

Half an hour passes, and Anthony approaches them on the stairs. "It's been some time you two. You think the groups are coming back soon?"

On his wrist is a boxy dark gray watch. The old man looks

at it and adds, "It's been about an hour and a half since they all left."

Kate views it too, noticing how thin his wrist is. "Don't worry about Hailee. They'll be back soon. Jason will be too."

The three of them look at each other without much to say.

"Hailee," Anthony repeats the name, "so she is the leader?"

It's not a question that they've thought much about. They all trusted Ms. Mack, and Ms. Mack trusted Hailee.

"We're a group. We do things for each other," Kate begins. She looks at Anthony, and then Marlon, hoping he is thinking the same. "Including her. She makes a lot of the decisions, but she cares about us, you know?"

"Of course. Joseline is the same. She's kept us alive, even when others were troubling us."

When it falls silent again, Marlon finally speaks. "So that girl, Joseline—she's not letting us stay here, right?"

Anthony's shoulders barely move as he shrugs.

"I don't know, kid. If I'm being honest, it's getting lonely in this factory. It'd be nice for some change."

Kate huffs. "Yeah, well our group keeps changing. We just want a place to live. I guess that's one thing Hailee hasn't found yet." She mumbles the last part.

"Just have some hope. Maybe we won't be separating after all," Anthony responds with an almost convincing smile. As he turns to leave, he spots people out the window.

Marlon sees them too. The window is thick making the image look blurry. He stands up and listens, but there's no noise coming from out there.

Anthony stays behind while Kate and Marlon jog down the stairs and walk towards the front. Kate reaches for her knife. The same knife she lost while trying to throw away some garbage. Marlon grabs his axe that sits on a table to the right.

Jason is in first wearing a cold expression. His boots leave snow on the ground. Avery steps in next, looking around the factory. Her eyes focus on Kate and Marlon. They lower their weapons and wait for the rest to come in. As Emily and Sarah walk in, Marlon inches towards the door. His friend should be right there.

The hopeful smile on his face is replaced with distress. The snow sinks into his clothes as he heads outside.

"Where is he? Ashton!" he calls out.

With no sight of him, Marlon finds himself back inside. Pictures of the dead ripping apart his friend appear in his mind.

The sound of Ashton's name brings flashbacks of what happened to the group.

Jason steps forward. His eyes are down, but he finds the courage to trace back to Marlon. "He saved us, but he didn't make it."

Marlon's jaw clenches, and he glares with fiery eyes at Jason. His axe clinks to the floor as he pushes Jason to the wall, holding him by the collar of his shirt.

"What happened?" Marlon's shouts echo through the factory.

The others turn their heads to the commotion.

"What happened to him?" The whites of his eyes grow red.

Jason pushes him off and reaches for his gun. One hand is held in front, protecting him from any future danger.

"There was nothing we could do, okay? You need to calm down. You need to understand, Marlon. There was another dude."

Hearing news of another man makes everyone perk up.

"Another person?" Kate questions, her eyes locked on the group.

Marlon doesn't break free from Jason's eyes. He searches

for some lie—someone he can blame.

When all he sees is the truth, he grits out, "Goddammit!" His body turns in every direction like his emotions are toying with him.

"Who? Who was the man?"

"His name was Elliot Francis." Upon saying his last name, Jason puts the pieces together. Emily too.

"Francis? Like Madeline Francis?" says Kate, a rise in her voice.

Jason looks out into the night. "Time was going so fast. I didn't even think about it until now."

"He looks—different," Emily begins. "He's not the same person he used to be."

The next words Jason uses are meticulously picked for Marlon. "He killed Ashton."

"So, you just left him out there?" Marlon spits out. "You guys are fucking sick." He turns around to hide his tears and to hold himself back from fighting.

Kate glances at him and then back at the group. "How are we going to tell Madeline?"

"We don't. Not yet at least," Emily says. "We're so close to getting that bunker. We can't let this get in the way. Especially not for Madeline."

Jason eyes the group. "She's right. Nobody says anything."

Not one person in the factory is unscathed by his eyes. Those who know, nod their heads. The ones in the back shrug their shoulders and continue their conversation.

"Well? Where's that prick now? Did you catch him?" questions Marlon. His hands are wet, and his face is puffed up.

"We're exhausted dude. Let us catch a break," says Avery, pushing through the crowd.

She sits down at a table, and some of the others follow behind. The four of them sit in silence with all the memories lapsing in their heads.

"C'mon, what happened out there?" Marlon pries as he trails behind.

He's trying to keep his face composed, but he's fuming inside. Everything in him says to run, find Elliot, and help Ashton. Kill the traitor and save the hero.

Jason glances at him, and then finally begins telling the tale.

* * *

"That's terrible," says Damien. He turns to Marlon. "He won't get away with this."

Kate stares at him, hoping to be of comfort but nothing comes out. She can't help him like he did for her.

"You didn't let him turn into one of those things, right?" he finally mumbles.

Jason shakes his head. "No. We made sure he was gone. He isn't one of them."

Nobody says anything after that. The cruel day has finally caught up and everyone is feeling drowsy.

"We need to get you guys cleaned up," says Tyler with a med kit in his hand.

Bandages, ointments, and other supplies are spread out on the table. They begin wrapping the straps around their wrists while Jason attempts to clean up his face. With Madeline gone, all the medical work will be done by them.

"Let me help you," says Anthony. He sets his hat down and looks at the supplies. Jason doesn't say anything, but he puts the stuff down.

As the old man finds a seat, he says, "I was a combat medic

stationed in the Middle East. My family lived down there."

"You were in the military?" Jason asks, his voice almost silent.

Anthony puts some liquid on a napkin. "Yep, but they found out that I was losing my vision and hearing a couple of years after I joined. All my friends got stationed away, and I would've been too," he says as he wipes the cuts. "I guess I'm lucky I got kicked out. Most of those guys are dead now."

Jason hides the pain in his wounds. He knows it's nothing compared to what's happened to the man in front of him. On one of the cuts, Anthony applies some white strips to keep it together.

Jason can't seem to look him in the eye. "I'm sorry."

"Kid, it's not your fault. I'm telling you this because people die—nothing we can do to stop that. We just have to accept that it's happened."

He wipes away the dried blood from Jason's face. There's a dark purple bruise forming below his eye, and his lip is busted.

"You could say that again."

Jason stares at his hands. His skin can't stand the snow. Anthony looks down at his colorless fingers, then at his face.

"You must be freezing."

Getting up from the table, the man looks around for a lighter. Eventually, he receives one from Tyler and starts up the flames on some newspaper.

Emily, Sarah, and Kate sit near the corner. Kate tries her best to wrap the bandages around their wrists.

"I can't believe I didn't recognize him," says Emily, looking at Kate. "I mean, we were in the same class for years. It's just been that long, I guess. His face, his height, everything about him has changed."

Sarah avoids looking at the two. "If I'm being honest, Elliot and those creatures aren't our only problem here."

"What do you mean?" asks Kate, tying off the strip on Emily.

Her silence is worrying, but their prying eyes cause her to reveal her mind anyway. "Well, I don't think Elliot's alone. There was this group, and we had a deal with them," she says, her eyes finally taking a peek at their expression. "I don't—I don't know if it's them or not. We came across them after Omaha got overrun. They were in a small city called Papillion. I think it's the city north of where we are."

"And Elliot's apart of them?" Emily interrogates.

"No, I've never seen him in my life. He could be. I don't know. But those people might come down here if the herd in Omaha has reached them. They could *already* be down here, and if they are, then we're going to be in trouble."

Kate starts wrapping Sarah's wrists. "What's so bad about these people?"

"They're smart, cunning if you would. But that's not it, they will do anything, and I mean *anything* to survive. They do things, inhuman things." She takes a nervous breath in while the two never drop their eyes. "They're cannibals."

* * *

I see the factory behind the trees in front of us. My hands are numb to the point of falling off. I should've brought those gloves from the mall.

People are shuffling around inside the factory. Emily and the others should be back. Hopefully, all of them. Angel and the others too. With Nathan taken away, we can't lose more people than we have.

Dylan sniffles next to me. This journey was dangerous. How did I allow this to happen? Was I so hunger-stricken that the dangers weren't present?

None of us have spoken to each other, not after the dead stopped chasing us. A silent walk. Every few minutes I'd recite the code in my head. Through the window of the factory, a body perks up. Hopefully, they'll see us. I don't know if I can keep up for long now.

We walk in through the fence and pass the tied-up zombies. I never realized how big it was until now. The cave and dozens of trees are all within it. My legs feel as though they are about to collapse, but I just need to make it inside.

"Hailee!" Emily calls and rushes over to me.

I brace her open arms and hug her with what little strength is left. My body aches.

She loosens her grip and looks at my wet sleeves. "You're freezing."

In seconds, she rushes into the storage room. Her boots tromp on the floor like a worried mom.

I haven't said anything about Nathan yet. I think I'd rather let Kira say it—if she even can. Out of all of us, she's the one who kept falling behind. Her feet would drag, and she'd keep looking around as we walked, behind us too.

I look at Dylan on my left, his face looks almost purple. Kira's is the same. We're freezing, literally.

"Glad to have you back," says Kate as she hugs Dylan and me. Her eyes wander to Kira, and then to the missing person. When she doesn't find the last member, she stares at me.

"He's—gone," Kira whispers. Her eyes don't turn to any of us, and Nathan's glasses are held harshly in her hand.

As Jason and Marlon walk up, my eyes are drawn to Jason's cuts and bruises that have been cleaned up.

"What happened?" My voice sounds weak. I feel weak.

Ashton isn't anywhere to be seen. Usually, he would complain about something like this. I shouldn't be negative, but how can I be positive when failure keeps haunting me?

"It's a long story," Jason replies, examining Dylan and Kira. "Wait—you said he's gone? You mean Nathan's gone?" His head barely shakes, and I wait for him to say what he's thinking. I know he can't keep it to himself.

"Fuck," he mumbles and looks at me. His face is washed with dread. The typical light in his eyes is lost. "Ashton's gone too."

Nathan *and* Ashton? My thoughts race around. If the girl was attacking us, that means there's more. Joseline's group might have been ambushed too.

Emily arrives with blankets for all of us. "We need to get you guys warmed up. Come over to the fire."

She hands them to each of us. I wrap it over my back and let the warmth sink in.

Emily helps me over to the fire. It's nice to know someone cares, even after the things I've done. Her arms guide me to a chair, and the bandages on her wrists catch my eye.

I lift them up, no blood has seeped through. "Bandages? What happened to you guys?"

Emily tells me all of what she knows. The cannibals, Elliot and Madeline, and the fight before with Ashton and Jason. I failed them all. The guilt is in every corner of my body. My sister comforts me, but she can't hide the truth.

Everyone needs an apology. I tell one to Emily first, and like all the other times, she forgives me in seconds, and then encourages me to talk to Dylan next.

And so, I do. Dylan stands in the corner with Jason. They

both look exhausted. When I approach, Jason heads off.

"I'm sorry," slips out of my mouth immediately, and Dylan smiles vaguely.

"For what?" he asks.

"There's a lot," I begin, "but mainly for bringing us into this mess. It was dumb, and we lost two people. I mean, I underestimated this place. I thought it would be easy to get the food and that this was finally our time to relax."

I want to tell him all of it, pour my heart out, but there's no point. I can't complain about what I caused.

"Hailee, these few months have been terrible. We're all hungry, and you just want to help, but you're not alone. You're not the only one making decisions. It's all of us. This world is cruel,"—he picks up my blistered hands—"so we have to stick together."

His words are sweet, but they don't cure my guilt. I know we're a group and that I'm not the only one making decisions, but I made this one. Had I given this all more thought, everyone would still be alive.

Two long arms wrap around me. The warmth of his body relieves some of the pain. My thoughts can wait. I hug Dylan back hoping he never lets go.

"I'm glad I have you," I whisper over his shoulder.

Wishing I could hold on forever, I let go of him.

"Same here," he says with a smirk. His eyes glimmer from the light of the fire.

The flames dance around, casting a fatiguing spell on me. After all that's happened today, sleep sounds like paradise. I stare off at the room below the stairs. When the others arrive, I must be awake. Even for the ones here.

"I feel like sleeping too," says Dylan. He views the corner where Kira sits. The lids beneath her eyes have puffed up, and she hasn't moved much.

"I feel terrible for putting her through this," I mutter, thinking back to the river. "The others too."

My eyes flick to the front door. It's just a few meters away from me. "They should be back by now."

"You're right, but they're smart. They'll be fine."

"Yeah, I hope so."

I leave Dylan to talk with the others. Jason sits across Emily and Sarah by the fire. His face looks gloomy.

"Dylan caught you up, right?" I ask, taking the seat next to him.

"With everything he knows, yeah."

"What about the cannibals part?" I watch his face turn to surprise. "Emily told me. Said something about how Joseline and the others made a deal with them."

"Cannibals? That's—wow."

"She also said they live in Papillion. Luckily, we didn't go there because she said these people are ruthless."

"You think they're the ones behind the attacks?"

"Yeah," I reply, rubbing over my wrist where the large cut still stings. "But I don't want us to worry about it. We're all hungry. When we get the bunker food, we'll leave."

He glances at the fire, his eyes never crossing mine. "Let's rest while we wait for the others, then we can talk in the morning."

"Yeah, I guess you're right."

THIRTEEN

ONE GROUP

I WAKE UP to the familiar bus pulling into the dirt path. They're back, finally. The sky is a black blanket, and there are barely any stars. Dylan's already up and talking to Jason. I rub my eyes and then look at the others. My heart aches. I shouldn't put all the weight on myself, but it's true that this all happened because of me.

My throat is on fire, and as I stand up, my legs feel immovable. After hours of searching and walking, my body feels worn out. The guilt doesn't mind taking a stab as well.

The weight of my knife is gone, and my gun too. I take a second to look at all the weapons in the room. In case of anything, it'll be nice to know where I can defend myself.

The light of the bus dies out, and people trot to the front. Everyone has already crowded around the door as they did for us. I approach the huddle and nudge my way to the front, hoping to see everyone all together.

Joseline steps in first. Her boots drop flakes of snow onto

the floor. Madeline and Ava are next. I lighten up when I see Angel's blonde hair through the others.

"Glad to see you guys are safe," I say, hugging Madeline. She frowns as I let go.

"Not all of us." Her voice is low, and she glances at Joseline.

Her eyes are tinted red, and her nose is too. I don't think it's from the cold.

"We found the code," she says. "It was on the door of a cabin."

I don't know if I'm imagining the rile in her voice. Perhaps I want her to be mad at me. I heard the tone in the others too, and I can feel it in myself.

"It was boarded up, and we went inside—"

She looks at her people, and they look back, their faces planted with grief. It's almost like they know something.

"We found people," Angel says. Concern flashes over her face as our eyes meet. "Zara and Thomas were their names."

"They took Todd," adds Madeline, "took our weapons as well. They had traps in the woods and near the cabin."

"Fucking hell," Marlon hisses from the back.

I walk to Angel and glance at the others. "Let's get you guys in better shape. We can talk when we're all feeling better."

Everyone settles down near the fire and some in corners together. Angel and I sit on the ground beside the flames. The fire is small, just a few pieces of wood in a steel bowl, but it's still warm. Small things can make a difference. I should start believing in that.

Angel wraps the blanket I gave her around herself.

"Thanks."

I barely hear myself say, "Yeah."

Her gaze is still fixed on me as I look back at the fire. Their faces are almost peeking out of it. Todd, Nathan, and Ashton. They trusted me enough to go, and they're gone now. That's three survivors I lost. I look down at my jeans. Blood is stained in spots all around. My hands have dirt seeped into the cracks.

"We're almost there Hailee," Angel whispers to me. "I can feel it."

Days like today only remind me of before when all we cared about was volleyball, grades, clubs, and homework. I breathe in, inhaling the same oxygen that's tainted all of us.

"I hope you're right. I can't feel anything."

She scoffs. "We'll make it through this. All of it, together."

Her blue eyes reflect the orange flames. Dylan and Jason sit down beside me. I want to say something, but with all the pain going around, I'm speechless. Every so often, my eyes find Madeline sitting with Kate and Joseline. Kate knows, most of us do too, and it feels wrong to keep it away.

Angel catches me looking at them. "What's wrong?"

My eyes flick to Jason. If anyone mentions it, it should be him.

"Go ahead," he says and stares back at the fire.

I turn back to her eager eyes and whisper, "You remember her brother?"

"Yeah, she never really talked about him, but yeah," she replies with the same level of voice.

"It's a long story, but he might be near us. Jason said he saw him. He has the same last name and hair color as her."

"Yeah, his name started with an E, right?" she asks and peers at Madeline.

"Yeah, Elliot. But we can't tell her anything. She'll become distracted and steer us away from the bunker."

Angel nods, staring back at us. "My lips are sealed."

After some time of just sitting, I tell everyone to come around. The next day we'll go to the bunker, and this nightmare will be over. Most of the people sit either on chairs or on the ground. Others are leaning against the wall.

The real map is in my hand, and a black pen that Sarah gave me is in the other.

Laying the map down, I glance at Joseline. "Let's start with the codes. Your group first."

She looks at Noah who says, "9, 3, 4, 6."

I can imagine the pain she is bearing. The others from the group nod their heads and assure the code. Everything seems related. Everyone that attacked us must be working together. And if that's true, I don't want anyone else to die, I'll even go to the bunker myself.

I repeat the numbers and scribble them down near the triangle on the left. Dylan watches me as I write our code down at the top with the circle.

"3, 7, 2, 4 is our code," I say and call for the last group.

Jason recalls his numbers, "4, 5, 7, 8." I say them back.

He nods his head, and the final code is written down. My eyes scan over the digits. The random numbers. Who knows if this will even work. My mind keeps building images of us opening the bunker. We'd see cans of food and bottles of water.

"We'll go tomorrow. I'll go alone if I have to, but I don't want any more of you guys to get hurt."

Dylan looks at me, shaking his head. "But what if *you* get hurt, Hailee? We're better together. We couldn't have expected this."

His eyes stare at me with concern, and it's too hard to say no. I hear others offer to go. The same people I picked in the beginning. After all this, they're still brave. I can't fail them.

"Okay, we'll take the same people we'd planned. Dylan,

Angel, Ava, Madeline, and Noah."

"I'll be there too," Joseline begins, "and I'll bring one of you."

Nobody seems to object, or maybe the one person I was used to objecting is gone.

"There is another thing we need to discuss," I say, knowing the battle we've already started, "the Cannibals."

Joseline eyes me, a sketchy look on her face. Emily and Sarah seem stunned as well.

"You know?" asks Joseline.

"Yeah." I turn back to the group. "We're weak, tired, and starving. The last thing I want to do is put everyone here at risk by these people."

"So, what do you say?" Damien asks.

"We should leave. If the Cannibals want this land, it's no use fighting them for it. I won't force you all to go, but even you know it's dangerous living here." The last part is said with my eyes on Joseline.

"We need to go back for him, for both of them," she says and barely notices me.

"I know, and we'll try, but I won't promise that we'll find them. We don't know what's happened to them, or where to even look."

She turns away, shaking her head. I need Joseline to stay with me. We may not know her and her group, but I have a good feeling about all of them. Even if there's a chance Todd and Nathan are alive, we would be leading ourselves into a death trap if we look for them. I stand up and scan the tables. A city map lies half open on one, and I bring it back to the group.

Once it's flat on the ground, we see the land clearly. The map displays Nebraska zoomed in with the states that surround it. I focus my attention on the east side. Between Omaha and

125

Lincoln, there's the town that Emily mentioned, Papillion.

"Do you know where we are?" I ask Joseline.

She points to a space a few inches below the town with the Cannibals.

"I'm guessing Sarah blurted something about them being here, right?" she asks as she pulls her finger back.

Sarah looks down, almost ashamed.

My eyes don't leave the area. "Omaha is overrun?"

Joseline nods her head and examines the cities.

We need someplace that's secure with supplies and walls. Another small building won't help. My eyes catch a city called Plattsmouth.

"It's further away from them, and with the food we get from the bunker, we could start an actual living here." I can see Dylan agreeing with me in the corner of my eye.

His face is calm as he watches the others. "The bus will have just enough fuel, and we can fill it up at the city. There is enough room for all of you to come." His eyes trace down all the members of the factory. Then his finger shoots to another small town above Plattsmouth. "And if Plattsmouth doesn't have supplies, we can go up to Bellevue or Council Bluffs."

"If we all work together, we can build the city up, or a section at least." I look around at everyone, especially at the people in Joseline's group. Their faces are down, shadowed. There's nothing I can say to make them feel better.

"What if the bunker doesn't actually have food?" Jason asks. His eyes don't leave a stare.

"Then we'll still go to Plattsmouth. We'll gather up as many supplies as we *can* find and stop at buildings between," I reply. "If we can find something to plant too, we could grow our own food. Emily knows a lot about it, and I don't doubt her."

Nobody says anything after that. Some of them have tuned

us out, waiting for this conversation to end. Joseline hasn't said anything either. Every few minutes, I see her stare off and think about something else.

"I guess now we all get some rest," I say and stand up. Snow has begun trickling down once again. All the events that happened today will be covered by a blank sheet. The start of something new.

The sun gleams on my forehead as I sit up against the hard bus seat. My head itches from the ragged knots making my hair their new home. The name of the city echoes in my head. Plattsmouth. Maybe the next place we can call home?

The bus is freezing, and my fingers are numb. My knuckles are healing, but everything else has yet to go. I open my backpack, which I rested on for the night, and look through the small number of supplies to find a water bottle. The plastic brushes my fingers, and I pull it out. Just like everything in my bag, it's ice cold.

A pounding is at the door. A straggler must've found the bus.

Emily sleeps against the window.

She must've felt me watching her. Like a sloth, her limbs stretch out slowly. A glance at the door should be enough.

She sees the dead man clawing at the glass that's now filled with smudges of slime. As she sits down in the driver's spot, I examine the man. I'm not sure if he's an old one, so my pocket-knife is my best bet.

His skin is tinted green and purple, and his eyes are blood-shot. Emily waits for my signal, and I nod my head.

The doors creak open, and the zombie reaches for me. With my free hand, I move aside his wavering arms and inject the knife into his almost bald head. As I take out the small blade, blood spills out, and he falls to the ground. The ruckus wakes up Kate and Jason.

Emily leaves the doors open as she walks back to her seat. I turn around to see who's awake, and that's when I notice Kira in the back. Her face is dull, and her eyes are almost lifeless. The guilt turns me away.

Jason is up and flexing his limbs. The cut and bruises on his face look no better than yesterday. Kate pulls out a small tube of lotion and rubs it into her hands. The sight of the bottle tightens my skin.

Marlon is seated between me and Jason. His head bobbles around as he starts waking up. Across from him, I see Dylan looking through his bag.

Everyone seems fine. I step down the stairs and move the man on the ground to the left. Joseline is tying up a new woman to the fence of the factory. The brisk air greets my dry face.

We make eye contact, but her silence is loud enough. Instead of trying to talk with her, I continue my way inside and see Angel and Madeline talking to Damien and Tyler.

The sun has shifted behind a thin cloud, and the light dimly shines through the windows.

I put the small knife away and head over to them. There are many new things I hope for at Plattsmouth. Maybe a weapon belt, an actual house to live in, or even strong walls to keep the dead out.

As Angel sees me, she brightens up. Her hands are out in front of her, covering something. Then with a smile, she reveals a pistol.

"For you. I noticed you lost all your weapons." She extends her hand a bit further.

"Thank you but—where'd you get this?" I take the gun and slide it into my jeans.

"I asked that girl Sarah for one. Told her it was for you. Out of all the people I know, I wouldn't expect *you* to lose all your weapons."

I think back to the girl who dragged Nathan down the stream. Everything that happened yesterday feels like a blur. Ashton's gone and yet, nothing feels different. Perhaps it's my way of grieving.

"Me neither," I reply.

Tyler shifts his focus to me. "So, what if one of the places we go to is flooded with those things? What then?" His black hair is matted just like mine.

"We'll see how bad it is. If it's a small herd, we can make it through."

I'm not even sure if that's the right thing to do, but I won't let them see my worry. They must stay strong.

"You think we could make it through a hoard?" questions Damien.

"We have a good shot." I look at them and know they're feeling scared. "You guys have survived in here. A hoard would be nothing."

Angel nods her head beside me. "Our group is strong, and you guys aren't bad yourselves. Those shits have nothing on us."

They laugh, but that doesn't mean they agree. They must hate me for losing their friend. I know the anger because I felt it when I lost Ms. Mack and my parents.

It would only take a few seconds for them to turn against us. Maybe the signs of it are already showing, and I'm just too oblivious to see.

FOURTEEN

THE BUNKER

I AM EXCITED about the bunker, but it feels almost greedy. Too many people gone just for food.

There's dirt all over me. It's in my nails and filling my boots. I can feel the grime in my hair, and the muck on my clothes. It's inside my body too, and in the choices I've made.

"Are we ready to go?" asks Dylan as he steps inside. He glances at the people and then stares at me.

"As much as we can be," I reply.

It doesn't take long for the others to come inside. Perhaps they're eager for the food too. The previous days feel like a dream—or a nightmare. I keep forgetting that they're gone. That's how I felt with Ms. Mack too. It was unbelievable.

"We'll give everyone a minute to wake up, and then we'll leave."

"Sounds like a plan," says Dylan, turning to the factory. "I'm going to go talk with the others."

He leaves to the other side of the building where Noah is

sitting.

Joseline has come back inside, and her hands work with diligence to polish an arrow. When she sees me approach, she sets her work down.

"Need something?"

I notice the blood on the rag, but I'd rather not dwell on it. "We're going to need bags and backpacks for the food, and maybe some more weapons. With those people out there, I don't want to put your group in danger."

She looks away. An obvious sign of secrecy.

"You've been hiding something. You can tell me."

"I miss my friend. That's all," she replies with a glance at the storage room. "Come, follow me."

Inside the room, the darkness blinds me at first, but my eyes adjust. Through the thick black, she manages to find three duffle bags.

Conversations still boom through the building as we exit the storage. Joseline heads to the front, and the others circle up. Dylan finds his spot next to me.

The quiet room reminds me of my class back in Cheyenne. Hardly anyone ever talked in Mr. Griffin's class. Nobody really liked health, and many of us didn't like him.

"All right everyone," I say, stepping in towards the group, "it's time to go. Ashton, Todd, and Nathan took the hits for us so we could be here. Their sacrifices will not go to waste."

I want to say more, something to help raise their spirits, but even I know that it's impossible right now.

"We'll take the bus to the bunker, but because of the Cannibals, we'll have"—faces of the group scan through my mind—"Emily, Damien, and Marlon inside the bus to stay on watch." Marlon scoffs, but he doesn't retort. The others don't either.

"Let's get everyone who is coming up here," Joseline says as she turns around to look at the bus.

Dylan picks up one of the bags from my hand. "Everyone else will stay here on watch. We aren't safe, but we're stronger together. Stay alert and help each other out."

When he straightens up, he sheds me a smile.

Soon, everyone finds their position, whether in the line at the front or in the back sitting on a chair. Angel jogs over to me before I step out the door.

"Are you ready?" I ask and match her pace to the bus.

"Hailee, you know I love food. Of course I'm excited," she replies, fixing the position of her knife, "but with everyone we've lost, it feels wrong to be happy. I don't know if this is survivor's guilt but—"

"I feel it too."

Her mouth closes, and she nods her head. The steps of the bus are muddy as we get up.

"I just hope it goes away. I feel sorry for them, but I don't want to be dragged down by sorrow. They would want us to get far, right?"

"I would hope so."

Dylan sits across Joseline and Avery in the first seats. Angel and I sit behind them in my normal seat.

Through the window, I see Tyler, Kate, and Jason looking at us. Their faces look exhausted. The bus doors close, and Emily starts up the engine.

After a few minutes of Joseline shouting directions and Emily twisting the wheel, we finally make it to what looks like the bunker. Tiny droplets of water sit on the window. That and the condensation disfigure my view outside, but the three code panels on the bunker that Joseline and Noah mentioned are there.

Emily exhales as the bus halts. "We're finally here."

My bag's fallen off my seat. There's some stuff in there that could help me out. The strings dig into my shoulders as I pull it over my back.

Those who are leaving stand up. The doors open, and we head out.

"We'll be back quickly," I whisper to Emily before I step down.

I take a good look at the outside of the bunker while the others come down. There aren't many trees around which made driving much easier. Getting out will be what's rough.

The land is flat, and the snow has piled up. It's a pretty sight. Sometimes I wonder why the world had to turn bad, why that rock had to bring its diseases to Earth, or why *we* lived out of everyone.

The cement doors of the bunker are almost threatening up close. Such drastic measures for food. When I was little, I would kill for something like this. But back then I had a bed to sleep in.

"It's exactly like the one my dad showed me. The color and everything," Noah says, and tries to look through the thick window of the door. It's shaded black making it as helpful as the door itself. I look down at the numbers on the map and back to the keypads.

"Do you know what the inside is like?" Joseline asks as she too tries to look through the door.

The keypads each display "Enter Code" with their shape next to it. I set my bag down and start entering the digits.

Each pad beeps and flashes green as the correct code is entered. On the last one, I hold back my smile and press the digits.

Beep.

The door trembles before it sinks into the ground. The sound of a machine stirs from inside the walls. Once the door is gone into the floor, the bunker becomes silent.

"That's not creepy," says Madeline as she studies the floor of the staircase.

Angel peeks down and then turns to me with eager eyes.

There's an awful stench flooding out, and from what I can see, there's a door at the bottom. The food must be behind it.

With one last look at the scene behind us, I pick up my bag and step inside. The others are behind me, but none of us really have the guts to go. We've been living with zombies for a year, but the look of this place is still haunting. The smell worsens as we go. The others notice it too. Angel's face has a sour look on it.

The outside gives us just enough light to see the steps. The room with the food is just behind this door. I wonder if there even is any. Joseline couldn't have confirmed it herself.

Angel pulls open the door to reveal a black room. Someone from the back shines a light inside. There is a soft growl in the corner.

The map fits into my jeans, and I take out the new gun that Angel gave me.

The light passes over a figure, and I whisper, "Over here."

The man sits in the right corner. On the ground, his body looks limp. There's a skull for his face, his eyes don't open all the way, and his hands don't bother reaching for us. He has a neon yellow uniform on. The fabric sags and bunches all over.

I take out the flashlight in my drawstring and turn towards the others. "You guys look around to find some sort of light or even the food. There could be more of these guys around so don't get hurt."

They nod their heads and scatter out. Dylan stays behind and sits on one knee.

"Looking for bites?" he asks as he fixes the zombie against the wall.

"Yeah, he's got no meat on his body. I'm worried that if he starved, he either didn't find the food—or it's not here."

"Yeah? Well, let's make our bet on the first one." He finds the zipper on the coat.

As he pulls it down, I see a light in the corner of my eye. Angel and Madeline stand by a lit lantern, holding more in their hands.

"They still work!" Madeline smirks as she turns on others.

She places the lanterns around the floor. Rustic tables sit on the edges of the room. The walls and floor are cement.

Dylan slides off the top of the suit to reveal the white shirt the guy was wearing. His arms are just bones, and as we take his shirt off, his chest is no different. Even as a zombie, he was starving.

My eyes shuffle down his body, examining his green skin. A small blood stain is near his stomach. I turn the zombie to its side and see the bite wound with gauze tapped on. Relief flushes over me. This man could've gone through anything. Maybe he died from this mark instead.

There's a thud from further in the room.

Noah curses as he stumbles back.

The noise is riveting. My heart is beating at an abnormal rhythm. I thought I conquered all that the apocalypse had to bring.

One of the creatures is sprawled on the floor near Noah. He views the body before shooting a bullet into its head.

Gasping for breath, he says, "Just another zombie."

Dylan goes towards him while I stay back. As the zombie

was approaching Noah, I caught a glimpse of something on the ground. Below one of the tables is a patch of disfigured floor.

"Help me move this thing," I call, walking to the wooden table.

Dust has collected at the top. The wood is a deep brown with scratches all over. Angel and Avery stand beside me, and the table finally budges. There's something there. A small black line separates the concrete platforms.

"Can I see your knife?" I ask Angel as my knees touch the cold ground.

She places her smallest knife into my hand. With the blade between the tiles and a few wiggles, I feel the platform shift. Debris crumbles down as the square lifts.

The idea of the food being gone was constantly in my head, but I'm sure it's in here. By the time the platform is pushed aside, everyone has gathered around the hole. My words have escaped. The food I've been dreaming about is in front of me. There must be about a hundred cans down there. Some bandages, medical tape, and other supplies are in the corner too.

The ecstatic feeling in my body seems to die out in seconds. My voice is cut short as footsteps come pounding down the stairs. With one hand already over my gun, I stand on my feet.

Two people come waltzing down. Their steps are light—cautious. Two big guns on each of them shine behind the light of a lantern. Guns that aren't just a pistol or a revolver. Guns that could end all of us in one pull.

"Drop everything you have," one of them says. She's a girl and likely younger than us.

"That food is ours," the other one says. A man in his twenties.

Angel and Ava look at me, but my eyes stare at Joseline. She and Avery are the only ones who could know these people.

I wonder what happened to the guys on the bus. We had them up there for a reason. How were these people able to come down here with them on watch?

"This isn't fair. We had a deal," Joseline shouts, distress in her words.

"Boohoo, things change," the girl says.

Her eyes look familiar. Muscles peek through her compressed shirt. She's the one who took Nathan.

Our eyes connect as she says, "You should've known this would happen."

I pull out my gun. "We haven't done anything to you guys, but you kidnapped our members and killed another."

A giggle comes out of her as Joseline's head hangs low.

"Wasn't I clear? Drop your weapons." Her voice is steady. There's no hesitation in her movement as she raises the weapon. This is a losing fight.

"Okay." It pains me to comply. I don't want to risk anything or anyone right now. "There, now can you tell us where our friends are?"

"The bags too."

I don't know why I'm taking her seriously. She's a kid and demanding *us* around, yet I still take off my drawstring. The others do too.

"Now our friends," I repeat, and the man snorts.

"You want to show them Cora, or should I?"

"Go ahead. It just might be the last thing they see if they don't listen to us."

He goes into her backpack. She holsters her weapon with precision, pointing the end at Joseline. His hand pulls out a fleshy object.

As all of it comes out, I know what it is. The hand of my friend is being held like a trophy. I wince at the sight. Blood drips down the cut-off. Could it be Nathan's or Todd's?

Joseline's member or mine?

Either way, it makes me sick. He throws the hand, and it drops on the table before me. The fingers are curled up, and the nails are long.

The Cannibal's arm goes back into the bag and pulls out something else. It's a dark gray watch with letters embellished on the side. It's Nathan's name. I'm reminded of the river, holding onto Nathan's arm, and regretting all my decisions.

"Now, your friends are alive, for the most part," the girl, Cora, says.

We're all silent and still like deer in the headlights.

"But, if they don't listen, they won't be for long. The same goes for you all."

"Where is he, Todd?" Joseline spits out. Tears are welling in her eyes. They both look at each other and laugh. Her question remains unanswered.

"I guess now, we need to find something to do with you all," says Cora.

"She'll want us to take them. All of them," says the guy.

They start bickering about something or someone. Cora hisses the man's name in an attempt to convince him.

Rob.

If I know his name, maybe he'll be more reluctant to kill us.

I don't pay attention to them after that but instead to the growling in the back. My mind keeps thinking about the bus. Emily is in there. What if they're hurt?

"Hey girl, what you looking at?" asks Rob.

I shake my head. "Nothing."

Luckily, he doesn't seem to care and continues to talk with Cora.

Neither of them sees the zombie hurdling down the stairs. They're frightened and lose their guard. Of course, one zombie isn't effective. The creature is down in seconds as Cora fires seven bullets into it.

"Let's just get the food before more of these idiots come down. You put it in their duffle bags, all right?" says Cora.

With his gun aimed at me, he nods his head.

"And you all, move over here." She shakes her gun to the right, and we follow into the corner.

Being attacked like this is embarrassing. We're like sheep in a herd, waiting for slaughter. I watch our duffle bags get stuffed with our food. It was all ours, and now they come here and take over everything.

The growling in the back has grown. This must be our chance. I can't let our food be taken away. My head turns just barely to see the others. I hope they hear it too. One snarl turns to many. Before I realize it, a pile of them tumbles down.

Cora turns her attention to the zombies. With her back turned and gun aimed without a care, our chance to escape is in front of us.

We're not sheep. None of us will be herded, and if that means killing the wolf, so be it. She stumbles back as my foot flies into her stomach. A desperate attempt to flee is taken over by the hands of the zombies rising to grab her. They wrap their claws around her waist and pull her down.

She cries out with an agonizing scream, and her hand with the gun raises.

"Rob, help me! You fucking coward!" she cries as blood splatters across her cheek.

Her face has contorted to horror as the monsters bite into her body, ripping up her shirt to feast upon the flesh.

This is it. She's gone.

Her gun aims down at us while the blood spews out of her.

Everything around me blurs. My ears fuzz up. The moment feels like it's been slowed down. In her distress, she still knows what to do. Her finger pulls the trigger, and the gun blasts hundreds of bullets at us.

We all duck.

After that, her body is lost in the crowd of creatures.

I hear a shriek. To my left is Ava on the floor. Her hands are placed over her leg and blood seeps between her fingers.

Madeline leaps to the injury and presses her hands down over Ava's.

I get up and recollect myself. Only one of us was injured, right?

As my eyes scan through the others, the silence to my right is worrying. There's fear painted over Angel's face. My eyes follow hers, and her breathing rises fast. Her back is against the wall, and one hand is placed over a bleeding wound. A shot to the stomach. The first gunshot to a body since the beginning.

She drags down the wall as tears build in her eyes. I know they aren't from the pain. Angel doesn't want to die. She never did. Everything snaps back as she falls to the floor.

"Angel! You're going to be okay," I burst, rushing down to her level. "Listen to me, it's all going to be okay."

Her eyes struggle to stay open, and the once livid body is limp. My hands reach over hers. As her blood soaks my hands, I feel my heart racing and a pit growing in my chest. My shouts alert the others. Dylan and Noah are over in seconds. Noah replaces my hands, and I step aside. In my head, my mistakes begin playing on loop.

If there's one thing I can make right, let it be killing those cold-blooded freaks.

I see the dark man crawling for my gun. He's not human anymore. He's just another Cannibal in my way. I've learned now that the best way to deal with them is to go through them.

"Get Angel back to the factory," I shout as I grab the gun away from the man. With two shots, he tumbles back, and I rip the machine gun off his back.

The zombies have finished eating off the rest of Cora. They rise from all the chaos, meat wedged between their teeth, blood spread all around their faces.

I aim the new weapon at the zombies coming for Angel and Noah. My bullets hit most of them, enough to clear a path. He picks Angel up and runs to the bus.

Once the rest of the monsters are killed, I drop the gun. The man on the floor lay motionless. If he's dead, good, and if not, I still have more bullets.

"Madeline, Avery, take Ava and go with them. Tell Emily to drop you off and bring the bus back here."

They wrap Ava's arms around their neck. Ava grunts as they get up and follow behind Noah.

The pain in my throat is too hard to swallow; the guilt keeps bringing it back. The air feels suffocating, and my mind seems to go blank.

A voice calls my name.

"They'll be okay. You need to stay strong for them," says Joseline as she looks at the amputated hand.

I see Angel's face, her body giving up, and I know that I've failed her. I failed all the others too.

"We have our food," Dylan says from behind me. "We don't need to harm them now."

I look back at Cora. Through all the blood, I can't make out her face. Bite marks are all over her taupe skin, and her outfit that was once green and blue is now a deep red.

"Rob," I mutter to the helpless man on the floor, nearing his body.

Joseline and Dylan follow behind. The engine of the bus roars, and the tires screech. We'll be here for a bit, might as well take advantage of it.

Rob's breathing is thick. His umber skin is soaked with sweat, and his hand is covered in blood.

"Hailee," says Dylan. His hand on my shoulder, "He didn't shoot Angel. It was the girl."

"Yeah, I know, but we still have to get answers."

My mind keeps replaying what happened, and each time it makes my blood boil. Nobody is innocent. They never were.

"Rob, where is Todd?" Joseline pleads as she gets down to his level. He's silent. His eyes look everywhere but at hers.

"Look, you're dying. You might as well just give us some answers," I say.

If Rob doesn't want to speak, we'll push him until he does.

Dylan steps closer to the man. "Rob, we could end this— no more deaths. Maybe you don't have to die either. This is your chance to make things better, don't you want that?"

I know that out of all of us, it'll be him who can get Rob to speak. The man looks at Dylan, deep in thought. Then he shakes his head and looks away. The blood in his chest spews out more, but he doesn't bother holding it. He'll be gone in a few minutes, but if we rush this, we won't get anything.

Dylan adds, "What is it you guys want? Food, water? We can help you and your friends."

Rob smirks against the pain. "They want you," he chokes out. "The meat on your bones. It's how we stay alive."

FIFTEEN

TO SAVE A LIFE

OUR EYES FLICKER around. The room is colder than before and more silent. It was obvious that these guys were a part of the Cannibals, but now we're face to face with one, and another lay dead on the stairs. My patience is diminishing.

"Who's in charge?" I ask.

His hands fix their position over the wounds, and he looks away.

Dylan grabs him by the jaw and forces his head straight.

"Tell us. You won't be alive for much longer."

"Why don't you just ask your friend over there," he says through clenched teeth.

Dylan and I look at Joseline. She stands behind us hiding herself from something.

"Joseline." My trust in her feels like it's shattering. Was it even there to begin with?

As her eyes make it to ours, she says the word, "Python."

"Python," I repeat the name through a whisper.

"What are you going to do to our friends?" asks Dylan, his eyes back on Rob.

The man's laugh is cold. His voice is hoarse as he says, "Eat 'em. That's if they don't listen."

I want to ask where the others are, but I know he won't respond. Revealing his location—anybody smart knows not to do that. Rob starts to choke, and the blood drips down the side of his mouth.

My mind is blank as I try to find any other question.

"Just end me. Unless you have something else to ask this dying man," he remarks.

Dylan lets go of his face, but the blood's still on him. Each second feels wasted, and a part of me just wants to ask where they are.

Maybe I can understand the way the live. Convince Python that she can change. "Why are you a Cannibal?"

He chuckles silently, coughing after. The blood from his mouth doesn't stop. "Long story short, people treated us like shit. We're returning the favor."

His breathing shakes more, and he's practically gasping for air. It's almost like the pants from a dog after a run. He's just another person shot. Everyone's dying all the time now, but what about Angel? What if this happens to her too?

"Please," he pleads.

His eyes glare at my gun. A dying man's wish—I can't refuse him. Just minutes ago, I saw him only as an enemy, but my rage has settled. I know Angel will be fine, and these two are already gone.

Despite that, my mind isn't satisfied. I need more answers, but there's nothing else I can do. His skin is already green, and he can barely hold his eyes open.

Rob is just another living zombie.

Once off the hard floor, my gun falls in front of his head.

With no more strength, he lets his eyes close, and his body doesn't flinch. If he weren't alive a few seconds ago, I'd think he was already dead.

The trigger feels too easy to pull. Rob doesn't make a sound as the gun thunders through the room. He's gone from this world, and I killed him. I look at the half-filled duffle bag next to him. There is still food left in the hole.

"Let's get these filled before the bus comes back," I mumble.

Everyone's weapons are lying on the ground. All of them fit into the duffle bag with enough room for the machine gun.

Joseline walks over to the dead ones near Cora's body.

She's one of them now. Her disfigured corpse rises. Those green eyes from the river are gray now. The rest of her face is covered in blood. Joseline's knife pierces her skull, and she falls back once again.

I notice something on her back, something Joseline has already noticed. She takes the bow off the girl and puts it around her.

The hand still lies on the table. Nathan's watch is on the floor. The screen is cracked like the ice at the river.

A piece of paper stuck on the wall catches my eye. There's a pen on the floor too. Once picked up, I see a message scribbled down.

Fernando, you were right. We have only a few minutes to live. The hunger is surreal, but the bite will kill us before. We have no way to end this. If you read this, we're sorry we didn't listen. It's too late now. We have already locked ourselves in. We can't support the poison the world has become.

I'm left with more questions than I started with. "So, they were bit before coming down here."

My hands fiddle with the watch. When I see the habit, I tuck it away in my pocket. Dylan and Joseline step closer to me.

"That explains why the food was still hidden," says Dylan.

Joseline fills the rest of the gun bag up with food. "Seems like they stocked up the factory and went to find the bunker. And since they built this place, they knew the codes."

"Right," I begin. "There seems to be lots of clusters of the dead around here. Maybe they got entangled with one."

"Probably," says Joseline. Her eyes glance at the hand. "The bus will be back soon. Let's pack the food before they're here."

It sits there and reminds us of those freaks. Nathan and Todd look different. Joseline knows whose hand that is, and I do too.

We fill up the bags in silence. The lights flicker every few seconds. Foods, a few seed packets, water, and medical equipment were all stored down there. The food is all canned, most of it being meat or beans. Guess we'll be eating a lot of that. I zip up the duffle bag and stand up.

Seeing bags full of food excites me. It's not enough to feed us all forever, but if we ration correctly and start planting the seeds, there is hope for a better future.

The bus squeals outside.

As we reach the top of the stairs, holding all the bags in our hands, I see Emily and Damien through the window. Marlon must've stayed back to help the others.

A small button with the word "Close Door" over it catches my eye. Bloody fingerprints are spread on the button.

I shake away the thoughts of everything that happened in

the last hour and walk to the bus door with the other two behind me. The bus doors kick open, and we climb up. Luckily, the duffle bags held everything from down there. Every bit of it matters.

Emily sheds a comforting face. "We got them back, and they're being taken care of. Don't worry, Hailee."

The only thing I can do is nod my head. Nothing can fix what happened. Dylan sits behind me, and Joseline is across from him. Just next to my seat, I see fresh blood. The sight feeds my guilt.

The bus doors close, and Emily begins to drive.

Once the bus parks, I'm eager to get up. Down the steps, I sprint, not thinking twice about falling, and stumble into the factory where Angel lay on a table in the back. Blood covers her abdomen.

Ava is sitting in a chair wrapping a bandage around her leg. Looks like she's better now. All the bags drop to the floor besides the one with the medical supplies.

Madeline, Anthony, and Noah crowd around the table, and I bring the bag over.

All their hands are red with blood. Angel is breathing heavily with her eyes pressed closed.

"Hailee, we need more rags, clothes, anything to stop the bleeding," shouts Madeline.

Nodding my head, I pull open the bag and push through the extra cans of food. The soft cloth grazes my hand, and my fingers hold onto it while I search for more. Beside it is a larger, more fluffy cloth, and I pull both out.

Anthony takes the supplies from me and nudges Madeline. She moves around as he applies hard pressure to the wound.

A wave of helplessness grows upon me. What if the bleeding never stops? What will I do if they can't save her?

"We need to seal the wound if she doesn't stop bleeding," Joseline echoes behind me. "There was a needle and thread in the bunker."

Her eyes show concern. For only knowing us for a week, I can tell she cares, even after losing one of the closest people she knows.

"That'll work, right?" I say, turning around to ask the two.

Anthony's hands still push on the cloth. "Yeah, that's perfect. Look for that hydrogen peroxide stuff as well to clean the wound."

I nod my head and run with Joseline into the storage room. There, we see Jason peeking into a food box.

"How's Angel?" he asks, worry in his voice.

"What're you doing?" Joseline is quick to interrupt.

Her worried face is now filled with outrage. Eyes look at me for an answer, but I have none to give.

"I know, this—looks suspicious. Don't worry, I'm just counting the food so if we don't find any in Plattsmouth, we can ration better," he says.

Joseline's expression doesn't change.

"Look, I've known Jason since we were five, he sticks to his word," I say to her.

"Okay, whatever. I have a good feeling about you, don't make me be wrong." She pushes past me and heads over to the corner. "We found some peroxide and other meds at one of the cities we passed before coming here."

Jason steps aside to reveal a small stash of liquids. The peroxide is in a dark brown bottle alongside medical thread and a needle. Joseline yanks them out and leads us outside.

"Were you telling the truth?" I ask Jason before he leaves.

"You don't believe me?" he hisses. "Right, of course."

His mouth mutters something before he leaves.

I don't bother calling out to him. Things are tough as they are, nobody needs another person who questions their judgment. Maybe I made a mistake saying that, but there are other things to worry about.

As I leave the dark room, Madeline pulls me aside.

"Hailee, there's something I need to tell you," she says with a grip on my arm. When I give her my full attention, she continues. "Ava's bullet went through her leg."

"That's a good thing, right?"

"Yes. It's one of the better things to happen, but for Angel—it's different. The bullet is still inside her, and we can't leave it in there for long or it could travel anywhere. And if it does, there won't be much we can do to locate it or to take it out. We gotta do this soon."

At first, I thought it wouldn't have been a big deal, but hearing that the bullet can go anywhere? When it comes to medical knowledge, I don't know any of it. But just that alone seems terrifying.

It's still day out—still early. There's daylight to be used. "How much time do you say we have?"

She looks to the side. "Well, when my mom was telling me about a victim who was shot, she said the bullet was almost to his heart by the end of the day when the cops found him. So, we should be getting it out about now," she replies.

Right now?

"Everyone is different. Angel's case could be better or worse, but she's lost a lot of blood already, so if we take it out now, it could harm her more."

Madeline presents me with two choices. Take the bullet out now and risk her dying or take it out later and risk the bullet going to her heart.

"Just stop the bleeding. We can take it out when we get to Plattsmouth," I say. Did I make the right choice? It's not *me* doing the operation. This choice could be another one of my mistakes.

Madeline nods her head and leads me back to Angel. I stand off to the side, unsure of what to do. Anthony hands Madeline the needle, and she slides the thread through it, tying a knot.

"Okay, we're ready," she says and hands the needle back to Anthony. "You have more experience."

He nods his head and raises Angel's shirt. Her pale skin is bleached in blood which continues to spew out. Madeline wipes off what she can, and Anthony leans over the table. A light shines over her body, Noah holding the lantern up. I see Angel looking towards me. Her hand is grasped in Noah's.

"You're going to be okay," I begin, taking this as my cue to approach her, "you're strong like stone remember?"

She smiles through the pain. "He's been staring at me for forever," she says, loud enough for Noah to hear.

Noah scoffs. His beady eyes seem to be connected on to hers. "You're not mine yet, so you can't leave me yet."

His words remind me of Dylan, and I look over at him talking to Jason and Kate.

Angel shakes her head. "Neither of those will happen, and you know, that's something a stalker would say, Noah."

Noah reassesses his words while Angel and I laugh. Seizing the moment, Anthony brings the needle close to her skin. We both notice it.

"Think of something fun," I tell her. "Like when that kid climbed the tall tree in the middle of our park."

Anthony pierces the needle into her skin. She grunts in pain, and her breathing has become shallow.

"And you remember how they had to call the fire department to get him down." I can't tell if it's helping or not, but it helps me, so I continue.

"The principal was pissed. She stood under that tree for an hour yelling at him."

Angel closes her eyes as the needle stabs into her again. The thread is tied after each time the needle pierces in.

"Almost halfway through, Angel. You're doing good!" says Madeline, rubbing her shoulder.

Angel tries to steady her breathing.

"Think back to the game, the game before all of this. We won the match, and we would be heading to State," I say once again.

"Oh yeah! Remember that great set you gave to Hailee," Madeline says. A smile cracks on Angel's face through her distress.

"It was an awesome set," she says through clenched teeth.

Anthony pulls the thread through the third piercing and starts on the fourth.

"My spike was pretty great too," I say.

"My blocks saved us a few times too," says Kate, approaching the table.

Angel looks at Kate. Something is stirring in her head.

Anthony sews into the fourth hole, and the bleeding is noticeably less. He ties the thread a couple of times and goes in once again.

"Just a few more," Noah begins. "This will be a great battle scar."

For the next few moments, we retraced that single night before the worst news of our lives came, like we were living it once again. That's when the people we lost were still alive: Ashton, the girls on the team, Ms. Mack—they were all alive.

My parents were alive.

Anthony finishes up the stitches with the last few knots. Angel managed to stay awake through the whole thing.

"Are we done now?" she asks, exhausted, but she still finds the strength to look at her wound.

Anthony places a hand on her shoulder. "Yes, you're good now, but you shouldn't move yet."

She looks over at me. I nod my head and collect my words.

"We're going to Plattsmouth soon. In a few minutes. Then we'll take out the bullet there," I tell her.

"Take out the bullet? But it's not doing anything now."

"If it moves inside you, it could go into your heart or your lungs," I reply, thinking back to Madeline's words.

"And in many cases, if it hits your spine, or if it already has, it can paralyze you," says Madeline.

Angel covers her face with her hand. Just barely, I see her wipe tears away.

"Okay," she says after a few moments.

"Okay," I echo after her, "let's get to packing then."

SIXTEEN

A NEW JOURNEY

I INFORM DYLAN about the decision. Like always, he agrees without any questions. The sky has started to warm, but clouds are still painted about. The locker beside me is freezing, and I'm sure the outside is too.

"This is our fresh start. A time to build ourselves up again," he says, a hopeful smile planted on his face.

"Unless this ends up like all the other times."

Most of the groups we find have denied us, and any city we've found has been overrun or robbed by others. It's been a helpless journey, surviving on the minimum supplies we could find.

"Still have hope, Hailee. We'll get there."

His eyes don't break from mine, and his face is steady. No extra actions or movements. It's like he's always calm.

"Okay," I say, looking to the side, "I'll have hope. We need to pack now."

Turning around, I see Joseline sitting beside Ava. Dylan

notices them too, and we head over.

"How's the leg?" I ask.

Ava takes her eyes off Angel and whispers, "It's better than her."

My eyes can't help but peek at Angel too. Darkness has surrounded her face, and her limbs move sluggishly.

"Yeah, but I'm glad you're okay. I didn't know what to expect when we went down there."

Her head drops down, but I know she's still listening.

"We have to fight for what we want, right?" she says, looking back up. Her smile is weak but sincere.

Dylan turns to Joseline, examining the rest of her group. "Your group is coming, yeah?"

Her brown eyes follow his gaze. She sounds reluctant. "Yeah. I think it's best for us all."

"Let's get your guys' stuff packed up then."

Her short hair barely moves as she nods her head. "I'll get some people on it."

Before heading off to Damien, I hear a whisper.

"Let's hope this is worth it."

Dylan and I agree to start loading the bus with our stuff. The brief number of supplies sit in the back. My hope is that they will triple. Maybe even more.

Kira isn't in the back anymore, probably finding more comfort inside. I told her we'd find Nathan, but after hearing what they said in the bunker, my confidence crumbled. Damien and Tyler arrive behind us with two bags in each hand.

"You guys can put them in the back," Dylan says, stepping aside for them to pass.

I move right, and they carry the bags to the last seat. Near the few supplies, they set the bags down and begin out.

"Can't believe this is happening," says Damien, following

Tyler down the steps.

He sighs. "Yeah, me either."

I don't take their words to heart. It must be hard leaving the place they've found comfort in for this apocalypse.

"Seems like they haven't moved in a while," I mumble.

Dylan chuckles. "Better than moving every week."

"Yeah? Well, that's going to change soon."

We head back to the factory, glancing at the trees that hear all our talks. Sarah and Avery are carrying bags to the front door. There are backpacks, drawstrings, and anything that can hold resources out on the floor.

Joseline's crew rounded up all their supplies. They kept a few bags empty for the things we find, so boxes are filled with other supplies.

I pick up one of the boxes. This one is filled with random items: combs, deodorant, some packs of ammo, and a camera with photos scattered. As I carry it out onto the bus, I can't help but pick up one of the pictures. It's a dimly lit room. Joseline and Todd are smiling into the camera. Their faces still look pure, young.

I wonder if my tan skin is wrinkled, or if my black hair is all muddy. It's rare to see mirrors now, and pictures are another story. It's been only a year, but it's been a terrible year. I'm sure I look older than I am.

The last of the supplies make it onto the bus, and a few people sit in their seats.

Emily traces over some of the controls in the bus seat. The orange seatbelt is strapped over her.

"What's the gas at?" I ask, approaching her.

"Almost empty. Dylan said it'll last a bit longer."

None of the icons behind the wheel are lit up. The vehicle

is still off. Dylan has always had good judgment.

"But it's enough to make it, right?"

"Yeah, but we'll end up stuck if we can't find anymore." Her hands wriggle over the wheel.

"Well, I guess we have to hope." I start down the stairs.

Joseline stands close to the door, her eyes gazing at the ceiling.

"We're ready," I say, trying not to disturb her.

She gives me a glance, her face moving solemnly. "Okay, I'll get the others. You can get your members on the bus."

I nod my head and walk over to the first people I see. Jason, Noah, and Angel.

"How are you feeling?" I say towards Angel.

"A little cold, definitely tired, but I'm holding up," she replies, looking at me. The bright glow in her face is gone, replaced by a pale white. Her lips are chapped, and her freckles have almost faded away.

"You look bad," I tell her.

She rolls her eyes. "Can't be as bad as that time you threw up at Madeline's house."

"You're not supposed to tell them," I whisper, eyeing Jason and Noah.

Despite Noah's laugh, the stare of Jason sends an uneasy feeling through my body.

"Well anyway, we're leaving now. Everything's all packed up."

"So, are we finally going to have a place to call home?" she asks. Her face struggles to show excitement.

"Can't make any promises."

I want to give her hope, but I won't lie about this. They deserve the truth, even if it's hard to believe.

She sighs, disappointed.

"Come on," I say as I help her up.

Her blonde ponytail has lost its elegance. The soft, well-taken hair is now dry and oily. Rough and tangled. I don't bother saying anything. She's had it rough.

Angel wanted to walk to the bus by herself, but I couldn't risk anything happening to her. We set her up against the wall of the bus in her normal seat.

I sit beside Dylan. It took only a few minutes to get the rest of the people. The weapons left behind at the bunker found their owners again.

The bus doors close. We watch as the factory disappears behind us. So many memories in just a few days. I feel like this every time we leave a place.

I talked to Jason, and he decided he'd tell Madeline about Elliot, about everything that happened yesterday. I can only hope he uses his words wisely. Ashton's death is getting to him. That can't affect the others too.

The landscape passes me like a movie. The drive is mostly silent. My mouth stays shut, words ready to fly out, but I know everyone is tired of all the talking. I am too.

"What do we do if the Cannibals are there?" I finally ask.

Dylan looks down at his black pants. His hair is overgrown and messy, but he doesn't mind. He doesn't mind a lot of things.

"I guess we try to compromise, and if they don't want to, we can go to another city."

I nod, but it's full of lies. A part of me doesn't agree with that, not after doing that exact thing over and over. There have been too many given-up homes.

As his head rises to look at the snow, he says, "That's if Plattsmouth isn't already occupied by others."

"I thought I was supposed to be the negative one," I reply, and he cracks a smile.

"I don't want us to die trying to find a home."

"And we won't," I say, holding back the "I promise".

He rubs over a cut on his right hand. "Sometimes, I wonder what's happened to those guys at the camp."

Ann and her fake government flash over my head. As much as I hated them, they had something that worked. Everyone was safe, for the most part, and it was like they had prepared for the apocalypse.

I stare at Dylan's golden skin. Though he looks different on the outside, his mind hasn't changed. His eyes still twinkle the same, and his smile never fails.

"I wonder too."

Some minutes pass by until Dylan asks, "What's the plan when we arrive?"

I think back to our previous calls when we went somewhere new. "We'll make sure no one's there, and then we find a gas station or some cars to siphon in case we need to make a run. After that, I guess we'll settle in if it works out, find a place to live."

The same old," he says through a grin.

Everyone talks for the rest of the ride.

Madeline sat back in her seat after talking with Jason. No expression on her face. Maybe she's too busy with other things, or the Elliot we all knew died the day he left.

An urban area comes into view. After seeing just buildings standing alone, a city looks nice. The bus avoids all traffic rules and drives above the speed limit. I look over at Angel with a hopeful smile. Her face doesn't look any better or worse.

"Let's take a drive around and make sure nobody's holed up here," I call out to Emily.

She slows the pace and says, "Got it."

As she drives us, I pay close attention to the buildings.

We'll need a place for us all to stay at, somewhere with supplies and sturdy walls.

There seems to be a school up North. The walls are dark gray, and there are signs on the large windows. The snow is only in patches around the parking lot, and some cars are lined in their spots. The building is big, and it looks newly built too.

My own school flashes in my mind. The place where we began this dangerous journey. When I blink my eyes, I can see the red brick walls and the dark brown roof of it.

We pass by dozens of other buildings, taking sharp turns and slowing down at certain spots. There are restaurants, dollar stores, bunches of houses throughout, and hundreds of other stores. This city seems like a great place, for now.

"The school looked secure, let's head there," I say.

Emily doesn't respond, but she changes directions. I can still see the cars that would flood these types of streets, and they all followed the rules of the road. Everything on the street had a purpose, but now it's all junk.

The school appears behind some evenly placed trees. The drive-in is long, and the parking lot is huge. There's a flagpole still up and mighty, with the flags eating up the wind they can get.

My thoughts can only be so nervous. This place could hold our success or our failure. Emily parks to the side in the drop-off lane. The bus could be parked on the walkway, and it still wouldn't matter, but I wish it did.

Just like arriving at the factory, I say, "Let's split up and look through the school. Remember anything and anyone can be in here, don't take any risks that aren't worth it."

I look around at everyone on the bus. After months of seeing the same faces, these new ones throw me off.

Dylan and Joseline get up with Jason behind. A few other

people stand up and stretch, eyeing the school. The white text above some glass doors reads "North Central High School". The building looks welcoming.

"Noah, do you mind helping Angel in," I say, heading towards the front. "We'll find a room for her to stay, and then we'll take out the bullet."

Angel looks at me, puzzled.

"We can't risk anything. Madeline and Anthony will help you. You'll be fine."

"But I feel fine now—" Her mouth clings open, but no words come out. She scoffs and shakes her head.

I know she's mad, so I'll just leave it at that. Instead, I walk out of the bus and onto the lightly snowed concrete.

The wind rustles like it did two days ago. The building looks mysterious with the dark clouds and foggy mist forming below. As I pull out my gun, the thought of my other weapons back at the river irks me, like a kid left behind at a store.

Everyone files out. Noah helps Angel down the steps. Her face is pale, not like someone being turned, but as though she's scared.

I soak in the landscape, much of which is snow. My eyes move fast, but they find the important details like the zombies limping towards us from around the corner. I guide the others to the front of the building, awaiting the hideous creatures to attack. A large crack is splintered over the left door. It doesn't budge when I try to pull it.

As the dead inch towards us, I let the door go and follow Dylan. His stance is slow, and each step is taken with caution. Jason, Marlon, and Ava are closely behind us. There are three in the front. The distance between us and the zombies is gone in seconds.

We kill the first five, each of us taking one. More stumble

around. This time, Jason and I take out those two. After a few seconds of waiting, nothing else shows.

Dylan inspects the side of the school. His eyes focus on the big windows, trying to find anything inside.

"Do you see anything?" I call out to him.

"They've got their blinds down," he replies and heads back to us in defeat.

The overhang at the front does little to prevent the harsh winds. The sooner we get in, the better. I take the butt of my gun and smash it against the glass. Shards of it fly down, and the pieces still stuck around the edges are easy to knock off. With careful balance, I peek through.

The frame of the door is big enough to fit us all, and I look at the others from the inside. The push bar for the door is now on the ground connected to shards of glass. I realize how foolish that was. An alarm could've sounded and alerted everything around us.

As everyone gets in, we walk down the halls. Half of them going the other way, including Joseline and Jason.

Noah stays behind me, while we leave Angel at the front. The plain walls with occasional posters of "Stop bullying," or "Get help here!" stare blankly at me. With the lights off, this truly feels like a scene out of a horror movie. However, every day of this life is a horror itself.

We peek into the classrooms. Half of us branching out again.

Anthony walks beside me and whispers, "This is the most adventure I've had in a while. When you're old, they think you can't handle death anymore."

I smile, unsure of what to say. He talks about death like it's an everyday thing. Ever since we arrived at the factory, I've seen more deaths than I have in months. It doesn't sit right with me.

"Yeah, that didn't sound right," he says, and then steps into a classroom with a tight grip on his knife. "I've just seen so many of my buddies die, and nobody can believe it. I've be-come—acquainted with death."

Stepping out of a room, I reply, "That's terrible. You're stronger than any of us."

"I'm glad you think so." His knife is held out by his side as he heads into another room.

The desks are disorderly, and blood has soaked the floor. We're yet to see a zombie in this school. It's strange. I don't know what happened here, but it won't stop me from making this our home.

SEVENTEEN

SETTLING IN

LOOKING FOR A good room felt tedious. All of them seemed the same: unsafe, crowded, and bloody.

Eventually, we come across one that seems fit.

There are tables, but only a few of them. The chairs are all stacked on top, leading a clear pathway in.

"This can work," I say to the others.

Tyler leans behind me to get a peek. "Yeah, it's spacious, kinda like the factory."

We enter the room, weapons drawn and quiet. Posters with encouraging messages like "Stay Strong and Carry On" and "Be who you are, everyone else is taken" are taped up. For being in a high school, this room reminds me of a class I had in elementary school.

"We'll remember this room then. Let's go check out the rest of them and meet back at the front." I head back out and search for another room.

Our examination continues down the hall.

Anthony mumbles something, but I don't catch it. His head looks down at footprints scattered all around the hallway.

Some of the prints lead to classrooms, others just stop at random points, but for the rest, they all seem to be going in the same direction.

"These prints, wonder where they lead," says Tyler. He faces the end of the hallway, trying to peek around the corner. I suppose I'm eager too.

"Yeah, but let's stay together. Footprints like these could mean anything."

As we arrive at the corner, many of the footprints lead to an outside door. The other ones, however, keep going down the dark hallway.

The school is not big, so walking isn't a pain. The marks are even harder to tell now as they lead us to a gym. Trophies sit behind broken glass cases and bulletin boards with torn-up paper.

As the double doors appear in our vision, I hold back my urge to open them. This place reminds me of the school in Cheyenne. Even the gym brings back the scenes of chaos. Tyler approaches the doors.

"Wait," I call out before he tries anything. "There's something in there." I step up to where Tyler stands, trying to peek through the window of the door.

My hope for a community of people is shattered by the blood and bodies on the ground. Others are sitting against walls. As I fix my head against the glass, the figures look clearer. They're not people, but zombies. Tyler wipes away some of the grim building up to see through. I follow his lead and wipe away what is on our side.

"What're you seeing?" Anthony whispers from behind. Kate peeks around us.

"Are those zombies?" she asks over my shoulder.

"Yep. All of them."

The sounds of another group lead me to turn around. I step away from the doors and squint my eyes to see who it is.

The spikes of dark brown hair and the conceited walk give it away. Jason leads Kira, Sarah, and Madeline towards the gym.

"You guys are here too?" he asks, stepping towards the doors. I sneak another view at the gym before turning back.

"We gotta stay quiet," I say, lowering my voice. "If they get an idea that we're here, we could be in trouble."

One of the stragglers still walking seems distracted. His eyes stare off at a wall until his head twitches, like a sixth sense is buzzing inside of him. There's a cabinet by the foot of the door acting like a barricade. A failed one.

The man climbs over it, his eyes never leaving the glass. He's already attracted the likes of others. Their eagerness sparks like wildfire. Each creature brings along a friend.

"Quick, grab something to barricade to door!" I shout at Jason, knowing they all have figured out we're here. "The rest of you hold it shut, brace for impact."

My legs are already on the move in search of something, anything, but it's all empty. Only walls of nothing, and frequent dirt covering the ground.

Those doors can be pushed from the inside. Any brainless fool can open them, and if one of them does, then the rest will follow.

I follow Jason down the hallway, but I know it's useless. There isn't anything, and there won't be anything for a long distance. He stops at the end, looking down at the marks.

"Do you have a knife?" I ask, turning to the doors of the classroom. There may not be anything to lodge the door with, but we can make something.

"Yeah." His face is concerned as he looks towards the doors of the classroom. "It won't be sturdy enough."

"It's our only shot. Right here," I say and point towards the middle of the oak door.

He shakes his head, but he knows not to waste time. The wood splinters down the middle as Jason plunges the knife into it. Then with a few kicks, the door falls into long strips. I pick up one of the biggest strips I can find, Jason grabs two more, and we race back to the gym.

The sight of the zombies is horrifying. The group tries to keep the door closed as best they can, but the hands of the dead reach through the barely open door. With the wood in my hand and my gun in the other, I shoot at some of the heads making their way out. With all these zombies in the way, we won't be able to close the doors.

The left side is clear, and Jason is quick to slide the wood through the handles. His presence feels empty as he stands beside me. While he punts some of the creatures back, I shoot. The door closes a fraction each time until it's almost there. Only an arm flails at the bottom, but we can't pull that zombie out.

"Okay, on the count of three, all of us push," says Jason as he places his hand on the doors next to Madeline.

"1, 2, 3!"

We all push against the zombies. The blood and tissue of the man with the arm squish against our pressure. The bone will be too hard to break, and more of the dead are already trying to push through. With the wood still in my hand, I put my foot down on the limb and yank the arm off from the body, the bone still attached. The doors close and zombie blood spews from below.

The plank fits into the handles of the door, and it holds. No matter how much they pound, they can't open the doors anymore. Their mouths chomp at the glass, hoping they can get a bite.

My body feels fatigued, but there are still tasks in front of me that need to be completed.

"Let's meet back with the others," I say through a desperate exhale.

"Holy shit," says Jason. His pale skin shines with sweat. "We need to keep people on guard. You never know when this'll break."

"You're right," I say, looking to the group for a volunteer.

"I'll stay back," Kira says. There's a look of determination on her face. "I don't have much to do, anyway."

"I'll stay with her," adds Kate. "Just in case something does happen, we'll have each other."

"All right. We'll come back for you guys and officially make a schedule to keep guard."

We split up to cover more ground. One of the groups is already back to the start as we arrive. Jason's group is there right after.

Dylan and some others have yet to come, but I know they all are smart. It must be a long route.

"Good, we all made it," I say as I see them walking in. "If you haven't seen, this place is a ticking bomb. The gym is filled with zombies. Too many to count, or to stay safe with."

Dylan's group disperses as he says, "We saw that too. It's best if we either kill them or leave."

"Yeah, exactly that." I turn to the doors behind me. The sun is warm as it approaches the horizon. "We'll board it up later. Kate and Kira are already on watch right now, and we'll rotate through people for the whole night."

"We wanna help," a tiny voice says from below. I see the

twins staring back at me.

"Well, those who are willing, we'll need some people to grab the supplies from the bus." I look back up at the others. "But only get the necessary items: flashlights, weapons, and stuff we'll need right now. Make sure to get those empty duffle bags so we can pack up the stuff we find here."

A few of the people go while a lot of the others stay back. I don't mind. It's only been a few days, but they've been long and exhausting for us, and for the people at the factory, this is something new.

"One more thing, everyone," I say just as conversations start up again. "Did anybody see any rooms we could stay in or any supplies?"

Madeline steps up for her group. "There was a health room with books about procedures, and the hallway was clear of zombies too."

"Good, anybody else?"

"We found the school's cafeteria," says Joseline. "Had to clear out a few of those things, but there's food packed in the corners—I think someone's living here." She flinches towards the cafeteria.

"Right, but how would they be living here with a gym full of zombies?" combats Jason.

"We'll investigate it right now, Joseline can guide us, and Jason, you can help look around," I say. Dylan's eyes fall upon me.

"I want you to come too," I whisper, "but who knows what might happen out here. I know you can keep everyone safe."

"Yeah, okay," he mumbles, turning away.

"The rest of you, besides Angel and Ava, will go grab the materials you find in the classrooms. Avoid that back hall with the gym. We need those zombies to forget we're here."

Joseline eyes Jason, but his face doesn't falter. They wait for me by the edge of the left wall. Dylan looks down at the carpet floor, but I hear him say something.

"Don't die over there, Hailee."

I feel bad, but there's no time to discuss it. We need to get situated before night. Just in time, a few empty duffle bags are brought inside. Those along with the ones found in the school should be enough for now.

I see Madeline go for one of them, but I stop her and say, "I need you to stay with Angel, make sure nothing happens."

She frowns with a slight groan, but still, she accepts the task and sits down with Angel on the pale green chairs.

The three of us begin down the hall.

None of us want to mention if people are living here. I chose them specifically, not just because they'll be helpful, but because our ideas are different. I know we each think differently, and that needs to be settled if we want to remain a group.

"About the people here," I start, "we need to decide what to do if they *are* here. I won't decide for the whole group."

"We'll kick them out," says Jason. His purpled face doesn't flinch. It seems like the cuts on his face have doubled.

"I expected that. What do you think, Joseline?"

"This was their place first. It should stay theirs."

From the corner of my eye, I see Jason shaking his head.

"We haven't had a decent stay in a long time, this place could be our next home," I say. Jason waits for me to speak again. "But they're people, and they deserve to be treated like ones too."

"You know, Hailee, why do you even bring it up if you know we're going to disagree." His walking slows down as he faces me.

"Look, our ideas are always going to go against each other. It's inevitable, so we need to face it now, and understand each other's views."

"That's pathetic. Aren't *you* supposed to be making all of our decisions?" he jeers.

"I never—"

"All the time you decide for us, and *now* you're giving us a chance? Is this choice just too hard for you that you have to throw it on to us? That's messed up."

"If you want to decide for the others, go ahead, Jason. We wouldn't be moving *anywhere* if someone didn't tell us what to do. If you want to be in charge, the pleasure is mine." As my voice echoes in the halls, I realize how angry I became.

"Why don't you both shut it?" Joseline shouts. "Jason, Hailee is trying her best to keep her people safe. And Hailee, you need to listen to Jason and your people." Her words are sharp, but her voice is weak.

We've stopped walking. Arguing is more important. Maybe this *was* a mistake.

Joseline's words echo in my head.

I need to listen to my people? I've been doing that this whole time. It's Jason who's making a fuss about this.

I scoff and walk into the cafeteria. They both follow me, sharing a look at each other right after. Joseline was right. Food lay in piles near one specific corner with a wooden door. It's an odd place for that amount. It's open for anyone to take. I don't say anything because clearly, they've already heard my decision.

We sneak over to the door. I take one quick look around the cafeteria. All the chairs are put up and aside, and the room is full of only natural light. Straight on, my eyes glare at them, especially Jason.

He stares back. My body feels on edge. When I see Jason,

I can't believe it's the same guy I've known my whole life. It's almost like Jason died instead of Ashton, and now Ashton is who I'm talking to.

Joseline drops the duffle bag outside and then takes a long look at it. Her head shakes, and she mumbles something beside me.

Jason opens the door and points his gun inside.

"What are you doing?" I hear myself say as my hand shoots out in front of him. Is this what he was talking about? Is this me being controlling?

He pushes my hand aside and steps in.

Two people, a couple, are below us. The sight of them on the bare ground is alarming. Aside from them, a pile of weapons in the corner has caught our eyes. I don't want to risk talking, these people could be dangerous, or worse—infected.

Jason manages to step around the bodies, and he makes it to the weapons. I look at the room, piecing together their living. Coats and bags are spread across the wall and pictures of people are hung up in the back.

One of the bodies is a man, and the other is a woman, both in their late twenties. They've probably been staying here since the beginning. With all the food in the cafeteria, there would be no reason to leave. My breathing feels too loud for the silent room, like every gulp of air is another sound to make them wake up.

Joseline waves a hand, grabbing Jason's attention, and then she hands him the duffle bag. He is careful to not let it drop, and the weapons are placed inside. A large rifle, three survival knives, and two pistols. The room is supplied with different necessities. A small box is on the floor to the left with what looks like ammo.

My feet step around the bodies to look inside, and my

thoughts are confirmed. Ammo of sorts fills up a fourth of the box, just enough to supply a few guns. As the room seems ba- ron enough, the time's come to figure out what to do with them. That argument led us nowhere.

I signal Jason to come out of the room as I make my way out. We shut the door, and with luck, it makes no sound.

"We've robbed them of their weapons, and we'll soon be taking their food," I say, turning towards the closed door. "We can't kick them out with nothing, especially not now. They'll come for us knowing that we stole from them."

"So? Let's just put some bullets in their head and call it a day," Jason replies.

The Jason I knew a few days ago would never say that. The words coming out of his mouth now are unbelievable.

"That could be us one day," revolts Joseline. Her eyes flash with disgust.

"Exactly, we need to settle something out with them."

"Okay, and when they come to kill us in the night, it's not going to be my fault," he says, and then walks towards the piles of food. A sort of disbelief and anger mixed into his brown eyes.

Heading to the door, I say, "We'll wake them up and hold them in custody until we know they're safe."

As my hand reaches for the knob, the door is flung open, and a large body tackles me to the floor. The blow knocks the wind out of me. My lungs beg for air.

A strong man is on top of me with one arm on my neck. When I go to take another breath, something so simple, it's blocked. I must not waste the only air that *is* keeping me alive. Limiting my breath, I search for a way out of this trap.

Joseline falls to the ground next to me, the same tactic on her. A knife blade touches my neck. With me squirming, there's no doubt I'll puncture myself. A flashback of Ms. Mack flutters in my mind.

"Use your nails, I know you all have them. Right into the eyes and then—they can't fight what they can't see."

With my strength weakening, I use what I can to dig my thumbnails into his closed eyelids. I push hard. I can't let him get away with this. Today isn't the day. That day won't be occurring for a while. As his grip loosens, my strength grows. I feel something warm on my neck, but it doesn't matter now.

"Ah shit!" he shrieks, clutching his eyes.

I can't tell what I did, but I did something. I get up and kick him down. With my pistol pointed at him, he's pinned to the ground. Seeing his knife right beside him, I sweep it away as his hand fails to reach it.

Joseline has turned the tables on the girl. They both stand there, twisting like an owner trying to calm their cat.

Though they came at us first, I still have a compromise on my mind. We all deserve a second chance after all.

"We don't want any trouble, don't make us have to—"

Two shots fire around us, right where we stand. I watch as the blood pools on the floor. A body thuds to the floor. My hand drops its aim on the man as his blood creeps out. It stains his shirt.

I step back, grasping what happened in these few moments. His eyes look at me, and he tries to say something, but the bullet is already in his heart, and he's dead in seconds.

"No more worries," Jason says with one of the pistols in his hand.

I look over at the other body, the woman's. Joseline draws back, stunned like me. Jason packs up the piles of food into the bag as if he didn't execute two people. Two people that could've been helpful, people that could've served a purpose to us.

When he sees our shock he says, "We don't have to worry

about them now. The food and weapons are ours."

I scoff, but I know whatever I say won't fix what's just happened

"How are you going to everyone about this?" Joseline demands. "You just murdered two people."

"They were attacking you guys. It's called self-defense," he replies.

"We kill the dead, not people," I finally burst.

"Like you killed that guy in the bunker? Or the girl? You killed them too, Hailee. You're not that innocent," he says as he picks up the now full bag.

My mouth hangs open as words try to form a sentence. I want to snark back—tell him what happened, but it's all just excuses. I guess I did kill them, but I had reasons. They were evil. They would've killed us, right?

They would've killed us.

I shake my head, hoping the spinning sensation that tortures me goes away. Get a grip, Hailee.

Joseline is silent. She looks at both of us with a mournful face. I step over the lifeless body of the man and grab his knife I kicked away.

Finishing off Jason's dirty work, I stab both the heads. Now he won't have to kill them again. Darkness has clustered the room just a bit more. It must be getting dark outside too.

"C'mon," I mutter and walk towards the hallway, leaving the dead bodies there to rot. Joseline follows beside me, her head hanging low.

Jason is behind us with the murderous weapon still in his hand, and the bag in the other. It clinks as he takes his steps. The walk back to the front is silent, just like the night.

The talks of the others echo louder as we arrive at the open room. All the bags that could hold anything are filled. Good. I look at Jason to make sure he'll tell them what happened with no lies or half-truths.

"What?" he asks, and the crowd of people goes silent.

"You're telling them. They'll know sooner or later," I reply.

He scoffs and looks at the others staring at him. "Two people were living there, and they tried to attack Hailee and Joseline, so I killed them."

As he says the last two words, I can see others in the group looking at each other.

"You—*killed* them?" asks Dylan with a puzzled expression. His eyes dart to me, almost accusingly.

"I did what I had to."

A hand over her knife, Ava asks, "You couldn't have tried to talk with them? Make an agreement?"

"If you guys were being attacked," begins Avery, "I don't see the problem with killing them."

I feel the tension rising and reply, "What's done is done. We can't change the past, but we'll move forward from this, starting with killing. We won't kill until it's the last option."

Jason turns to me, his face looking attacked. "So, you'd rather have to split the resources *we* gathered with some low lives? They would've just stolen it in the end."

"You took their food and supplies too," says Joseline, "and then you killed them as if they were part of the dead." Her eyes hunt him down.

"We would've tied them up and made sure they were trustworthy," I hear myself say. "If Joseline's group didn't let us into the factory, we would still be on the road with no hope."

"That's not the same. We didn't attack them—we didn't try to kill them."

"If you were encountered by three strangers who took your stuff," Joseline begins, "you would've done the same thing they did, Jason." Her hand is over her knife as she approaches him.

Teaching Jason is pointless. He never liked being wrong in school. I'm sure he hates it now too.

"I wouldn't have been so stupid to get myself killed like that."

"Okay, drop it," I say, pushing him away before he takes a step. My eyes don't break the stare. "We need to get settled and figure out what to do with that gym."

The room is quiet. I see Angel looking at me, Emily too, even the twins. They don't show it on their faces, but it's like they're scared. Not of the zombies, but of someone else.

EIGHTEEN
PREPARATION

THROUGH THE SILENT tension, Tyler draws in our attention. "Now that they're gone, we could just stay in the cafeteria."

It sounds cruel, but it's true. If they were living here safely for a year, then it must be okay for us as well. This could be our shot at a new beginning.

Nobody dares an eye at Jason. None of them want to be his next victim. The argument keeps coming back to me. The things Jason said weren't all wrong. I killed those Cannibals too. Am I just like him?

We put all our supplies into the cafeteria and unloaded some of the duffle bags, including the ones with stolen supplies. For safety in the front, we stacked chairs over a cabinet to block the door. This way, if any zombies do come around, they can't get in.

The cold floor isn't a comfortable bed, and the bus might just be better, but at least we're together and in a more secure building. I recall Kate and Kira still at the gym. Those two gunshots must have them confused.

The others found some tables and are preparing to get Angel's bullet out. It's been too long with it inside her. What if I made another mistake?

Dylan stands off in a corner looking at the pile of food. When I find him, I ask, "Do you want to go on watch with me?"

"Sure," he replies. His eyes never leave the floor.

"You okay?" I ask, despite our limited time.

"Yeah, I'm fine. We should try to barricade the doors."

"There's too many in that gym to keep locked up. It'll be hazardous quickly."

He fixes his position against the wall without glancing at me. "Just for tonight. I think we're all exhausted."

He says he's okay, but Dylan always looks at me straight on.

"Right, there isn't much, but I'm sure we could add some more wood."

"All right," he says and walks towards a door. He takes Marlon's axe and sends a crack down the middle. With a few kicks and throws of the tool, the wood breaks into large chunks.

Dylan hands me a few pieces and grabs some of his own as I lead us towards the gym.

Kate and Kira light up as they see us arrive. They stand up from the floor and stretch themselves out.

"Is everything okay?" Kate asks, her eyes analyzing our bodies. "We heard the gunshots."

It still brings me rage when I think about this last hour. "Everything's fine. Jason killed two survivors in the cafeteria."

Standing in disbelief, she mumbles, "That's terrible."

"Yeah it is," says Dylan. He eyes the creatures in the gym. "Is the door holding up okay?"

"It hasn't moved, but it will soon," replies Kira dimly.

She stands taller, and her tired eyes are gone. Perhaps she's getting over what happened at the river, or maybe she's turning into Jason: angry and careless.

The handles are filled with wood now. The sight of the saliva on the windows is sickening.

"Why don't you guys get some rest and go ask others if they want to take watch later in the night," I begin, "we'll stay for now."

They turn the corner, whispering something to each other.

Dylan's head faces me, but his eyes stare away. He looks exhausted. The darkness of the school has killed the lights in his eyes.

"You must be angry."

He laughs to himself, thinking of a way to reply. "Well, I'm just a little—frustrated."

"C'mon, you can tell me."

This time, his eyes lock onto mine. "Okay. It's about Jason. You know I trust your word more than anything." His head turns away. "When he told us he killed two people, I was in disbelief. Not just because he murdered someone, but because *you* didn't do anything. Hailee, they were humans, just like us. It's not fair they died."

"I know—"

"But you tried moving past it. Jason's my friend too—but he can't go off and kill people because he's upset. We're all upset."

My words are empty. I never thought of it like that. What would Jason look like to an outsider? A killer, that's what, but aren't I one too?

"What do you think then? As a punishment."

"We have to separate him from the rest. He can sleep in

another classroom away from us, with no weapons either. It'll give him some time with his emotions, and if things go wrong, he can handle himself. He clearly showed that."

I nod my head, imagining myself in a lonely classroom.

Dylan watches me, and I pretend to not see him.

"I'll tell Jason—and the others." His voice trails off as he walks away.

The wall catches me as I sit down. So much has happened in the last few days. I feel like exploding. Giving up sounds like paradise, but I know it's wrong.

Seeing the others almost scared of Jason reminded me of who we are. We're survivors trying to find a home, and here we are instead, running away from cannibals because of my mistakes.

How many times have I promised them all a home and failed each time? Maybe I *am* failing them. Maybe I'm becoming selfish.

The zombies growl again. Something about their low raspy voices brings me peace. My thoughts calm down, and I stare at them. Women and men, all kinds of people brought together for some reason.

Each of them, despite their appearance, are similar. There's blood all over them. Small circles are scattered across their chests. Some have dozens while others have one or two.

I'd try to figure out what happened, but after that bunker, my liking for puzzles has died. My head rests on my hand, and my eyes have grown tired.

I sit in silence for many minutes, just waiting for one of those zombies to step through the door and attack.

Dylan's steps catch me off guard. I get up with weak legs and meet his eyes. Usually, he'd crack a joke, but this time he's silent.

"It's okay, we can sit," he says and finds the floor beside me.

I follow and ask, "Is he mad?"

"Yeah, he'll be fine though." This time, Dylan looks at me again.

"I know. I just hope he knows why we're doing this."

Dylan feints a smile and then glances to the side.

"What?"

"You must really care for Jason."

I never think of my thoughts about Jason as care. Maybe that's why I didn't act against him back at the front.

"I've known him for forever. I'm worried he's become like Ashton. What if everyone becomes like that?"

Dylan finds my hand. His darkened eyes stuck on me. "They won't. We have our ups and downs, but in the end, everyone knows it's the living against the dead." He turns to the zombies.

"Yeah—about them," I begin and look at the horrific creatures. "You see those bullet holes? Almost all of them have it. And the ones who don't have bite marks all over."

His head shifts to the door, a puzzled expression planted on his face. "Sounds a lot like murder."

"Right. It could have been the couple who did it, but that just doesn't seem right."

"I'm not in the mood to solve another mystery," he says with a chuckle.

"Don't worry, I'm not either." I look around trying to find a new topic. "Have they started the operation on Angel?"

"Crap, I forgot to tell you. They're going to start soon. Angel said she wanted you there, you better get going."

My muscles feel on fire as I get up. "Okay, take care," I say and begin my way.

Arriving at the cafeteria, chatter fills the silent hallway. Jason is there sitting on the ground by himself. He twiddles with his fingers until he sees me. Like a frozen bug, he doesn't move.

"I'm not here to do anything to you," I say. "I was just going to tell you that you should go on watch now. Dylan's by himself, he'd appreciate some company."

"Not by me. If you haven't seen, we aren't really buds." He raises his head and squints to look at me.

Flashbacks of the couple appear in my mind, and then I turn to them still rotting on the ground. Everyone sits as far away from the mess as they can.

"Then you can work it out. While you're at it, you can figure out what to do with those bodies."

Mumbles come out of his mouth as he looks to the side. Then with a drooped body, he gets up. A cautious feeling falls over me as he walks by. The same feeling you get when walking alone in the dark.

I shudder it away and head inside the cafeteria.

Angel sits against a box on the school table. A nervous look on her face.

"Hey," I say, approaching her.

Her face seems relieved. "Hailee, I'm glad you're here."

Madeline is beside her. There's a textbook on the other table lying open. Anthony and Kate stand on the other side. Noah sits in a chair not too far away.

"He's finally leaving you alone," I whisper.

She laughs, her nose scrunching up. "I know right. Poor guy. He's going to lose all his hair worrying about me."

"We'll, he won't have to worry anymore 'cause you're going to be okay, and then you can finally help me out. I could really use you right now."

"Obviously, I'm a very needed person."

"Yeah, you really are," I say with a smile matching hers. "I guess we should start then."

"Yeah, who knows where this bullet could be," begins Anthony as he examines Angel. "But you said you haven't felt pain anywhere else but *there,* right?" He eyes the blood on her stomach.

She shakes her head.

Madeline sets a box down with what looks like medical equipment. "We don't have much to ease the pain, but Joseline said she noticed some meds in that storage area."

"I'll go check. Any sort of names I should look for?"

Anthony's eyes light up as he thinks to himself. "Any pain-killers. From what I remember we used what we could get our hands on. Morphine, ketamine, opioids like—"

"I'll just bring it all," I cut him off and hurry over to the storage area.

The realization occurs only after I see the bodies. The blood is still there, and the bodies seem alive. Seeing their dull faces is horrifying, and the stench is worse.

The sooner they're out the better. I shake away the nerves, not just the ones coming from the bodies but from the surgery. One of the only surgeries we've done. I want to believe it'll work but—will it really?

The doorknob twists open, revealing the dark hideout. There are two shelves that I hadn't paid much attention to on my right. Some knives fill the top few slots, but at the bottom is a bucket too big to fit. To my surprise, a few med bottles and other bags fill it up.

I bring it back to the group, stepping around the bodies. Before I can set down the plastic bucket, Anthony starts looking through it. His searching worries us all, and the disappointment on his face after is worse.

"These won't help. I mean maybe the Oxy, but most of these are anti-depressant pills."

I see Madeline's face tinkering, and then she says, "This might sound strange, but couldn't we just get her high? Then the pain will be less severe, right?"

She looks up at me, and I just shrug my shoulders. I wasn't one to take drugs, but I remember others offering me all sorts of things.

"That's—that's not a bad idea. You young kids always have something up your sleeve."

He searches through the bucket again and pulls out two plastic bags with a title too blurry for me to see. There are pills in all sorts of colors inside.

"LSD." He flicks the bag with a finger. "I knew a guy who got high on this. We'll watch out for you in case something happens, however, it can't harm you—that much."

Angel looks at him with a disoriented expression. "Okay, but are you sure those are what they say they are? What if they switched them?"

Anthony pulls one of the pills out and brings it to his eye.

"The three letters are engraved in it. We'll just have to assume it's true," he says as he puts the pill back in and wipes his hands.

"Look, once we get this done with, things will start feeling normal again. Well, the new normal," I say, holding onto her shoulder.

"There's not many, but one should do. Let's have you take it when we get there. Then after the surgery, if it really hurts, we'll give you the Oxy."

"Are you sure I'll be okay?" her voice quivers.

"I'm positive," he says. As he smiles, his crooked teeth

peek out as though they were waiting to be displayed. He turns to me. "And you should prepare some food for after. Her body will need fuel to repair."

I nod my head and glance at the pile of food.

"You aren't planning on doing it here, right?" Madeline asks as her head eyes the people sitting around.

"No, we found a science room across the school," I begin as Anthony nods. "The tables were big, and there were barely any chairs. The room was spacious too."

As Anthony helps Madeline pack up some stuff, Noah walks towards us.

"Where are we going?" he asks, smiling at Angel.

Madeline replies, "It's time for the surgery."

"Okay, let me help you move her."

He heads to the other side of the table. Anthony pushes while Noah pulls. They slide the makeshift carrier to the doors, drawing people's gaze. Angel wants to seem fine to them, so it's better if I don't mention the surgery.

Following the table at its slow pace, I see Angel taking her last few glances at the cafeteria. The rubber on the legs of the table claws against the floor.

Madeline walks beside me. Bandages, rubber gloves, water, and other items stuffed into a cardboard box in her hands. The pills shuffle as she takes each step.

"You have everything?" I ask her. She snaps out of her daze and looks at me.

"Hope so, I got what Anthony needed. Oh, and here." Her eyes search inside the box, and then her hand reaches in. Pulling out a dark silver-colored knife, she says, "I know Angel gave you a gun, but you like to do things the silent way, so I thought it'd be helpful."

I stuff the blade into my jeans. "Thanks. I should really

keep track of my weapons."

She smiles. Her eyes are fixed on me in an almost unsettling way. "Are you feeling okay, Hailee?"

"What do you mean?" I avoid her stare.

"Well, this whole week's been rough. Just a few days ago we still had Ashton and Nathan. Even this morning, Angel wasn't shot, and our only thought was food. But now, with all these things that've been happening—and I'm not saying it's your fault but—they're taking a toll on you."

I don't want to believe she's right, but I know it. This all happened because I was so desperate for food, and then the bunker. Then everything just led to another.

"I know, and I don't know what to do anymore. I can't just stop or try to take things back."

"You need to give yourself a break and focus on what really matters. Sure, food is a necessity, but we need to stay united. That thing with Jason. I've known both of you since we were little, and I would never imagine him to do what he did."

"Me either. Guess Ashton dying changed him."

"I don't think it's just that, Hailee," she whispers.

I look at her, trying to think of a reason for Jason's change.

"Jason wouldn't kill random people because of someone who bullied him. There's gotta be something more."

"But what would that be?"

"For the months I was in psychology, we learned that humans do a lot of things to get what they want. You can tell that without even being in the class. Anyway, I think for Jason, he doesn't agree with what you're doing, so he's lashing out."

All I can think about is the fight we had while coming to the cafeteria. Just moments before disaster.

"You guys fought about something, didn't you?" she asks, nailing it.

"Yeah," I say as we turn down the hall. Luckily, we went the opposite way of the gym, avoiding Jason. "He wanted to kick out the survivors, leave them with nothing in the cold."

"And that's not what you wanted. You've probably heard this a lot, but to stop people like Jason from causing harm, you either end up sacrificing something of yours or you use violence before it gets worse."

Violence or sacrifice.

Before I say something, Anthony announces, "We're here. Let's spread out the supplies, and have you take your pills."

I look at Madeline one more time, and she takes a shaky breath in, her blue eyes darting around the science room as we enter. The chairs and desks haven't moved, nor have the dull windows and brick walls. The thought of them taking the bullet out makes me itch all around. This is really happening.

Noah and I stand on the sides of the table, while Anthony hands the bag to Angel and a water bottle.

"I hate pills," she grunts as she looks at the baggy with marker labeling it as LSD.

"At least you'll get to be high," I say.

She smirks. "My first time on drugs, and it's here, minutes before a big surgery."

"And I thought Madeline was going to be the first."

Madeline snorts from afar. "Me too."

She takes out lanterns from the box and turns them on. The shadowed room lights up, but the corners are still hidden. The materials are lined up next to Angel's table, most of which are Anthony's from the factory.

I turn back to Angel who's already placing the pill in her mouth. Then with a few gulps of water, she washes it down.

NINETEEN

SURGERY

I MADE A few trips to the cafeteria and the gym where Dylan and Jason surprisingly made up. Jason didn't care if he was isolated for the night. He was more upset about not having his weapons, but he'll have to live with that.

Tomorrow will be better. Angel will be okay, and we can finally make plans to build the place up.

Emily and Damien have started making real food by cooking beans and other bland ingredients from the dozens of cans collected. All our efforts towards the bunker have helped. We're not surviving on granola bars or expired food anymore.

Half an hour has passed. Angel's showing signs of a trip. She's tried to get up many times with claims of a flowery and beautiful zombie awaiting her presence. Every few minutes, the room fills with her babbling about the wondrous and intricate thoughts she sees. Her endless talking stops when Anthony puts on some rubber gloves. The snap as the rubber hits his hand wipes away any joy in Angel's face.

As Anthony brings tools to the table, Angel says, "Those are *not* going in me."

"Well, we got to get the bullet out somehow," he says, and then motions us to come over.

Something tells me she's going to be in a lot more pain than we expect. Maybe she'll pass out and won't feel the rest.

Madeline approaches from behind with materials in hand. She sets them down, just a few inches away from Angel's twisting body. The old man lifts her shirt and reveals the bandaged wound.

"Seems like she hasn't bled a lot, that's good," Madeline says as she puts on some of the blue rubber gloves.

Anthony takes a final look up, and then with caution, he unwraps the white cloth. "Keep her down. We can't have her shake too much during this."

Noah and I share a look of agreement. I'll grab onto her shoulders while he holds down her legs.

The bloody bandage is tossed to the side while Anthony peeks at the wound. The knife in his hands hovers just centimeters above her purpled skin.

"Is that bad?" I ask.

Wiping off the excess blood, Madeline replies, "It's most likely just the bullet moving around, but that's good. It hasn't gone too far, so this should go by fast." Her eyes watch Angel as she does.

Angel's face wrinkles up. "That tickles."

Anthony picks up the knife, inching it closer to the string. "The blood might start spewing, or it might not. We'll get it out quickly and then sew her back up."

Madeline goes back to the table and searches through the box to pull out more materials. The needle, thread, and gauze are set down near Anthony.

Anthony catches a glimpse of all our faces before he brings the blade to the string. With the blood removed, Angel's skin looks drained of color and raw.

The first loop rips apart by the knife's pressure, then the next, and soon all of them are undone. As the string pulls out, dots of blood start growing again.

I notice Angel looking at her wound. Her eyes dart across her stomach, looking at every little section.

"You guys see it moving?" she questions as her head falls back onto the table. Then with just her eyes, she stares at a new target. "The zombie—the zombie it's—Ivy?"

Eagerly, I turn to where she looks at. The thought of her sister being here stuns me. The doorway is empty, with nothing but silence in the hall.

"She's not here, Angel. Remember, they're still in Texas," I say, hoping she'll get over it.

Her head bobbles as she tries to get another view of the front. She hasn't brought up her family for months, saying that when she does, it just brings up negative thoughts.

"No, she's right there!"

Anthony notices the rise in her voice. "She's going to start moving. You two need to use all you got on her."

Noah and I nod our heads and keep Angel pinned down to the table, but she really isn't trying to get up. Lucky for us, her body begins to rattle as Anthony seeps his fingers into her abdomen. She was easy to keep down when human skin wasn't in her, but now it's like her strength has tripled. I feel Madeline staring at us, and she decides to hold down Angel's hips.

"Don't eat me!" Angel shrieks. Her eyes flash with fright. It's better to just let her talk through this madness.

"I've got it," Anthony says.

His hand adjusts to Angel's rapid movements. He pulls out

a bronze and bloody bullet, with half of it gone. His face is hidden by the shadows, but his sigh makes it obvious that he's frustrated. The bullet is placed on a clean napkin. Angel's wriggling calms down.

"All right round two," he says and sinks his hand back into the body. The now purple glove dances around.

My ears feel like they've been shot with a gun as Angel screams.

"Give me a rag, Madeline!" I shout. She reaches with one hand to grab a clean rag next to her and hands it to me. With my one arm still on Angel, I try to hold both shoulders down and shove the rag into her screaming mouth. "Bite down on it."

She stares at me with anger for shutting off her only source of emotion, and then compliantly, she bites down. Her lips flare open, and her jaw shakes.

"C'mon," Anthony rumbles. His hand squirms through the layers of tissue, "I think—I think I have it," he says as his hand struggles to pull out the rest of the bullet. "It's deep in her tissue. This is going to hurt like hell—keep up with keeping her down."

Angel looks around, biting with all her power into the rag. Her limbs have weakened as her strength is put onto the cloth. Seconds pass by of struggle in all of us, and then Anthony pulls out the other half of the bullet. It's too hard to tell the color of it. The only thing we can see is blood. As he sets the half down next to the other, the two parts look completely different.

"You're going to have to sew her up, Madeline. My hands are covered in her blood."

She looks at him warily, then takes a big breath in. "Okay, yeah—I can do it."

Her eyes never leave the needle and thread as she brings it over to Angel. Anthony adjusts his fingers to give an opening to the skin while keeping it together. She takes a final look at him, and he nods his head. With clean blue gloves, she pushes the needle into the skin. The same screams are back, but this time muffled.

"You're doing good, just keep going," Anthony says as he moves his fingers in awkward positions to help Madeline. Just like the first time, she pierces Angel's skin with the needle.

Angel's cries, alongside her struggling, come closer to a stop with each puncture of the needle. Madeline managed to re-pierce most of the holes, which should've taken off some of the pain, but Angel's cries still sound agonizing. I can almost feel the needle in my own skin too.

Madeline ties off the string and then cuts the rest of it with the knife. The room goes silent. Madeline and Anthony look at each other in relief, and Noah and I step away from Angel. They take the rag out of her mouth as her cries have stopped.

Though quiet at first, Angel begins talking once again. Every couple of minutes, I see her smiling to herself or staring in odd directions.

The two begin cleaning up the bloody mess while Noah and I stand off to the side like before. Through the window, the blurry stars watch us.

"How long will the LSD last?" I ask Anthony, my heart aching for Angel.

She hasn't acted anything like this since around fifth grade when she was still just a kid. Her parents made her mature after that. Taking care of her other sisters and helping them out was just part of her role as the eldest child. Emily went through the same, and she complained about it every day.

"Hours," Anthony replies. "It could be seven or eight, or the effects could even get to thirteen. It'll be hard to tell, but since the effects came onto her so fast, they probably won't go soon."

"Can she eat?" Noah asks as he inches towards the blood around the table.

"Sure. Nothing her body will have a difficult time to digest though, so keep it to those liquids and mushed-up foods."

"Aw man," I hear Angel whine, "so I can't eat those fruits from the can?"

"Don't you hate those?" I reply.

"Yeah, but you need to be open to anything. Maybe they'll taste different."

"I can smash them up for you—if that works?" I ask, turning to Anthony for an answer.

"That'll do."

"And what do I do with her after? I don't want the others to see her like this or get scared."

"You can leave her in here. From what I've seen of your friend, she doesn't seem like she'll try to harm herself intentionally. She won't be able to go to sleep though, at least I don't think. You can get people to check on her every few hours. That way if she does start to slip into a bad trip, she'll be with people to keep her safe."

And to think that this would all be over after the surgery. I guess it's just a few more days and then you can finally settle in, Hailee. It seems like I have been telling myself that a lot lately.

Madeline and Anthony finish cleaning what they can and put everything into the box. They leave the room, abandoning the rags soaked in blood, along with the drops of blood under the table. I walk to Noah who is staring at Angel. She's trying to get up on her own.

"Noah, can you help her eat? I need to get some other stuff done. I'd appreciate it."

"Yeah, no problem," he replies and picks up Angel.

"And I saw some clothes in the closet near the people. You

can look for a new shirt or something."

Even saying "the people" still haunts me. Seeing them on the floor reminds me of Rob. He was helplessly laying there, and I shot him.

"You killed them too, Hailee, you're not that innocent," Jason's voice rings.

Noah nods his head and walks out the door with Angel. Her head moves around, and she tries to keep it still with her hands.

The room sits lonely without the ruckus of surgery. I glance over the still posters, the encouraging words don't provide any light, but I guess "Stay Strong..." is good enough. With one last look at the dead room, I exit and begin my way to the gym.

The hallway traps me in my thoughts, like when showers were still a thing. I could think about anything and everything. The same goes for this plain hallway.

Being plain is good now. It always was, I suppose. People didn't do anything to you because they forgot about you. But is anything *really* plain? Zombies are still roaming in the gym of this hallway.

After all my thinking, I make it to Dylan and Jason. The growls of the zombies haven't settled down yet, and the chatter of their voices bantering with gentle manners feeds the silent walls. Their conversation dies out as they see me. I try to piece together what to say. So many ways to start this conversation that might just turn into an argument.

"Angel's surgery went well, for the most part," I say, my voice echoing back through the halls.

"Good for her," says Jason as he picks at his fingers.

Dylan eyes him. "For the most part?" He focuses back on me.

"Lots of blood, and LSD. She's high out of her mind," I

say.

"Sign me up. I need to get out of this shit hole for a few minutes," pipes Jason. An unamused expression on his face.

"Few hours you mean. She's going to be on it all night and for most of the morning," I reply, trying to shake off the monotone in his voice. "Anyway, I need to get going—I'll send some people down so you guys can go take care of those bodies."

As I walk away, my mind can't help but peek at them. Dylan looks at Jason with a sore look, and their odd talks continue as I turn back around.

"You didn't tell me about the bodies," says Dylan.

Jason scoffs. "I forgot, okay?"

They tune out as the corner passes by. I don't think our group will ever be the same.

TWENTY

RECOVERY

ENTERING THE CAFETERIA, my eyes search for two eligible people. They can't be injured, too tired, someone who's already watched, or a child. Noah and Angel sit on the floor against a wall with Noah feeding Angel peaches from a copper-colored can. Injured.

Will and CJ are playing with Sarah, Damien, and Tyler. They're busy with the kids, I probably won't bug them unless it's my last resort. Madeline and Anthony are talking near one of the cafeteria tables we managed to unhinge, but they're too tired to keep watch.

Joseline and Avery talk in the distance. Joseline's bow is strung onto her back again. They both seem ready for a battle, maybe staring at zombies will be of interest to them.

Before I approach, my eyes dart across each person that has not been seen. Kira and Kate already kept watch and Ava's leg won't do her any good if the zombies break out.

As the night passes, our hunger begins to take the best of

us. I know Emily will help me with rations. With a bit of spice and seasoning, she could make any canned food feel straight out of a restaurant. I could call up Marlon. It seems like he hasn't much to do nowadays, but with him losing his closest friend, he probably doesn't have good focus either.

The two girls it is. Their conversation falls short when they see me coming. Mouths close and weak eyes trace on to me.

"Hey, don't mean to end your chat but Jason and Dylan are going to take care of something, so can you guys go on watch? We'll figure out a better schedule later—"

Joseline jolts up. "Yeah, sure. We've been needing something to do."

Avery scrunches her face and eyes the door, but taking a hint from Joseline, she stands up.

"Thanks, I appreciate it," I reply. They head out of the cafeteria with long strides. Now for everything else that's to be done.

First is food. Every minute I'm reminded with a growl of how empty my stomach has become.

I find myself a seat across from Emily at the lunch table.

"Hey, what's up?" she asks, delighted at my presence.

"Hi, my mind's a jumble, but I need to talk to you about the food."

She smirks, laying her arms on the table. "Whatever you need."

"You're hungry, right?"

"Yeah, of course, and seeing all that food isn't making it better." Her eyes lead mine to the pile of cans near the closet and the bodies. Just in time, Jason and Dylan walk through the doors and to the decaying corpses. I'll just wait and see what they've decided.

Turning back to Emily, I say, "We need to start rationing.

How much do you think we would need for at least a bit more energy? We need to maintain the food until we've found a proper schedule."

"If you really want to fill us, I'd say a few cans. As much variety as we can get is best, but I get what you mean. A can of beans should do the trick, and there's plenty over there."

"Okay, so a can per person, that'll do. Do you know how many cans we have, of everything?" With a group the size of ours, those cans are going to be gone fast. We'll need to start checking the city to find some more supplies.

"Not yet, but I'll get on it. Anything else you need?"

"Not really, just trying to figure everything out." I laugh to settle my nerves. "Are you able to cook for us all the time?"

"Hell yeah. Do you remember my dishes back at home?" she says, standing up. "I'll start planning meals and counting those cans."

"Thank you, Emily."

I lean in for a hug. Her arms wrap around me, embracing me with a warmth that I really needed. "Tomorrow, we'll fix ourselves up. We'll start living and making this place a home."

"Looking forward to it," she says, trailing away. "You're doing great, Hailee."

The rest of the night was hazy. We put Angel back into the science room after feeding her some more food. Jason slept by himself in one of the rooms by the front, and we gave him a can of food for the night. I talked to more of the people, getting input on what they all were hoping for. Some said a shower, more food, a nice bed, or other things that make me hate the apocalypse even more.

We switched people on watch throughout the night. The zombies rattled down as everyone prepared for slumber.

As the silence grew on me, I finally felt at rest, and excited for the day ahead.

Dylan and I decided to take the morning shift, so that way we could both talk through everything we needed to do. So far, the shifts have been for three hours. That way, we can all still sleep and we're not going through too many people.

A blank paper sits out in front of me. "We've got a lot to do in a few hours. We should prioritize our main worries," I say as I pick up the pen in an odd position. A year of holding a knife and a gun will do that to you.

"Yeah, you said Emily will take care of the food, right?"

"Yeah, and if she ever needs help, we'll be there, but I think she knows what she's doing. What we need to do is start developing a plan for—that." The moans of the zombies capture my eyes. I can't help but investigate their cold, dead faces.

"Okay, so develop a plan for the zombies," he says, looking at the paper. I nod my head and write down his exact words. "We'll also need to check around the city for supplies, people, or any possible threats."

I write down the next bullet point. Both of us continue to discuss all the things that need to be done, and a well-developed to-do list now awaits to be done. There's no doubt that as we continue to advance—that's if we do—more things will need to be done. I'll just take it piece by piece. That's how we got here.

"This should be good. Let's start waking up the others," says Dylan, stretching out his legs as he rises. "I'll send some people down."

"Okay, we'll need to get the group together to talk about this," I say with another look at the paper.

"Yeah," he begins, peeking around the walls until his eyes catch a board behind me. "We should set it up here. It lets everyone get a look at what's going down in this place."

My eyes follow his to the corkboard. "Sounds good. You

go ahead. I'll wait for the others to come before I leave."

He disappears behind the corner, and soon after Madeline and Noah come around. If I didn't know, I'd assume they were zombies. Their steps are sloppy, and their faces are distorted.

"You guys don't look very good," I say as they approach.

"We don't feel good either," Madeline replies, her voice groggy.

Before I worry, Noah says, "We're just tired. More than normal. That cafeteria is a shit bedroom."

"Well, good morning to you guys too. We'll figure out a better place for sleeping soon." I fold up the paper and begin down the hall. "I'm going to go check on Angel."

"How long are we going to stay here?" Noah calls.

I shout back, "Just for thirty minutes. We're getting the group together soon."

Neither of them says anything after. I turn the corner on the right and head towards the science room.

Hopefully, Angel's recovery is going well. I can only hope she hasn't hurt herself. I pull the handle of the door, hoping to see anything not disappointing. There, Angel stares at one of the posters in the far corner.

"How're you feeling?" I call to her.

"Bored, though my mom and dad are keeping me company."

Guess she's still on it.

"Well, at least you're not hurt. Does your stomach hurt?"

She nods. Her new shirt is a worn-out blue, and she wears the same rustic green jacket. "It's like every time I move, my muscles are trying to tear apart."

"Do you want some pain meds? Maybe some food?"

She stares at me strangely. Her eyes dart around my face and to the wall. I wait for her to say something, but her mind seems confused, like something that shouldn't be happening is.

"Hailee—why are you doing that with your face?" she asks, a strange scare in her voice.

I laugh at first, but the more her words sink in, the more I realize she isn't joking.

"Doing what?"

"The—your eyes, and your face. Why are you grinning so big?" She stumbles over her words and then looks around. Her eyebrows raise, her breathing quickens, and her lips frown. "Stop talking. I—I can't hear you. There are too many of you. Just be quiet, please!"

"I didn't say anything."

I've never seen her act like this until now. Her knees shake, and she slides down the wall, confiding herself to the corner.

"Just stop—just stop talking, please!"

"Okay. I'll leave. Just stay calm, Angel."

No matter what I say, it won't help her face this. Anthony mentioned this happening. He said it's best to leave and let her handle this. Angel turns to the wall and covers her ears. I shut the door, and not even a click of the handle escapes.

Sprinting down the halls, I look for Anthony. Madeline may have been easier to find, but she doesn't know about LSD as well as he does. I find him standing beside the closet door, examining the crimson stains on the floor.

"Anthony," I call, rushing into the cafeteria. He looks in my direction. "It's Angel. She's panicking, and she isn't acting like how she was before."

"Don't worry about it, kid," he says, turning towards me. "She's probably having a bad trip. Just leave her be. It's best if she faces it alone."

"I know, but what if—"

"She's going to be fine. Even though she is on LSD, her

conscience is still there. She would only hurt herself if she has wanted to before."

Angel never talked about her feelings. It would make her feel them worse if she did. I suppose I overreacted, but she scared me. Not once did she push me away, until now.

"Let her take her time. The drug will be wearing off in a few hours anyway." He notices my reluctance and adds, "Trust me, Hailee. I've been alive a lot longer than you."

I calm myself down with a few deep breaths. "Yeah, you're right."

Maybe I'm the reason Angel flipped. It's not like she was screaming before, it only happened when I came. I should just accept that.

I decide to take a break outside—the urge to pee being a part of that decision.

When I come back, most of the people are with cans of beans, some sort of fruit, or soup. Dylan sits at the table with the food, asking Anthony what he wants to eat. Anthony picks up a can of soup and then walks off. The stack of food on the counter takes up all the space. A dozen or more cans sit underneath the table.

Dylan hands me a silver-colored can of garbanzo beans as I sit down, and then he picks a can out for himself.

The paper of tasks is pulled out of my pocket, crinkled. We stare over the list and open our cans of food.

It doesn't take long to devour them. The hunger paired with the desire to get stuff done is no match for the cans. It hasn't snowed yet, and the ground has started clearing up. Maybe spring is on its way, and then summer too. Days will be warm and light, and maybe we can grow crops by then.

My hopes shouldn't rise too high though. It's still winter,

and we have other things to do.

Everyone gathers at the gym doors where the mindless zombies haven't figured out how pressure on a door works. Most of the group have seen the horrors going on inside the gym, but the people who haven't stare with wide eyes. Will and CJ both seem intimidated, terrified at that.

Everyone stands in a half circle around Dylan and me.

Sometimes I wonder how this all came to be. I was a scared girl just a year ago, and after my parents died, the only parental figure I had was Ms. Mack, but just like most people, she left me too. So, how did I become the person in the middle of the circle?

"We've called you all here because there's a lot of things that need to be addressed," I begin. "Dylan and I've made a list to talk about some of the things we need to accomplish, and we've taken suggestions from you all—the ones that we can do at least."

"Finally getting things done," someone mumbles from the back of the circle. Dylan and I both ignore the likely suspect.

"We plan to split up everyone into groups, getting through everything together. In the next few days, we will build this school up, collect resources, and make this place a home."

"Last time we split into groups," says Jason again, "we lost three people. One of them is dead, and the other two are likely gone as well."

I notice Joseline looking away and Kira glaring at him.

"I know, and it was all my fault. I shouldn't have let you all go knowing what could've happened, but because of it, we have all learned to be stronger and smarter. We can't slow down or stop because of tragedy; we all know that. Splitting up is the best way we'll get through this. It's dangerous, and if you don't want to be a part of this, you're free to go."

Some of the people look at me like I'm crazy or as if I'm a tyrannical king, especially Jason. Others nod their heads, understanding what needs to be done.

"The first thing we need to figure out is this," I say, looking at the doors. "This door could break at any moment. With us in here, we need to take care of them as soon as possible."

"Does anyone have an idea?" asks Dylan, his stance unwavering. "Whatever we do needs to be stable. If this does become our permanent home, these zombies can't be a danger."

Ava leans against the wall before suggesting, "We could do what we did at the front and keep the doors shut with cabinets. Or anything heavy."

"That's what we were thinking. Anybody else got an idea?" continues Dylan.

"We need to deal with them sooner than later—might as well kill them," says Jason. He looks back at the creatures lumping at the door.

"That's also a good idea," Dylan says and then looks at me, "but we need more weapons to do that."

I catch Jason scoff and turn away. Nobody else speaks, each of them looking at us with eyes that have been drained.

"All right then. For now, we'll keep the doors shut with anything heavy," I say, waiting for Dylan to start the next topic.

He graciously takes the paper from me and views it. "This next task is going to require a lot of people. We need to gather all sorts of things: food, ammo, guns, blankets. Honestly, anything to help build this place up, and for us to survive."

"And are we sure this school is our new home?" questions Avery. Her hair is pulled to the front, and she twists the ends. "What if the cabinets don't hold, or trying to kill them goes wrong? I mean, how are we certain that *this* is the place?"

"The school is big enough for us all to fit with space for

everyone," I say, looking at the others. I'm sure they all have been thinking about this question. "We can't be certain that this zombie problem will be taken care of, but we'll deal with it soon, and in the meantime, we can advance this place."

"And if things do go South," adds Dylan, "there are hundreds of other buildings to check out. And that's what we need some people doing today."

He then hands me back the paper, and I read the next line in my head. "Next up, we'll need just a few people to look all around and inside the school. Assessing the potential of each classroom, like what rooms can be used for storage, medical care, sleeping areas."

Everyone nods their heads, this time complying.

"We also need people to find building materials for the front door and walls. You guys will look out for any wood planks or bricks, and other forgotten necessities," Dylan says.

The crowd is silent, listening to us with attentive ears. It's peaceful, the group listening and the feeling of finally getting stuff done. Maybe Jason is right—he is a lot of times. We've been stalling this whole time. We should've done this months ago.

"And that brings us to the last thing we need. Hygiene and self-care," I say and fold up the paper. "We're all gross, bloody, stinky. Everyone will go through a series of fixups. This way, we can start this new home with better care for ourselves too. Once we've assigned the groups, and completed our tasks, we will all do some grooming, but don't expect too much as most things are basically unobtainable. We'll try our best to figure out those later."

"Does anybody have anything to add?" asks Dylan.

Either everyone is too tired to speak, or they truly have nothing to say as nobody makes a sound.

"Okay then, let's get some groups assembled," I say, looking around for potential members. "We'll need a group of two or three to build up this door. Add anything heavy but don't make the pile a mess. This'll go by pretty quick, so you'll probably work with the group who's assessing the school to find some items."

The healthiest people here will need to go check the city, so anybody injured or needed here will do. "Ava, Anthony, and Emily. You three can find some items to block the zombies. This way, Anthony can stay here and help with any medical problems, and Emily can stay to help organize food issues." They nod their heads, accepting their task.

"Sarah and Kira, do you two think you can look around the school? You'll need to clear the area and plan out rooms with specific purposes," asks Dylan.

They look at each other hesitantly and nod their heads.

TWENTY-ONE

THE CITY

WE SPLIT THE rest of the group up, keeping anybody unfit for the city inside the school. Splitting up wasn't smart last time, but today things will be different. Everyone is alert now. They know the risks.

"Let's hope these cars have gas," says Dylan as he gets up from beside me. In his hand is an empty gas can and a siphon. I stand up after him.

Avery is one of the first to rise as well. Among all of us here, she knows the most about cars. On our first day with the factory people, I recall her rambling about engines and motor-cycles. Her dad was a mechanic and taught her stuff while they lived on a reservoir.

Emily opens the doors, and we file out. Once we can find cars, she'll go back to the school and help the others.

We decided on the groups in a few seconds. Everyone has gotten more comfortable with each other, so nobody really objected. Avery and Madeline are going to find ammo with me.

The car shop in front of us reads "Auto Way Motors".

Luckily, the parking lot is packed with vehicles for sale. Now we just need some keys, or Avery, to help us get into them.

Approaching the concrete walkway, I see Avery gazing at the building. The brick walls, red title, and advertisements on the windows sell the whole car shop vibe.

"You know where they'd keep their keys?" I ask as she turns around with a face wiped of expression.

"Probably locked away in some safe or something," she replies. Then to be more sincere, she looks me in the eye. "I know a few ways to start up a car, you know that, right?"

"Yeah, that's what I was hoping for. How long will it take for about three cars?"

"Depends on the car, really. My dad knew how to hot wire them when he was younger, but that was when cars weren't as advanced. They were easier to get into, but I know a trick that'll get into some of them. Just give me some time."

"Okay, no worries. As long as you can get the cars started and working, take your time," I reassure. "Also, I was wondering if we can use these on and off whenever we want?"

"Yeah, but it'll wear down the car. We'll need a new one after a couple of times." She pulls out a screwdriver that was tucked into her pants. "Don't worry about it right now. We'll be okay."

I nod my head after every word, only understanding a few. Come to think of it, there wasn't much I was amazing at before the apocalypse. It was always volleyball and academics. Not like Jason with aces on all his tests, but I was decent. There were a few clubs I joined, and I only stuck around to become president. Maybe I'm running my own club now.

Avery turns to the parking lot and says, "I'll start trying the cars."

Once she leaves, I glance at the door in front. It's made of glass, and the opening times are displayed.

On the far left of the building, large glass panes reveal some of the cars that are inside. A few are raised, and some have parts missing. That must be a service area.

People have gathered around to explore the inside. The door is locked, but it doesn't matter. I pull out a case of picks from my bag and use two of them to jiggle inside the keyhole. With a few clicks and odd positions, I rotate the lock pick, and the door is open.

"These keys are probably stored away somewhere safe, but we'll still look," I begin. "Keep your eyes on your surroundings and each other. Look for any type of key, and maybe even a safe."

Once they all look ready, I open the door. The entrance is mostly welcoming. Cheap red chairs are placed around a coffee table with car magazines spread throughout.

Behind the service desk is an almost silent growl. The ragged face peeks behind the table, eager to see the new guests that have entered its building. Another zombie reaches out to try and pull itself up. They both crawl over the wooden desk, pushing aside the papers and knocking over the computers. Another one rises as the other two stumble onto the floor.

I pull out my knife as Joseline takes out hers. We kill the two with ease as the third one makes it over the desk. A shiny object flickers from his waist as he falls. Jason stabs the zombie before it can make it to us.

Walking past the two, I reach the last creature where Jason towers over the body. He sees the silver reflection that hangs from the zombie's pocket. A small black shape with a silver stick at the bottom. A car key. This will open at least one of the cars out there making Avery's job a bit easier.

An irritated sigh leaves Jason as he plops onto the chairs.

Dislodging the car key from the pocket, I notice all the other junk attached to it. A flashlight, lighter, and a small picture of a guy and his family. At least he's back with them now. Their bodies can rest.

"This'll get a car started for us," I say, getting up and holding the key to show everyone. "Let's get a group going. We can't waste any daylight."

I walk past Jason and to Kate whose group is getting wood and other necessities.

"You'll be going around parts of the city to get stuff, might as well get started now."

She takes the keys and looks at the rest of her group members. They begin filing out. Before Jason exits, his eyes glare at me. His face doesn't look any better.

I keep thinking our friendship can be fixed, like one day we'll forget about all that's happened and be close like before.

The sunlight is warming, but the remaining snow on the ground pushes off cool air. The concrete is stained dark with patches of light gray growing throughout. The winter was short, snow only fell a few times. This apocalypse is almost like our punishment for ruining the planet.

I hear a rattling noise from outside and peek through the window to see Avery opening the hood of a car. She's focused. I can't imagine what's going through her head. Usually, Nathan and Dylan would work on the bus when it needed to be fixed.

My attention draws back to the warm room and all the people inside. Some have already started searching while others are waiting.

We look through the whole place from head to toe. In the service area, another zombie was lodged under a car. I could barely look at the sight of him. His bottom half was completely squashed. The blood and guts spewed from the sides where his skin exploded. His legs were still intact, but they flattened, opposing each other. That must've broken a few hip bones. Just like the first one, he had car keys in his pocket.

Everyone gathers in the parking lot once again. Dylan siphoned some gas for the bus, and his group now prepares to leave. Avery got two of the cars started.

Madeline and I join Avery in a deep red SUV. I don't recognize the brand. That must explain why it was easier to break into. The car smells fresh, just like how a new car would. I sit in the front seat with Madeline graciously taking the back.

Being in a vehicle other than the bus feels different. Dylan's car begins driving off, him in the driver's seat with Joseline next to him. Seconds after, the bus drives off as well.

"Are we ready?" Avery calls to both of us, sounding a bit annoyed.

I look back at Madeline who hasn't bothered fastening her seatbelt.

"As ready as we can be."

The engines disrupt the quiet sky as Avery pulls the car out onto the roads. They're empty and lonely. The buildings aren't any better either. Without many zombies, this place feels like a ghost town. Everyone here must've gone to the school for safety, and then they were shot dead. I suppose it's better than being eaten alive.

"This town is a lot smaller than Cheyenne," says Madeline, peeking through the window. Her eyes flick to the driver's seat. "Avery, what town did you live in?"

"Sioux City, but I moved to Nebraska a few years ago," she replies, taking a right turn.

I notice tattoos on her fingers. "You guys said you weren't

at the factory during the start of this, right?"

"We were in Lincoln—with a group who claimed to know the cure to this disease. They just tested on people and zombies, hoping they would find it along the way."

Madeline leans forward. "So did you guys run from them?"

"Something like that." Avery goes quiet, probably piecing together what to say so that she doesn't reveal much. "Joseline lost her brother to one of the tests. He had helped us for a few days when this all began, so it was heartbreaking for us all. We decided to revolt, and a lot of the others agreed."

Sounds too familiar. The Air Force Base was no different. I look at Madeline, and her pondering expression matches mine. She remembers the base too.

"We dealt with something similar," I say.

"Yeah? Well, it looks like we both think being on our own is better. All those places just wanted to trap people."

Avery makes a left turn, and we start heading down a long road.

"All the evil people become leaders," she continues, "and the ones who fight back are usually killed or punished."

We talk about them for a while. Avery explains their story while Madeline and I explain ours.

It's hard to tell what a gun store is. After all the storms, lots of the buildings have been wiped out or broken down. Luckily, this car is filled to the brim with gas. Those few wrong turns won't cost us much. "Main St." is plastered on a green sign to my right.

"We're in the central area," I say, viewing the start of the buildings. "There should be a gun store around here."

Slowly, Avery drives the car while Madeline and I peep out of the windows, looking at buildings. A cafe, a jewelry store, and another auto shop.

"There." I point at the store, catching Avery's attention.

The bottom half is covered in what looks like black metal. Intricate designs in shades of green are displayed near the middle of the building. It doesn't look like a gun store, but the "Shotguns, pistols, and more" sign written in big white letters through the window sells it.

An empty flagpole is attached to one of the frames, and other text is written throughout to help advertise the store. Avery sees the building and pulls the vehicle into one of the many empty parking spots. It doesn't matter how good the parking is, no cop is going to give us a fine.

"I always hated bad parkers," Avery says as she opens the car door.

Most of the road is wiped out clean. The streetlights tower over a once alive city.

The top half of the building is plain brick just like most of the top halves of buildings on this street. I take out my knife that's stained red from the previous zombie at the auto shop.

The snow might almost be gone, but the wind hasn't given up. Maybe Plattsmouth isn't such a good place.

The opening times are written on the door alongside posters of missing dogs and job opportunities. I raise my knife to my chest as the door creaks open.

The shop is narrow like the hallways in the school. It takes me just seconds to register the empty shelves and broken glass. Only a gun or two are hooked onto the plain white walls.

"Everything's been robbed already," I say under my breath.

Avery sighs and looks at the shelves. "If somebody's been here, they could've robbed the other stores too."

She walks towards a black rack with a lonely gun that has been knocked over. Glass shards are spread around the carpeted floor. This place is a disaster.

Madeline steps towards the main desk after taking a look at the glass. "At least they left a few guns, and we already found some with the people in the closet. We really just need ammo."

I join her, noticing a zombie on the ground with a bullet through its head. There are sounds of clattering as Avery picks up the guns she can. Every single rack, shelf, or display case has been looted.

"You're right—and maybe those two were the ones who robbed this place," I say, trying to follow Madeline's optimism.

The desk has a glass display attached to the front. The broken glass has only a single revolver left in the case. I pick it up, examining the black color before opening the magazine.

Empty.

"We really do need ammo," I mumble.

On the other side of the desk is a better surprise. There's a dozen or so boxes of bullets. Not ideal but better than nothing.

"This is good. We'll be able to last a bit longer." Madeline peers behind me. She squats down and searches through the boxes.

An open one has ammo splattered across the floor. I bend down to examine the black box. ".38 Special" is written across the top—the ammo needed for the revolver in the glass case.

Madeline catches my smile. "You found the right one, didn't you?"

"You can tell?" I reply, picking up the bullets and shoving them back into the box.

"I see the smirk on your face."

Compared to a machine gun, a revolver is nothing, yet I still admired it when I was younger. I guess that's stuck with me. The first gun I'd ever fired was a revolver. Maybe its easiness is why I liked it.

We pick up the rest of the boxes, getting any stray ammo as well. Avery stole the rest of the guns, and it only took one trip to the car. Madeline and I put all the ammo boxes in the back.

The seat is cold from the wind that howls through the broken glass by the driver's seat.

"Let's keep our eyes peeled for one more spot," I say, holding on to the handle at the top. "With this store being raided, we might need some more guns."

Avery pulls out of the diagonal parking. She maneuvers the car to go back the way we came from, opposing the street laws.

"Right there," Madeline calls out. Just a few yards down is a shop with the name "Quick Shot". A picture of a gun is on the right. The title is almost concealed, but I still feel stupid for missing it.

Avery brings the car into a slot. What looks to be a hair salon is next to the building. That might be helpful later today.

We rob the store of what we can, but to no surprise, it's already been raided. We get about four guns and a few boxes of ammo.

As I enter the car with guns in my hand, a black figure catches my eye. Looking back at it, the roofs are empty. Must have been a hallucination. I didn't get much sleep anyway.

Another passes by as I begin turning away. This can't be a hallucination now. The figures are gone as fast as they appeared. The buildings opposite the gun store are tall. Tall and slim like they were made for jumping across. There must be people up there, but do I want to scare everyone?

"What's up, Hailee?" calls Madeline from the back. My focus snaps back, guns still sit in my hands, and the car door hangs open.

I sit back down, closing the door. "It's nothing, just looking at the buildings."

Avery checks out the wires at the bottom. "We should come here again, lots of shops that could be useful."

"Yeah. We'll be needing more resources again," I add, stealing another view of the building.

As Avery begins driving away, my eyes scan across the roofs just hoping to not see another figure, and yet I do. The man dressed in all black bolts to a brick building with a rim and hides behind it. It's a large rim made of what looks like black stone. My eyes nearly turn away from it, but the figure never appears again.

TWENTY-TWO

HOME SWEET HOME

GOING AROUND THE town, I kept thinking about those figures. Were they hallucinations, or were they real people? And if so, do I want to rattle everyone up again? We're getting settled in, and I don't want them to feel unsafe or lose trust in this group.

Madeline puts a hand on my seat, steadying herself. "I think we're good on weapons. Maybe there aren't any knife shops here."

"Guess so, let's head back then," Avery replies, looking left and right before taking a turn onto another street.

Madeline says something, but my mind has already fallen back into its cycle. At times, the figures stare at me through the window. They watch the car drive by, and then they disappear.

One of them calls my name.

"Hailee?" Madeline grasps my shoulder. "You okay?"

"Yeah. Let's head back," I reply.

Avery looks at me concerned but ultimately turns back to the wheel without a question. Madeline stares at me, puzzled.

She can't know if something is wrong, not yet.

"What?" I ask, averting my eyes to the city.

"We need you *here*. If you have something on your mind, you can tell us."

I would tell her, but I'm not certain I saw those things anyway. I only snuck a glance at the building before we left, and nobody was there. She'll start thinking I'm crazy.

"I was just thinking about the school. We're finally getting somewhere, building a new home."

"Sure," she says, falling back into the seat with a faint smile on her face.

The rest of the ride is silent aside from the occasional clatter of guns. The thought of those figures haunts me the whole way.

Avery parks the car into one of the handicap slots. The slots in front of the school are empty, however, the parking lot on the left, likely the teacher's lot, is packed with cars.

We fit all the guns and ammo into one bag. One of the only benefits of not finding a lot of stuff. I make sure to keep the bag steady, any of them could be loaded and ready to fire.

Through the shattered window, Damien and Tyler lean wooden boards against the wall. The sun still shines above, leaving enough daylight to get more work done.

After crossing the concrete path, I say to them, "I'm glad you guys found some boards. I was beginning to think that this town wouldn't have what we were looking for."

"Yeah, we checked around the city," Damien begins. "No shops or stores that had any of these. We came across a few houses with wood projects inside their garages."

Tyler sweeps his black hair aside. "And the people inside were dead, so we took some of the pieces. These work, right?"

"Yeah, they're perfect. We'll be able to secure the front

door and maybe even the gym doors with these, thank you, guys."

I head down to the cafeteria and arrive at a silent room. Kira and Sarah are sitting together at a table, both displaying a dull face.

Next to the closet, the duffle bag is placed on the floor. It'll be best to keep the weapons all in the same location until we can sort them out. I set the stuff down with caution. The pile has grown, and the mess has too.

I approach the girls who seem to have nothing better to do. "How's it going?"

"Good. We've planned out a few rooms, like that science room Angel is in. It'll be our medical area," Sarah replies.

She pulls out a piece of paper. There's a rough sketch of the school with arrows and labels around it. Her pale hand holds it out, and I accept the offer.

On the paper, an arrow points to an imaginary line around the school labeled exterior walls. Another arrow points to the cafeteria. This one is labeled meet up and food services. Other arrows point to other rooms, some are sleeping rooms, and others are supply or tool rooms.

"This looks perfect. I appreciate the work. We'll start making these official," I reply.

Sarah smiles, and Kira only glances at me. She's probably remembering Nathan once again.

Sarah takes the paper back. "We also went through every room in the school, clearing out any other zombies we found, so now this school should be zombie-free, for the most part."

"Okay. Thank you, guys. We're going to hand out food soon, so you guys are done for the day."

After leaving Sarah and Kira, I greet Emily who looks over the food and water.

"Hey," she says, "We've patched up the door. There were some fridges and couches in the teacher's lounge, so we used those and stacked them up. Those zombies can't even shake the door now."

"That's amazing."

She offers me a seat, but I deny it, telling her that I won't be talking for long. Our conversation is short. Her face lights up when I ask about her plan for growing food and serving it.

She explains without hesitation. With the new cans of food, she'll be able to make proper meals without using as many cans as we have. In the spring she'll begin growing seeds, and though it'll take time, she still expects to have some food grown by the end of fall.

As I finish talking to everyone, Dylan's group arrives through the doors. Noah and Joseline walk beside him, and they all hold cardboard boxes that they've set down at the front. I leave Anthony to go check out what they brought. Since those guns in the store were wiped clean, I can't expect much with food.

As Dylan sees me, he approaches. "Not a lot of food, but we got a few other things." His eyes lead mine to the boxes. "Some of the food hasn't reached its expiration date yet, so we decided it'd be nice to have food with taste."

"That's good to hear. Emily said she'll be able to grow crops during spring, so maybe we won't have to worry about food soon."

"Nice. I'm looking forward to it."

An awkward pause starts to form. Now would be a good time to tell him about those figures—hallucinations—whatever it was, but do I really want to?

"You should go get the rest of your stuff," I spit out.

"Emily's going to start making food soon, and we need to get everyone through the clean-up."

With a laugh to himself, he agrees and leaves the room. Joseline and Noah have already left, putting Dylan alone in the hall.

Now the clean-up. I must've been vague about it because even I don't know what we need to do. All I know is we'll come out looking a bit better than before.

For everyone to hear me, I'll need to stand up somewhere tall. Lunch tables will do. I find one and climb onto the table part. This one is connected to the one Kira and Sarah sit by, just a few tables down.

"Listen up everybody," I shout out. After doing this hundreds of times at each place we go, meetings are becoming easier to handle. Before, I would be full of anxiety and worry. Even with Dylan by my side, I feared messing up.

The people closest to me are the first ones in the newly forming circle. I see Anthony's face, almost like a proud father, looking up at me. Soon after, others hear me and begin walking over, and as they do, everyone else gets the memo.

These circles have always felt intimidating. I don't think that feeling will go away. All their faces stare at me, and they wait for a sound. They're waiting for *me* to say something, this is my cue.

"Now that we have most of the things we need, we'll be making another step towards growing. We all are filthy and covered in muck. So, for the rest of today, we'll try to clean ourselves up," I begin.

Perhaps it's the food, or having shelter, but it's the first time in days that I've seen some of these people watch with genuine faces.

"Everybody will go grab their bag from the bus if they

haven't already. If you were from the factory, then you don't have one. But don't worry, everything that's in our bags we've found to make some more for you guys."

The bags are light, but they contain many things we all need. Some have items that others don't, but we all have the basics to help us feel cleaner. There are toothbrushes, combs, and some of us have deodorant, hand sanitizer, scissors, and more.

Ms. Mack thought of it during the one month at the school we had food and water. We all started to look like the zombies outside. The food and water kept us healthy, but on the outside, we looked terrible.

"Emily will be serving lunch soon. I must warn you all— we're going to be running low on food and water soon. It's going to be a constant battle trying to find some. Hopefully, as months pass by in this place, we'll start to grow our own food."

Heads turn to the cans of the food on the table. Many of them scrunch their eyebrows. They probably think the large pile could sustain us for at least a year. That's what I thought too, but with a group this size, we're taking it down faster than we can find it.

Just in time, Dylan's group arrives with more boxes.

"After you get your bags, you guys will divide amongst the classrooms. Remember to spread out. We need to cover all areas of the school in case anything happens."

Some of the people look around at their future roommates.

"If you were in the factory, come talk to one of us. We will show you guys what's in our bags and try to get you guys similar items."

Dirt crumbles off my boots as I get off the platform. Some people start dispersing out, and my eyes catch the paper next to me.

"Before you all go," I say, straining my voice in hopes that those down the hall can hear, "everyone should write their names on this paper."

When I see the others come back, I hold the paper up. "This way, we can keep track of you all without being behind you. I'm sure you'd all like that. Once you have written your name, you're free to go find a classroom to stay in."

Near the entrance of the cafeteria, Dylan talks to Noah and Joseline. As the three of them didn't hear part of what I said, Dylan must be explaining what they missed. Meetings like this rarely came. Every place we went to had some sort of problem.

Roughly every week we've done these clean-ups, but for most of them, they've been on the bus. People would take turns to get out and do what they needed to while the rest of us either stayed cramped in the seats or stretched outside.

The paper fills with names as the line disappears. Noah and Joseline are the last to put their names down, and they head to the hallway after.

It's just Dylan and I left in the cafeteria. I head over to him, clumping up words in my head to find what to say.

"You want to share a room?" I ask him as we start heading out.

He chuckles softly. "Was just going to ask you that."

"So, that's a yes," I reply with a smile.

His laughs confirm it.

"Great. Let's head to the gym, I want to see how the doors are holding."

Walking beside each other, we arrive at the gym. The doors don't seem to have budged. Stacked in front of them are fridges and couches. There's no way the zombies will get out.

A small sliver of the window is left at the top and bits of it peek through the legs of the couches, but it's secure, and that's what matters.

We head over to Angel to see if she's gotten the memo yet. As we enter the room, I catch her golden locks against the wall. Her skin is gaining back its color, her eyes are shut comfortably, and her body lies still. She must've put herself to sleep.

I'd wake her but she was up all night yesterday on a trip. Once she gets enough rest, I can give her some food. The room is dark and almost scary. Even the halls are like that as the night approaches. We head back into the hallway, neither of us saying anything until we're far away.

As we go through the whole school, it seems like there is a group in every corner. Noah wasn't happy about being so far from Angel, but Joseline and Ava made him feel better. And it's not like we're trapped in these rooms either.

The only place I could think of best would be the middle. Being closest to everyone—but also being the center for any attack. I'm fine with making that sacrifice.

Since the doors to the gym are sturdily closed, the only lookouts we'll need now are for the front doors. The windows of the door are broken, meaning anyone or anything could sneak in. Kate and Sarah agreed to stay on watch during the night.

A welcoming room stands in front of Dylan and me. Spanish words are written around the walls. The room is full of greens, pinks, magentas, and yellows. Dia de Los Muertos posters are hung up alongside posters of Latin countries. I regret not taking Spanish.

The room is across from Jason and Marlon. Their room is full of computers and chairs that crowd around. The room itself seems cold, almost creepy too. The map of the school that Sarah and Kira made said the computer rooms were for anything technology. Obviously, Jason takes it, dragging along the one person who forgave him.

I didn't think it would happen, the two of them. After Ashton's death, Marlon *was* mad, but he started to realize who his friend truly was. He saw him as a bully, and it brought him closer to Jason. Perhaps Marlon wants to rewrite his story, or maybe he hasn't changed, and it's Jason who's different.

We finally enter the room, quiet at first. After talking the whole way through the halls, the silence feels calming.

"This seems like a good room," says Dylan, shining a flashlight around. "I used to take Spanish in high school."

"Really? All I know are the basic words."

I set down my bag and open it up.

"You would've liked the class."

"Right," I say through a weak smile. "Well, you'll have to teach me someday."

Boots clank down the hallway. I twist my head to see Jason and Marlon exiting their room.

"We should probably start too," I say, examining all the items I took out: a toothbrush, a small tube of toothpaste, a hairbrush, and a stick of deodorant. There are more items in the bag like my lip balm, pocketknife, nail clippers, a pair of socks, and a half-working flashlight.

There's a list forming in my head of what I want from the store. Lotion is at the top. When I saw Kate with it, I knew I was missing out. This winter has damaged my skin, and I know there will be more snow coming soon.

Jason used to keep count of the days after our phones died. Who knows if he is still at it.

Dylan repacks all his stuff. "All right, I'm ready," he says and throws the drawstring over his back. I put away my stuff as he waits for me.

The clean-up goes smoothly. My teeth feel fresh, and I was able to wash my face with the water we had. Emily took the snow that was still left outside and began boiling it. The dinner was nice too.

I can tell everyone is getting used to things. I feel it too.

My hair feels cleaner. We don't have enough water or a river to wash our hair efficiently, so the grease will continue to build up. I was able to redo it though, but no braid this time. The oils horridly revealed my scalp, so I kept it in a low ponytail.

After that, everyone went back to their rooms, and we ended our night. I slept for a few hours. Maybe the thought of the bandits woke me up.

Dylan lies beside me. We pushed a few chairs to the entrance and made a small little bed with two blankets. One on the bottom and one on the top. Usually, I'd be freaking out sleeping next to a guy, but with Dylan, I don't feel it. With all that we've been through, I can't imagine life without him. The warmth of his body puts me at ease.

Even if Dylan's presence is welcoming, my mind can't draw off whatever I saw. For the last few hours, I hadn't thought about the three, and now it's all I can think about. Three black figures skipping through the buildings. What if they manage to come to ours? The front door is barely patched up, zombies still crowd the gym, and we're starting to get comfortable. A perfect attack to strike would be now.

I can't let that happen. I won't.

My body begs me not to get up, but I can't listen to it right now. With what strength is left, I get up, forcing my limbs and joints to awaken themselves for a journey in the night.

Stumbling around, I eventually find my bag resting on a desk. Silence and the depths of the dark surround me. It's eerie for sure. I'm not scared, but my heart can't stop accelerating.

One thought keeps crossing my mind. How will *I* take down three, if not more, bandits? Bandits, I guess that's what I'm calling them now if they *are* real.

I tell myself I'm smart, and that I shouldn't do something dumb and make things worse, but my steps have already continued. My mind is on a set path.

This group can be dealt with, and not through fighting. We can live in Plattsmouth with these guys in peace. Sharing resources, giving each other help—two strong groups growing together, making history.

I open my bag, careful not to wake Dylan. I'd need him in times like these, but I can't. He'd want to tell everyone else. Let everyone know, and then try to deal with the bandits.

The flashlight grazes my hand. At the touch of the ridges on the side, I yank it out. My arm works tiredly to put the bag on the ground.

As I step onto the marble tiles, I peek into the computer lab. Not for Marlon, but for Jason. There's an almost clear view of the lab from the hallway. The left corner is the only hidden side, and neither one of them is over there. I flash the faint light into the room, hoping to not aim at anybody's face.

Marlon sleeps alone against the two walls. His position is like Angel's. Sleeping in the corner, a blanket is scrunched over his knees and legs. We gave everyone a choice: a pillow or a blanket. Marlon chose the blanket, but Jason chose the pillow.

I move the light just barely to the side, hoping to see Jason's brown hair and pale face on a pillow, but only an empty one comes back. The white pillow sits against the wall. There is a head indent in the middle. It's unlikely that he's going to the bathroom—I had caught a glimpse of him walking over to a tree during the clean-up.

It doesn't matter anyway, there's no time to waste on Jason. If he gets himself hurt, it's on him. He knows what he can do, and the consequences of what he does. Right now, I'm worried about those bandits.

I draw the flashlight into the black hallway. The pale blue light casts my path. My steps are taken with caution. The school isn't safe yet, and anything could be lurking in the dark.

TWENTY-THREE

BROKEN FREE

AFTER STAYING AT this school for about two days, the hallways have become familiar. I stopped at the cafeteria where the guns were before arriving at a corner of the hall.

I look around to make sure Kate and Sarah are there. As it's been a few hours since starting their watch, they should be waking up a few others to switch roles with. One part of the office is in front of me, with the entrance of the school to the left. Neither of the two are sitting at their post. That's not good.

Maybe they had to use the bathroom. There's no need for me to get worried now. Plus, those bandits will do more harm than a zombie that has stumbled inside. My flashlight finds the floor and clears a path.

I reach the front doors. The glass looks the same with just some more planks plastered on. We decided to lock the doors at night, but the open glass at the bottom can still let us in and out. I fit through the hole without a struggle.

I turn off the light in my hand. The flashlight will be a nuisance if things go south. Soil lines the front of the school, and I bury the light there.

My hands scan around my waist. My pistol and revolver are there alongside my knife. Good.

With a final look at the school, my heart begins to jump. This could be my death. This could be the last time I see my friends. But I am doing this for them.

My steps are quiet on the concrete. The stars glimmer in the black sky, the wind whistles, and everything around me feels at peace.

At first, I couldn't see it, the figure. It's black and blends in with all the darkness, but after a couple of seconds, I can make out the spiky hair and tall posture. He must've caught me staring as I hear his formal tone.

"Hailee, what are you doing out here?" he questions, a rise in his voice.

As I step closer to him, I see a small light shining on my feet. It's Jason. Only a few members of the group have a gun with a light. We were lucky to even find some. He's not supposed to have any weapons for a few days, and why would he need an SMG in the night?

"Well, since you have a gun out here, I'm thinking we both saw those figures." The words slip out of my mouth.

"Clever. There were two of them near us," he says and turns to the field of trees.

"I saw three. They were jumping from the roofs, right?"

"Yep."

The darkness envelopes us. The light on the gun doesn't do much to help us see. I'm not even sure that I'm facing him.

His body has already begun taking off. "So, five. Could be more spying on us. Let's find out where they are tonight and see if we can take them. If not, we'll go in with reinforcements tomorrow."

"I thought you used your head," I say, following behind.

The gap between us widens. It's clear he's set on his way. I snatch his hand and yank him around.

"You really think we can roam this city and not get caught by anything? A couple of pathetic guns aren't going to help us take down a group. Then everyone will get scared—"

"If the danger is gone, then our safety returns. Don't you understand that?" he replies and breaks free from my grip.

"If the 'danger' is bigger than us, then it only grows if we try to stop it."

"No. I'm done with your plans and lazy attempts at keeping us safe. Nathan, Todd"—he looks at the floor, shaking his head—"Ashton. They're all gone or dead because you thought we could walk for miles in the fucking cold for a bunker we didn't even know was true. I'm not following your ideas anymore."

"Look, I know I made a mistake—"

"A mistake, Hailee? Ashton is *dead* because of you!"

The word rings in my ears.

These past few days, I've started to realize that what happened at the factory was one of the worst things I've done. Letting Jason be right kills me, but he always is.

He stares at me, and if it weren't for the dark, I don't know what I'd do.

The memories lapse in my head like a movie. I stood by and let those freaks hurt and kill my friends. It was all a mistake, and I'd give anything to go back and fix what I did.

"If you go and fight those people with no idea where they are," I begin, barely holding my head up, "you'll just be doing what I did. You'll be putting us in danger and making a decision you'll regret."

I can tell he wants to retort, deny all I say, but he knows that this time, I'm right. My eyes have adjusted to his face, and I see that same Jason face from school. The one that hated being wrong. He searches in every corner of his mind to prove me wrong.

In his silence, every small noise can be heard. The heavy stomping behind us is just one of the sounds.

My head flicks around, hoping to catch a glimpse of whatever it is. Who knows what could be out here, and just that alone is worrying.

Jason shines his light, but it's no use. They are too far out. We start running to the right of the school as the steps die out.

Doors are scattered around the side of the building. We scan the walls trying to find a clue. Soon enough, the hallway door crosses Jason's light. The left window has been shattered.

A person wearing all black with guns strapped to their belt runs through the open window and across the light. Jason runs after him, but I grab his hand.

"If they were inside, who knows what they did? We have to make sure everything's okay first—"

"Fuck off, Hailee. This is our chance to get them." He swats my hand off and tries to go, but he's stopped once again.

"If you really want to go on your death wish, I won't stop you, but if people die inside when *you* could've saved them, that's on you."

His hand falls, and he stands there. But Jason doesn't like wasting time, so he heads to the door. When he doesn't leave, I know that Jason still has his smarts.

"I need my flashlight. You go ahead and meet me at the front."

He doesn't say anything, but he jumps through the window. Everything around me has started to disappear. I'm only focused on the bandits, the zombies, and what matters. My body feels like it's taken control. I run to the front with the cold, darkness, and silence chasing me.

"Hailee?" A girl calls.

I recognize the bubbly tone. "Sarah? What're you doing out here?"

"Just had to take a pee. What're *you* doing out here," she replies.

I contemplate telling her. Everything about these bandits could be cleared up if I did. But what if the bandits didn't do anything, and I just scare everyone, or have they already created havoc, and seconds are being wasted?

"I don't have time to explain right now. We need to get inside and check on everyone. Can you round them up and give every group a flashlight or two?"

"Yeah," she says reluctantly. I can't see her face, but her voice puts the picture in my head.

"Thanks, and where was Kate?"

"She was going to grab people."

I don't want to get mad. The bandits snuck in from the side so it wouldn't have mattered that they were gone.

"Okay. Well, while you go to find the flashlights, look for her too. If she was in the halls, something might've happened to her," I say, and then hand her one of my guns. The pistol that Angel got from her. "Now let's hurry."

I run to the front as she follows behind.

"Wait, what happened? Who's they?"

"People came in. They're gone now, but we need to make sure everyone's okay."

We make it to the front, and I crash to the ground where the flashlight is placed. My nails clump up with dirt.

Sarah has already gone inside.

I rub off the dirt on the lens and flick the switch. The light comes to life. Quickly, my body pulls itself through the door, and I head to the front of the school.

Jason stands beside the empty lobby with Marlon by his side, both holding guns.

He inches closer to me, his head down. "Hailee. The zombies are out."

Which zombies? He couldn't mean the ones in the gym.

"No, they can't be. We secured them up."

"The couch was pushed aside," Marlon begins, "and the window was cracked open. Someone did this."

From what I can tell, Jason's looking at me. He must not have told Marlon yet.

"We'll have to act fast. Sarah's rounding everyone up and giving them flashlights, so it's on us to take those guys down."

"How? There are dozens of them. We'll be devoured in seconds," says Marlon.

"I got an idea." Jason leads us towards the hallways. "Let's draw them into a room with a window, bust open the glass, and shoot them down from there."

That's one thing Ashton couldn't do, think on his toes.

I shine my light down the hallway. "Yeah, that'll work. The office has those types of doors."

We head down the right hall. The office is just a few feet away. A large door with a window, perfect for his plan, sit alongside the wall. The door opens, and we file in.

It's a friendly room. Hopefully, Kira and Sarah cleared this area of zombies.

As Marlon and Jason walk inside, there's a shuffling of feet. A pile of the dead come running, and the door slams shut before they reach inside. The slime of the zombies starts fogging up the glass.

"Jesus!" Marlon cries out.

Their faces seem no different, but their speed has doubled. "They're faster than normal. That's—weird."

Jason eyes the doors. "They must be so hungry for food that once they finally find it, they want it as fast as possible."

"So, they're evolving?" Marlon puts a hand to his head.

"Seems so."

Jason pulls out his gun, and I step aside to let him do the honor.

With a weak inhale, he aims the gun at the window and shoots. The glass doesn't break much, and his aim kills one of the zombies who was drooling all around.

Good. Jason's plan will work.

The creature falls to the ground, and another one takes his place. Some of the zombies peek up from the bottom of the glass, while some are shoving each other to get in frame. Fortunately, we don't need to hold the door closed; they haven't evolved to open them, yet.

"Let's try not to waste our ammo," I say as I raise the light to their faces.

The end of my gun aims right at one of the zombies on the left side. Marlon aims at the ones on the right side, while Jason gets the ones in the middle. Together, we shoot down the ones we can.

Something about their grueling eyes freezing and their bodies falling brings me joy. I kill the last zombie. A girl about Emily's age. Her hair was wet with grease, and her skin was practically falling off.

After the gunfire, the silence feels more haunting. I put away my gun and approach the door. The metal hinges creek open.

"If they're evolving, we'll need to be careful," I say. "They can attack us better now. Our goal is to just get rid of them and make sure everyone is safe."

I flash the light at their chests. It gives just enough to make their faces appear. Marlon's eyes have deep bags, meanwhile, Jason's pale skin is a slight red color.

"In the dark, they can easily take us out," says Jason.

"You're right. Your idea seems to work well," I reply. "If we can draw in small amounts of them, we'll be able to pick them off. Getting them over here shouldn't be too bad, doing it safely is what we'll need to look out for."

"What about the others?" protests Marlon. "Kate, Sarah, they're still out there. They could be getting eaten right now." He glances outside.

Angel flashes over my mind. A gory picture of her on the ground with zombies digging into her body. What if she's the one getting eaten right now? From the drugs, she passed out like a baby. What if she doesn't wake up, and they've gotten her?

"Well, this is great," Jason remarks. "We need to get something done. Those zombies will get to everyone by the time we think of anything."

He steps out of the open door. The dead bodies are piled up outside, and their blood soaks the floor.

"I need to get to Angel—and everyone else. We need to make sure they're safe first before we do anything else," I say as I follow behind him. My light waivers around, luckily revealing nothing.

Jason nods his head and steps towards the left. "You go for her. Marlon and I can look for the others."

"Okay, if you can, get everyone outside at the left hallway door. The opposite one of where—"

"Got it."

Marlon walks behind Jason without a question.

To the right of me is the hallway, and Angel is just at the end of it. She's smart. She wouldn't let zombies get to her. She wouldn't allow herself to get bitten here, not like this.

Or is this another one of my misjudgments? She's asleep. She won't be able to protect herself.

No—no she'll be okay. She'll be sleeping peacefully in her corner, dreaming of the life we used to have. She'll be seeing our volleyball game and imagining our plays.

I step over the bodies and make my way to the hallway. Going to the science room so many times, all the possible routes have been engraved in my head, but the zombies lurking within haven't.

I hear the growling and footsteps of a group of them. There must be only three or four.

I set the light down, and it casts over the zombies in my path. This shouldn't be hard. This is for Angel. I have to make sure she is okay.

The first zombie runs at me, arriving faster than the others. My knife stabs into his skull just as the creature reaches for me.

I pull the weapon out and pierce it into the approaching one. It falls with its friend. The next two zombies drag behind. The third one is a lanky male. His dark brown hair is sleek and straight, and his glasses are almost off his face.

Blood is all over my knife, and more is yet to come. The zombie is much taller than me, by at least a foot. I won't be able to reach him properly. Lifting my leg off the ground, I go for the back of his knee.

Cold claws grasp around my leg, stopping any movement. The fingers tighten, and I try to break free, but it's no use. The strength of it seems impenetrable.

The other zombie is unfazed by my attack and looms closer to me. This can't be where I die—I still have to save Angel.

The light barely skims the zombie that clings to me. His facial features are blocked out by the darkness. I can only make out his body eagerly flailing to get mine. His legs lay out in front of him, and he bends his body in half.

His head lolls to the side as he relies on his hand to keep him up. I can't get the foot unstuck, but I can rest it on the floor. I shift my weight to the grabbed foot and lift the other to kick the tall zombie away from me. Now it's just me and this eager one on the floor.

My knife feels unsteady in my hand, but still, I try to aim at the zombie's head. His head wobbles around, getting this knife in might be harder than I expected. With my free hand, I pin the zombie's head back. He tries to free himself but it's like his legs don't work. I hold the knife carefully to his skull while his teeth threaten to sink into my hand.

I swing my arm back and hurl it at the head, but only the air greets me. A heavy body crashes into mine. The weight of it presses against my torso, and the blow sends both of us sliding down the hall.

The creature growls above me as my eyes search through the darkness. I must've hit the light while falling because now the hallway is a thick blanket of black, and my hands are weaponless.

I can't see anything. For all I know, more could be coming. I need to get up. I need to get this off me, this isn't my time.

Not yet.

Not now.

Angel is waiting for me.

"Hailee," her voice echoes. I may not be able to see, but I sure can hear and smell. Its foul breath leaks over me as I push against its shoulders. The cold floor soaks through my shirt and sends shivers through my back. Where's my knife? The light?

Anything?

With my left hand, I keep the zombie above my body while my right searches around for something. The flat hallway, the one that I've walked across so many times, is empty. More of them are coming, and I have nothing.

"Hailee!" The voice shrieks louder.

I'm coming for you, Angel.

The strength in my arms rejuvenates, and I launch the zombie off me. As it lays on the floor, stunned by the push, I pick myself up. If I miss this hit, my leg could end up in this guy's mouth. Quickly, before it gets up.

I stomp with all my power, and the soft bone of its head crushes beneath my foot. No time to sulk over this zombie. The glint of the flashlight catches my eye.

The mutant that started this all sits beside it. My knife sits a few feet away. I pick up both and then look at the sitting zombie. This time I won't wait. My knife injects into the skull, and its mindless body goes numb.

The sound of running feet comes closer. It doesn't hit me until the zombies do that they're running. This time, two of them pile on top of me. The one on the bottom snaps its prowled teeth hoping for a piece of my flesh. The other isn't any less feisty.

Angel's voice doesn't call to me. It doesn't bring me any help. It doesn't shout for my strength, for my aid. Only silence is in this hall, and the snarling of these two freaks.

My flashlight and knife stay in my hands while I use my knuckles to keep them away from me. It won't be of use though, another zombie's steps shuffle in. Louder and louder until it falls on top of the two zombies.

Their strength overpowers mine. No amount of incentive can help me now. Their gruesome, green, and chilling faces stare into my soul. I've no choice but to use both my hands now.

At this moment, I start to think that maybe it's for the better. Maybe if I just bend my arms and let the zombies get me, I won't have to watch all my friends die. I won't have to face more guilt. I won't have to live in this cruel world.

"Hailee!" A voice calls from one end of the hallway. The same end I came from. It's a boy's voice, a boy I am familiar with.

"Hailee!" he shouts again.

Dylan's tall build hovers over me as I struggle with the three zombies. Soon enough, I feel the pressure of them release as Dylan stabs his knife into the first one. Then the next, and as the last tries to reach for him, it drops dead too.

Just like that.

All of them are dead, and the hallway is clear.

I help myself to my feet and run to Angel. She's okay. She has to be okay. We left her with a knife, we healed her wound, and—we left her alone.

Dylan chases behind, and the light in his hand bounces around. The door to the room is right there, just a few feet away. The tall zombie marches back, and unlike the previous time, he's met with a knife. Now there are no zombies to pull me back, and instead, a person who's always there for me.

"Angel?" I step inside, scanning every inch of the room.

The blinds are barely open, and they reveal the foggy night. It's silent. Silent as in nothing's here. Silent as in Angel's either okay or dead.

I flash the light around the room, and as Dylan enters, he does the same. Together, we manage to locate some sort of body sitting against the teacher's desk. As we get closer, I realize the body isn't Angel's, but a zombie's instead.

"Angel..." I say, hoping those images in my mind aren't

true.

Behind the table, Angel sits with a tired face, and her chest rises. Three zombies, all dead, surround her. She opens her eyes, and they light up as she sees us.

TWENTY-FOUR

A MESSAGE FROM AN ANGEL

I FALL TO Angel's level. Dozens of different words want to come out. In the light of my flashlight, I can't tell if she's okay, but the sound of her breathing brings me relief.

"Hailee," she says through a broken gasp, "glad you found me."

"I'm glad you're okay," I reply.

A wad of spit clogs my throat. It seems like she's just out of breath from killing. Her smile is weak, and she glances at the zombies around her.

"I never told you—"

The people flash over my mind. Angel must be stressed already. Revealing the bandits will just make it worse.

"What?" she whispers.

"We need to find the others. Someone opened the gym doors—the zombies are all loose," I reply, hoping my change of topic was subtle enough.

She smiles once again, this time with a soft laugh.

"C'mon. Dylan and I will lift you. We don't have time to waste. Jason and—"

"Wait, can we just wait here?"

I look at Dylan for guidance. Have the drugs not worn off? His face is just as clueless as mine.

"You don't get it, Angel. Someone opened those doors. They could be anywhere around us. I need to make sure everyone's safe. We have to get to them before someone gets hurt."

I feel like I could ramble on about the things I need to do. Everyone looks up to me, and here I am, confused about my next step.

"No, Hailee. *You* don't get it. I can't leave. I'm too afraid to even move…"

Each time her eyes blink it's like her lids refuse to open again.

Dylan steps closer. "Angel, are you okay? Did something happen?"

She looks at him like she wants to speak her mind. The same look she'd give the teachers when they said something she didn't like.

"I—I'm okay. My stomach hurts a bit, but really, I just want to sit here for a second." She then looks at me. Her face is drained of energy. "Months, Hailee. Months since a decent home—a decent place to live. Something to live for." Her voice shakes as she speaks, and her breathing has become aperiodic.

"Months we just ran. We ran until we could find what we wanted, and how many people did we lose? Too many. Our high school, that Air Force camp, all those towns in Nebraska. They all became lost causes."

She wants to say more, but with all the words said, she starts wheezing. Her eyes are almost lifeless, the determination wiped clean.

Slowly, she catches her breath. The world around me feels foggy. Maybe I should just sit here like Angel wants.

"Are you ever going to stop running?" she asks, holding her eyes to mine.

I feel ashamed being here with her. She always thought I made the right choice, and now she's finally lost trust.

"I'll stop running, Angel. I'll find us a home. I know it's been exhausting for you, but I promise you, I'll find a place to go back to."

Her eyes have gotten weak, barely able to keep open.

"Not me, Hailee. It's too late."

Too late?

"No…" I begin. "You can't—it's not too late. There's still time."

The words feel like mere thoughts. My legs aren't squatting anymore, my body isn't tense. The only thing I can and want to see is Angel. My hands are empty, and my body is slumped over. She takes my hand into hers and with what muscle she has, she keeps her eyes open.

"Don't waste your breath, Hailee."

Her hands draw mine towards her shirt, leaving it by the collar. Images of Angel being eaten by the zombies keep appearing in my head. Each time, they're pushed away, alongside all the thoughts of her death.

Her eyes look past me, just waiting. The usual eagerness Angel provoked is gone. The darkness has seeped into her. The color of her skin is now a pale, sickening green. Her face is sunken in, and Dylan's light barely illuminates her.

The moments slip by too fast. My heart races and tears fill my eyes. Just look at it, Hailee. Know it's there, and then move on. Everyone is relying on you.

But are they?

They could go without me, I'm sure.

Jason is smart, Joseline has been leading her group long enough, and Dylan knows what's best. It would be fine without me.

"Open it, Hailee," Angel's voice echoes in my head this time.

I pull aside the collar of her blue shirt, revealing the disfigured blood and skin. Red is splattered around a horrifying bite mark. Her chest is paler than I'd ever seen. Purple colors surround the disgusting sight, but all I can think about is her beautiful smile.

The memories of before creep into me. The jokes we always laughed about, and the late-night chats every day. Staying at her house whenever I wanted, and her doing the same. Braiding each other's hair and clogging up the slides.

"We always went to the mountains," she croaks. "They're connected to the ground, and they face any disaster that comes, Hailee. They live *with* the trees and animals, and they never move. They don't need to." There's fear in her voice, but still, she continues. "Be like the mountains, Hailee. Find the home and don't move."

Dylan rests a hand on my shoulder. "Hailee, you know what you have to do."

I want to wake up and end this nightmare, but each time I try, everything is still the same. It's a nightmare come true. An endless dream is present in this reality.

The tears are slipping out of my eyes too fast for me to wipe, and Angel can't even look at me. A part of me is boiling with rage.

Why did she have to get hit with that bullet? Why did she come with us to the bunker? Why did we leave her in this room? Why didn't she defend herself better?

Why did any of this happen?

"Hailee," she says through what little breath she has left.

My fists have crumpled into balls, and my teeth are clenched together.

Her weak voice only makes me want to cry out even more. To find every person who caused this and bring justice to Angel. I get up, my legs tired like I've been on an endless jog.

I try to speak, but only let out a quiver. My gun sits cold in my hand, two bullets remaining. There's enough for both of us.

I can end all of this if I really want to.

"Don't keep—don't keep running."

Tremble washes over her face, and tears stream down. This is the first and last time I'll ever see this horror on her face.

"Find our home, Hailee."

Find our home.

Through a blurry vision, the gun aims at her head. A once blue shirt is now red with blood.

"I will, Angel. I love you so much, and I promise to find that home."

The shot sends despair across my body. Her lifeless figure doesn't move an inch, but her presence disappears. The tears only continue, and I feel Dylan holding onto my arm. My gun falls to the floor, and I let myself crumble into his arms. His shirt dampens as I sob with all the anger and guilt running through my head.

* * *

"We're reaching the finals," says Angel, but her voice is frail.

The semi-final for Regionals stands before our eyes, and we're playing in them. We've been dreaming about this for weeks, battling each team to victory and getting one step closer to the end each time.

So why are we losing?

8 to 12, the scoreboard reads. The other team is in the lead.

It's not a big score, really. Four points, but they're demolishing us. The girls on the other side wear their blue and gold jerseys with pride. Even they've worked so hard for this. They're all tall, and I'd like to think that tall people make more mistakes—but these girls are careful with everything they do. Four points. Soon it'll be five, then six, seven, and then a win that's not for us.

"Hailee," says Angel from the middle of the court. It catches my attention but doesn't keep me focused. She only nods her head, and I feel a sense of pressure building up.

The referee blows the whistle, and the crowd is silent.

8 to 12.

The number looms in front of me on the big scoreboard. I hear a smack and see the white volleyball float to our side. A jump floater. They've been using those on and off, and we lost 19 to 25 last round because of them. The ball can float, meaning it can wobble and slide in the air, leaving its placement confusing for receivers.

Bella receives the ball with a set. She's just gotten used to them. It's not perfect, but they never can be with a serve like that. Angel faces me, and I know she'll set to me. She's been doing it all round, and it's the reason we're losing.

"Not to me," I think, hoping she can feel my worry.

Another touch. This time a set that goes high into the air. It gives me time to run up, but the blockers on their team know. They know to shut me out once again.

I make my run-up, foot after another, and jump with all I have. Gravity pulls the ball down, and it falls right in my path,

247

but I must've waited too long. It's low. I can't do anything now. I have to spike, I have to hit it, I have to—

My body did what it needed to. It spiked the ball, but the towering hands stopped it once again. The ball pounds into the ground with the same force as my spike. Another defeat against the tall towers.

I don't turn to face my team. We always huddle together as a way to comfort each other, but this time I can't. Just sub me out, Whitmore, please.

Someone approaches me. She puts a hand on my shoulder and turns me around.

"You're losing yourself, Hailee," Angel says. "What happened to thinking in the air? The Hailee that wasn't afraid of blocks or her opponents?"

I stay silent. Not because I don't want to speak, but because I'm speechless.

"Hitters are supposed to jump high. They attack the other team, but you can't jump high and attack without any thought. We both know this team is dangerous"—the ref blows his whistle—"but we're dangerous too."

The ball floats to our side again. This time, Madeline is the one to receive it with a set. The receive is a few feet short of Angel, but it's high, giving her time to reach it. Knowing Angel, she'll set to me, hoping for me to make a change.

She sets the ball to Aieslynn. The blockers must think that I'm hitting as two of them stay on my side, leaving Aieslynn with only one.

She sends the ball barreling down. Her long legs give her an advantage. She can hit fast spikes both long and short. This hit drops short, just a foot before a receiver.

The ref blows the whistle and draws his hand to our side. One point down, sixteen more to go. Sixteen more points until the victory is ours, but only twelve more until defeat.

One rotation follows through, and now I'm in the middle with Angel positioned to the right and Kate to the left. Kate takes Bella's position, and in return, Bella plays in Aieslynn's. She's our sharp defense. It brings me hope. Maybe with Bella behind me, getting blocked will be less scary, yet nothing feels different.

Bella hits a fast jump serve over the net. The ball lands only a foot away from their libero who gets the ball up. It's off from the setter. Now I'll need to focus on my blocks.

Kate and I switch positions just before the setter gets the ball. It's a backset to the left, to the same hitter that blocked my shot. If I want to prove I'm on her level, I must block her.

I don't jump in like I do for hits. My blocks aren't deadly either, so timing has to be my friend. As the ball flies to the left, my feet shuffle in sync while Kate follows from the side. To-gether, we jump, and I focus on the hit, watching how the hitter swings her arm back. It's going to get blocked. It has to.

The light tap of the ball brings me back into the game. A feint. Bella dives for the ball and gets it up behind me. It's not a perfect save, but it reaches Angel.

With Kate still in the middle, I become the left hitter once again. The same position I got blocked on.

Kate jumps just seconds after the ball hits Angel's hands. She slams it down hard into the floor, and the blockers miss her shot, shaking their heads as they recollect.

We gain two more points over long rallies, putting the score to 12 to 13. The other team calls a timeout. They can tell we're gaining on them, but the feeling I normally get isn't there. My body feels like it's grasping for threads at each point. I'm falling behind, and I can't feel myself catching up. Those rallies took out my energy too. Maybe I should just sit out for the rest of the match.

"Doing good girls," Coach Whitmore encourages.

The girls huddle together. Sweat drips down faces, and hair sticks to skin. We fought hard for these last few points, and we are barely getting them.

"I know you guys are all tired, wanting to give up, but hey, we still have another match to fight. Another round to get that victory, and we're going to get it." She looks at me and asks, "Anybody have something they want to share? Maybe tips to help each other?"

"I think we all need to stay in the game. No losing focus," Aieslynn says. Her voice doesn't sound confident.

The other girls nod their heads, *acting* like they will change how they've been playing. It's not their fault that we're losing, it's mine.

Coach nods her head too, eyeing the other team. "Well then, if there's nothing else to add, you guys are ready to fight again. Remember, the other team isn't perfect. They'll mess up at some point. Don't give up just yet. We're winning Regionals, all right?"

Regionals. All this fighting for a pathetic title. It's not State or Nationals. Just a couple of schools from around here, so why is this such a grueling match? Everyone has been waiting for this fight. All our friends are in the bleachers. I can see Jason, Ms. Mack, and even Ashton in the crowd.

The match continues, and their points rack up. 14 to 17. Losing once again. Eight more points for them, and eleven more for us. This might just be another loss because of me. Bella got the balls up, and the sets were perfect, but the walls in front of me were just too good.

I panic, and then the spike falls into their trap. I can feel

Whitmore itching to call the timeout, but it'll be our last one, and I don't know what to do differently. If I don't change, it'll be another loss.

"Call it Whitmore," Angel says from the back row.

Angel has been nailing all her sets, and still, her focus is strong. The focus I wish was in me. I could score if I had it. It's just fingertips away.

The whistle blows, and I look over at Whitmore. Her hands are in the t-pose for a timeout. The teams go into huddles once again.

I can already feel the wraith about to come down on me, but I'll face whatever scolding I need to get back into the game.

This time, Angel talks first. "Hailee," she begins.

"I know, I know," I say before her. "I'm falling into their blocks. I'm losing it for us."

"You're not wrong, but don't forget about all those other games. The ones where you carried us to victory. You got us here, and now you'll get us to State."

In the matches before, I felt like I could surpass any blocker. Most of the girls I faced were my height, and they weren't as quick as my hits. But now? Every time I jump, their hands are already there.

"It's easy for you to say."

"Hailee." When she says my name, the guilt in me just rises.

I feel the others watching as she pulls my shoulders to face her. Her blue eyes spark with a motivation that I haven't seen since—ever.

"This isn't only your battle. You have me, Bella, Madeline, Kate, and everyone in those stands. It's six versus six, not one versus six."

I don't say anything. After all, we're losing because of me. Trying to fight everything she says will just make me worse.

"Stop jumping into the spikes without thinking. Everyone has flaws, and this team does too, you just need to find them before they score more points. You've done it before with other teams—you can do it now too."

Look for their flaws. The words replay in my head. I nod, but I still feel the same. Another tiring battle is upon me. Those two girls seem perfect—indestructible—but maybe I'm wrong. Nobody is perfect.

"To State, right?" Madeline adds while patting my back.

Kate pulls her hand into the huddle. "This is our victory."

Coach didn't have to tell me anything. She trusted Angel that much. The rest of the girls put their hands in, and we say our classic shout.

"One, two, three, Sharks!"

I feel a new confidence growing in me, like I'm prepared to take on whatever challenge this match brings. I prevent myself from looking at the scoreboard. It'll only bring me down. The court starts to feel silent, empty almost. Us six against the people on the other side of the net. It's just a normal six-on-six. A match that *we* will win.

The whistle blows, and the other side serves. This girl is weak, and she only does a simple overhand. The ball reaches Tatum, another one of our outside hitters, and then to Angel in a perfect motion.

Between Kate, Madeline, and I, Angel chooses me. The same person who lost so many points.

My confidence drains, and panic flushes over me. My feet move, but my mind only thinks of one option. I haven't even seen the blocks or how the receivers are positioned. I must feint it. Hit the ball so lightly that it simply floats over the blockers.

A feint is risky, but it can be helpful. It also shows a sign of weakness, a sign of being cornered. Angel sets it up, and I feint it right over the blockers.

The libero sprints for the falling ball but barely misses. The ref blows the whistle and the score changes. Still, I refrain from looking.

The rotation shuffles, and I'm in the back row. My serve isn't good, but my aim makes the other team hustle. Aiming at their weakest player means more chances for us, even if it seems cruel.

Their formation is broken, and Kate stops their weak attempt at a play. We gain another point this way, and I can feel my spirit rising.

Our joy is cut short when the hitter forces a block out. I know the score is close. The audience's eyes are on us.

We set up another play, and Kate slams the ball straight down the court. Their receiver gets it, but it flies into the stands. We rotate once again, and this time, Bella is serving in replace of Kate.

After a few rallies, I stand back into the original hitter position. Bella is behind me, and Aieslynn is on the right side. The other side hasn't let down on scoring, and they maintain a lead.

I glance over at Whitmore, and she whispers to me, "*You are going to win this for us.*"

And that's what I plan on doing. They keep counting on me, so I guess the only thing I can do is live up to it.

The other team stands tall, but like Angel said, they must have holes. Their strongest blocker is sitting out, meaning a chance for me to surpass them is there.

I'm in this position for a reason. My spikes won it for us last time. I'm ready to not fail my team. I'm ready to bring this win, and I'm ready to go to State.

The game begins with Tatum's serve. Aieslynn switches with Angel to be in the middle. Her blocks are the second best to Kate's. I can feel the other team about to take a risk, setting their weak spiker because they think they'll win.

The girl isn't tall compared to her teammates, but she's still taller than me. With Angel here too, our block won't be at its peak, but I'm not going down without a fight.

My legs lurch back, and I wait for the set. I don't jump in, and my mind starts to tune out all the noise and distractions. My body feels at ease. It's like every move I'm about to make has already been calculated.

The ball sets towards the left, right where I am. I hold off the jump until I know for sure the spiker will hit it. There's a decoy spike by the back row, but none of us are fooled. Then as the ball reaches the spiker's zone, all three of us explode up and block the ball without hesitation.

Cheers roar across the gym.

The score continues to grow on our side. Angel sets me the ball, thanks to Madeline's receive. Their blockers stand in front of me just like before, but this time, I know I won't mess up.

The tingling feeling is still inside me, and my body is reacting with my mind, not against it. As I jump, the blockers jump too. Just two of them, and they're standing away from the left antenna. There's enough room for a straight, and that's what I do.

My body angles towards the left and lines up a hard shot down the line. The receiver doesn't get there in time. I hear the glorious whistle blow and chants shouted by the bleachers.

On the next play, there are three blockers instead of two. They know they need backup to stop me. It leaves Aieslynn's side wide open, and through that, we score another point.

We lose one point from a serve. Tatum must've gotten too excited by our rising score of 22 to 21. Now with the loss of this point, it's 22 to 22, but all six of us know the momentum in our plays will keep us going.

The second round ends with a victory for our team. The score was close, 25 to 23. My spikes passed through their hands, whether it was with wipes or cut shots. Angel's words brought me out of my losses, and I scored the winning point. We all celebrate with the crowd in the stands, and Angel tells me that she is proud.

"I knew you had it in you. I never once doubted you."

"Yeah, yeah, I know," I say through a wide smile. "Now let's win this next one."

TWENTY-FIVE
NOTE IN A BOTTLE

THE SILENCE ONLY lasts for so long. Zombies begin their way through the door. These ones are just as fast as the other mutants. Dylan lets go of me first and shines his light at the hoard.

"Hailee," he calls.

I look at them, but the feeling I used to get when killing those freaks is gone. The tears took it all away, and I'm left with emptiness.

"Hailee," he says, this time louder and with a shakier voice.

One of the fast zombies tries to pounce at him, but just like always, he dodges and kills it in a flash. I barely see his face turn to me. My head is still relapsing over Angel, but my body moves on its own. It picks up the gun and flashlight.

Dylan faces another creature and kills it in an instant. He stands ready to take on any that dare. I hold my gun with both my hands, the flashlight sitting between them. This is just a nightmare, right? That's why I feel so weird. Bandits and zombies don't exist.

But they do, and I can't keep pushing that thought away.

The next three come almost in sync at Dylan, and him being closer to the doorway makes him a bigger target.

Don't keep running. Find our home, Hailee.

The words replay in my head until I finally aim my gun at the creatures. Dylan kills two of them, but the other attaches to his back. Its head wobbles around trying to find the best angle to bite into Dylan.

I take aim and fire. Dylan lets go of the zombie's head, and it falls to the ground. He gives me a strong look of reassurance and fear. Then without a word, he grabs my hand and leads me to the door.

As we step into the hallway, I whisper, "The cafeteria."

He turns around and lets go of my hand, barely nodding his head after.

My face feels sticky, and each time I think of Angel it gets worse. Angel's shadowy figure is just sitting on the ground with zombies next to her. I feel the memories of us seal up into a box. This won't be the last time I see her.

My knees hollow out, and I collapse onto a table. My face is hidden beneath my arms as the weeping takes over my body. The emptiness in me is unbearable.

I don't care if the zombies come. I don't care if they take me with them. At least then I'd be with Angel.

My hands squeeze around the gun and light, and then the rage settles into me. The rage against the bandits, the rage against the Cannibals, and everyone who denied us a home.

My cries are short, but they take out all my energy. Fog has taken over my sight, like everything that just happened has put me in a state of delusion. Can I just close my eyes and forget about all this?

A warm hand falls on my back. It's comforting but doesn't

change anything.

Angel's smile, her bright blue eyes, her charismatic self, and everything else I loved about her flashes through my head, and then her dead body. Her pale face and lifeless eyes, the bite mark, the gunshot.

With a few breaths, I find the small courage to calm myself. My hands aren't tense, and my body feels loose. The thoughts blur around my head, with only one in focus.

I lead Dylan out of the room. We begin in silence, listening to the sounds of the night. The growls of disgusting creatures fill most of it, and when we meet a large group of them, I attack with no thoughts.

The first dies simply, a stab through the head. The second dies like the first, and the momentum of the knife being pulled out helps me kill the third. I don't see the fourth, but I feel its presence on my left. With the sound of his growl, my knife launches into him. Dylan stands beside me, his light shining against the mutants.

The next two are gone in seconds as my vision clears up. The last one follows their demise. With each kill, I imagine myself saving Angel. I'd have reached her. I'd have killed those freaks before they could even touch her.

At the end of the hallway is a turn to the gym. The failed prevention of zombies, and more of my pathetic mistakes. The sound of glass breaking brings me out of my rage. A shattered green bottle lies in front of me, and someone runs away outside. I turn to Dylan for a brief second, and then focus back on the bottle.

My light flicks over a small yellow note with something scribbled on it. Falling into temptation, I lift the note up.

Dylan watches over my shoulder as the note is opened. In red ink, it reads,

Glenwood, Iowa,
Her name is Mia. She hangs by the library
She might be able to help you

Dylan looks at me first. I have to blink the mist in my eyes away. The last hour has gone by like minutes, and everything that happened seems so vague, yet the memory of Angel reels in my head over and over.

"Let's think about it later," says Dylan, taking the paper from my hands.

I don't reply but instead nod my head. He stashes the note, and we walk beside each other to the gym.

The couches come into view of the light first. They've been pushed off the fridges, leaving the windows wide open. As we inch closer, Dylan's light reveals the cracked glass. Puddles of blood, new and old, sit below the door, alongside the red covering the shards of glass still in the door.

The sight somehow doesn't bother me. My mind traces back to one thing, and that one thing is putting me in a haze.

Despite Dylan looking around for another clue, we both know the obvious answer as to what happened. I hear the footsteps of other people in the dark.

Jason flashes his light in our direction. It illuminates our bodies, but he's careful not to shine it in our eyes. Dylan brings his light to them too, revealing Jason's stern face and Marlon's tired one. Others are behind them.

"You guys are alive, good," says Jason. He mumbles the last word.

From the back, Madeline asks, "You guys find Angel?"

A knot forms in my stomach, and I stare at the ground. My mouth opens, but nothing comes out. Her words are stuck in my head until I finally force something out.

"She's gone."

Nobody utters a word. Not a question nor a comment.

Jason is staring at me. He shakes his head and looks away. Madeline and Kate look at the floor, hiding their faces. Despite all my tears, I still need to stay strong. Angel's wish *will* come true.

Something else Angel said finds its way to me. The mountain. The message was almost like the one in that cave. It feels taunting. I'm not a mountain, none of us are.

Looking at their gloomy faces, the guilt starts forming again, especially for Dylan. I stole the sorrow away from him. He must be hurting too. Being with us for a year, he's made hundreds of memories with Angel.

"The mutants. They got her," I mutter as I wipe away the water in my eyes. The air feels thick as I try to breathe in. "We're going to Iowa."

Dylan's gaze falls on me. The others stare too, all of them confused with such a random decision.

"So, we're just leaving this place?" questions Jason. "We finally found a good home, Hailee. You just want to throw it away—like you always do?" His face doesn't seem antagonizing, but rather concerned. "And—and what about Angel? We're just going to leave her body here with those bandits?"

His group doesn't seem surprised. He must've told them. I never got around to telling Dylan, but it seems like he caught on. I hate how he's never mad, how he takes everything with the best intent.

A part of me agrees with what Jason says. After all, Angel told us to stop running. Even before the apocalypse, Angel always knew what to stay when times got rough.

The other part of me wants to flee. Another battle with a

group of people, more bloodshed, and more people lost.

"I can't let any more people die. It's too dangerous here with them. There's someone in Iowa," I begin, waiting for Dylan to pull out the note.

He hands it to Jason who shines his light on it. They all read it as I continue.

"She could help us. We need a way out of here, so I'll reason with those guys outside by myself."

"What?" asks Dylan, pulling my shoulder so I can face him. "We're in this together. If something happens to you, you need another person."

"I don't want anybody to—"

"No. It's not just you in this group."

His words remind me of Angel. I regret not listening to her more often, so I won't make the same mistake with Dylan.

Jason hands the note back to me. "As long as you don't put anyone else in danger, do whatever you want. It's time you start being a good leader."

The hallway is silent once again. Jason's words hurt like a knife to the back, but recently, this is how he's been. I would argue his statements, but there's barely any energy in me, and I know they're true.

"Guys..." Marlon's voice trails off as he takes the light of Jason's gun. He shines it to the left, revealing bloody writing on the wall.

The smell starts to register, and I feel like puking. Iron, rust, and a hint of vomit flood the hallway with their putrid odor. I point my flashlight with Marlon to see the red text written in thick letters.

LEAVE NOW OR YOU'LL WISH YOU LEFT SOONER

"What the hell—" says Madeline before gunshots blare through the back door.

The window on the right shatters, and bullets clink to the ground.

"Get down!" Kate shouts as her body flails to the floor.

Soon we're all on the ground. The shots only last for some time. The bandits are either giving up or finding a new way to threaten us.

"Meet with everyone in the cafeteria, and don't come out until I say so." I get up, still staying low, and start heading down the hall. "Tell the others about the note and that we're moving soon."

The words shouldn't sound right, but they've been used so often that it's expected with every new home. I won't let that keep happening.

It may sound cruel, but even if that girl doesn't let us into Glenwood, we're staying. Whatever happens, happens. That city is ours now.

The others get up with caution. Dylan trails behind me as we sneak towards the shattered glass. There's nothing outside, no figure still roaming. The note is in my hands, and I look at it once more.

"Together," says Dylan, standing beside me.

My eyes drift to the science hall. Angel's body still sits there. Nobody can bury her or give her a funeral. She wanted to live, and because of my mistakes, she's gone. My throat feels heavy, and I close my eyes before the tears come back.

A part of me wants to go outside and kill every one of those bandits, but I know Angel. She liked killing the dead, not the living.

We push open the doors and walk around the school. It

hurts knowing Angel isn't around to be with me. I can't hear her voice ever again, or see her smile, and all those days that we would sit around laughing until it hurt are gone. She barely lived her life—the same life she wanted to make the most out of.

I swallow the pain growing through my neck. Now that I'm outside, the people in the trees are clear to see. Their stares are haunting, but I don't look away.

After the corner, I see more bandits on top and around the bus. In front of the front doors are four bandits with large guns. Some of them in the back have bottles and lighters just inches away.

I hear a thud from behind as a bandit hops down from the roof. How'd he get up there? And how big is this group? Jason and I wouldn't have been able to pull off killing them.

"This isn't all of us," the bandit from behind says with a masculine voice.

I feel a gun push into my back. The front of the weapon pinches my spine. Dylan is held at gunpoint too.

His hands raise. "Look, we don't want any trouble. We'll leave okay, we got that—"

"We'll find a new place. We saw the message on the wall, okay?" I interrupt.

If Dylan says something about the note, it could harm our chances of getting there. I won't risk that.

"Let us have our bus, and we'll be out of your hair."

"We want what's in the school," the man says. "Your stuff, and the food."

After so much effort to get enough for all of us, there's no way we're losing that.

"No—no you can't have that. It's ours," I begin before the man pushes the gun further into my back. That won't stop me though. "It's ours. We have people in there who haven't eaten a proper meal for weeks. There are children in there."

"You came onto our place. Everything here is ours," the bandit standing to the left says. He's another man, an older one too.

"Look, we didn't find the food here. Maybe we can work something out," replies Dylan.

"Seem's like you don't understand," the one behind me says. "Food for freedom. You ignored our warnings. Give us your food or we'll take it."

"What's not to say our group won't fight back? You killed my friend in there. The others are mad."

"We don't care about your friends. This city is run by us, everything is ours."

Just then, another bandit comes from towards the bus. This one has a short black ponytail coming out of her mask. A large blade rests on her back, and a red pen peeks from her front pocket.

"M.P., we have enough food. Let's just force them out," she says.

"No, we don't. The winters are too long. We need the food to survive."

"Don't they need it too? What happened to your humanity, M.P.?" Her eyes fall onto mine and then Dylan's. "You told us that we are the last of humankind. We must stick together if we want our world back."

There's a growl in the distance, and zombies illuminate out of the darkness.

The guy behind me, M.P., doesn't lose his focus, nor does the other.

"Drop your weapons," he says.

The bandit in front of me turns to the incoming zombies. The ones near the bus are alerted too. They all raise some form of weapon and prepare to attack.

"Must've come from out of the city," the bandit behind Dylan says. "T.B. and I will keep these two close by, you go help them."

M.P. switches with the female, T.B., and goes off to fight the zombies.

It doesn't seem like a lot until the darkness consumes the zombies and growls are heard from all directions. It's hard to make out where anything is coming from. I would offer up my flashlight, but these are the same guys who killed Angel and are forcing us out.

"It looks like there's too many of them. None of us can see clearly right now—"

T.B. cuts off, and I feel the push of the gun let go. Shots are fired aimlessly as the lady shouts, "Dammit! Get this bastard off me!"

I turn around reluctantly. It's hard to tell what's going on, but I hear the ragged voice of the zombie on top of her. My body acts without a thought, and I stab my knife into the mutant runner just before it can bite.

TWENTY-SIX
THE SAME STORY

IT'S HARD TO see through the suffocating darkness. My body must've moved on instinct. Fighting zombies for a year now puts a new level of alertness over us all. The bandit catches her breath and stands up. Her hand reaches into her back pocket, pulling out something. With a click, the light flashes on, and I can make out her black mask and clothes.

She doesn't say anything and instead stares blankly at me. Our eyes are locked until I fold under the pressure.

"Thank you," she says through a wispy breath.

I just nod my head and look around at the other bandits. Most of them have some sort of light protruding out of their weapon or hand. Three more zombies come in from the side, and this time the other bandit helps the woman. Together, they take the three of them out with ease.

Her light illuminates the zombies well. Their pale skin, dull eyes, and expressionless faces. All the things that bring me back to Angel. My head drops to the ground. They can't see my tears.

The zombies around the bandit and the ones in the school continue limping towards us. There are too many of them, and they just keep coming.

As each one approaches, a bandit kills it in seconds.

This is the first time in months where we aren't the ones killing. Both Dylan and I just watch as they take out the swarm in minutes, or perhaps the zombies have found a new target. A hoard of them surrounds M.P.

His composure hasn't changed, but his hands tremble as they slice at each mutant. He takes out the amount he can, but while the other bandits are off near the bus dealing with their own swarms, only Dylan, the three bandits, and I are left. The three of them try to fight off the growing swarm but it's too much for them.

Just let it happen, let them all get eaten. They freed those monsters that killed Angel. *They killed* Angel.

Dylan runs to their aid and pulls out his knife. Just like that, for the same people kicking us out, he goes and helps them. Is this some sort of test? A test of humanity? I feel myself draw towards them, and soon enough, my knife is in my hands, ready for whatever zombie comes our way.

With all five of us, the hoard empties quickly. A pile of the dead lay below us, and I hear the bandits sigh in relief.

M.P. waves the flashlight over us all. Out of breath, he says, "Thank you."

There's some sort of mental challenge going on in his brain. He wants to say something but can't tell if he should.

With the other bandits watching him, the pressure must be on. "We *are* the last of humankind," he says, "I suppose if you two helped me, the best I can do is be nice. Take your stuff and leave."

I don't react, and Dylan doesn't either. If anything, I feel worse. Angel couldn't be avenged, and I stand here selfishly.

We went inside and took out all our food, weapons, and anything else we owned, repacking it into the bus while all the dozens of bandits watched in silence.

I look at the school as my body walks me to the bus. My heart tells me no. This was supposed to be *our* home, and now it's just another lost town. Angel's still in there, rotting. I didn't even bury her.

The others has already found a seat on the bus, and every face is full of sorrow. It's dark, and they're all tired. They're sick of running. I want to cry as I start stepping up the stairs, but I'm dry of tears.

A cold hand brings me out of my thoughts. One of the bandits has a grip on my wrist. It's the girl from before, the one I saved. She pulls my hand out and forces my fingers over a large brown sack.

"For saving me when you could've run," she says and heads back to the front of the school.

There's something I need from her. I hear myself say, "Wait."

She turns around while the other bandits watch her. She's alone in the parking lot, but her family is guarding over her.

"Could you"—my eyes dart to the room where Angel is in—"bury my friend. She's in the science room. That's all I—"

She nods her head and runs away before I finish.

Is she even going to? I hate that I left Angel in there, and I hate that I left her alone. When I sit down in my seat, I curl into a ball and stare at our lost home.

The bandits turn their heads, watching us leave the parking lot. The moon is vivid tonight, scarred from everything that's happened. All the horrors, fights, and zombies.

Emily already knows to head west to another home. The map Dylan holds guides her to the town. To the place that I won't give up no matter what. That's what Angel would want.

The sky is still dark by the time we reach the new city. Just like all the other ones we've visited, it's not much different. I clutch the brown bag in my arms, unopened. All of us are too tired to find the library or a map for it, so instead, we park outside an apartment building on the outskirts of the city.

The group is big, but luckily each of us fit into a seat by ourselves, so sleeping isn't an issue this time.

I set up my jacket and lean my head against the glass. My eyes stare at the ceiling, hiding all the thoughts roaming in my head. The thought of Angel on the ground with the bite continues to haunt my mind, and each time it does, my feelings of regret increase.

I feel a small tear slip through my eyes, but I brush it off before anyone can notice—not like they could anyway.

Somewhere in the night, I thought about Ashton, Nathan, and Todd. My nose clogged up as the tears never stopped, and eventually, I was asleep.

In the morning, I find myself still holding the brown bag. All our supplies fill the bus's top shelves. Jason is up again before any of us, but instead of staying on the bus, he's sitting above. The small exit at the top is cracked open with fresh wind blowing inside.

Winter is supposed to be ending, but the bus is still freezing inside. We were lucky enough to hold off the worst of the cold in a small town with a few nice people. Nice people. I thought it wouldn't be hard to come by, but everyone only looks out for themselves in the end. Whether it's eating human flesh or letting zombies loose, all of it is just to protect themselves.

What I did back at the school still creeps up on me. How could I have let them get away with killing Angel? They wanted our food too, and I was about to let them.

I shake the thought away. It's about the present now. This home is ours, no matter what. I'll do whatever I have to because this time, I won't let this place go.

More people in the group wake up. Their eyes are dark, and smiles seem rare now.

I walk to the back where part of our food and water is kept. The new bottle in my hand is half-emptied in seconds. With a new place, we must find more supplies to sustain ourselves.

As I sit back down in my seat, Jason comes through the top and finds his own. Dylan is awake, along with most of the group. Usually, I'd direct us all to search around, but my heart feels too heavy, and I only want to sit on this bus. Every time I look over, I wish to see Angel on the bus seat. She would smile at me, and then we would laugh about something. Now I cannot laugh without feeling selfish.

The bus doors open, and a shock of air bursts through. It forces me up and outside. My body aches from the night, from all the walking around and fighting zombies. None of us got any sleep, but maybe this place will bring us better fortune.

Dylan follows behind me. His eyes are red around the pupil, and his light brown hair is a mess. I'm sure I look the same.

"We should find the girl," I say as I pull out the note.

Dylan notices the brown bag on my shoulder.

"That girl gave me it."

"You didn't open it?"

I shake my head. "Not without you."

Once reading over the writing, I push the note back into my pocket and look at Dylan who's eager to see inside.

A flowery smell comes from within, and it strengthens as I open the rugged top. It's a few pounds or so heavy, and the inside is filled with plastic bags. I pull one out. There are three small potatoes with vivid green stems and dirt caked around them.

Taking out a couple more, I notice the pattern of the gifts. There are tomatoes, beans, radishes, roses, and dozens of seed packets.

"It's a bunch of different foods and seeds," I say to Dylan who analyzes the bags.

"They must be for growing." He puts the cucumber seeds back inside. "This could help us."

"Yeah, probably. We'll keep these safe for now until we find Mia."

I head back inside and hand the bag to Emily. Not only do I trust her with everything, but she knows about planting food too.

"This is great," she begins, "we might be able to grow our own food someday."

That's if we can keep our home.

I glance at everyone on the bus. Everyone is up, but I'm sure they all wish they could sleep forever.

We left our other cars at Plattsmouth, meaning that once again, the bus is all we have. Cars, food—there's a lot to worry about, but for now, I can only focus on Mia. Can this girl really help us?

Turning back to Emily, I notice her put the sack next to the peddle.

"They'll be safe here. You guys are seeing that girl, right?" she asks, turning her attention to me.

I nod. "Yeah. Her name is Mia. It'll be Dylan and me. We don't need her to feel threatened."

The others seem to have heard, and I turn to them. "We're leaving for some time now. Search the buildings if you want. Just stay together and—don't get hurt."

Joseline glances at us from the back. I haven't talked to her since yesterday, before Angel was gone. She knows about the note, and said she'd rather stay on the bus with the others while we go.

We first head into the run-down apartments, checking out the empty area and picking up a map of the town. Luckily, no zombies were inside, or around the area either. The pastel yellow panels for walls remind me of the buildings in Cheyenne. One of them was Angel's house.

I clutch the map tighter against the growing winds and locate the library roughly one mile away. Many buildings are along the path, any of which could host this girl.

The city is not big, but the walk still feels long. No zombies were sighted outside, but maybe they're all holed up somewhere like the gym. We don't waste time searching the buildings.

The small library sits on the side of the road near some other houses, all of which look old. From the outside, you can't tell that the brick building is what we're looking for, but the map says it's true.

"This is it," says Dylan, doubtingly.

There is a glass door atop some steps. White pillars hold the portico up, and a small sign is at the top that reads "Public Library". On the walkway is a flagpole with a flag still waving.

Dylan approaches the door with his knife out. Then he looks at me. "Ready?"

My head nods, but my heart feels worried. We're going in with no idea of this place or Mia. What if she's not alone, or what if she doesn't even exist?

TWENTY-SEVEN

THE GIRL WITH AUBURN HAIR

THE LIBRARY IS small, just like the town. The floor is made of carpet, and the walls are an off-white paint color.

Because of the size, it'll be easy to find Mia. I hold my knife out and peek around inside before entering. There are signs around the walls about reading and others about the genre of books. We walk through the doorway and find ourselves surrounded by stories. The shelves aren't very tall and only sit an inch below me.

"It's a small place. We can find her fast," I whisper. The quiet room boosts my sound.

Dylan nods, and we walk past the shelves. There aren't many windows, but they let in enough light to see. Dust covers the tops of books, tables, and the old-looking couches. Beside us is a picture labeled "Survival Books".

"The base always read these kinds of books," Dylan says, gazing at the long shelf.

I think back to Angel. She hated reading and anything to

do with it. The only things she did read would be the subtitles on movies.

My body flings to the sound of stepping feet.

A girl my age stands facing me with a gun pointed towards my chest. A stand-off is what this feels like. The girl has bright blue eyes like Angel and auburn hair tucked into a low ponytail. She wears a gray shirt with the sleeves cut off, and black pants. On her shoulder is a small backpack. This could be Mia—or someone dangerous.

Who are you?" I say before her. After taking the words out of her mouth, she looks for something new to say.

"I can say the same for you."

Her body doesn't even twitch with the large gun in her hand. A determined look is on her face, and it doesn't change. I won't take any risks right now. This girl could be anyone.

"We're just stopping by, looking for a place to stay."

"Just the two of you?"

I hesitate before nodding my head.

Her eyes squint at me, gazing at my knife. "Lower your weapons."

I glance at Dylan, and he brings his blade down. With a frustrated sigh, my hands lower. Though this is a rough spot, something tells me that I can trust this girl. I don't want to follow my gut, but my head has been wrong lately.

"Put them on the floor and slide them to me."

"How do we know you won't kill us right after," I say, ready to bring my weapon back up.

"You're the ones looking for a place."

"So, you might let us stay?" asks Dylan.

"Weapons on the floor."

She didn't say no, but even if she did, it wouldn't matter. We'll make this place our home. No more running.

We'll have to mention the note at some point if this girl is truly Mia, so it may as well be now.

"Do you know who Mia is?" I say and reach for the note. My hand is slow, showing no sign of danger. The girl steadies her aim on me.

"Heard the name, why?"

The note is in my hands, but should I even show her? What if she doesn't like Mia and tries to harm us for being allies? It's crazy to think about, but with a gun pointed at me, my mind is swarming with thoughts.

I hand the note over and watch as the girl reads it with a bothered expression.

"Who gave this to you?" she asks. Her tone changing from secretive to confident.

"Somebody sent it to us. You know where we'd find her?"

"I am her. Those guys sent dead weight my way."

"It's not like that," Dylan says. "We went into their city, and they unleashed this pack of zombies on us. That's when we got the note."

She scoffs, eyeing Dylan. "Weird."

Easing up, her expression turns to curiosity as she rests her gun. "I don't trust you all yet, but I guess you can stay with me. What are your names?"

"I'm Hailee."

"Dylan."

"Hailee and Dylan. And you said it's the two of you?"

Silence falls over us. I look at Dylan, and timidly, he nods his head at me.

"There are a few of us," I reply, trying to get the words out fast so she doesn't worry about the lie. "Look, we've been on the road for a while, so however *this* ends, I plan on staying here."

"I can see why you would lie," she says and stares at her own weapon. "By a few, you mean like five?"

"It's more than that," says Dylan, "but we all have things to offer. We'll help you more than you'd think."

She looks at us for a few seconds, her eyes darting to her gun, then back up.

"I don't like large groups," she mumbles, "but I'm willing to make some compromises. I've been lonely lately, so I'll just hope you guys are good people." She doesn't wait for a reply and continues. "We've just met, so I won't spill my background to you guys. For now, let me take a look at your people, and we'll go from there."

We bring her back to the bus. This time, the walk is filled with Mia explaining the city design. She also told us how she's been living here, and we told her about Cheyenne. Dylan and I decided to not tell her about the Cannibals, yet.

Some of the people sit outside the bus like Jason, Kira, Kate, and Marlon. CJ and Will sit near some dead trees. The sun is warm, and it shines over their conversations.

"You don't plan on staying at these apartments, do you?" asks Mia, looking at the buildings.

"Well, we got here in the night. It seemed like an okay place to stop at," I reply, leading the three of us towards the bus.

Jason is the first to see Mia, and then Kate and Marlon. They're on their feet in seconds, hands over weapons.

"Who's this?" Jason questions as he reaches for his gun.

Mia stares back at him, holding her own with an aim at his feet.

I step between Mia and the group. "Relax. She's the reason we're here. Remember that note at the school? She's Mia."

"And you just trust her? Who knows what she's done or

the people she's been with? What if she's not the same girl?"

Dylan draws towards the three of them, hands held out. "Calm down, Jason. What other choice do we have? She can help us, and we can help her."

"And it doesn't matter what she's done or the people she's been with. We've all done bad things. We all know what you've done Jason."

His mouth curls, and his eyebrows crush together. "At least—"

"No, we're here for her. We aren't going to be violent."

Mia lowers her gun first and analyzes the others.

In a low tone, I say, "Don't mind him. He's lost a lot of people—like the rest of us. He just can't handle it as well."

Jason can hear me, and I want him to. He walks away, mumbling something to himself.

I guide Mia to the inside of the bus. Everyone is spread out amongst the seats, and they turn around as we get on.

"Everybody, this is Mia, the one from the note. If we can help her, this could be our new home," I say.

A few of them look confused, some happy, and some with plain, dull expressions. A couple of people greet Mia, but nobody asks questions. Angel would've been the one to do that, or even Ashton.

"All right, let's talk," I say to Mia as we head outside. We find a spot on a curb next to some dead grass. Joseline joins us.

"The first thing we need to talk about is where we can all sleep," I begin. "I know you don't like large groups, so we'll stay away from you, or however you want."

Mia nods her head. "I like to jump around places. Learn something new about this town every day. There are a couple of houses that I like to stay at near the library."

Her eyes glance at some of the old buildings by the road. "I don't mind where you guys stay, but from my experience, everyone crowded in one area—" she pauses, her mind relapsing.

Her mouth hangs open, but she holds back what she wants to say. "It leads to disasters. Anything can happen to you all at once. Sooner or later, people are hurt and—just try to stay separated."

"You're right," says Joseline. "We got lucky at the school. A lot more of us could've gotten hurt."

Her words make it seem like Angel's death is just another number, and Todd's too.

She must've seen me react. "I'm sorry, Hailee. I didn't mean it like that."

"It's fine," I reply, fighting away the memories of Angel. "No point in hiding anything now."

I go on and tell Mia about the beginning of all of this. Once the story reaches the factory, Joseline adds by explaining the Cannibals. As the story continues, Mia's face changes to a sort of realization.

"You said one of them was a young adult, right? Did she have brown hair, pale skin?"

Joseline looks to the side. "Yeah. Her name was—Zara, I think."

"Zara," she repeats. Her voice is barely alive as she says the name.

"You know her?" Dylan asks.

Mia nods her head, blinking a few times to kill the memory. "It's a long story for another day. You said those Cannibals captured your friends?"

My fingers play with the dead grass. "Yeah, Nathan and Todd. They killed another. His name was Ashton."

Mia gets up, sorrow on her face. "I think you guys might want to see something."

We tell the others we're going off somewhere, and none of them fight back. They're like sitting ducks just waiting for an order.

Mia leads us down the roads, her legs faster than before. Eventually, we arrive at a small house near the library. The panels are dark green, and the windows are white with dirt stains everywhere. The roof looks broken and old.

"This is one of the houses I stay at. Personally, it's for the color," she says as she steps through the gate.

There's a wooden fence surrounding the house and a small front yard with dead grass. A cement walkway heading towards a porch and a rusty brown door greets us. On the porch is a table with a candle and lighters. Below the table is a painted rock of two girls. I barely catch the name "Mia" written in the corner.

She opens the door, and a ring echoes through the house. I look up and see a small contraption connected to a bell.

"It's Mia," she whispers.

So, there *are* more people.

She walks to the right, and the three of us follow. There's a small living room with old furniture, and a person lying on one of the couches.

It takes a second to register his face, blonde hair, and lanky body.

"Nathan..." I mutter. My feet barely take a step as the air flies out of me.

Mia steps aside, letting us meet. Joseline looks at Nathan and then searches around the room for someone else.

"Where's Todd?" she says through a breaking voice.

Nathan helplessly looks at her, and then back at me. Dylan comes closer as well, a relieved look on his face.

"He—he didn't make it," Nathan's familiar voice says.

Joseline holds back her tears. In a way, she knew this had already happened.

"Where's the rest of the group? Is Kira with you guys?"

"They're all back at some apartments. How are you feeling?" I ask.

As I look at his bare face, the memory of his glasses and watch flash through my head. They're in one of the bags back on the bus.

"I'm okay, I hope. Probably some sprains from the fall. It's been days though. I was with the Cannibals and—it's a long story. It's better if I tell everyone at once."

"Can you walk?" Dylan asks.

"I think so," he says as he tries to get up. His stance is off, but he's able to walk with a limp. "I want to see the others," he says with a glowing hope.

We make it back to the bus. The same trip we've been on for a while now. The apartments don't seem like the best place to stay if we're going to be meeting at the library often.

Nathan eagerly looks through the bus windows, his head flinching at every person around. Jason is the first to see Nathan, and the other ones outside see him too. Down the steps, Ava and Anthony come.

Following behind them is Kira. She takes slow steps, and when she sees Nathan, her eyes light up, and she runs into his arms. Dylan, who was helping Nathan stand, steps off to the side, and we all watch as they hold each other closely.

"I thought you were dead," she feebly says.

His smile is warm as he holds her closer. "You gave up on me that easily?"

They let go of each other. A few tears slip out of Kira's eyes. Other members of the group come up to Nathan with positive greetings. Everyone's glad that he's back, even Jason.

As Joseline's group sees Nathan, they begin to ask about Todd. Soon there's a huddle of everyone around Nathan, and he rests on the bus steps, readying to spew his story.

"After the river carried me down, I passed out. The girl carried me out and stayed with me until I woke up. We were in the middle of the forest. The girl was small, but she wasn't afraid to hurt me. She'd already tied my hands up and stripped me of all weapons. She also tied a cloth around my eyes so I couldn't see where we went.

"Eventually, we made it to this camp where she let me see. There were tents, a metal fence, and a fire. A small building too, but I never got the chance to go inside. I don't think I'd want to. I saw your friend, Todd. His hands were tied up like mine on a tree. He was happy when he saw me. I stayed at the camp for a couple of days, but for Todd, it was less."

Nathan stares at the other group with a gloomy face. They all know what's coming, it's obvious.

"By the night of that day, they told us they could help. They said that if we became cannibals—we could survive this world. I overheard a few times of some incoming zombie herd. They said they needed to move camps soon, and they asked both me and Todd if we would become one of them. They only took one answer. Todd said he would never betray you all. He said he'd find his way back to Joseline. The next day, I woke up to Todd with only an arm and a leg. The other limbs were bloody nubs. He was alive but barely. I guess they didn't kill me because I said I'd become one. So, they put me to the test. I had to eat a part of that kid."

Nathan's voice breaks down. We knew Todd was dead, but

why like this? I look over at Joseline whose tears are piling in her eyes. Some of the other members are also crying. Nathan inhales. His head shakes away the torturous memories.

"In the evening, they started trusting me. They thought I was finally becoming one of them, so they got careless. In the camp, they stopped supervising me every day. A lot of them took trips away as well. I snuck into one of the tents with guns, grabbed a few, and began my way here. On my way out, I found a pair of car keys and drove through a few cities until I thought I was far away. That's where I found Mia. I think the Cannibals are coming soon. They'll be moving 'cause of the herd—if it's even true. No doubt they'll end up around here."

My head still registers his last few words. It's all a lot to process: Todd's death, this zombie herd, and the Cannibals. Does the running and fighting ever end?

Despite the sorrow amongst us all, I know we'll be seeing those freaks again. This can't weigh us down.

"We have to start preparing now," I say, looking over at Mia, and then to the rest of the group. Though they all look dark, there is a determination pushing its way out.

We won't let their deaths go to waste. The Cannibals don't stand a chance now.

TWENTY-EIGHT
PYTHON

MIA SHOWED US her secrets to surviving for the rest of the day. She has traps placed in locations around the city, warning her of any zombie signs. The traps are simple rat traps connected to wires along trees, and when a zombie triggers the wire, the trap closes and the wire falls. If any wire is down and a trap is closed, she knows something has come through.

She also showed us how she keeps herself clean. There's a stream to the west of the city. She uses either a water filter that she found a while back or she'll make her own version. On some days, she'll boil her water too.

By the time her tour of life is over, the sky has snuck behind a black sheet. All the things she mentioned make me feel like I'm living in this world wrong. From her gadgets to her intelligence, I know she'll be useful.

We sit around a bonfire where Emily and Damien cook food. Mia helped them start it, and she gave them the utensils.

"Those bags are pretty smart," she says, heading towards

our group. "I'll have to do that one day. All my stuff is scattered around the house."

The fire isn't far from the house we visited, and the bus is parked down the road. We've decided to split up the people into the houses around the neighborhood. Everyone is close, yet not together.

"I thought of it with my teacher last year," I reply. "We had different members then."

"I bet."

The night feels peaceful. There's a warm feeling in the air, but there is silence too. The silence before it rains, or the quiet as the water pulls back in a tsunami.

I can only hope nothing bad happens.

Emily finishes cooking the food. The cans we used from previous days are used again.

We hold the makeshift bowls out like baby birds to their mother. Emily scoops out a portion of the beans and canned vegetables. Eventually, all of us have a warm, half-appetizing dinner in front of us.

Angel would've loved this. A warm meal under the bright stars.

I sit next to Dylan with Kate and Madeline a few feet away. Jason sits back against the house staring at the dead grass. Avery sits with Sarah, an empty spot left for Emily. Mia takes a seat next to Dylan, and I can tell Jason keeps eyeing her.

"Thank you again for taking us in," I say.

"I didn't have much of a choice. You would've taken this place by force anyway, but it's okay, I understand. When zombies take over the world, life gets pretty crummy."

"You can say that again," adds Dylan. His head turns to the trees on the left. "You know if there's any wildlife around here? Rabbits or squirrels? I could use some meat."

"I'll occasionally stumble across a critter, but I like to let them live. I like to see them survive and have a family, know that they'll be making more food for me."

Dylan lightly laughs. I feel a smile crawl on my face. With Mia around, we can get a lot more done.

I woke up the next morning with Emily next to me. Just like old times when we slept in the same bed. I sit there for a bit before finally deciding to get up. Being in a bed with no worries about zombies and feeling safe—this is something I haven't felt in a long time.

I pass by Noah who sleeps on the couch with a pillow. He's dead silent. Dylan is in the other room, or possibly outside.

I make my way to the street and see a few people sitting around. Mia's there along with Jason. She holds up different equipment, showing the others.

Before heading over to them, I go back inside and grab a bottle of water. At night, we were able to distribute most of the food and water we had into the houses. The bus is parked near the group, and I can see the library in the distance. My stomach feels like a pit. It hasn't growled like this for months now.

The morning takes a while to pass. Everyone wakes up and eventually, we all circle around Mia as she shows us her tools. She has a makeshift showerhead, lighters, watches, and a box of survival knives. She also mentions her recipes for things like toothpaste and shampoo.

After Noah woke up, he finally talked to me. He was silent for the whole ride here and all of yesterday. I've only seen him with Dylan and Ava.

It's like I should be feeling worse, more upset that Angel's gone, but when I look at these people, I know that we still have a future to construct. Being controlled by grief won't get us anywhere.

Perhaps like Ashton taking over Jason, Angel has taken over me.

Mia packs up her stuff and carries it into her house with help from Madeline. Madeline hasn't said anything about Elliot since we told her. Her head must be buzzing with thoughts now that we know the Cannibals could be coming.

Thinking about Elliot reminds me of Jason. The snow at the factory, and Ashton's death. I glance at him, and he has this surprising spark in his eyes. A twinkle that I haven't seen in many days. The ones he'd get when he'd talk about something he loved, or when he answered the question right in class. It's subtle, but it's there. I don't say anything about it. It'll go away if I do.

There's a roar of a car in the distance. It grows louder in seconds. The sound of the engine goes on for about a minute, and no one utters a word.

We all knew this was coming. We knew it would be soon, and they decided on today.

The Cannibals.

Faces turn to me, and my vision traces to Nathan first, then Mia, and then Joseline.

"Everyone, load up on weapons," I say and assure their eyes. "If it's the Cannibals, we'll be prepared to attack, and if any of us get caught, stay hidden until there's a sign to fight."

They begin shuffling towards the buses and houses for weapons.

Mia sprints over to me. "I've got a sniper in my house. I'd use it, but I'd prefer to be closer to those guys in case of an emergency. You know of anyone who could use it?"

My mind traces through people. Dylan's a good sniper but he'd also want to be close to the Cannibals, Jason hasn't used one of them, and I don't know about Ava and Noah either. The next person I can think of is Emily. Dylan was telling me that she was a good shot.

"Give it to Emily, my sister. I think she'll use it well."

Mia nods her head and goes off.

I head back to the house and pick up my revolver. My knife is already tucked into my shirt, and I've got a spare gun in my back pocket. I'll fight if I need to, and I won't lose another home.

It only takes a few minutes for everyone to find some sort of hiding spot. People are peeking through windows, on roofs, and behind fences. Dylan and I crouch behind a small bush near the house we settled in. Noah is above us on the roof with an assault rifle.

There are only two ways for the Cannibals to come into this neighborhood, and they're through the roads.

Minutes pass in silence until the sound of a gun dragging on the floor kills it. Joseline is inside the house on our left. Her face is barely visible through the window, but she nods her head at me, worried. This must be them.

There's a rumble of gunfire atop us all. The bullets fly into the houses, shattering windows and cracking wood. Any zombie nearby must be approaching now.

The sound stops in seconds. Still, none of them have said anything. I don't risk peeking, and Dylan doesn't either.

There's another round of gunfire above our heads once again, followed by a voice.

"We know you're hiding," a girl says.

Her voice is a higher pitch, and it almost rings like a snake. The words are slurred, yet they're clear enough to understand. She's loud. No doubt everyone can hear her.

"Save us the trouble, we'll make your deaths painless."

Nobody moves. If she fires a gun through the fences, it's likely that she won't hit any of us unless she shoots for a while. By then, she has to run out of ammo, and if not, the few above will get her.

There's a weird sense falling over me—a guttural feeling to go somewhere else, like someone is coming.

"Well, I suppose we'll just take you by force," she says.

I don't see how she'll do it. There's more of us than there are of her group. I'm able to sneak a look at her. They are all loaded with large machine guns, smaller guns too, and knives. Each of the members looks lively. Their health is incredible.

The girl speaking is the blonde one. Her hair is almost platinum. It's long and braided. There are four other people with her. One has brown hair, a darker man with large muscles, and another with short black hair and beady black eyes. I don't see Elliot anywhere, but there could be more of them coming.

Eyes are watching us. I can feel them.

A throat clears behind us, and as I turn around, I'm met with a pistol pointed at my head. There's another one pointed at Dylan.

They must've come from around the houses. With ours being on the edge, they got lucky. What happened to Noah then? Or had he not seen them?

"Listen or get shot," one of the guys holding the pistol says with a southern accent.

I hold my hands up, just like with the bandits, and stay silent. Dylan does the same. He gives me a worried look, but I try to remain calm. If we show any sign of weakness, it will make them feel stronger.

"Walk," the other says, and we begin to the center.

I know the group can see us in the street, but hopefully, they will listen to what I said before.

Python, I assume, stares at me with a grinning expression. It's an evil grin. The kind you get when you see the person you hate fail. Too bad for Python, I'm not going down without a fight.

"And what are your names?" she asks.

I look at Dylan but don't say anything. If Todd or Nathan told her anything, then she might be looking for specific people, the leaders.

"You aren't talkers. I can understand. Joseline must be lurking around here, right? You're a part of her group." Her words are more chilling up close.

The pistol on my back pushes into me.

My legs find a stance, and I stare at the girl. "If you kill us, you won't get any information."

My confidence is withering as the thought of being killed lurks in my mind.

"I know your friends are in those houses. Just a few bombs, and they're all dead." Her eyebrows raise as her smile widens.

"We can work something out. We were here—"

The pistol kicks into my back. I fall to the ground in front of the girl who now towers over me.

Her revolver meets my head, a snake carved on the handle. "Joseline and I've already made a deal," she hisses. "Why don't you bring her out? She'll tell you about it—unless you want your friends to die."

A deal? Joseline never told us anything about that. A door creaks and footsteps approach from behind me. I don't turn my head. I already know who it is.

"Leave them, Python," says Joseline. "Don't forget that you broke the deal first. We'll leave and stay away from you. Just—don't hurt anyone." Her voice is booming, but a nervous plea is within.

I want to say something, tell Python that this is *our* home, and we aren't leaving it, but anything I say could result in a bullet through my head.

"Oh, leaving so soon? But we're getting hungry. No good meat on the road here. Though your friend was a good meal, we still need more."

The thought of Todd by that tree haunts me.

"Python, we'll leave you alone, please," she protests. I see her eyes holding water, but she shakes away the tears. Her hand turns white as it clutches her bow.

"You've always been beautiful with that. It takes a while to master those. A lot of time and patience to become efficient," says Python, inching closer to Joseline. "It takes time and patience to survive this world with efficiency too. The right ideas fall into place. Don't you see us? We look like we're from the modern world. Our skin is strong, our muscles have grown more than yours could ever, and our blood is filled with everything it needs. It's all because of the meat on our bones. I'm sure you have plenty of members, Joseline. Just spare one for me."

Joseline turns to the ground, eyes shut.

It's as if Python is trying to convert us too. In seconds, a gun now aims at the blonde-haired girl. She's quick to bring out her own gun towards Joseline.

"This again, my dear friend?" Her snake eyes dart at us, and her gun switches between Dylan and me. "Which one of these two would you like to see again?"

There's a large rumble of growls and thuds in the distance. None of us can see what's really going on, but as Python looks towards the sound, I search around the houses.

Noah is still on the roof with one of the Cannibals behind him. A gun sits by his head. Emily and Anthony are on the other houses, and both are too far to help Noah. I see Emily pointing her sniper at Python, but if she makes any move towards her, the three of us could be dead.

"The herd is coming, and they've gotten faster. We need to run," Python mumbles. With a hesitant moment, she flicks back to Joseline and shoots.

Falling. That's how my heart feels as I see a body hit the floor. It's Joseline dodging the bullet. She barely escapes and points her own weapon. Python leaps behind one of the house fences and hides. The bullets miss her.

The Cannibal behind me grabs my hands, but I won't let him take me.

My elbow hits his face, and he uses a hand to console his nose. With only one hand he tries to shoot me, but his aim is off. I'm able to duck and lunge. He falls to the ground as his nose floods with red. I fight off the gun from his hand and point it at him.

The other Cannibal grabs me from behind. He holds my arms with the same muscles that Python talked about. There's no way I'm getting out of his hold.

There's a large thud, and the restraint loosens. Dylan is behind the now fallen man with a gun in his hand.

A grenade can of some sort finds its way near the road. At first, it seems like a bomb, but white fog begins seeping out.

The running of the Cannibals dies in seconds. The smoke glides through the air, eventually swarming everything in its sight. I can only make out the ground that's a foot away. The gas stings my eyes and makes my wounds burn. The one on my neck is the worst.

A helpless gun shoots from the roof, doors open, and familiar voices shout. A hand grabs my arm and pulls me inside, but my eyes are too foggy to tell.

I crouch to the ground, trying to focus on anything. My neck burns, and my wrists are no different. I was lucky not to breathe in much of the gas, but now my nose feels like it's been pierced by wasps.

"Holy shit. Something's coming," says Jason.

I look up and Damien and Joseline. She hovers with a worried look. There's a med kit out on a chair and water.

"Keep your eyes open," she says and pours the water onto my face. It's uncomfortable, but I feel it helping. I blink a few times and dismiss the pain from my mind. There are more things to worry about.

I rub my eyes and try to catch my breath, and then I look at Joseline and can only think about what Python said. An agreement, yet she never told me. She risked the lives of my group by not telling us. Maybe it would've been better if we didn't stick with them. It's only been trouble, death, and pain ever since we met.

"You never told us about a deal," I say through clenching teeth.

"Look—"

"What was she talking about?" As I say the words, I think back to the factory. Sarah was talking about a deal too, and she also mentioned the herd in Omaha. It's all coming back.

We stare at each other until she finally faces defeat. Turning to the floor, she shakes her head. "When we first came to the factory, we wanted to go north to the same city Python was at. Her group started giving us trouble then. They killed some of our members, and we killed some of theirs."

Her eyes glance outside. The room is silent, and she's forced to continue. "I always knew we would lose against them, so I offered a deal. We'd leave their city, stay away from them, and not hurt any of their members as long as they did the same."

Despite being on the ground, my eyes never leave hers. "So, did she break it first?"

Joseline doesn't respond, let alone look at me.

With a hand on her shoulder, Damien says, "Just tell them the truth, Joseline. We're already in a fight, and those zombies will be here any minute now. Hailee's on our side."

Her face finds the floor, and then me. "It was an accident. A group of their members were in our territory, near the factory. They were trying to find more supplies just like us. When I saw them in the woods with our stuff, I didn't know what to do, and I acted with anger. I shot one of them with my bow, and then the other with my gun."

Anger and forgiveness fight their way through me. My feelings are jumbled up into a knot. I'd follow my heart in this situation, but my heart is lost.

Jason views our huddle, an urgency flaring on his face. "We're a group now—like Damien said. It's not you and your factory people anymore. We're in this together."

He turns back to the glass window. Something has caught his attention. "We don't have time to argue or chit-chat. That herd is coming."

There must be a part of him that's angry. A part of him that wants to harm everything in his path, but he's calm. I suppose the chaos calms him down.

"He's right. Whatever happened—happened," I say, facing Joseline with a kinder look. "It's the present that matters. If Python wants this place, she won't get it without a fight. And this herd of zombies—we'll get through them too." My body finds enough strength to stand up. My eyes still sting, and I feel gross all around.

Damien peers through the window with Jason. "The first of them are here."

My legs ache, but I carry myself to the glass. A long line of zombies is out there. Some of them are walking, others are barely jogging, and the ones at the front are running like the ones at the school. At this rate, they'll be pounding down on our door in minutes.

The other groups must be planning out what to do too. Maybe it's for the better that we're separated. I don't want to risk going outside. Python's group could be lurking, trying to take us down with the zombies.

My mind traces back to the first month of all of this. The school with Ms. Mack. There was a swarm just like this, smaller of course. We had already set up our supplies and food. We could've run, but the school was our home when everything else was taken over. A few of us planned a way around them.

A kid named Daniel Hart and his father Mr. Hart figured out that the zombies couldn't detect humans when we smelled like them. With that in mind, we only had minutes to act before the swarm caught up to the school. We covered every door and window with the blood of zombies. We put some of them by each exit and barred off all the doors.

His idea saved us all. The swarm passed for the most part. Some of those grueling creatures got stuck in parts of the school, and others decided they wanted to stay on the land, but the bulk of them left, and we were okay.

"Jason, do you remember the first month of all this? With Daniel, and that swarm at the school."

A light goes off in him. He takes his attention away from the swarm and looks around the street.

"Hell yeah. They won't detect our scent if we cover everything in their blood," he says slowly, recalling the memory.

"You guys mean," begins Damien, "cover everything—in blood? You think it'll work?"

"We know it'll work," Jason says. He's confident. I admire it, but there are some flaws to using the same plan.

"No zombies are around that we could get inside," I begin, viewing the glass, "and we won't be able to tell the others unless we find a way to get their attention through the windows."

I look over at Joseline. Her face is shadowed, and her eyes are zoned out. She must still be thinking about Python and the deal. From behind her, near the kitchen, I see Will and CJ hiding. They've watched us all along.

"Joseline," I say, approaching her. "The past is the past. There's a hoard of zombies out there, and we need your help. The only way we'll get through them is if we work together."

She looks up at me blankly. I stare back, hoping that my eyes can convince her to forget about the deal. We look at each other for a moment, and her eyes break away first. The silence is interrupted by a weak sigh, and then Joseline glances at the window.

"So, we're covering everything in guts?"

TWENTY-NINE
THE HERD

I GO BACK to the window and look outside next to the others. Even Will and CJ are peeking from afar. We're all looking at the incoming swarm and standing there like deer in the headlights.

There will be some that come faster than the others. The mutant ones that've adapted to their bodies.

Though there is a risk to doing this, it's our only shot. "We need to warn the others. I'll go outside and tell each house the plan. You guys go out and stay on watch. Once the zombies come, we'll kill what we can and bring them inside."

The three of them look at me and nod their heads. Damien heads for the door and opens it with caution.

As he's about to leave, he turns to Will and CJ and says, "Stay silent guys. If anything happens, you guys hide somewhere no one can get you."

I begin down the street, keeping my eyes peeled for Python. My legs fall into a rhythm when they run, like sprinting for the ball in a match.

Turning to the hoard, a buzzing feeling takes over my body. In the end, those grueling creatures horrify me, and seeing them all together like that is the icing on the cake. That thundering sound is them.

Everyone agrees with the idea. Some of them come out to catch the zombies too. If Python were to attack us now, we'd both be in trouble. The zombies don't care what side is right or wrong, they just want to eat.

Piles of two or three mutants sit outside each house, and everyone starts back in. The next lines of zombies have reached the back houses. They're close enough that I can see their faces and expressions, what clothes they're wearing, and which side they're limping on.

I see Angel in the crowd too. Her peachy skin is now green, and her golden hair is wet and dirty. The blue shirt she was wearing has been ripped apart, and she stares at me.

The growing sound of the others pulls me out of the daze. It's just another one of the creatures.

The air is cold, the sun is barely out, and the house has a menacing smell inside. Jason leans over one of the zombies and digs his knife through the stomach. All of us hold our breaths as the disgusting scent of blood and iron escapes.

There is another zombie beside it. I bend down and get ready to sink my knife in, but I stop myself. It's not a zombie on the ground. It's Angel. Her face is sunken in. The whites of her eyes are full of red, her hair is matted up, and her lips are crinkled. She's the same one in the swarm.

I stare at her for a long second hoping she will wake up and be alive. That's when her head lifts. She's slow at first and then builds up consciousness. Her hands reach for me, and I let them come. A gaping mouth with flared teeth begs to take a bite.

An arrow pierces into her head, and she falls. And when

she does, the image of her breaks too. It wasn't Angel, it was just another zombie—another taunting figure.

"Hailee, you okay?" asks Joseline from behind me. Her bow in one hand and an arrow in the other.

"Yeah. I'm fine," I say and cut open the zombie's stomach.

My mind can't be doing this right now. I need to focus. Angel's dead, and there's a tsunami of zombies outside.

The room is silent as we lather the blood over the walls and windows. I shut the curtains, enclosing us in darkness. We take some of the blood and put it on ourselves too. Now the scent will never go away, but at least the zombies will.

Damien peeks outside. His open neck is covered in blood. "The first line of them is here," he whispers.

As he closes the curtain back up, I catch a glimpse of the hoard. Thousands of them, all in a scattered line. Each of them looks like the other, yet different. There's no route that they're following. It's just an aimless walk in hopes of finding food.

The rumble is louder than ever. I hear Joseline whispering to Will and CJ. Jason and I sit across from each other behind one of the couches. Damien sits just a few feet away from us.

At first it was unison the way they growled, all together in harmony, but now I can pick out the sounds of each one. It's messy and threatening. You wouldn't think a zombie is that harmful until you see it in this. Until that same zombie comes after your friends when they aren't alert. When that same zombie kills someone you loved.

My knife is still in my hand, covered in rotten blood. I keep it out because who knows what'll happen in these next few minutes. I close my eyes and focus on the sound outside.

Thousands of footsteps have passed through. I wonder how the houses next to us are doing. What about my sister and Dylan, or even the Cannibals?

Soon, the darkness fades away, leaving a gray shadow over the room. Jason and Damien have become visible.

Every time I hear a loud growl, my breathing stops. Back at the school, I felt safe with everyone around me. No matter what, we would have each other's backs. And now? It's just a few of us against thousands of them.

I didn't feel very scared when Angel was dying because I knew she was bit. She was gone already, and there was no hope. I didn't feel scared when the bandits came to the school and let those zombies loose. I was so focused on everything else that I just kept moving forward. And I didn't feel scared when the Cannibals took our people. Maybe it's because I hadn't known them yet, or just that I wasn't close with them.

But I'm scared now. I don't want to accept it, but I must. I'm scared this hoard is going to break in, and I won't know what to do. I'm scared the zombies will find my friends in the other houses. They'll find Dylan, Emily, Kate, Madeline—anyone.

I don't want any more deaths. I don't want to keep fighting. I just want my old life back. To be a classic teenager who's on her phone all day. The girl who goes to school and lives in a world where everyone isn't infected by some disease.

I can't tell if those creatures are passing by or not. All the footsteps together seem like they're moving, yet not. There's no smell in the room besides that of the dead, so there's no way they smell us.

The fear in me hasn't gone away, but I am starting to face it. I can be scared and still think straight.

The silent room is broken by Joseline's whispering. Her arms are wrapped around the twins. Those two have been quiet this whole time, but maybe the zombies are scaring them too.

I put a blind faith in Joseline to keep them calm. If they

scream or shout—or make any noise—the creatures outside will know we're here.

The large thud is like a cannonball to our ears. Everyone turns to the cause. A painting has fallen on the ground, and one of the twins shrieks in pain.

Joseline hushes the kid. She tries to cover the mouth of what looks to be CJ, and he stays silent, clutching his hand. But the noise was too much.

At first, the zombies around us stop moving, and then they head for the window. From the small crack of the curtain, I see the grueling face peeking inside.

He pounds on the door, drawing in all his friends around the house. Soon there are dozens, and then hundreds of them using all the strength they have to get inside.

The pressure grows on the door. It starts to thump and shake.

I look over at Jason and pounce up. "Quick, the sofa!"

He rises in seconds, and we push the sofa to the door. It won't hold them all back, but it'll buy us some time to escape.

"We need to get away from here," I say and begin looking around.

My hand tightens around my knife, and I prepare to fight whatever comes inside. There isn't much time to think, but I see the staircase near Joseline.

"Let's go upstairs. We'll decide from there."

I could be sending them all into a trap, but anywhere away from here seems safe to me. Joseline and the twins go up first, and the rest of us follow behind.

The staircase leads us to a small room with three doors leading to parts of the house. There's a splintering sound, and then growls louder than ever downstairs.

The sight of three zombies all trying to push their way in

steals the breath from me. They managed to put a crack in the door, the lock still on.

"Shit," Jason mumbles, pulling out his gun.

I stop him, my body almost frozen in fear. "The blood's still on us, there's a chance they'll go away. Just use your knife for now."

Joseline draws her bow and aims it at the bottom of the stairs. Two zombies hurdle over the sofa and begin up with unsteady legs.

I look around the room. There's a bookshelf I could use to block the stairs, but how long would it take to move it? They'd reach us anyway. There are paintings around the room, but they too serve no use.

A window where the sun glistens through is on the left. I twist the lock at the top, and it opens, letting in a harsh breeze.

Joseline and Jason have started killing the zombies coming up. The crack in the door has spread throughout. One by one, the zombies crawl up. As they die, a pile at the bottom of the staircase grows.

I peek out of the window and look up. The sky is now filled with clouds pebbled around. The roof is just a foot above the window. If we're careful, we can get up onto the roof and away from the zombies.

"Over here," I say and signal the others to come around.

The two at the stairs look at me, but don't move. I step back into the room and let Damien look outside.

"We can get up to the roof. Those guys down there won't be able to."

There's an agreeing silence until Jason asks, "How're we going to get down then?" He talks with his back to us, allowing him to kill the approaching zombie.

"We'll figure something out. The houses are close enough,

we can jump around if we need to."

I look at Will and CJ whose faces are pale with worry. Their eyes are petrified, and their small bodies are shaking.

I walk over to them, trying not to show my own fear. "All right you guys, it's best if we get you guys out of danger first. Remember, we must stay brave if we want to live, right?"

They nod their heads with reluctance. I lead them to the window.

Will looks outside, his hands clinging to the frame. "We're gonna fall!"

"Don't look down, buddy," says Damien. His pale hand comforts Will. "We'll be right here to help you up."

"Who's going first?" I ask.

CJ steps up to the window while Will backs away.

"I will," the kid says.

Whether it's the guilt he feels from downstairs, or because he truly wants to help, his courage makes me feel better.

My hands wrap around his waist, and I lift him up. "Okay, just step up on the ledge."

As I look down, the drop looks scarier than I imagined. Anyone would be scared of this, but we all have to go if we want to live.

Damien stands beside me, and we both hold his hips.

"We've got you, CJ. Now you need to climb onto this next part." I let go of one hand and point at the beam between the windows.

He carefully steps up. Damien is halfway out the window helping the kid. The beam is small, but CJ's feet manage to stand on it.

"Can you grab onto the roof yet?" I ask.

"No," he says with worry. From what I can see, his hands are far from the roof.

"Okay, I'm coming out," I say, stepping through the frame.

My foot plants onto the ledge, and I stare at what's below. The pain all around my body has disappeared. All I can think about is the fall, our bodies crashing to the ground.

I feel a small hand grab onto my shoulder. CJ looks at me with a clueless expression.

I hold onto the top rim of the window, steadying my balance. "You're going to have to stand on my shoulders, all right?"

His head nods as I lower myself. His tiny feet press against my jacket. The wind pushes against us, and the lingering smell of blood makes it hard to focus.

"Hold onto the window."

My legs straighten out. One of my hands holds onto CJ while the other grasps the window. Damien watches as CJ grabs onto the roof. His hands barely hold on to the end.

I lose the grip on the window to help CJ further up, and as my hands reach for his stomach, his shoes slide off my shoulders. His tiny body grazes past mine, and desperately, I try to find a hold on him.

"CJ!" Will cries.

The small hand clutches mine. CJ dangles from the ledge, and there's nothing but terror on his face. My other hand grasps the window, and my body is slanted. CJ's green eyes are stuck on me. The zombies stare at us from below.

No time is wasted as I lift the kid up and send him inside. He doesn't say anything, but his face tells enough. Damien wraps his arms around CJ, trying to hush his breathing.

Trying to recollect, I spit out, "CJ, I'm so sorry. I don't know what I was thinking."

CJ glances at me and then burrows himself into Damien's stomach.

I almost lost another person because of a stupid decision. Ms. Mack said I was amazing at making them, but now, the mental strain is catching up. I'm not as quick as I used to be, not as smart, nor as decisive.

Looking at the roof, the fear scaffolds inside me, but I know I must do this instead. The breeze hits me hard—but it calms me down.

My hands can reach the roof when I'm on my toes, and my fingers grasp a few inches over. The roof is short, meaning the climb up will be less difficult.

There's no place I can grip properly, and my hands are too wet with blood to try anything. Instead, I search below and feel a small indent, almost like a pull-up bar. I hold onto the crevice and use all my strength to get myself over.

My arms pull, but my body doesn't move. All this time, I thought fighting zombies had made me stronger, but my body is weak and exhausted.

Don't give up yet, Hailee. There is a swarm of creatures below just waiting to tear into me, and I can't let them.

Slowly, my head rises above the roof. I let go of one hand and grab my knife. Once stabbed into the roof, it stays sturdy. With all my weight on it, I bring the rest of my body up.

I turn over with my back to the roof and stare at the clouded sky. It's a challenge to keep my eyes open as the energy begs to come back. The snarls are almost calming up here, and I can feel myself drifting away until a voice echoes in my ear.

"Save the others, Hailee!" Angel calls from nearby.

I look around and see nothing but the city. It's like a reminder of what this is all for. The reason we haven't run away again. This *will* be our new home.

"I'm up!" I shout to the others and pull out the knife. Will and Damien stick their heads out of the window. "Let's get the kids up first," I say to Damien.

The thought of one of them falling stays at the back of my head. I won't let anything happen to them, not this time. I'll risk my life if I must. I put the knife back into my belt and lean over the edge.

Will shakily stands on the ledge. His eyes show no trust. I can't blame him. His brother almost died in front of him because of me.

Damien's expression seems disappointed, but upon looking at me, he softens his gaze. "Hailee's got you, Will. You just have to trust her."

He begins lifting the kid. Will stays silent and slowly raises his hands. It's hard to sit properly on the roof. The slant puts me at an awkward angle.

I stand on my knees and lean over. One hand holds tightly on the side of the roof while the other reaches out for Will. My fingers touch his, and then I find his palm.

"Ready?" I ask.

He nods his head, and I pull. Damien lets go of Will as my arm brings him up. My other hand reaches his.

Will lifts his legs and uses his knees to get on the roof. I let go of his hands but keep mine nearby as he finds his balance.

"Good job, Will," I say and put my hand on his back. "Now we can get your brother up."

It's surprising to see CJ not full of anger when he looks at me. Instead, he has trusting eyes.

"You saved me, Hailee, I believe in you."

A smile finds its way onto my face, and I reach out for the kid.

Damien and CJ, both make it up to the roof, and now the other two are left. Joseline shares her worry from below. If they try to get up, the staircase will be filled with creatures in seconds.

"There's a bookshelf to the left of you guys," I say, leaning over the roof. "If you can push it down the stairs, it may give you both enough time to get up."

There's a second of silence, and then I hear Joseline's muffled voice.

"On the count of three. One, two, three!"

The crashing sound of zombies and thudding tell me that they've already pushed the bookshelf down. The zombies must be piling up if they were that eager. I look over the edge and see Joseline ready. She hands her weapons to me and then grabs my hand.

Damien and I both pull until her waist is level with the roof. Then she bends her legs and climbs up, turning back down to Jason.

He stares out of the frame with a determined look. He wants to get up, but so do the zombies.

I hold my hand out. All the blood has dried up, but the sweat has increased. Damien stands to the side, holding out a gun aimed at the ledge.

My arm works tirelessly to pull. Jason has one hand in the indent, and his body slowly rises. With one final tug, his head should be above the roof, but instead, his body doesn't move.

One of the creatures has a hold on his leg. Other zombies push through the window with their hands all reaching to grab him. If they were smarter, they could get him, but they barely miss his foot.

Jason's confident face floods with wary as he views the figures below. Damien shoots one of them, but the others are hiding inside. Trying to shoot them could mean falling off the roof.

Jason kicks his foot around. One of the zombies falls back,

which leaves two on his feet. His dark brown boots withhold the strength of those freaks, but I feel my own chipping away.

Joseline sees the struggle and offers her hand to him. He hesitates, but he knows we're here to help. They link hands, and Jason turns back down at the creatures. He kicks off another zombie while Damien shoots. There's just one raspy hand left, and it's gone with a kick.

Jason makes it onto the roof and lays on his back. His dark blue jeans are covered in blood and dirt. I feel myself sitting down, and the others do too.

Our breathing harmonizes with the grueling sounds. We're somehow safe against the sea of creatures, and now, we wait.

THIRTY
AFTERMATH

THE LAND COVERED in creatures captures my eyes. The ones far away don't sense us, but the ones in the house are eager to get a bite. We're the only ones on the roof. The only ones in plain sight. Python and the others are nowhere to be seen, and the zombies aren't packed into one area to reveal a hideout.

Once my body slows down, I stand up and examine the roof. There must be a place where we could wait out the hoard—where we would hardly be seen. The shape of the roof is almost like an L. The back left has a protruding bit while the rest is just straight.

"This is terrible," I mumble, sitting back down. The sight of the zombies makes me nauseous.

"They're not going to leave us. They have nothing better to do," Jason pipes. "If we want them to go, we need a distraction. Then they'll forget about us—and if we're hidden from them, they'll just move on."

The only things I have on me are my knife, gun, and the

belt holding them. Neither of the three could be used as a good distraction.

"You're right," says Joseline, looking down at her weapons. "They're only going off sound right now, so they'll forget about us, but I have nothing on me."

"Me either," I add.

Damien holds something tight in his hands and brings it out. "I—I have this recorder thing. Before the apocalypse, Tyler and I recorded us playing hide and seek with Cyrus. It's about a minute long of talking. I could turn up the volume all the way."

"It's okay Damien," says Joseline, "you don't have—"

"No, I want to. There's no point in me holding this anymore. Cyrus is gone—he *was* gone. I wanted to hold on to him for longer, but it was just selfish. We're in a new chapter of our lives. If I could help in any way, let it be this."

I look at him and see his unwavering expression. "Thank you, Damien. You're going to be the reason we all live, and maybe after all of this, the recorder will still be there."

He chuckles, shaking his head. "You don't have to lie. I just want to help—and live."

His eyes steal a glance at the hoard, and soon all of us stare at the evermoving creatures.

"They'll see us again if we stay up here," I say.

Over the edge, the hands still rattle around the window. Green and brown flesh with wicked nails pound against the walls and glass.

"We won't be able to go inside, either."

My eyes trace through each weapon here. If only we had Angel's machete, then we could cut through the roof.

"Over here!" Joseline calls from the front.

Will and CJ are next to her leaning over part of the brown panels. The ones by Joseline are lighter in color. A noticeable difference.

She pulls on the off-colored shingle, and it snaps. More is ripped off, revealing a gray mat under.

I pull out my knife and use my free hand to find where the wood of the roof is. Three beams graze my fingers, and I place my hand between two of them. My knife pushes through the felt and feels another side.

Jason does the same between the next two, and together we rip off the mat. The space is small—not big enough to fit Jason or Damien. If Joseline and I squeeze, we can fit through.

"We have to get rid of this middle beam." I try kicking it off, hoping it was weak just like the shingles.

"We could saw it off with our knives," Jason says. "Mia's got plenty of them."

Now he wants to use Mia as a favor. Just yesterday he was criticizing her.

Joseline hands her knife to Jason, and he begins sawing the wood.

It takes time, but being on this roof with zombies below means we have nothing better to do. Luckily, they haven't torn down the house yet. Maybe they're already forgetting about us.

It's a good thing Angel's not here. She wouldn't have to see what a mess we got ourselves into. I wish nobody had to see this.

Jason pulls off the wooden beam, tosses it inside, and then squeezes through the opening. Will and CJ go in next, then Joseline, followed by me, and then Damien. The short roof forces us to crouch.

I lead the others to the far side of the opening. This way we can see the daylight while also being far away from the zombies below. After analyzing the area, Damien and I head out.

"Are you ready?" I ask.

He looks at me with half sadness and half acceptance. "Let me hear it one more time," he says and plays the audio.

Nobody utters a word as the click of the recorder begins the sound. Damien and Tyler are laughing together as they search for Cyrus. There are giggles in the background, and Tyler saying long sentences in Mandarin.

Talking fills up most of the sound, until the end when they find Cyrus. Cyrus is surprised they found his "best" hiding spot, but clearly, he's hidden there many times. Their giggles are free of worry.

When life was still normal, I wanted an escape from school and the endless stress of being sixteen, but not this. I would do anything to get it all back.

"I'm ready," says Damien, standing up as tall as he can.

I go back inside and peek through the hole with the others. All of us watch Damien solemnly walk to the swarm. He brings the recorder to his face and kisses it. After looking at it one more time, he turns the audio up and plays it. Then his arm pulls back like a tennis player about to swing, and he throws the recorder deep into the hoard. I can't see his face, but I'm sure it's full of grief.

It falls to the ground with a thud, the audio still playing. It's hard to see what's happening, but I can make out the swarm of zombies heading over to it. The ones at the back of the house start limping to it as well. It's louder than I imagined. As the audio plays, Damien walks back to us. His eyes are red, but he seems calm.

One of the zombies holds up the recorder and brings it over to his mouth, trying to chew it. The other zombies reach for it as well. Two of them get a hold of it while others push against each other. As all three of them pull, the recorder snaps, and the audio turns off.

I look at Damien who flinches at the sound. "It's okay. Most of the zombies drawn to us left. Now we just wait."

All of us sit feet away from each other in the left corner.

My mind wanders to the outside. To just an hour before when Python was threatening to kill us. I'm not letting her or any of her group have this place. If it means I have to kill her, I will.

Ms. Mack would've wanted me to talk with them, but she isn't here now. The times are changing. Everyone in this world has become tainted with both the disease of the zombies and of evil. Nobody is good anymore.

I look at Jason. He isn't good, and he knows it. It could be written on his shirt, and he'd wear it proudly. And Joseline—she puts up an image of being good, but even she has killed people. And Kate told me what happened with Damien. He kept his zombie brother locked up so that he wouldn't have to leave him. Though it was out of love, he didn't set Cyrus' soul free. In a sense, we're all tainted strangers hoping that we're on the right track.

Will and CJ are the only pure ones, but can we call them pure when their eyes have seen humans murdering each other, monsters rotting away with only one goal in their minds, or even ruthless people who eat others to survive?

"We'll find Python after this. If she doesn't want to leave, we kill her. The same goes for her group." I break the quiet.

"Yeah, if they haven't died yet," says Jason under breath.

He sits to my right, Joseline sits to my left, and Damien is across from us with his knife in hand.

"Do you really think we can kill them?" asks Joseline. Her voice is quieter than before. "They're dangerous, and they'll kill anyone to get what they want."

"We used to have more people. Strong fighters who were

killed by Python," Damien adds, glancing at Joseline who comforts herself to the ground.

"Well, now you have us, and we outnumber them," I say.

"They can still kill us," Jason says. "They have guns, smoke bombs, and who knows what else?"

He rises and walks to the open roof, peeking out. Seconds later, his head shakes in what looks to be frustration. In the corner away from us, he finds a seat.

"They're not going away anytime soon," he mutters and lays down on his right side. "Might as well rest if we're killing those freaks."

Will and CJ have already flattened like Jason. Damien and Joseline hesitantly follow their lead.

I lean back against the wall of the roof and close my eyes. Thousands of thuds vibrate the home as the zombies pass by the town.

Closing my eyes like this feels risky. What if Python were to attack now? Still, all I can think about is how much my body aches, the chaos and fighting from these past few days, all the deaths, and Angel.

Her dull gray eyes as she turned, and her colorless skin, aside from the gushing red mark on her collarbone. I can't help but think that all of this was a mistake. If we had just left when we first arrived, maybe we would've found our own town to stay in. There wouldn't be Cannibals chasing us down, and we could've found a group with stability.

Tears slip down my face. I hate what I've become, and the fact that I let so many people down. I failed them, and I failed myself too.

This fight with Python, despite who wins, will make us the losers. Winners don't lose people, winners have confidence. They don't let people die because of dumb mistakes.

I'm not a winner.

I didn't fall asleep. My hatred against myself kept me up, but the time passed, and the hoard thinned out. Damien and the twins are already up and looking outside.

I stand up and let my body wake up from the position I was sitting in. A clear goal is in my eyes. Kill Python. As I walk to the roof, the three sit down in the corner. Joseline and Jason make it over to me, and we look outside.

The land that was once covered in zombies is now empty. Stragglers still roam around, and some of them still cling to our house. The sun sits in the middle of the sky, beating down heat, and the wind's whistles never stop.

Within the growling of the zombies, the sound of an engine sputters. There's no visible car in the distance, so it must be behind the houses. I look at Joseline, and her face is the same as Jason's. None of us say anything, but we all have an idea as to what's happening.

I feel my breath go silent, my mind focusing in. This is the time to fight them. The time to avenge my friends.

The air is almost worrying as I step outside. None of the Cannibals are in sight, but I know they're lurking somewhere.

"The only way we'll get down is from here," I say and head towards the front of the roof. There's no porch to the house, but we knew that when we went up. "The windows have ledges. We can hop around from there."

Jason goes first. His fingers flush white as he clings to the roof. His feet stand on the window's ledge, and he climbs down. His eyes in the sunlight glow.

Damien goes next, following the same path. The drop isn't much, but it'll be felt. Will goes next with CJ right behind. Both are caught by Damien. Joseline and I are last. We make it down safely, but the pressure of the fall tingles in my feet.

The stragglers have already made it to us.

Ahead is Jason. He's making strides to get to the sound of the car. I must not be the only one with a goal to kill Python.

The door to the house beside us creaks open. Five people come out, and amongst the crowd is Noah and Tyler.

Damien runs up to Tyler and wraps his long arms around him. Joseline and the twins go with them. While some of the others kill the zombies, I approach Noah.

"You guys heard that too?" I ask, glancing at the sound of the engine.

"Yeah, we saw that the herd cleared out as you guys came outside." His face turns to the ground, and then back up at me with a fickle sigh. "We're going to kill them, right?"

There's a look of revenge in his eyes. I've been seeing that look often.

"This place is going to be *our* home. We'll do what we have to."

Looking at the others, my voice raises so that everyone can hear. "Python's around here. Let's kill these strays and make sure everyone is okay."

Jason doesn't say anything as he continues his path to the car. He's been killing most of the dead ones on the way. I don't bother saying anything to him. He's smart, and he'll figure it out.

Nobody else has come out of the houses yet. It's just our two groups, but I don't want to think of the worst.

I begin my way down the street with my mind on high alert and my heart beating quickly. An odd sensation runs through my gut. I can't tell if it's a bad feeling or just my body aching.

A bad feeling it is.

The door down the road opens as Python steps out. She

has an arm around someone with a gun pointed at their head.

The long black hair and red flannel make my heart pump more than it should. Emily is in the arms of Python, and she's the one with the gun to her head.

The two other Cannibals step outside, Ava and Kate in their hands. They are pushed to their knees with barrels behind them.

"Python, why don't you just leave us alone?" I say, keeping my face straight.

My eyes are locked on the hostages, but I know there are still more members inside the houses, and Jason must be hiding or already at the sound of the car. He wouldn't come back right now.

"Alone? You're never alone in this world," she says with the voice that I wish would disappear. "Had Joseline not killed our members and taken the bunker that was ours, maybe this wouldn't be happening."

"What's done is done. We don't have to fight. We can work something out," I pause, looking around at her group, "and if you don't want to, we'll still win this fight."

"I think you're forgetting, Hailee, that I hold the life of your precious sister in my hands."

I can't help but look at Emily's terrified eyes. I know what she's thinking.

"Just let me die, Hailee. Save the others and yourself."

But I can't live with that. I promised myself and everyone that no one would die. If I try anything now, Python and her members will kill those three. Who knows what they've done with the others?

"We outnumber you guys. Even you know that there are more of us around here. Why risk your life for revenge?"

"We don't have much to live for anyway," she replies, and

I can almost hear a real voice beneath the slur. A pause falls between us, but I know there's more she wants to say.

"There are evil people all around us. Even if we don't kill you, Hailee, someone or something will. It's the same for everyone."

I know what she says is true. That there's no chance any of us will live till we're old. We aren't going to die of natural causes. Frankly, our natural cause is a zombie bite or murder. But that doesn't make this all okay. Peace is still an option, yet only some see it.

And only some want it.

THIRTY-ONE
A REASON TO KILL

MY PARENTS ALWAYS told me that evil people were out there. People who'd do anything to anyone for no reason. I didn't believe them. How could anybody be so cruel? Even people like Ashton weren't only jerks. They were still humane.

Python is the first. The first to be the cruel amongst the nice.

We're all going to die. I knew it when Angel died, I knew it when Ms. Mack died, and I knew it when my parents died.

"But that doesn't make it right," I reply. "Maybe, Python, you've forgotten our old world. You forgot that we lived in peace before this."

"Don't fool yourself. There has always been conflict. And now there's just no limit for revenge—no limit for justice."

"You call eating people justice?"

"We do what we must. Eat, sleep, and fight," the Cannibal holding Ava says.

He's the one who found Dylan and me. Touched by the

South, his skin is freckled, and his voice is deep.

"You don't *have* to fight anyone, Thomas," replies Nathan.

The other Cannibal snickers. He's got a thin black beard, and his hair is put into a low ponytail. "You must miss your friend, right?"

I see Joseline look away, an enraged expression planted on her face. The Cannibals continue bickering as Nathan and others argue back.

It's tempting to pull out my gun now while everyone is distracted, but I'm sure Python will pull the trigger the second she sees me. It won't matter anyway. I see a figure crawling out of the house.

Sarah uses the last of the strength she has to get in a ready position. My body holds me back from saying "no".

Without hesitation, she jumps onto the Cannibal on the left, Thomas. Python and the other one jump to the shouts of the man.

It's time. I pull out my gun and shoot hoping to hit either of the two.

The bullets miss, and I feel a drop in my heart. My one chance and I screwed it over. Yet, Python is lying on the floor, and Emily is sprinting away to a house. She must've saved herself.

Ava is freed from the help of Sarah who lies on the ground with barely any movement. Nathan fires a shot at the other Cannibal, and he's hit in the arm. The pain frees Kate.

It's now or never.

The three of them hide for cover near the fences as they bring out their own weapons. The others behind me hide too. We've already outnumbered them by almost triple the amount, but I know Jason is alone near the bus where more of them could be. He can't handle them by himself, and I haven't seen

Dylan either.

I hear shots bursting around me. Not everyone is hidden yet. Through the shots, I can almost hear them piercing skin. Maybe it's the Cannibals getting hit. I must believe that, or I'll lose my focus.

The house to the left is still closed. I crawl to avoid any of the shots and see Python crouching behind fences on the right. Others are still inside houses. Once I can find everyone in the group, we can make a plan to take them down.

It's dawned on me that Python doesn't care if she lives, she just wants to kill as many of us as she can. We were only lucky that Sarah saved us from the house, but the moment I shot at her, I saw it in her eyes. An evil hatred that was destined to kill.

She would've shot Emily, and then as many of us as she could before she herself was taken down. People are going to die, and I don't want to believe it, but I have to if I want to kill Python.

Those still outside seem to be in a gunfight. The two sides inch further down the street as the Cannibals attempt to flee. I don't look back at those on the ground, those injured, or those still fighting.

When I make it to the steps of the house, my body barely rises to open the door. It shuts behind me as I stand up. There's nobody inside. Only the zombies with stomachs cut open are on the floor. The house is tiny and dark. It stinks of blood and the dead as well. Footsteps bolt up the stairs on the right. I raise my gun/ aiming for whatever comes out.

Anthony's figure is just barely visible. With a sigh of relief, I lower the gun, but my mind is still alert. Behind him, Madeline, Avery, and Marlon step out. They form a cluster just a foot away from the stairs as another figure steps out.

I catch a glimpse of something odd. As my eyes scan each

of them, something seems off about Avery. A nub is in place of what used to be a hand. There's a thinly wrapped bandage around it with blood stains. The others are covered in blood too.

As the other person comes into my vision, I recognize the red hair and familiar face from before the apocalypse.

Elliot.

There's a surge of rage that flies over me. I look at the others with the feeling of betrayal.

"Hailee," he calls my name.

It's just like when we were kids and would sleep over at Madeline's. We were still young, and the Elliot we knew was just an older brother to us. He left around that time, and I haven't seen him since.

But those aren't the only things I think of. I think about the Cannibals. The Elliot that I knew was from before all of this. When I look at this one's pale face and double-colored eyes, all I can think about is Ashton, Angel, Todd, the bunker, and the paranoia just a few days ago.

"What are you doing here," I croak.

"I don't want to be a Cannibal anymore. I don't want to hurt you guys," he says, taking a step closer.

My gun finds his head, but I don't place my finger on the trigger. It's not weakness, just hope. That's what I tell myself. A hope that is telling me not to fire the shot—to take his word.

A feeling too similar occurred to me before. I didn't blame those bandits for killing Angel, but they were the ones who let the zombies out. They kicked us out of another home, and I let them. Each thought just brings my finger closer to the trigger.

"Hailee, don't," Madeline shouts as she steps in front of the shot, her hands held out.

My mind focuses back, and I drop my arm.

I stand there in silence with their eyes watching me. The rage is ready to burst, but it stays inside. If I let my emotions control me, I'd become someone terrible. Someone I never want to be.

"What happened to your hand," I finally mumble.

Avery almost hides the wound. "I got bit."

Why hasn't she died like Angel then? Why is Angel gone, and she is here?

"He cut it off. I don't feel any sickness or symptoms. All I feel is the pain. Elliot saved me."

My eyes don't leave the empty spot where Avery's hand once was.

"So, it works," I mutter, closing my eyes to prevent any tears from starting.

As I do, I see the old Elliot in my head. The one who cared for us all like we were family. I don't think I can forgive him, but I can let him be with us. It's not me who has been hurt by him.

"Python is out there. Jason's trying to keep the other Cannibals from stealing the bus. He's all alone. Some of you guys need to go help him—and protect each other while you do."

They nod in silence and then step out of the door leaving Avery behind. I don't say anything to her. The thought of killing Python is the only thing flooding my mind. The other Cannibals don't bother me. They all follow a leader anyway.

I walk outside from the back door and leave Avery to rest inside. The air feels thin and dangerous as I touch the concrete. The house has a small patio, and the grime from the zombies has covered the fences. There's no time to look around. I must catch Python.

A gray and yellow bomb lands at my feet.

My head spins with hatred, and I sprint to the left.

The fence slows me down, and the smoke catches up. It floods the air in seconds. My eyes burn again, but I tell myself to continue. Every chance I had, I didn't take it, or I blew it. I won't fail this time. I'll end this battle.

Now or never.

The words repeat in my head. I hold my breath and escape the smoke. I catch a glimpse of platinum hair as a girl runs into a house down the street. I'm quick to follow.

With each step putting me closer to the house, I see Angel running beside me. The setter who never failed. The one who knew what to say.

Python's wicked face flashes in my mind. She shatters the image of Angel and replaces it with her own. A snake is wrapped around her leg, and her eyes don't leave mine.

"This is our home." I push through her image and sprint to the front yard. My lungs fill with air as I approach the door.

Once the door opens, my gun scans around the area. Blue sofas and a round wooden table are on the right. The walls are painted a teal green with knife cuts all around. Bullet holes are equally placed in perfect positions.

My foot touches the carpet, and then the other, just like at the river. A kitchen is on the left and a door is at the end of the room.

There's no noise, but I feel Python's presence. I turn to the only spot still unchecked by my eyes, behind the door, and see the familiar blonde hair and pale skin.

The knife attack is fast, but I'm faster. It skims my shirt leaving a small cut, but now I can see her face clearly for the first time.

She has a thin mole above her lip, and her cheeks are colored red. Her eyes are green, but not the innocent kind, the kind that a snake would possess. It's mixed with a shade of yellow, and it looks almost as if the pupil is stretched to be long.

There's barely time for me to move as she elbows my already cut side. The pain stings deep, and I can feel my shirt sticking to the blood.

The month at the Air Force Base taught me that a good fighter can let their body do the work. They can move without thinking, and the mind is then used to make the final move.

With as much strength as I have, I use my fist to deal a grueling blow at Python. Her body spirals backward, but she turns around like it didn't affect her. I still have the gun in my hand, but everything is going too fast to take a shot, and my adrenaline has me in a fighting mindset.

I go in for a kick to knock off her balance, but she grabs my leg and readies her own over mine. She's trying to break it just like the Base taught us. I use my other leg to jump and kick her back. I'm sure she didn't expect that.

Barely catching my balance, my leg finds the floor, and her back slams into the wall, yet her strength hasn't diminished. In all honesty, it only seems stronger.

Her knuckles dig into my cheek. The force sends me back, almost to the ground, and my body struggles to move. Still, I fight the pain and stare at her. She's smiling with red-tinted teeth.

The pressure of another punch hits my face. A cool feeling slips over my cheek followed by a warm liquid. With one final punch, my face goes numb, and I fall to the floor.

She holds her knife out like a butcher ready for slaughter as she squats down to level with me. I don't look at her face. She can't see that I haven't given up.

My leg pushes out and hits hers as I raise myself. Her balance is thrown off, but she doesn't fall. I throw my fist at her cheek. The memories of Angel carry through with it.

Blow after blow, I keep hitting her until I feel no strength in my arms. She's backed up against the wall, and her pale skin is filled with red blood.

My mistake must've been stopping. I don't feel the pain at first, but I know something is wrong. Just like the cut on my side, I feel the warm gushing liquid stick to my shirt.

She pulls the knife out, and I inch backward. If I try to fight now, I could risk losing my life. Even breathing is scary now. Nothing hurts, but everything does.

The same evil grin shines against her beaten face. My legs are starting to feel loose. A flash of heat pierces my skin. I haven't felt sick like this in a long time. My palms grow sweaty, and I drop my gun.

Is this how Angel felt? And Ashton, Todd, and everyone else who died like this?

They're all by the window, standing outside. They look at me with grief—like I failed them. I stare at them as my body crumbles to the ground.

Their bodies turn away, disappointment on their faces, and one by one, they begin vanishing. Am I failing them again? All the promises I made just to end like this?

I'm sure someone will come. They always do. I always end up relying on the others. I can't help it—I'm not as strong as I think.

Angel's the last one to leave. Her skin and body seem healthy again. Her eyes don't break contact, but her body's ready to go.

"Wait," I whisper.

It catches Python's attention. Maybe she thinks I'm saying it to her. Angel stands at the window with her body begging to walk away. Soon, her face drops to the floor, and she doesn't peek at me again.

Despite everything telling her to go, she still stays. She must be disappointed in me. All she wanted was a home, and she trusted me to find it. I'll show them all. I'll get justice for them. I'll get justice for Angel.

I stand against the pain. The aches pounding throughout don't mean anything. I know my body is crying for help, but if I don't do this now, who will? The chance is in front of me. I'll take what I can get.

"This isn't over," I say. My teeth grind against each other as I muster up enough energy to fight once more.

I swipe a glance at Angel looking at me. There's hope in her eyes now, a small smile too.

"You killed my friends, you killed Angel," I say, squaring my shoulders toward Python.

"Angel. Too bad I couldn't—take a bite," she says through a smirk.

An incentive to fight. Her attempt at making me angry is just another reason to fight. I smack the knife out of her hand and punch her already bruised face.

"Angel would've killed you faster than I will."

"Are you sure she wouldn't just get shot again?"

The sound of the gun echoes in my head, and I notice the Angel outside with blood all over her shirt. Her face is the same as it was at the bunker. Her blue eyes trembling with fear.

The pain of loss stings in my eyes and throat. I can't let myself die like this too. Die at the hands of a group that's pure evil.

Her boot pushes me back. I somersault to the ground with my head hitting the floor hard. I end up on my elbows, lying flat. My brain pounds against my skull, but I still look at Python. Her face is practically dismantled, but she still has the smirk. She still has the energy to fight, and yet, I feel myself running out of it.

Just a foot away, she towers over me. "I'm a terrible person. That's what you're probably thinking."

She jolts her leg at my side, sending me tumbling to the right. I lay on my back now, the knife wound exposed, but I fight through it and plant myself on my stomach.

"I wasn't like this, Hailee. I had a sibling too. I had a family. But terrible people will always find you. They do what they want and don't think twice about you." Her knife glimmers in the light with my blood dripping from the tip.

"If you can't beat the evil, you might as well join them."

"You're wrong," I say through my depleting breath. I raise my head to face her. "You gave up. You're just weak—"

"You think I'll listen to the bitch on the floor? You're just another body to be eaten now, Hailee. What should I cut off first: legs, arms, or maybe your fingers one by one?"

"How about we start with you?" My hand finds the gun just a few inches from my side, and I point it at her. Everything tells me to pull the trigger now, but my mind tells me to wait.

Though my body trembles, I put myself back on my feet. "I'm sure you were a good person, Python. But that was before I met you. The snake I know is the one holding the knife."

She doesn't flinch at the weapon. "You're not some saint either. Had you not sent out those people in the freezing cold, maybe they'd be alive."

There it is. My recurring mistake that caused all this. It stings when she says it, but there's nothing I can do about it now.

"I know I made a mistake that I can't take back, but you know one thing, Python? We all have control over our own lives. They were free to do what they wanted—and you are too. You can still change. It's cliché, but it's true. You're not confined to a Cannibal."

The room fills with silence. No growls or gunshots. Then there's the sound of heavy breathing. Python's eyes look fatigued. Her face looks as though she's in a kind of pain within. Her hands tighten their grip, shaking from the pressure, and her legs wobble.

"Did Elliot tell you that?" she asks under her breath as she smiles at the floor. "He ate the most skin out of us all." She looks up at me again, her eyes fixed on mine. "You have it better than me. Not because you fought for it—but because you were given it."

Her mouth frowns, and her stare fills with hatred. With a hand still wrapped around the knife, she loses balance and drops to her knees.

"You all think that as long as you fight and protect each other, you'll live, but what about inside of us? The diseases everyone forgets about until it happens to them?"

"What are you trying to say?"

A single word flashes through my mind. Something I haven't thought about. It's never affected me before. Cancer. I don't know much about it, but I know it kills, it's hard to beat, and there's no cure.

"You're thinking the right thing," she says, not bothering to stand. "I know it's back. I'm at the edge of life, and there's no helping me. Eating human flesh helped my body fight, you know? I'm only here because of it."

"But you killed countless others."

"You think they cared about anyone but their own? I wasn't the only one in my family with a disease."

As she pauses, I find my arm already down. The gun no longer points at her, but she doesn't care. She continues.

"My brother had autism. Every group we went to turned

us away because they knew we would just be dead weight, the weak ones."

I stare at her eyes full of water. They don't seem piercing anymore, but rather, they look like those of a girl. A girl who was handed a terrible life.

"I guess they were right, but I still blame them. I blame every venomous snake who denied us."

She drops her knife, and the sound of her painful breath fills the room. Even her slurred voice is gone and filled with a hoarse tone instead.

"I'm already gone. I don't think I'll make it to next week. You've ripped out the only life I still had, but I don't blame you."

Dropping to her level, she can barely hold contact with my eyes. Her hand traces over the cut on my cheek. It stings, but I don't move it away. Python's face flinches every few seconds, and she looks away.

"I can't continue living, but I hope, Hailee, that you never give up on the dead weight. You aren't a terrible person. I know you can help."

She grabs my hand with the gun and raises it to her head. Distress paints itself over her face. Her body is killing itself from the inside, and there's no hiding it. An incurable misery is upon her.

"I don't want to die by my own body," she says and tries to steady her breathing. "I know it's coming. I would rather speed the process up. You've won this battle, so it must be you."

"What about your group? They're out there fighting for you."

"Those shits out there mean nothing to me. They don't care about anyone. For them, this is all an excuse to be evil. I want you to do this. All I ask is that you bury me in the soil."

It takes me a second to recognize what she's asking, and when I do, I nod my head. Her eyes don't break away from mine until she knows I'm sure, and then she allows herself to close her lids. Her lungs suck in the tainted air.

Tears slip down her face as she mutters something to herself.

Her body becomes still. There are no sounds of breathing, no tears that drip, and not a single movement. This is it—just like Angel.

I pull the trigger and watch her body slump over.

THIRTY-TWO
THE LOST MEMORY

JASON MAKES IT inside the house at the end of the street. Shots are being fired outside, but he doesn't let it affect him. And now, he sees a crowd of people heading his way. Amongst the crowd is Elliot Francis, the same person who killed Ashton.

He can't decide if Elliot is a hero or a villain, but he knows he feels a harsh resentment against him. After all, Elliot's a murderer and a ruthless Cannibal. He succumbed to the new world. He's not the same person he used to be. Nor is Jason.

The group makes it behind the fence. The Cannibals outside are too busy with the others to fire at them. They crouch over to the front door and open it.

Joseline has tagged along. With Python and Hailee off somewhere, and the other Cannibals shooting outside, this is the only place she'll really be able to help.

Jason grasps his gun. He's already thinking of ways to kill the Cannibal in front of him—and maybe even the traitors with him.

"Jason, wait," Madeline says, stepping in front of Elliot. "He's going to help us fight the others."

Jason glares at her. His brows furrow. "Did you forget? He killed Ashton. He probably ate Todd, and his friend shot Angel. This guy isn't your brother anymore."

His gun aims past Madeline and at the redhead. "He's just another piece of shit. I'll take him out quickly."

"Kid, calm down. You're fighting the wrong people," says Anthony, his eyes wide with caution.

"Or maybe you're trusting the wrong ones."

"Jason, you know Ashton was the closest person I had to a brother," says Marlon, stepping closer, "but he's not here no more. Right now, we're fighting those Cannibals on that bus, and Elliot wants to help."

"Elliot *killed* Ashton. You know that, right?" He doesn't look away from Elliot who's hiding in the crowd.

Elliot looks back at him, his mouth barely open. "If you kill me, Ashton isn't coming back. Even killing the Cannibals won't bring your friends back, but we can stop them from taking more."

His footsteps are taken with caution as he inches closer to Jason. "They want to hurt you, Jason. Your friends too. That bus is leaving anytime now with all your supplies inside."

Jason stares in the direction of the bus. The window is barely open and not enough to see standing there. The sunlight casts against his eyes making the brown resemble the rage inside. Instead of using his eyes to look, he uses his ears to hear the engine's rumble. It's enough to convince him to let it go, for now.

Jason knows he can't go alone—he'd be outnumbered. His sigh is loud, and it's followed by a shaking head. The others stare, waiting for a response.

He'll need to know how many Cannibals are outside. He peeks behind the brown curtain of the house and sees the bus. Two of them, both tall with muscles, stand outside while two figures are inside.

There's a red car with its trunk open a few feet to the right. Already, there are supplies inside. The ones from the bunker and the school. If Jason wasn't incentivized enough, he is now.

The plan fits seamlessly together in his head. With a few reconsiderations, he knows what he needs to do and begins telling them each of their roles. Now it all depends on them to take it into action.

The group sneaks to the back of the house. Luckily, there's a fence providing some amount of cover. Marlon and Jason stay back while Elliot, Joseline, and Madeline go to the house on the right. Anthony stays inside watching the bus through the window. He has a gun, and though he can't fight up close, his aim is still steady.

Marlon and Jason fire the first shots. They draw the attention of the Cannibals outside and inside. The bullets cause the two inside to move like ants before they get stomped. The young man, who looks sicker than the rest, begins firing. The two outside run for cover behind the bus.

The Cannibal on the right is the same one that was with Python when they found Hailee and Dylan. Joseline seizes the chance and fires an arrow at his neck while Madeline steadies her aim. The guy looks towards the house with his hands over the wound, and it's not long until Madeline fires the killing shot at his skull.

His body falls to the concrete giving Elliot time to run. He sneaks past the guard on the left who's too busy fighting Jason and Marlon.

His body sticks to the back of the bus like a spider on a

wall. He's careful not to make any noticeable movements or sounds. From there, he must fire a shot at Zara. The only way they'll get to her.

Marlon and Jason struggle to hit a shot on the man. His physique tells the two that he's had years of defensive and offensive training. Too bad he's fighting against people that are stacked with anger. The gunshots boom in an odd pattern. First the bullets from Jason and Marlon, and then from the guy. Neither one can find a lead.

Elliot calms his nerves and stares at the brown-headed girl. He lived with these people for months, and they became a family. He tells himself that his real family is waiting now.

Inside the bus, Zara and the other Cannibal are crouching low. They know they're under attack, and by being on the bus, they're just waiting to die.

A bullet is fired at the Cannibal. Elliot watches as the guy clutches his side, only to be shot in the head after. Now it's just the two up there.

He raises his gun in silence. His lips are sealed shut, and he draws only the slightest of breath. Since she's crouching, Elliot only sees her through the closed window. But even then, he can fire through the glass and hit her. This is his one chance, and if he fails, he knows what the others will think of him. What his sister will think of him.

"I never liked Zara anyway," he repeats in his head.

Sure, he may have been close with some of the Cannibals, but Zara was never one of them. She often stole from him and the others. She would make things go her way, and the only person she'd listen to was Python. In a crazy way, she treated Python like a king.

With a new form of revenge, Elliot readies his gun at the girl. The memories of living with her and the others flash through his mind as he sees her crazy expression.

Her familiar face views him from the glass. An eerie smile draws his attention away from her gun being brought out. She aims and fires in one second. All in one second, she destroys their plan.

Madeline and Joseline watch Elliot fall to the ground. He makes no sound as his pale skin rushes with red. Beneath him, a pool of blood swarms the concrete. His face stares at the sky, his eyes too, like they finally chose which side they were on.

"Elliot..." Madeline whispers.

Her voice sounds fragile, and her mouth clings open. Joseline looks at her eyes as they grow buds of water, and she doesn't move from behind the fence.

Joseline hops over, muttering something in distress, and then runs to the view of the bus doors. She sees Zara smirking to herself, and a bullet shot through the window. The arrow is already in her bow, but it misses by an inch. Zara was quick to dodge it, and she now ducks for cover.

Madeline approaches Joseline who strings up another arrow. She holds out her gun and heads for the bus. Joseline chases behind her, staying close to the exit.

The Cannibal can hear footsteps coming up, and she hides in one of the seats.

As Madeline climbs the last stair, she loads the pistol and fires at the helpless Cannibal in the back. Though he didn't kill Elliot, he's still to blame. All of them are.

From outside of the bus, Jason and Marlon hear the firing of guns. Jason doesn't know what's inside that bus, or even if his people are still alive.

They approach the scene and turn the corner where the dead Cannibal lay beside the wheel. Elliot's body is there too, lifeless and covered in blood.

Madeline must be enraged, but the Cannibals already have dozens of guns and bombs. If she makes a mistake, it could cost the lives of everyone.

The sound of a body falls like a beat to a drum. Marlon looks at Jason as Jason looks at the back door. He opens the hatch eagerly and sees the young guy splattered on the ground. This is what they wanted. An end to the Cannibals, and if that means death, so be it.

They both step onto the bus, pushing aside the man and preparing themselves for the dangers Zara might bring. Down the aisle, Madeline stands with a look of determination. Her eyes are red, and her skin is too.

She aims her gun as she walks, peeking between each seat. It's like she's forgotten how dangerous the Cannibals are.

Jason stares at the right aisle while Marlon looks at the left. Neither can see Zara until she creeps out on the left, spotted by Marlon.

He catches her brown hair and the grenade in her hand. His body moves on his own as he bolts to Madeline yelling,

"Get down!"

A cold hand grabs him, and he finds Zara clutching on with all she has.

"If I'm dying, I'm taking you down with me."

Her smile is full of hate, and she glares at Marlon. With her mouth, she yanks the needle out of the grenade, her eyes never leaving his—and they don't notice Jason.

He shoots twice at the Cannibal, one missing over her head and the other hitting her shoulder. She jolts in pain and loosens her grip giving Marlon the chance to run. He sprints faster than ever to the front of the bus. The grenade clanks onto the metal floor behind him.

He doesn't give even a glimpse at the aisle, trying to save as much time as he can when he hears the terrifying boom. The heat is strong against his back. The flames pinch at his neck and clothes, crisping the back ends of his curly hair. He falls forward, whether intentionally or accidentally, and stares at the ground.

Chunks of the bus fly everywhere, many of which hit the group. The fresh cuts all over Marlon's back begin soaking his gray long-sleeve shirt.

The smoke seeps outside through the shattered windows. All the metal frames are broken, and flames threateningly grow on the seats.

Marlon tumbles to his side in agony, but he's glad Madeline escaped. He's glad nobody else was on the bus, and that nobody he loved has died again. His vision is blurred, and the fumes of smoke around him fill his lungs.

"Marlon, stay with us," Joseline shouts as she dashes past Madeline on the ground and towards Marlon's side. Anthony steps out of the house and hobbles to Madeline, a hand on her shoulder.

While he helps her up, he says, "We need to get him inside and start treating his wounds."

Madeline brushes off his aid and walks past all of them without a glance, getting back on the bus.

None of them stop her.

She sees Zara first, sprawled on the bus floor with burns scattered across her body. Her skin is distorted, almost like a zombie, and she hasn't moved yet. Jason stands near her head and lowers himself to her level.

The fire crackles beside them, and at any, moment the engine will burst from the heat. They'll have to leave soon if they don't want to end up like her.

Jason stares at the brown hair now covered in charcoal. He wants to shoot her as much as Madeline does, but Madeline wants to see her suffer more. She wants to leave Zara as a zombie, forever trapped in a body she can't control.

Jason studies Madeline's face, trying to see how she must be feeling.

"Don't kill her," Madeline whispers. "Let her suffer. She doesn't deserve the freedom of death."

"Madeline—"

"Don't kill her."

Jason averts his eyes at the disfigured person. Her finger twitches, and then her shoulders move. She begins to lift her head, and with a low, broken voice, she says,

"You're just—like your brother."

Her mouth forms into a smile. Her face is covered in dirt and dust, but her features are still just as evil.

The fire on the seats fills the gaps of their words.

"I don't care what you think. You're going to be a zombie for the rest of your life. All alone, but this time you—"

"We have to kill her," Jason interrupts. His eyes drop low like a man who's tired of his life. "Keeping her alive—it'll only remind us of what she's done."

"You know, I don't care what you think either." She bends down and grabs Zara's foot. "I'll put her in one of those houses. You won't have to see her."

"No," he replies, "you can't let her control you."

His half-open eyes widen at the sight of the gun. The barrel points at his head with Madeline on the other side.

"I'm doing this, okay?"

"You think Elliot wants that?"

"Just shut the hell up!" she cries out. "You don't know a *thing* about Elliot."

"You're wrong. If Elliot wanted Zara to suffer, he'd done it already, don't you think? He had all this time with her. He would've done something by now."

"She killed him. He would want her to suffer, I know him."

"Madeline, look at yourself. This isn't right. Those Cannibals have done terrible things. It's better to take them off this earth than leave them as another monster."

Tears rain down Madeline's cheeks. She looks at Zara's still body, and then at Elliot outside. She remembers the way Elliot looked just minutes before this. The way he'd comfort her, and the way he would protect her from all the bullies around.

She also remembers when he left. He had said to her the day before, "It's better to leave you than hurt you forever, Mads. If I stay, I'll only be a reminder of all the bad things I've done."

Zara's foot falls out of Madeline's hand, and then the gun falls too. Her head hangs low as she storms out of the bus. Jason stares at Zara and raises his gun.

"Mia," she spits out, "tell Mia that—I was the reason she got bullied."

Jason looks up to the sound of someone climbing onto the bus. Mia stands at the front with a large gun in hand. She walks to Zara with a grim face.

"I already knew, Zara."

The Cannibal doesn't bother moving her head. She doesn't want to see Mia. She can't tell if it's the guilt she feels or the anger, but whatever it is, she lets it control her.

"Of course you did."

All her words are slow. She's starting to lose the evil in her, and it's being replaced by the evil of the dead. Her body stays limp with only her lips moving. There's also the sound of suffocated breathing as she tries to get enough air to speak.

"Let's just—get this done, *Mia*."

Her words feel like venom as she says Mia's name. It's the
same way she said it in high school when all the girls would beat
her up or steal her food. *Mia.* Zara would say it with a long M.
She'd let the end dangle on her tongue. Only three letters, but
it killed Mia every time she heard it.

Even now, it fills her body with hatred and memories of
something she thought she'd buried. *Mia.* A sickening word.

"Mia," Jason says with a gentleness he's not used in a while.

His eyes stare at hers. He'd had his share of getting picked
on by Ashton, but he never decided if it was serious or not. Not
until that day in the snow. The day Ashton died. That was the
first time he'd ever been beaten up. The memory of that and
the aftermath still plays in his head.

"It's up to you."

He backs away, only looking at Mia.

She draws in a shaky breath. "This isn't for me, Zara. It's
for you."

Zara turns her head to get a glimpse. This will be the last
time she sees someone.

"You ruined my life, and you ruined yours too. You tainted
it with hatred and bitterness. I'm setting you free. I'm—setting
you free," she says, repeating the end in hopes of believing it.

With a single bullet, Mia kills the girl. The shot disappears
into the air amongst the dozens of others. Each one of them
has hit someone or something. They kill some, injure others,
damage the walls, and break windows.

By now, everyone has held a gun, and by now, everyone
has ruined their life.

THIRTY-THREE

SELFISH

THERE IS A low thud as Python sprawls across the dirty carpet. I look at her with dazed eyes, contemplating if I should carry her out or not. If the other Cannibals see their leader dead, they'll either surrender or fight back with more power than before.

I decide to leave her inside until everything soothes out. Maybe all the gunfire I heard outside means no more Cannibals. No more Cannibals. A week ago, I didn't think I'd ever say those words. Even just a few days ago. Even yesterday.

The door creaks when I open it sending chills down my spine. The pain in my stomach is starting to settle in, but I can't stop now. Snow sits in patches around the place, and the sun has lit up the air. Python's blood on my knuckles has dried into a deep orange color.

My body wants to collapse and let everyone else take care of this aftermath. I don't even know what's happened to Jason, or any of the others outside.

Something in my head keeps tiptoeing around, but it won't

show itself. It's almost like a missing feeling, but I'll have to ignore it. If I keep trying to remember, everything else will be forgotten.

I creep past the row of houses and onto the main road where the shots were first fired. The bodies look blurred. My vision must've tanked because of the bombs, or because my health isn't as good as it used to be. Three people lay on the ground near the fence and another near the door. Two of them have moving limbs like a signal that they are alive, and the other ones are still.

Across from the bodies lay a Cannibal, and upon stepping closer, more of them can be seen throughout the sidewalk. A horrifying shoot-out that I can't tell is for the better or worse. Four of my friends for only three of theirs. Who knows who else is hurt?

Who else is hurt?

The memory snaps back like a rubber band. The forgotten memory that irked me in my head is filled. I haven't seen Dylan at all. He wasn't here after the wave of zombies, he wasn't here to fight the Cannibals, and he wasn't there when I killed Python. He disappeared, but I know him. He didn't do it intentionally.

My steps quicken as I head towards the others. A part of me wants to just ignore them and find Dylan, but I know he'd be disappointed if I did. But he's not here.

Their faces haunt me from the ground. Tyler, Kira, Ava, and Sarah. Nathan hovers over Kira, clutching his arm. The sight of them changes my mind. I can't leave without helping them. They're my friends—all of them.

I make it to Ava first. The bandage on her leg is bloody, and her arm leaks red.

She squints at me, and her face winces in pain. "Hailee, you need to go help Dylan."

Her eyes reveal the terror within, and as if pointing with her hands, she stares at the house where Sarah lies.

"He's up there."

The others beside her capture my heart in guilt. Is it right to leave them?

"Are you going to be okay?"

"I'll have to be. But Dylan, they hurt him."

The last three words echo in my head. Ava watches me sprint off to the house. Thoughts about Dylan spiral inside of my head, and as I approach the door, Sarah's limp body throws my stomach in a knot. It feels wrong, but I still cross over her and run up the stairs.

"Dylan?" I call once, only once. Too many emotions are flying through me. Worry, hatred, grief, shock. I don't know what to feel.

The ladder to the attic sits in the corner waiting for someone to climb it. It's as if it's calling me to go up. Each step I climb is like a punch to the gut. What's happened to him? I try to calm my breathing. If I panic against another Cannibal, I'll end up making things worse.

I wait to show my hands above the opening. Not until my eyes can see what's inside do I want to reveal myself. I'm only an inch or two away when I see Dylan's head leaning forward. My worry gets the best of me, and I throw myself up.

When I see Dylan's body clearly—him sitting alone, legs stretched out, head falling forward—the same image of Angel flashes through my mind. I couldn't and still can't believe what happened to her, and I don't think I can handle another one of my closest friends to be taken by this hurtful world.

A friend. That's what I keep saying Dylan is, but a part of me knows he's not. Nothing happened between us, but so much did. In one year, he became one of the best people I know.

I never let myself believe it, but the feelings inside of me were never forgotten the first day we met. I never forgot the way my heart fluttered with excitement. I was ready for whatever challenge the universe had for us. It was almost thrilling fighting the dead by his side back at the school. Whatever he said, I followed. I trusted him despite not knowing a thing about him, and I still do.

Was it a sign of love, or just a good friendship? Seeing him in this state is pushing out all my feelings. What if I never tell Dylan the way I feel, and it's too late?

"Dylan," I choke out with the last of my strong voice. Anything I say next is going to lead me into a wreck of tears and emotions.

Inching closer, I see bruises all over his face. Cuts are on his arms with the blood running down. His body looks exhausted. I drop my gun and fall to his side. My throat feels heavy, and I blink over and over in hopes that the tears don't well up.

It's silent in the attic. No breathing from either of us, one of us too scared to, and the other—incapable.

My final moments with Angel replay in my head and each part of me begs that this doesn't end the same. I can't let it end the same.

My hand presses against his shoulder, and I call his name again like a magical spell, and maybe on the third try, he'll wake up. His bruises will fade, and he'll be healthier than ever.

Zombies were just a fictional story too, and here they are now.

"Dylan…"

I can't look at him anymore. My mind wants me to just give up. "Put him out before he becomes a zombie. He'd want that."

While my heart tells me to wait. "He must be in there, even if he becomes one of them."

I close my eyes in hopes that the choice will take over my body so that I don't have to choose. And I guess it works. I hear a small sound. The sound that I never thought would bring me so much joy. The sound of breathing. It's not coming from me; I can feel my face rushing with blood from the lack of oxygen.

My eyes jolt open, and I see Dylan smiling just slightly at me. Without a thought, my arms fly around his weak body. His skin, tanned under the sun, is warm, and in his arms, it feels like it's just us on the planet.

He laughs without an actual sound, and his hands wrap around me. I sit there for a while with my face resting on his shoulder. Though nobody in this world is safe, I still feel like I am when I'm with him.

"I'm so glad you're okay," I say and force myself to let go.

He looks at me as though he wants to say something. His mouth opens, but no words come out. Instead, I see his face inch towards mine. My cheeks feel red as he presses his lips against mine. Emotions buzz inside of me, this time with excitement and love.

He backs away just seconds later, but I wish he'd stayed. I wish we could hug forever, even if everything around us falls apart.

I don't know what to say, but I smile. One of the most candid smiles I've had in a long time. Maybe it's selfish of me to feel like this when my friends are hurt outside, and I've killed yet another person, but it doesn't matter. Sometimes you have to be selfish if you want a better life. When you give all that you have, there's nothing left for you.

* * *

I brought Dylan downstairs and set him up on a couch.

The house was once again silent, and even outside felt calm. I saw the smoke coming from the bus. Gray puffs filled the sky, and the smell of it stung my nose. Madeline told me what happened as she treated Dylan, and that the Cannibals were all dead. Her bright smile was gone, and her words were short.

Those uninjured checked up on the ones hurt from the gunfire. Kira and Nathan were shot, but their injuries were taken care of. Tyler was shot two times, and though we could have done surgery, he didn't want us to waste resources on him.

He kissed Damien goodbye and let us take his life. He didn't want to turn. "Not like Cyrus," he said.

Sarah too. She didn't have the strength to speak, but her eyes told us her answer.

For Elliot—for Angel, Tyler, Sarah, Ashton, and all of those who died on the way, we decided to form a memorial for them. I'll never get over their deaths, even when I feel better, because I know things could've been different. That thought is going to haunt me no matter what.

The memorial will honor them all because, without them, we wouldn't be here. Without the fight and sacrifice, we'd still be on the road looking for food.

I still want to cry and let out the overwhelming feelings tossing around in my head, but my eyes have gone dry. I loved Angel more than I could imagine, and I still do. Her pretty smile and attitude will never leave me. All the parts of her that annoyed me are the parts that I miss the most. I'll just tell myself to live on, for her, because I know that's all I can do now.

As for Python, I did what she said. Her ideas didn't align with mine, and she was a terrible person, but I don't want to be the same. I buried her in the woods far away from us all. And for the Cannibals, we tossed them in the flames of the bus that swarm every inch now. The engine exploded, putting an end to our beloved vehicle.

The bus is a memory I'll never forget about too. It may have only been around for the apocalypse, but it was one of the last things we had that reminded us of the old world. Those rides to games where we'd sing and annoy the driver, or field trips to Denver where we'd never want to leave.

The sun sits just above the horizon. We've already started building the gravestones for those gone. The bus still burns high in the sky, and some of us have even brought around a few chairs to sit and watch. There's still an unsettling feeling around, like someone is lurking, but maybe that's just because it's the apocalypse. Being safe is something that won't happen like it did before. The dead will always roam, and the living—well, terrible people will always find you.

I can't help but wonder if the loss will ever end. If this life of misery ever gets better. The memories from before are starting to fade, and the idea of going back to normal seems impossible.

The government has already given up on us. Who knows where the hell they all fled to? We haven't heard from them in forever, but it's not like I would want to anyway.

I've found a new family, people who care about each other. We are all bonded by this apocalypse because we're alive.

Maybe this is the universe's way of telling us that in the end, all we have is each other. When everything is gone, it's just us. The dead and the alive. We are all that is left behind. It's up to us if we want to survive.

AUTHOR'S NOTE

I was in sixth grade when I began writing the story of Hailee. In the corner of my classroom during some free time, I thought it would be a fun idea to write my own take on zombies. It was around that time that my passion for fictional creatures and survival books really sparked.

The TV shows and games about zombies were some of my main inspirations for writing. By age twelve, I had watched and played almost all the popular media.

Hailee, or also Haley, was the name I had been using for any online games or accounts. It was almost like a fake name for me, so it was best that I used her for the story.

Technically, *What's Left Behind* is the second book of the story about Hailee, but the first was entirely sloppy, unoriginal, and you could find plot holes on every page. Not to mention, the book ended up being only seventy pages long. I never intended for it to be anything but a way to kill time.

I finished that book in seventh grade after abandoning it for months. The only reason it was "finished" was because of my computer class where I had unlimited access to writing.

I won't ramble on about the first, unseen book, but I find the startup of *What's Left Behind* to be interesting, and how far the story has come is incredible.

After seventh grade, my mind was flourishing with ideas, but I didn't want to overwhelm the second book with too many of them. When I started the first chapter in eighth grade, I had zero idea of what the storyline would be, but I still wrote, hoping it would form along the way. (The zombie hoard and the bunker were some of the ideas that made it to the end). After the first few chapters, I realized how much potential *What's Left Behind* could have, so I pushed through. A lot has happened in those years. Some good things and some tragic things, but what hasn't changed is my passion for this book.

As of writing this, I am currently a junior in high school, finally making something out of the story of my younger self.

In the beginning, this book was also full of plot holes, childish writing, and no true story, but I knew I wanted it to become something, so I turned it around.

Finishing the story for me was like making my younger self proud, and it was a way to show my determination despite all the obstacles. School, stress, lack of motivation, and writer's block are just a few examples.

It has been hard. I won't lie. I can't speak for all authors, but I struggled a lot when writing and editing this book. The publishing process was incredibly difficult as well, and countless times I thought, "What if I just quit?"

That's when my mom and sister both pushed me to keep going. My mom, upon telling her that I was writing a book, was ready to help me publish it and asked me often when it would be done. My sister reminded me of all the work I had accomplished, and to not waste that effort.

Even a few of my friends, online and in real life, awaited the publishing of my book.

With all these people ready for me to produce this story, and my younger self's dream of having her own book, I knew I needed to finish.

That is the best message I can offer to anyone reading this. Don't sell yourself short on the work you have done. If you've come so far, you might as well push through. Even if that means only writing a page in a week or barely fixing the margins and calling it a day. Any amount of effort contributes to the whole.

To the creators out there of both big and small ideas, I hope you continue what you are passionate about and see things to the end.

I would also like to thank you for picking up *What's Left Behind*. I hope my passion can aid you in yours.

I do not have much contact information to offer, however, if you would like to ask questions or send a message, please email me at aaniyapatel208@gmail.com.

www.ingramcontent.com/pod-product-compliance
Lightning Source LLC
Chambersburg PA
CBHW030634020726
47493CB00006B/1708